MW00990701

The Water Lords

In the same series:

The Chemical Feast: Ralph Nader's Study Group Report on the Food and Drug Administration, by James S. Turner

The Interstate Commerce Omission: Ralph Nader's Study Group Report on the Interstate Commerce Commission and Transportation, by Robert M. Fellmeth

Old Age: The Last Segregation: Ralph Nader's Study Group Report on Nursing Homes, by Claire Townsend

Vanishing Air: Ralph Nader's Study Group Report on Air Pollution, by John C. Esposito

The paper used in this book is composed of 100% recycled fiber.

Ralph Nader's Study Group Report on Industry and Environmental Crisis in Savannah, Georgia

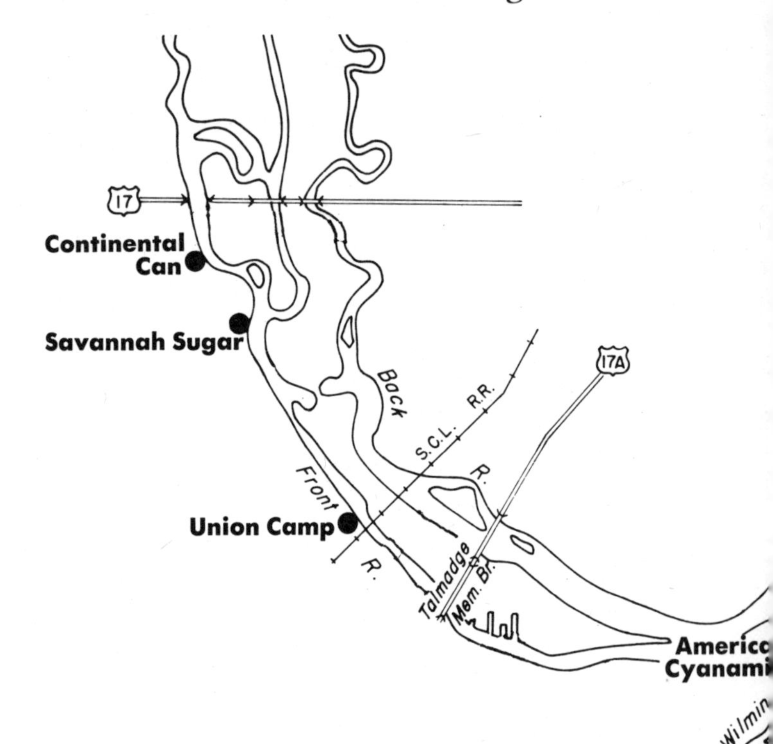

CITY OF SAVANNAH

Source: US Army Corps of Engineers, Savannah, Ga.

The Water Lords

BY *James M. Fallows,* PROJECT DIRECTOR

GROSSMAN PUBLISHERS NEW YORK 1971

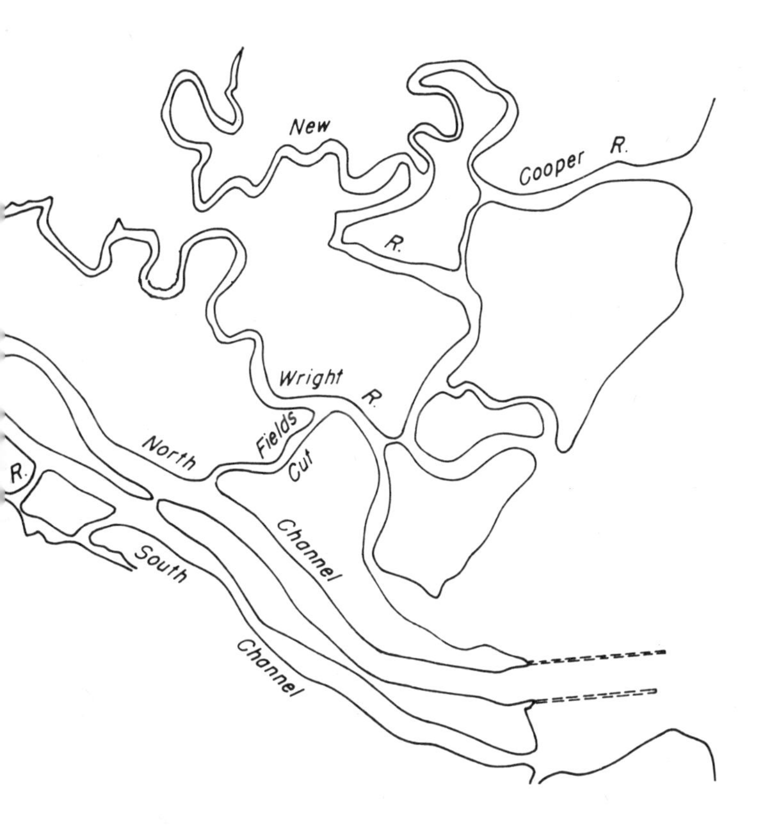

Published in 1971 by Grossman Publishers
44 West 56th Street, New York, N. Y. 10019
Published simultaneously in Canada by
Fitzhenry and Whiteside, Ltd.
SBN: 670-75160-X
Library of Congress Catalogue Card Number: 70–149318
Manufactured in the United States of America.
First printing.

All royalties from the sale of this book will be given to The Center for Study of Responsive Law, the organization established by Ralph Nader to conduct research into violations of the public interest by business and governmental groups. Contributions to further this work are tax-deductible and may be sent to the Center at 1156 Nineteenth Street, N.W., Washington, D.C., 20009.

Members of the Savannah River Project

JAMES M. FALLOWS received an A.B. in History and Literature from Harvard in 1970, and is now studying law at Oxford as a Rhodes Scholar.

SUSAN FALLOWS is a member of the class of 1973 at Scripps College in California.

ROBERT E. FINCH, JR., received a B.S. in Zoology from North Carolina State in 1969 and has studied medicine at the University of North Carolina.

MELANIE MASON is a member of the class of 1971 at Radcliffe.

NEIL G. MC BRIDE received an A.B. in English from Hamilton College in 1967 and a J.D. from the University of Virginia Law School in 1970. He is now Southern Director for the Law Students Civil Rights Research Council, in Atlanta, Georgia.

RICHARD W. MIKSAD received a B.S. in Mechnical Engineering from Bradley University in 1963, an M.S. in Applied Physics and Thermal Engineering from Cornell in 1964, and an Sc.D. in Oceanography from M.I.T. in 1970. He is now a Research Assistant at Imperial College in London.

DIRK M. SCHENKKAN is a member of the class of 1971 at the University of Texas.

TERENCE J. SEYDEN has studied chemistry and psychology at Armstrong State College in Savannah.

J. OWENS SMITH received a B.S. in Forestry and Wildlife Management from the University of Georgia in 1959 and is now a member of the class of 1971 at the University of South Carolina Law School.

JOHN P. WILLIAMS received an A.B. in English from Davidson College in 1969 and is now a member of the class of 1972 at Vanderbilt Law School.

DEBORAH ZERAD is a member of the class of 1971 at Radcliffe.

MARY ADAMS, who did historical research for the project, is now a member of the class of 1974 at Hollins College in Virginia.

Projector Coordinator: HARRISON WELLFORD

Project Sponsor: RALPH NADER

Foreword by Ralph Nader

It can always be left to industry to tout the benefits of its operation to the community. The short and long range costs to the community, however, are not included in the balance sheets, the income statements, the company literature or statements. Such disinterest does not inhibit the costs from spreading and deepening and accreting corporate power to perpetuate and shield the companies from the just indignation of the citizenry. There is nothing particularly unique about the treatment accorded the people and environment of Savannah, Georgia, by large industrial corporations. Knowing and unremitting destruction of rivers and their usefulness to human beings, contamination of the air that people draw into their lungs, scarring of the land with poisons and debris, the impairment of people's health and property with total impunity and, as in Savannah, a massive taxpayer's subsidy for so doing, are macabre portraits that can be drawn for many cities and towns in this country. The many general or abstract descriptions of such situations by the media or government, whose specifics are most often restricted to the recitation of statistics, do not convey the dynamics of the human tragedy and the rupturing of man's relation with nature to the point where nature abused is turned against man.

In the summer of 1970, nine students and a young lawyer under the auspices of the Center for Study of Responsive Law, settled down in Savannah to study the environmental tragedy that has encompassed the city and its friendly people for decades. The students' reception was cordial at first; and later in the summer, due in no small part to their sincere dedication and the willingness of Savannah residents to accept them as fellow human beings rather than as "outsiders," the reception from many in this historic city turned into calls for assistance. The task force was humbled by these requests —many ranging across the spectrum of human problems. The students, realizing their inability to solve these problems, learned firsthand about the vacuums of citizen power which lead to such victimization by business, government, or other arbitrary power centers.

Led by their Project Director, James Fallows, the task force began to document the intricate story of how companies set up shop around Savannah in return for exacting concessions from the city which insured the depletion of the municipal treasury, the foisting of excessive costs on other, smaller taxpayers, and the ravaging of the environment. The students show how interwoven are the issues of corporatism, ecology, taxation, and government, and how decisive is the impact of the first on the other three situations. They show the aesthetic deprivation from the pollution, impairing the sensitivity and feeling of the children who reach out to touch the River's waters and get burned from the sulfuric acid dumped by American Cyanamid. They show how massive contamination of the River has repercussions on drinking water, fisheries, recreation, health, and comfort. With its Moloch-like thrust, Union Camp—the largest paper bag plant in the world—is seriously exposing the precious treasure of fresh ground water to saline intrusion by its voracious pumping of such water for its industrial use. The ample flow of Savannah River water is not adequate or suitable for human use because of what Union Camp and its corporate brethren have done to pollute those waters.

The facts in this report compel an ethical conclusion. These Savannah-based companies are outlaws. The violation and defiance of even the most modest laws does not fully reveal the enormity of the lawlessness. A self-answering question needs to be asked: by what right, legal or moral, do these companies destroy the property and health of innocent neighbors, and jeopardize the resources that our generation holds in trust for future generations? One might expect that destruction of public and private property by such pollution would require, at least, compensation for damage rendered. No. All these devastations are considered the price of progress, but the victims pay the price, not the perpetrators, who profit handsomely and suppress known technologies that could make the Savannah environment an aesthetic and healthful glow in the nation.

If this report has an impact, it will be in two areas.

A more widely shared evaluative framework for corporate crime in the community will begin to emerge and citizens who share these values will see in them an impetus for decisive action to change the conditions and preconditions of this environmental epidemic and economic plunder. What this report calls for, in simplest terms, is for the industrial companies next to Savannah, and other similar operations around the country, to pay their taxes and their environmental way—just as any small, non-corporate citizen is expected to do. The double standard that coddles corporations breeds immense cynicism and disrespect for the law and permits industries to lie, to deceive, to corrupt political processes, and to manipulate the law in order to be permitted to continue destroying, piece by piece, the natural resources of land, air, and water, in what we used to call "America the Beautiful." Tearing down the country by this relentless environmental violence will inflict ever increasing suffering whose poignancy is sharpened by the awareness that the solutions—through resources and technology—are at hand but unused.

Preface

The time is coming when the South will no longer exist as a separate and exotic province of the American experience. Many of the old monuments of regional distinction—one-party politics, one race of voters, one-crop agriculture, one-industry towns—the old symbols of a monolithic South, are vanishing. The South still enjoys its share of faults, but its blemishes are increasingly the faults of other parts of the country—standard American faults. While positive in some areas, this trend can also have melancholy results.

In too many areas, the South is making a pell-mell dash to catch up to something that is essentially sorry and shabby in the rest of America. The South is buying some brands of progress which it would better shun: alienation from work and the land itself, the ugliness of brash new cities and suburbs, a runaway bulldozer mentality; the narrow vision that sees polluting smokestacks as simply obelisks of progress, that smells in polluted air only the scent of jobs. I am speaking of that blind boosterism, often found in Chambers of Commerce and business associations throughout the South, which would make industrial wastelands such as Newark, New Jersey, the models of the Southern future.

Since the collapse of the Populists, Southerners have become increasingly tolerant of corporate abuses which needlessly reduce the safety and beauty of their work and leisure environment. These attitudes have attracted some of the least responsible corporate enterprises to the South. It is now time to start counting their costs to the quality of Southern life.

Environmental pollution is a good place to start. The South, which prides itself on its open spaces and natural beauty in contrast to the congested and polluted North, is now being polluted at a faster rate than any section of the nation. Seventy-five per cent of all pesticides used in the United States are used on Southern soil. Southern whites have 30 per cent more DDT in their tissue than

Northern whites, and Southern Negroes have twice as much. Every year industrial pollution claims new rivers and lakes at an accelerating rate.

In part this attack on the Southern ecology reflects the vulnerability of an underdeveloped region which desperately seeks new industries for more jobs. When impoverished communities have to cajole industry with cheap land and tax shelters, few are inclined to bargain for environmental values and longer-range economic costs. Consequently, many industries exploited the traditional Southern indifference to the ugly side effects of new industry as long as jobs were being provided.

There are signs that Southerners may no longer be willing to invite in any industry with no questions asked, but with secret strings attached which ultimately erode the independence and health of a community. They are beginning to think twice before they agree to mortgage the safety and beauty of their natural surroundings which are so much a part of the region's identity. In the past in the face of an uninformed public, the bargaining advantages were all on the side of the polluters. Now when the latest census figures show the South to have the highest economic rate of growth in the nation, the old "payroll" blackmail is becoming an empty threat. With labor, tax, and land costs all very favorable to industry, the South need no longer worry that industry will fold its tents and steal away if the public requires it to be a good citizen. An aroused public may well find it possible to have more jobs without losing their birthright to a safe, natural environment. At least in the South, there is still something left to save.

There is a deep Populist sentiment in the South which is emotional about the environment and exploitation of Southern resources by outsiders. Yet, this feeling has lain dormant as established Southern leaders have either encouraged the exploiters or rationalized their costs. With this project in Savannah, we hope to help the public learn the facts about the threats to its environment so that they can avoid needless capitulations to industry in the future.

For a democracy to work, the people must have the facts to make real choices about conditions which affect their lives. We have provided the investigative resources to dig out the facts. The rest is up to the people of Savannah. They must decide for themselves whether the price they have paid for "progress" is too great, whether the polluters are making genuine efforts to clean up after themselves. When citizens lack the facts to answer these questions for themselves, "public policy" permitting needless pollution of air and water becomes the cruelest kind of taxation without representation—the tax may be exacted from the health, safety, and beauty of a community, not directly from its pocketbook, but it is taxation nevertheless.

Strolling through Savannah on a summer night when the wind is not blowing from the direction of Union Camp, it is easy to become sentimental about the Southern way of life. The South has had more than its share of those vices of the spirit which have led to national trauma—racial injustice, intolerance of dissent, indifference to the poor—but it also has some peculiar virtues which, if cultivated and preserved, might protect this region from some of the failures of mainstream America. I am speaking of the Southerner's sense of place, his sense of continuity with a past, his attachment to the soil, the irony and wisdom which is distilled from a collective memory of defeat in dealing with problems of race and poverty beyond the capacity of technological gimmickry to solve. These virtues are deeply rooted in Savannah, but they were not strong enough to shield this graceful city from the smog and stench of a corporate polluter, an invasion far more threatening to its quality of life than General Sherman ever was. It was the task of this project to find out why.

Harrison Wellford
Project Coordinator
Washington, D.C.
December, 1970

Contents

Foreword by Ralph Nader ix

Preface by Harrison Wellford xiii

Introduction xix

1. The River 1
2. The Last Resource 13
3. The Floating Crap Game 24
4. The Lesser Evil: American Cyanamid 40
5. Papering the Earth 46
6. Polluting the Earth 64
7. Three Pulp Mill Towns 75
8. Union Camp's Divining Rod 113
9. The Smell of Money 128
10. The Making of a Company Town, 153
    I: A Present for Mr. Calder
11. The Making of a Company Town, 171
    II: Representation Without Taxation
12. Bringing Down the Law 189
13. Bringing Back the Water 217

In Savannah and Beyond Savannah: Conclusions 244

Appendices
1. The Other Side: John E. Ray III's Speech of the Savannah Rotary Club, October 19, 1970 256
2. What to Look for in Your Environmental Quality Control Law 264
3. The Second Oil Spill 270

Notes 275

Index 287

Introduction

By the time we arrived in Savannah in the middle of 1970, water pollution and the "environmental crisis" had become such bland and shopworn topics that everyone—from Richard Nixon, to candidates on all sides in the 1970 Georgia elections, to most of the nation's largest industries—could join under the wide banner of saving the environment.

We did not intend our work to be one more item in the already substantial literature of ecological disaster. We did not want to issue another death certificate for another river. Any American who has had access to newspapers or television in the last year knows that something is wrong with the balance of nature. The people of Savannah have known for years about their river and did not need us to tell them that it was polluted.

We did want, however, to look for answers to the next logical environmental question: what can we do about it? By tracing in detail the sources of the problem in one specific example, we hoped to find ways to eliminate the causes. At the start, we did not know that this work would take us into so many areas that have no obvious connection to water pollution—county tax structure, air pollution, industrial marketing philosophy, and the other topics that fill the chapters of our report. But it soon became clear that we had no other choice. The surest guarantee of a simple-minded, ineffective study would have been to concentrate entirely on the filth in the river. That was our focus, but we found that we had to include other fundamentally connected questions. The same economic and political arrangements that have ruined the river also fill Savannah's air with obnoxious and dangerous contaminants. The same corporate thinking that impedes cleaning the river also shortchanges the public treasury. By discussing many more of these questions than we had initially expected, we feel that we have covered problems that apply in every part of this country.

Apart from the content of our study, we found another troubling sign in Savannah. Time and again, the city's residents assumed that we, as well-publicized "Nader's Raiders," had some special, secret tactics for eliciting information. That attitude may, in part, reflect a well-deserved respect for Ralph Nader's remarkable investigative achievements. But it can have disastrous consequences, when it leads to the feeling that only special, outside groups can do the investigation.

We used no special tools in our study, no secret contacts. Aside from the freedom we had to spend an entire summer studying one relatively limited topic, we did nothing that anyone else in Savannah (or any other city) could not have done. All that is required is time, and the willingness to use it studying files and conducting interviews. The sooner that people understand how simple the process is, the more quickly they should begin to use it on their own local governments, their own industrial neighbors, their own universities and professions.

As such scrutiny becomes more common, however, it is likely to meet increasing obstacles. There are laws that force government agencies to open themselves for public observations; the laws and their application vary, but the citizen knows he has some protection, however vague, however theoretical, for his right to know. The protection disappears in dealings with private companies. Their decisions can be more important than any the government makes, but private companies can make themselves virtually impenetrable.

We met different versions of this resistance in Savannah. Continental Can and American Cyanamid, two companies whose policy comes straight from corporate headquarters in New York and New Jersey, did everything they could to seal themselves off. Union Camp, playing its accustomed role as Savannah's leading citizen, allowed us several interviews. This company has certainly learned a lesson from the summer: because it was initially more open than the others, we were able to find out much more about it in a much shorter period of time. The implications are clear—next time, any investigator will have a harder time with Union Camp. Across the country, companies whose public comments have later been turned against them will decide that clamlike secrecy is the best policy in the future.

In the long run such tactics cannot succeed. American Cyanamid, for example, refused to tell us whether it was releasing chlorine gas into the air. With enough time, investigators could check state records, interview engineers, or even look up the specifications on Cyanamid's patents. These steps can be painfully time consuming, but serious investigators must realize that they sometimes provide the only way to find the missing information. In the meantime, until that far-off day when corporations have no reason to conceal any of their practices, the public must convince them that secrecy is not worthwhile. When corporate decisions affect the public welfare, the public must demand to know about the decisions. Public protests and legal sanctions can eventually make secrecy more costly than full public disclosure.

In a report like this, which contains a full supply of criticisms, we should begin by giving our praise and thanks to those who deserve them. The Georgia Water Quality Control Board, and especially its director, R. S. "Rock" Howard, deserve the gratitude of the people of Georgia. They have our thanks as well, for providing a model of dedicated and open government. The city manager of Savannah, Picot Floyd, also took the remarkable and much appreciated position of welcoming the scrutiny of the city government. Because of this and other attitudes, the city of Savannah is fortunate. Many of Savannah's private citizens also gave us help and advice during the summer. We are especially grateful to two of them, Ogden Doremus and Richard Heard.

The eleven members of our project cooperated throughout our research, and we share joint responsibility for our findings and conclusions. A twelfth investigator, Mary Adams, worked only on the material contained in Chapter 1. The writing in this report is almost entirely mine, and I take responsibility for its shadings and style. Neil McBride wrote parts of Chapter 12 and helped edit the report.

James M. Fallows
Savannah, September, 1970

The Water Lords

1
The River

There is the rich history that has been made along its banks, so that, as I look upon it, I see it running across the map as a thick red line, for there is the red-earth blood of the hills and the lowlands in its waters as a symbol of the fertility on which it draws.

Thomas Stokes, The Savannah

Them paper bag people are fiddlin' with our livelihood. What's more important, a damn paper bag or us making a livin'?

Shrimper in Savannah

Most of us just thought it was a dirty old stream, without any hope.

J. C. Lewis, Mayor of Savannah

There are not many cities like Savannah left in this country, a fact that draws different responses from different people. Many young people leave, complaining that the town has no life. Other families move in to stay, saying that it is a good, calm place to raise children. Whatever its miscellaneous virtues or shortcomings, Savannah has a special, quite charming place in American culture. The relaxed pace of Southern towns is one aspect of it; but in that Savannah is no different from a hundred other Southern cities. The stately old houses are another part; but again, cities from Oxford, Mississippi, to Charlottesville, Virginia, have the same antebellum architectural heritage. Somehow, however, the mood of Savannah is distinct.

The city is not all history and old houses, of course.

The plastic and neon of post-1950 America have made their mark here as elsewhere. On the outskirts south of town, the predictable cluster of 7-11 stores, burger stands, and shopping centers look the same as their counterparts in Anaheim, California, and Newton, Massachusetts. Savannah's suburbs have grown in the last ten years, and the plastic signs have followed. But so far, this influence has mercifully spared the heart of the city —the several square miles nearest the river, where the city first put down its roots and where it now retains its memories. In this area, Savannah not only preserves but still uses the relics of its past. The result of this harmonious acceptance of the old is a refreshing surprise for visitors accustomed to the dingy, bland, chaotic appearance of American cities from Pittsburgh to Atlanta to Houston. Parts of New Orleans retain the same antique flavor as Savannah, as do the older portions of San Francisco when the traffic calms down and the smog blows out to sea. Nearby Charleston, whose imposing old mansions loom over the waterfront, is probably Savannah's closest equivalent.

In its central area, ramming up against the river and extending for several miles inland, Savannah seems part of another century. When James Oglethorpe and his Englishmen arrived in 1733, they scrupulously laid out the city streets, allowing plenty of room for parks and gardens. Savannah now remembers that it was the country's "first planned city," and a short walk through its downtown streets shows the wisdom of the planners. At two or three block intervals throughout the central area, Savannah's streets temporarily give way to small plazas and squares. Some of them have fountains; some, statues of heroic Confederates; some, gardens full of color. In these squares and the streets around them, trees drip with heavy Spanish moss.

Midway through the 1960's, Savannah began to pay serious attention to the aged houses that fill the downtown region. Instead of razing them for parking lots or skyscrapers, the city began to restore them. The work still goes on, but already rows and rows of graceful restored houses stand, looking much the same as they must have in the eighteenth and nineteenth centuries. Elaborate wrought-iron work (originally brought to

Savannah as ballast for sailing ships) swirls down from many of the balconies and doorways. Less self-consciously than Williamsburg and other deliberate monuments, Savannah has successfully recreated a historic setting where modern people live and work.

Like the days, nights in Savannah are often hot and thick, but during the worst parts of the summer, frequent, brief, violent thunderstorms leave the trees and houses with a cool, washed look in the evening. On those nights when the air is so moist that it seems to merge with the river, when hundreds of tiny insects scramble across Savannah's sidewalks, the old street lights go on near the resurrected houses, and the town seems peacefully removed from the pressure and garishness of American life. In its calm isolation, Savannah offers something few other modern cities can give: surroundings that are actually pleasant to be in.

The houses, the fountains, the wrought iron would probably never have appeared in this corner of Georgia if a river had not run through Savannah. From the day Oglethorpe's boat sailed through the estuary and beached where the city is now built, Savannah's life has centered on the river. The city hall sits at the river's edge, looking out at what was once a spectacular stretch of water. Along the river front are the ruins of "Factor's Walk," the offices and wharves where cotton dealers once made their fortunes. Savannah's boats have carried different cargoes in the years since trading began, but the port has always been the core of the town's economic life. The people who made their money from the river also took their recreation there; swimming, boating, and fishing made the town a miniature paradise for many of its residents.

They had a good river to work with. Clear mountain streams from the forested Blue Ridge mountains in the Carolinas and upper Georgia run together to form it. For 300 miles, the Savannah is a large, forceful river, forming the boundary between South Carolina and Georgia. As it moves down toward the sea, it picks up red Georgia silt and earth, and the river itself turns red. Before the English settlers arrived, the Indians called the river "Isundiga"—"blue water," but the name was probably as much a misnomer then as today.

Like other rivers in the wet Southeast, the Savannah is a mighty river. Visitors from drier portions of the country are usually impressed by the size of the river as it passes through Savannah. What they rarely realize is that they are seeing only half of it; shortly before it reaches town, the Savannah splits into two channels. The regions that feed the river are blanketed with an average annual rainfall of 46 inches—more than any other part of the country except the Pacific Northwest.[1] The run-off from this rainfall creates an average *daily* flow in the river of 7.2 billion gallons of water—about 10,000 gallons per day for each of the citizens that live on the river's banks.[2] In the days before men tamed rivers, the flow swung between extremes of flooding and low water, but now two large dams upstream hold back huge lakes and release a steady flow of water.

With such a dependable and seemingly unlimited supply of water on hand, the people who lived by the river naturally assumed that they could do almost anything they wanted to it. There are no records to explain whether the Indians who lived by the river used it for sewage disposal, but on the very day that the English settlers arrived, they used the Savannah as their toilet. As the little colony on the river grew, it eventually set up a sewage system; it collected the wastes from each house and sent them straight to the river. There, mingling with the billions of gallons of fresh water, the human by-products conveniently disappeared. As long as the population remained small, there was no problem.

While using the river as their garbage dump, the early colonists also began another kind of campaign against the river. With single-minded determination, they set out to correct all the mistakes nature had made in designing the river basin. The engineering mentality which, in 1970, inspires the Army Corps of Engineers to close off half the river as a sediment basin is nothing new; its roots lie in the "harbor improvements" that began as early as the eighteenth century. The first real flashes of engineering ingenuity, however, did not come until the Revolutionary War. Then Savannahians, properly fearful that English ships might sail up the river and cause trouble, decided to block off the river. The eighteenth-century equivalent of the Corps of Engineers towed several large ships out to the mouth of the harbor and sank them. When that war and another with England had passed and the city had survived, the Corps of Engineers completed the project; in 1826, it pried a $50,000 appropriation from Congress for "removal of obstructions at The Wrecks."

During the Civil War, which held less bitterness for Savannah than for the rest of the South,* townspeople thought up another idea for keeping enemy boats out of the harbor. Instead of going through the costly procedure of sinking ships, the people of Savannah tried to drink the river dry. "I remember a time when we were not clamoring for so much water in the Savannah River," an old-timer reminisced in 1892. "It was," he said, "a time when every Savannah man regarded it as his patriotic duty to drink as much Savannah River water as possible in an effort to lower the water in the river." [3] A nice idea, but one that required either a bigger town or a smaller river. If the river's flow then was anything like it is now, each thirsty Savannahian would have had to put away more than 100,000 gallons of water a day—about 75 gallons a minute, 24 hours a day—to make a dent in the river.

During the first two centuries of the river's colonized history, when the Savannah seemed predestined to serve as a sewer, a few voices offered warnings. Midway through the eighteenth century, when river trade was beginning to grow, the town passed a law against throwing tree stumps into the water. But serious concern about the quality of the water—not just its floating debris—had to wait more than a hundred years. In 1879, the city newspaper published an analysis of the problem which, in its sophisticated understanding of the situation and its pungent language, has not been matched:

* According to local accounts, Savannahians were appropriately aware of what might happen to them if General Sherman came storming into town. So they decided on a strategy of friendly persuasion. Whatever Sherman's intentions at the beginning, a short time with Savannah's hostesses mellowed him and his troops. Sherman gave Savannah to President Lincoln as a "Christmas present," and the city escaped with no serious damage. Now, most residents are proud of their city's shrewd tactics, but some malcontents remain. Guides at Savannah's Fort Pulaski, which is now in excellent shape because it saw little action during the war, say that they would feel much prouder to be at some bombarded ruin like Charleston's Fort Sumter, "where the real men fought."

The sewage of the town is incessantly added to this vast accumulation of decomposing organic matter, creating a compound highly charged with elements destructive of animal life. In the ebb and flow of the tides this immense stratum of fermenting filth is alternately exposed to the concentrating rays of the sun and again covered with water, and is always sufficiently agitated to liberate the imprisoned gases.[4]

Despite the dangers of tree stumps and sewer gas, the river was still in good enough condition to serve many of the town's needs in the eighteenth and nineteenth centuries. It carried navigation, as it does today; but it also provided good fishing, a place to swim, and —incredibly—a supply of drinking water. In a way that modern Savannah can barely imagine, the river was the focus of the city's social life. An historian of nineteenth-century Savannah recalls,

There was a time, when the river was teeming with social activity as well as maritime. The populace thronged to the waterfront to view the balconies on River Street, which were in their day as much a status symbol as boxes in the horseshoe ring at the Metropolitan Opera.[5]

For a long time, from the founding of the city until the 1930's, the Savannah River served many needs of its community. No one user—commercial, recreational, or municipal—destroyed the river for the others. Cotton ships did not drive away the fishermen; pleasure boaters interfered with neither socialites nor merchants. If there was ever a model of balanced use of a natural resource, this was it. Much of the balance was accidental and, if the municipal sewage had been more voluminous, or if the industries then were as grossly polluting as the factories are now, the balance would have tipped many years earlier.

Like so many other aspects of Savannah life, the river's big change came in 1935, when the Union Bag Company (now Union Camp Corporation) brought its factory to town. There had been industry on the river before Union Bag; near the time of World War I, the Savannah Sugar Refinery built a factory several miles upstream from the city. But whatever pollutants it released—together with the untreated wastes from the city's sewers—were a relatively small concern compared to the torrent of filth that came from the paper mill. One year after the paper machines first ground into operation, a Savannah civic committee made the first anxious comment about what was happening to the river. "With the ever increasing industrial development in the area," they said, using the veiled language so customary in Savannah's references to Union Bag, "it is necessary and advisable that a study be made of the problem of industrial waste pollution, and a constant check maintained on this potential menace." [6]

That was hardly the kind of warning designed to swing the city into action, but it was one of the most direct statements Savannah would ever make. For 30 years after Union Camp came to town, the river paid the price for the city's neglect. Soon the city paid too. Where once there had been many uses for the river, now there was room for only one. When Union Camp used the Savannah as its sewer, no one else could use it for anything.

Savannah's casual admission that its river is polluted often hides the full extent of the aquatic slum the city has created. Even without studying the technical data, visitors can begin to appreciate the damage after a boat trip down the river.* Upstream, at Union Camp, the normally muddy river gets a large dose of dark coffee-colored waste. For many yards downstream from the plant, the two kinds of water do not mix at all; the pollutant spreads out from the factory in a long, brown wedge. A line of foam runs along the edge of the pollutant and finally spreads out over the river when the mill wastes blend in.

As the river makes its way down through the city, it gives off the unmistakable odor of human excrement. This is no great surprise, for several large outfall pipes dump the untreated sewage of more than 100,000 peo-

* This is not always so simple to arrange. The Corps of Engineers and the U.S. Coast Guard keep boats permanently docked in the main channel of the Savannah, but many private boat owners refuse to take their boats into the river. In September 1970, a young adventurer making a kayak trip from New York to Miami paddled into the Savannah dock and quickly pulled his kayak from the water, saying that he didn't like the thought of what the river would do to his rubberized craft.

ple into the river. At times the water in front of City Hall literally boils as pockets of hydrogen sulfide and methane gas rise from the wastes on the river bed. The situation remains the same for several miles, until the river undergoes a final calamity as it passes the American Cyanamid factory. There, some 690,000 pounds of sulfuric acid flood into the river every day, killing fish and running into the marshes alongside of the river. The river water near the plant, often as caustic as concentrated laboratory acid, has seared the skin of small children who have unwittingly dangled their arms in the water.

As many Savannahians take pains to point out, even the water that flows into the city from points upstream is not entirely pure. The chief upstream source of pollution is Augusta, 160 river miles from Savannah. Like most of the other cities on the river, Augusta and its industries have chronically refused to treat their wastes. For many years, however, the sheer volume of the river's flow was enough to dilute and absorb the pollutants before they reached Savannah. Or so it seemed. It was only during the nationwide mercury scare of 1970 that Federal authorities discovered how far-reaching an effect Augusta's pollution could have. Because one Augusta factory, run by the Olin Corporation, leaked mercury into the river, fish along the entire downstream stretch of the Savannah had stored up dangerous concentrations of mercury. Late in the summer of 1970, all of the river between Augusta and Savannah was closed to fishing because of the contamination.

Dramatic as that step was in demonstrating the extent of the pollution, it caused only a small flap in Savannah. Savannah's portion of the river has been so dismal for so long that mercury was only the latest disaster. The government did not have to make the lower portions of the river off limits to fishermen; the State Water Quality Control Board had done that several years earlier because of industrial and municipal pollution. Even before the mercury ban, fishermen on the lower 100 miles of the river often found that they were unable to sell their catch. Customers understandably objected to the vile, oily taste the fish picked up in their brief passage through the industrial region near Savannah.

In an otherwise clean estuary, mercury might also have built up in the flesh of shellfish, creating a serious threat to oyster eaters. However, the river's existing pollution eliminated this possible mercury hazard as well. Federal authorities did not have to rush to pull oysters off the market because, for more than 20 years, the oyster beds of the Savannah estuary have been condemned because of sewage contamination.

It takes a lot of pollutant to do this much damage—about 100 million gallons every day from Savannah's major polluters. A frightening array of poisons and contaminants rides out every day from the industrial and municipal outfalls: sulfuric acid and several metal compounds from American Cyanamid, raw human sewage from Savannah and the small surrounding cities, and, overwhelming them all, pulp mill wastes from Union Camp and its smaller neighbor, Continental Can.

Although the chemical components of pulp mill wastes—wood sugars, bits of cellulose, natural wood adhesives called "lignins"—seem less obnoxious than sulfuric acid and human sewage, in Savannah they do much more damage to the river. More clearly than in most other areas, the blame for Savannah's pollution falls mainly on one source: the world's largest kraft paper mill, run by the Union Camp Corporation.

Technically, the story is this. Like many other rivers and lakes, the Savannah River's most important pollution problem is oxygen-consuming wastes—products that, while not necessarily toxic themselves, use up the dissolved oxygen in the water as they decompose. The result is water so poor in oxygen that fish cannot survive. When the oxygen consumption is due to the biological breakdown of organic material, it is called "Biological Oxygen Demand" (BOD); when it is due to purely chemical reactions that consume oxygen, it is called "Chemical Oxygen Demand" (COD). Both forms of pollution are measured either in pounds (one pound of BOD means waste that will use one pound of the river's dissolved oxygen in a set period of time, usually five days) or "Population Equivalents" (PE). Each PE unit is theoretically the amount of oxygen-consuming pollutant that one person would produce as sewage in one day; numerically, it is equal to about one-sixth of a pound of BOD.

Using these standards, the Federal Water Pollution Control Administration has calculated that between 1,000,000 and 1,250,000 Population Equivalents of oxygen-consuming pollution (equal to the raw sewage produced by the populations of Pittsburgh and New Orleans combined) flow into the river every day. Of this total, only about 13 per cent comes from human beings. The rest is from the city's industries; and to say "the city's industries" is, for most purposes, to mean Union Camp. Most recent figures, collected for a 1969 water pollution conference in Savannah, show how heavily one mill can add to the pollution load:

TABLE 1–1

Source	*Oxygen-Consuming Pollutants Per Day (in Population Equivalents)*
Union Camp	696,000
City of Savannah	108,000
Continental Can	80,000
Savannah Sugar Refinery	29,850
GAF Corporation	18,650
Hercules, Inc.	17,900
City of Savannah Beach	16,700 (during summer)
Certain-Teed Products	14,000
Two other industries and four small towns	24,160
Total:	*1,005,260* *

Source: Federal Water Pollution Control Administration Conference, October 1969.

* At the same 1969 conference, Charles Starling of the Georgia Water Quality Control Board reported that American Cyanamid, whose acid pollution problem had long been known, might also be contributing to the oxygen demand on the river. Unlike the other industries and cities, however, Cyanamid's pollution would be not Biological but Chemical Oxygen Demand, because of the iron particles released in its wastes. Starling estimated the amount of this pollution as 150,000 Population Equivalents. If he is correct, it would make Cyanamid the second largest polluter on the river, and it would drop Union Camp's share of the total pollution load from 70 per cent to 60 per cent.

In other words, Union Camp is responsible for 80 per cent of the industrial pollution, and 70 per cent of the entire oxygen-consuming pollution load on the river. Although this kind of culpability should, ideally, convince Union Camp to hurry to repair the damage it has done, unfortunately, this has not been the case. While the other industrial polluters, contributing their relatively minor shares to the river, have moved with some degree of good faith to correct their problems, Union Camp has been the slowest and least successful of the important factories to carry out its treatment plans. Only the city of Savannah, which is still searching for tax money to build a sewage treatment plant (see Chapter 3), has made less progress in the last five years.

One of the most pathetic aspects of Savannah's plight is that the river's condition cannot be blamed on benign neglect from the state and Federal governments. In the last decade, a series of investigators and enforcers has come to Savannah to make reports, think up solutions, and issue orders. The Federal government held two enforcement conferences, one in February 1965, and the other in October 1969. At the first conference, Federal and state officials ordered all industries to cut their pollution by 25 per cent; at the second session of the conference in 1969, the industries faced a 1972 deadline for reducing their pollution by 85 per cent from the 1965 level. Since the first session, the Georgia Water Quality Control Board has ceaselessly badgered both the city and its industries to get the job done.

But despite all the hours of effort and the dollars spent on pollution control, progress can most optimistically be described as meager. Measurements taken show that the river is in no better condition than it was before all the "enforcement" started. A few of the polluters—most notoriously, Union Camp—sometimes put out *more* wastes than they did in 1965. The City of Savannah, which was told in 1965 to build a sewage treatment system immediately, still has not broken ground for this plant. Meanwhile, the residual pollution in the marshes and river bed has increased; more and more streams that run through the Savannah's estuary network have been closed to swimming and fishing; the river shows few signs of recovering.

How has it all gone wrong? The roots of Savannah's failure reach into many corners, from legislative weakness to industrial deception, from the technical problems of sewage treatment to the marketing theories of the paper industry, from the biology of the Savannah estuary to the company-town arrangements that have strangled the city for years. The details of this story differ from those in other cities, but the general pattern should offer important lessons for many other towns that sit over dirty waters.

2

The Last Resource

> *We can bequeath our children cities of iron and stone and aluminum, but we had better be sure to give them water to make them livable.*
>
> Senator Robert Kerr,
> Land, Wood, and Water

On the rare occasions when they do think about their river's pollution, the people of Savannah usually see it as an annoying but hardly critical problem. Like the downtown traffic problem, it seems more a nuisance than a genuine crisis, like an economic slowdown or drug use among the local youth. To most residents, cleaning the river seems one of the luxuries the city should try to obtain, both to make Savannah more attractive to tourists and the much sought new businesses, and to maintain a sense of civic pride. It comes slightly ahead of such frills as a city zoo, but far behind projects like a $40 million freeway to the plusher suburban areas, historic restoration of downtown houses, or construction of an elaborate new coliseum *cum* civic center. It would be nice to fish in the river, Savannahians realize, and nicer still to swim and boat there. But not quite nice enough to justify either excitement or money for the project.

Too few residents of towns such as Savannah realize that only a quirk of geographical circumstance has let them continue so long in their nonchalant attitude toward their rivers. Like American pioneers in the days before the frontier closed, the people of coastal Georgia think that there is no end to it all—that the water that runs in their rivers, falls almost daily from their skies, and rides gently in and out of their marshes will be there forever, in dependable and usable supply.

Already, cities throughout the rest of the country have learned how dangerous that assumption can be. Even the once moist Northeast, after its agonizing mid-60's droughts, has come to understand what the parched states of the Great Plains and Far West have known for years: water is precious, and not to be squandered. They now know that the health and growth of their communities depend more on water than on any other resource. They are learning the hard way the consequences of misusing their water supply.

Only two areas of the country have managed to postpone the inevitable day of watery reckoning. The coastal regions of the Southeast and parts of the Pacific Northwest—both areas with abundant waters and relatively few people—still operate under the comfortable assumption that there is enough water to go around. But even for them, time is growing short. Savannah's spectacular mistreatment of its underground and surface water supplies shows that even the most bountiful resource can disappear with alarming speed (see Chapter 8).

While exploring the many ways that people in one Southern town have abused their water, it is essential to remember just why this story is important. If water were merely a replaceable commodity that the Savannahians alone stood to lose, then there would be no reason for tracing it in such detail. But the messages that emerged from the exploration of Savannah's problem are important to every other part of the country—from Phoenix to Seattle to New York. These cities, like every other city in the country, depend on water; all face the disastrous consequences of its misuse.

Water is a substance basic to our survival. Next to water, all other resources pale in worth. Without it, the proud achievements of technical man would lose their value, civilization would collapse, and life would cease. It is also a limited resource, one that needs to be conserved and properly managed. We have no more water today than our ancestors did; our descendants will have no more than we. We cannot approach its use with the same mentality we have applied to so many other resources; that once it is used up or spoiled, we will be able to find something else to take its place. The way in which we use our water today will determine whether our children—or we ourselves—will have enough water in the future.

Human bodies are made of at least 70 per cent water; like the societies they compose, the individual bodies need an adequate supply of pure water. Water replenishes the cells, discharges the wastes, cools, cleans, and nourishes the whole body. To fill all these needs, the average American uses 3.8 million gallons of water during his lifetime. If our bodies cannot get the minimum necessary water supply, they react in a biologically predictable manner. They weaken and fail, and eventually the irreversible processes of degeneration and death begin.

The modern society we have built needs water for the same reasons as individuals, but its needs are grossly swollen reflections of private use. In the days before heavy industrialization, men could feel secure if they had enough water to drink and wash with, and enough lakes and rivers to provide recreation and some food. Now, like it or not, none of us can escape the environmental costs of the factories and consumer goods our society has produced.

The coming of industrial society has complicated water problems in two important ways. First, we must find enough water to fill industrial needs, if we want to maintain the output of our industries. But at the same time, we must protect ourselves from the very plausible threat of drowning beneath the deluge of water-borne pollution and wastes. Until we decide that it is time to produce fewer material goods, to cut back on the products and by-products of our industries, we have no choice but to find the water our technical society needs.

Our modern water demands are nearly insatiable. For example, it takes two and one-half gallons of water to make one phonograph record; five gallons of water to process one gallon of milk; eight gallons to process one pound of sugar; 150 gallons to make the paper in a thick Sunday newspaper; and 300 gallons to make one pound of synthetic rubber. It also takes 40 gallons of water to grow the feed a hen needs to produce one egg, and

350,000 gallons of water to grow one ton of corn for cattle feed.

The United States now uses about 1,600 gallons of water each day for every one of its citizens.[1] But of these 1,600 gallons, only 150—about 9 per cent—go to the private citizen's physical and domestic needs.[2] This 9 per cent goes to water our gardens, fill our bathtubs, run down our sewers, and quench our thirst. The other 91 per cent goes to feed the technical demands of our hyperproductive society.

The industrial demand is a quickly increasing one. America now uses seven times as much water as it did in 1900, and twice as much as in 1945. By 1980—in less than ten years—the use is expected to double once more.[3] At that point, the nation will face a crisis in its use of fresh water. By then, our use will be dangerously close to the maximum amount of water that nature and man can provide. By 1980, something will have to give; someone will have to cut back or suffer. In view of the last few years' history of water use, it is uncomfortably clear who the victim will be. The average citizen today uses twice as much water as an American of 1900 did; industries have increased their use seven times in the same period. As a small fish in the pond of big users, the individual citizen—and the town he lives in—have reason to be afraid.

To understand the limits on our water supply, we must temporarily put aside some of the convenient statistics doled out in high school science courses. It does not matter that three-fourths of the earth's surface is covered by water, or that if the earth were a uniform sphere, there would be enough water to cover it all to a depth of 800 feet, or that the earth contains about 325 million cubic *miles* of water.[4] Those figures are impressive, but totally misleading. The important factor in calculating our water supplies is not how much water there is, but what fraction of that water is usable. Only 3 per cent—about 10 million cubic miles—is fresh water. From the start, we face the fact that 97 per cent of the world's water is in the oceans. Even the most efficient processes for removing salt from sea water use huge amounts of energy to produce minute volumes of fresh water. Unless the next 20 years bring some technical breakthrough that cannot be imagined now, there is no way that ocean water can provide a practical supply of water.

We must, then, count up the fresh water resources available for our use. All the water on earth circulates in a constant, endless cycle; at some point during its eons of existence, each drop of water will pass through each of the phases. Water from the oceans evaporates into the atmosphere; from the atmosphere, rain falls, and then soaks into the ground or runs off in rivers to the ocean. At any one time, however, there is a rigid statistical distribution of water in each phase. These statistics show how severely limited are the sources we can tap for water.

Fresh water is distributed mainly in forms or places that make it almost unusable for normal human needs. Seventy-five per cent of the fresh water is frozen in polar ice caps and glaciers. Another 14 per cent is buried in ground water reserves too deep for most wells.[5] Tiny amounts are stored in other unusable forms: 0.06 per cent as soil moisture, and 0.035 per cent in the atmosphere.

That leaves only a small amount—about 11 per cent of the world's fresh water total—in forms that towns or industries can easily use. Almost all of it is stored as ground water at depths of less than 2,500 feet. Only 0.3 per cent of the fresh water total is in lakes, and one-tenth that amount—0.03 per cent—flows through all the world's rivers.

The United States' share of the world's usable fresh water comes to about 1,200 billion gallons per day (bgd). Much more water than that falls on the country as precipitation; with its annual rainfall of 30 inches, the American landscape receives an average daily shower of 4,300 billion gallons.[6] But about 70 per cent of the total rainfall never enters usable reserves; it is lost by evaporation, enters deep ground water pockets, or goes to support trees and other forms of natural vegetation. This is far from "lost" or "wasted" water; it is necessary to preserve the balance of the earth's life cycle. But for purposes of supporting human life, we must concentrate on the amount in rivers, lakes, and shallow ground water reserves. This portion—1,200 bgd—is what we must depend on for domestic consumption, industrial use, recreation, navigation, and power generation.

At first glance, even when compared with the large number of people who must use it, this seems like a comfortably large supply of water. The United States Geological Survey, a perpetually optimistic prophet of the nation's water resources, has gone a long way toward bolstering that impression. At every opportunity, the USGS releases reports like this one from 1960:

The United States is in the happy circumstance of being well supplied with water. After nature takes its share of water which falls as precipitation, there is available for man's use about 7500 gallons of water per day for every citizen in the country. Of this available water, we presently use about 1 gallon out of every 5.

In a national sense, then, the country is not likely to run out of water in any foreseeable future.[7]

In the decade since this report, both the number of people using the water and the amount each person uses have risen. But even so, using USGS logic, we would still be in a safe position if it were not for one other problem: there are practical barriers to using all of the 1,200 bgd of available fresh water, even if this country were desperate enough to make the aesthetic and biological sacrifice of draining every lake and river. Because the water is usually not located where it is needed, water storage and transportation systems become a necessity. The more a society tries to juggle the distribution of its water, the higher the cost it must pay for its benefits. The most fanciful engineering projects, with elaborate storage tanks and 100-mile pipelines, may lead to only an infinitesimal increase in the water supply. Even the cheery USGS warned:

. . . the benefits derived from storing water follow a law of diminishing returns. . . . Each increment of controlled flow requires a larger amount of reservoir storage space than the preceding increment, and consequently each increment costs more than the preceding one. Furthermore, with each increment of controlled flow, the surface area of the reservoir is increased, which permits additional evaporation. Storage capacity in a basin may become so great that *the most recent increment of storage water will be dissipated by evaporation.*[8] (Emphasis added.)

In quantitative terms, estimates of how much water we can dependably use vary. In 1955, the dependable supply was about 315 bgd; one analyst has since estimated that the supply will rise to 515 bgd by 1980.[9] The Public Health Service says that the maximum amount of water the country will ever be able to depend on is 600 bgd.[10] Optimists from the Senate Select Committee on National Water Resources, however, foresee the days of the 800-bgd supply.[11]

Using even the rosiest of these predictions, the point at which supply cannot fill demand is coming soon. In 1960, the nation's towns and factories used about 270 bgd of water; in less than ten years, the figure had risen *37 per cent,* to 370 bgd.[12] By most conservative estimates, the country's water use will rise *another 80 per cent in the next ten years,* to 630 bgd by 1980.[13] That means that sometime soon, probably before 1980, the country will start asking for more water than it can provide. Predictions showing water use of 900 or 1,000 bgd by the year 2000 are meaningless; there is no way to use more water than the 600–800 bgd we will have. When the time comes that the country finally realizes it is dealing with a limited resource, there will be several possible decisions.

We may decide to cut back on the 40 per cent of our water that now irrigates crops; then we will have to figure out where to find food for our own country, let alone the rest of the swelling world. We may decide that we can do without some of our industries, and that they can do without some of the 50 per cent of our water supply they now use. We may decide that doing away with air conditioners is worth the 2 per cent of the water supply it would save. Or we may decide that agriculture, industry, and indoor comfort are all so crucial that human beings will just have to get along with fewer baths and less frequent sips of water.

There is, of course, an alternative. It is the only course open to us if we want to head off the long-term threat of death by dehydration, and the more immediate danger of losing all the aesthetic and biological virtues of our natural waters. Until this country and the rest of the world come to their collective senses about the need for strict population control, it is almost inevitable that

TABLE 2–1

Water Use, 1950–1965 (in billions of gallons per day)

User	*1950*	*1955*	*1960*	*1965*
Industry	77	110	140	170
Irrigation	79	81	84	87
Public Supplies	14	17	21	20
Total	170	208	245	277
(plus— conveyance losses in agriculture)	?	29	26	33
Total, all uses	*?*	*237*	*271*	*310*

Source: USGS.

our water use will keep rising—as will our use of other resources. But, unlike the possibility of controlling other resources, we have reason to be optimistic about the chances of controlling our water supply.

When water is "used"—for drinking, for manufacturing, or simply for watering crops—it is very rarely "used up." Of the nation's total daily water use, about 22 per cent is "consumptive" usage—water that is not immediately returned to lakes or streams. Nearly all of the consumptive usage takes place in agriculture, although a small amount leaves manufacturing plants as part of the finished product (one ton of dry paper, for example, contains 15 gallons of water). Most of the water—more than 275 billion gallons per day at current rates—simply flows back to the surface sources where most of it came

TABLE 2–2

User	*Consumptive Usage*	*Per cent of Consumptive Usage*
Industry	3,600	5.5%
Irrigation	52,000	85%
Public Supplies	3,600	5.5%
Rural Supplies	2,400	4%
Air Conditioning and Miscellaneous	Approx. 400	Insignificant
Total	*62,000*	*100%*

Source: U.S. Geological Survey Circular 456, "Estimated Use of Water in the United States, 1960."

from. There, if it were not so grossly polluted, it could be used again and again.

Already, almost every city that takes its water from a river is practicing an unintentional form of water re-use. Along the Ohio River, for example, a gallon of water may pass through four different municipal or industrial water systems before it reaches the Mississippi. The problem is that this re-use has, until now, been far too chancy and coincidental. In the next few years, the demands we place on our rivers' buffering capacity is bound to increase. We will pour in more pollutants upstream and try to draw out more water downstream. This is where the problems of water supply and water pollution become inseparable. Unless we make a deliberate effort to clean the water we put into our rivers, we can be sure that we will run out of usable water, and very quickly.

What this dual problem requires is a complete inversion of the abusive, careless philosophy with which we have regarded our water. One of the first changes must come in our water laws, which now make water pollution a "free" practice, one with no price tag. It now costs an industry absolutely nothing to dump its garbage into the water; others must absorb the cost. The next town or mill downstream must pay to purify the water; the fishermen who depend on the river's healthy life cycles must also pay, and the costs they endure amount to a subsidy of the polluters. In a more equitable system, each source of pollution would pay to cleanse the water he puts back into the river. Only a system under which industries pay for each pound of pollutant they put out —instead of saving money for each pound they do not have to treat—will give American businesses the incentive they need to clean their wastes.

In practice, this means that cities will have to spend some money, and businesses will have to spend a lot more, to cut down their present amounts of pollution. Although human beings produce large amounts of pollutants in the inescapable performance of their bodily functions, industries produce much more.

Human sewage is dangerous because of its bacterial content, but the stunning volume of industrial pollution still makes it the most formidable threat to the future of our waters. For example, industrial sewers emit three times as much waste as all the cities of the country together and are thereby chiefly responsible for the single

TABLE 2–3
Estimated Volume of Industrial Wastes Before Treatment—1963

Industry	*Waste Water Billion Gallons (Year)*	*Standard Bio-Chemical Oxygen Demand Million Pounds (Year)*	*Settleable and Suspended Solids Million Pounds (Year)*
Primary Metals	4,300	480	4,700
Chemical and Allied Products	3,700	9,700	1,900
Paper and Allied Products	1,900	5,900	3,000
Petroleum and Coal	1,300	500	460
Food and Kindred Products	690	4,300	6,600
Transportation Equipment	240	120	*
Textile Mill Products	140	890	*
Rubber and Plastics	160	40	50
Machinery	150	60	50
Electrical Machinery	91	70	20
All Other Manufacturing	450	390	930
All Manufacturing	*13,100*	*22,000*	*18,000*
For Comparison: Sewered Population of the U.S.	5,300†	7,300‡	8,800§

* Not Available.
† 120,000,000 persons times 120 gallons times 365 days.
‡ 120,000,000 persons times 1/6 pounds times 365 days.
§ 120,000,000 persons times 0.2 pounds times 365 days.
Source: Federal Water Pollution Control Administration, "The Cost of Clean Water, Volume 1: Summary Report," 1968, p. 17.

most important kind of water pollution—waste products that consume oxygen, making the water uninhabitable for fish and other living organisms, and destroying the river's capacity to absorb other kinds of wastes. The chemical products industry alone produces more of this "Biological Oxygen Demand" (BOD) waste than all municipal sewers. The second most polluting industry, the pulp and paper mills, come closer each year to matching the municipal BOD total.

Within its gentle Southern boundaries, Savannah and the streams that surround it contain most of the elements of the national water crisis. Although the problem grows more acute, the people have still not had to deal with it. Only the fish and other inhabitants of the lush coastal marsh have suffered so far from the pollution the city has placed in its river. Since their uniquely abundant source of ground water has not yet been exhausted, Savannahians have not had to think about re-using river water at all. The time is coming for Savannah, however, as for the rest of the country, when survival will depend on putting the old, negligent ways aside.

3

The Floating Crap Game

You just can't tell people to stop flushing their toilets.

Rock Howard

Like most other people, the citizens of Savannah are not used to peering into their sewers to learn the great lessons about life or law. There could be worse places to look. As Savannah's experience shows, the simple task of trying to build a sewage system can bring together and display all the classic flaws of municipal government.

With very little effort, a scholar could make a full-time occupation out of studying Savannah's sewer crises. The "sewer" files in the city government offices are several feet thick, and the transcript of just one of the court cases involving the sewage system occupies 35 miles of recording tape. Added to this are the overlapping bureaucratic problems of six or seven forms of local government, two Federal departments, and at least one state agency, all writing memos and issuing orders.

The complication is unfortunate. It makes the problem seem far more subtle than it really is. Two sets of figures and dates sum up the problem concisely: in 1965, when the city of Savannah first learned it would have to build a plant to treat its sewage, engineers said the project could be done by 1968 and would cost about $10.8 million. Five years later, when construction had not yet begun and the Federal and state enforcing agencies were becoming seriously irritated, the cost estimate had swollen to $21 million and the city was working hard to finish the plant by the middle of 1973.

A formidable array of obstacles and problems have

played a part in creating the five-year, $10-million gap between the first sewer prediction and the most recent estimate. On its slow road to completion, the sewer plan has run into legal barriers, technical questions, and several economic objections. But by far the worst problem has been political.

A crew of politicians with their eyes on re-election has discovered that the sewage system will cost a lot of money without making anyone very happy, at least in the short run. And so plans for building the sewage plant have made their way to the bottom of the municipal priorities pile. Meanwhile, the city's leaders have found other projects—like shiny convention centers, crack-down programs on Savannah's version of hippies, and campaigns to make Savannah an "All-American City"—which cost much less but produce more visible results. Showing rare flashes of imagination, the city government has guided its favorite projects through hazards that would have turned back less diligent men. At the same time, Savannah's government has watched as its sewer plans have neared the brink of success, only to be pulled back by petty, sometimes unimaginable problems.

Like excretion itself, sewage treatment is not a popular topic for conversation or thought. Since Savannah's founding, the city has avoided serious consideration of its waste by sending its sewage untreated to the river. For the first century or two of Savannah's history, all the sewage went directly to the Savannah River. When the city started spreading so far south that the sewage would not flow easily to the Savannah, the sewage pipes were aimed at the creeks and streams to the south. During the 1950's, the city tried to cope with part of this problem by installing a few oxidation ponds and a treatment plant for wastes from the suburbs; but the main city sewage—about 16 million gallons daily, all that 135,000 people produce—still went straight and untreated into the Savannah.

Whether people wanted to think about it or not, the sewage had an inescapably bad effect on the river. If the Savannah had been in better condition to start with, the addition of millions of gallons of raw sewage might not

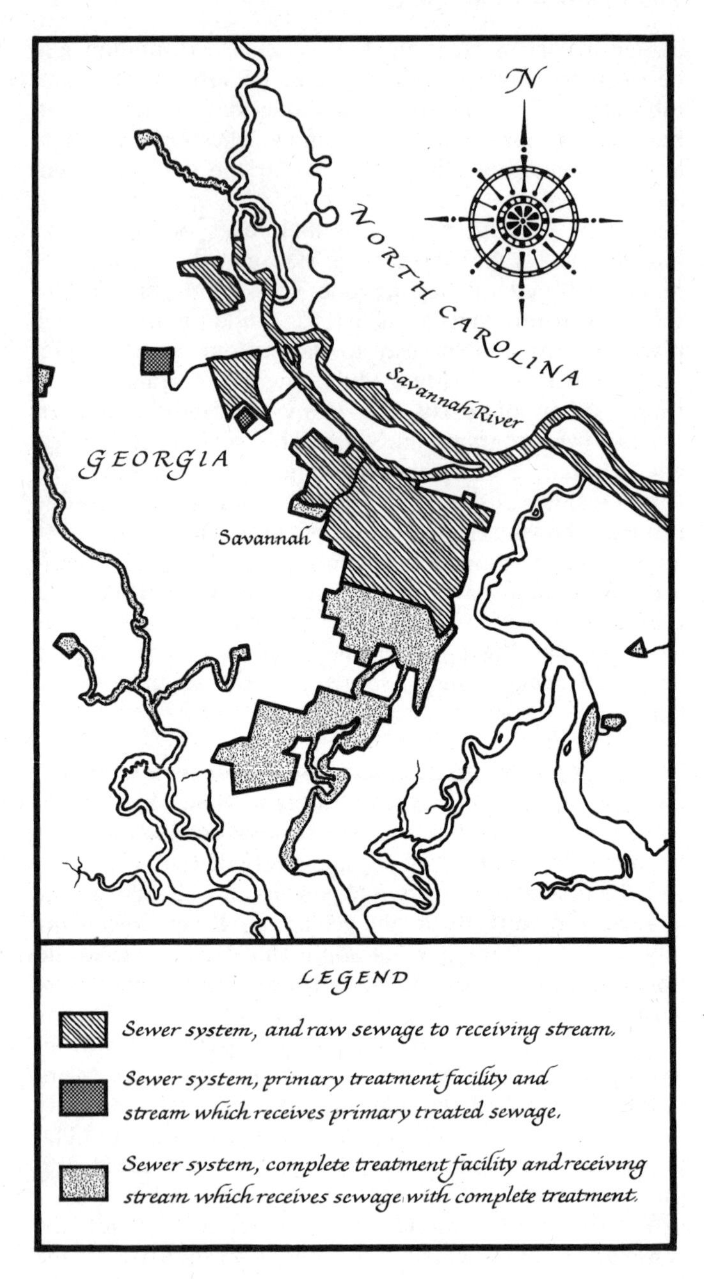

Source: Georgia Department of Public Health

have been catastrophic. But, burdened as it already was with industrial waste from upstream, the river was in no shape to handle human sewage as well. The effects of the overloading show up in several unpleasant ways, from the unmistakable scent of rotting bowel movements that rises from Hayner's Creek and from the Savannah near City Hall, to the increasing number of No Swimming signs that line the shores.

The peculiar problem that human sewage poses is that, unlike most other kinds of pollutants in the river, it is more dangerous to men than to animals. Human sewage contains bacteria—both the relatively harmless "fecal coliform" and more dangerous forms of disease-causing bacteria. This is no serious problem for the fish who are not usually susceptible to human diseases, but it is a constant danger to any humans who happen to eat fish harboring the bacteria. Thousands of acres of oyster beds in the river and surrounding marsh have been condemned since the 1940's for just this reason: while the oysters themselves may be perfectly healthy, they contain bacteria that is harmful to humans. The same dangerous bacterial contamination caused the Chatham County Health Department to declare several rivers and creeks off limits for swimmers.

As they have endured several other strange materials in their air and water, Savannahians have managed to endure the sewage. Only in the rarest cases have they become upset—or at least upset enough to do something about it. The most notable example involved the people of Vernonburg, a small, plush residential community several miles south of Savannah. The townspeople, who had moved there to enjoy a scenic location on the Vernon River, were understandably unhappy when effluent from two Savannah sewage plants began flowing through their small creeks and rivers. Although the effluent was "treated," it turned the creeks it flowed through into "open sewers" and made life generally unpleasant.

"The creek's condition has the power to alter the mood and quality of life for those who live around it," a newspaper story describing the situation said. "Even those who've given up all ideas of using the creek find it impossible at times to sit in their back yards or use their swimming pools because of the stench." [1]

So Vernonburg's residents filed a suit and won. They forced the city of Savannah to add the nearby treatment plants to its master plan for treating sewage. When the whole system is finally built, it will solve the Hayner's Creek problem by piping the effluent up to the already filthy Savannah.

Even this one example of citizen action against pollution shows why more ambitious projects have bogged down. The people of Vernonburg got what they wanted by making someone else—some other city's group of taxpayers—do the cleaning up. Apparently Vernonburg saw no irony in the fact that its *own* sewage still went into inadequate septic tanks, instead of into the sewage system it has refused to build. Neither did some of the leaders of the suit against Savannah think it peculiar that they were executives of Union Camp, which produces a far greater load of pollutants than the trickle that runs through Hayner's Creek.

Since most of the people of Savannah have not been in the fortunate Vernonburgian position of getting someone else to do the job, they have chosen another approach: that of learning to live with the problem. The pinnacle of this pleasant obliviousness probably occurs at Savannah Beach, where bathers often frolic a full 100 feet from the pipes that discharge city sewage.[2] According to the state Water Board, the danger zone extends at least 1,000 feet away from the sewage pipes.

The formal history of Savannah's modern sewage problem begins in 1965, but the city had ample warning before then that trouble was coming. Throughout the early 1960's, the county grand jury, city study groups, and even the U.S. Public Health Service reported that the city had to do something about its raw sewage. Under the liberal city administration then in office, Savannah actually did begin to do something. By the time the Federal water pollution conference came to town in February 1965, city manager Arthur Mendonsa was ready with a comprehensive plan for treating the city's sewage. The Federal and state officials at the conference were satisfied, and they told the city to begin work on the plan so that it could be finished by 1970.

The sewage treatment plan—designed by the Atlanta

engineering firm of Wiedeman and Singleton with their Savannah collaborators, Hussey and Gay—was the one the city relied on for the next five years. Immediately after the enforcement conference, however, there were no signs that the city was doing anything at all. Mayor Malcolm MacLean, a lawyer shrewdly sensitive to the political whims of his constituents, figured that he had enough politically unpopular projects on his hands because of his relatively liberal management of the city's integration problems. "Two issues in this town," he later said, "race and taxes." Having one issue, MacLean saw no need to bring in the other. "No politician in his right mind puts on a tax right before an election." [3]

Despite the lack of publicity, much of the quiet work continued. Mendonsa saw that preliminary engineering studies and contracts went ahead, and he reported in 1966 that the project was on schedule. After the election, MacLean thought, the sewage plan could move into high gear, complete with the tax increase that would undoubtedly be necessary to pay for it.

For MacLean's administration, however, there was no "after the election." The voting public, apparently fed up with six years of MacLean's generally progressive policies, swept him out of office and brought in J. Curtis Lewis and his team of aldermen.*

To understand the events of the next four years requires a closer look at Lewis. In traditional Savannah sociology, the town's well-to-do class has generally been split into two large groups. On one side are the "cultured" or at least "cultural" rich, families who regard themselves as the modern version of the old Southern planters, patrons of art, history, and music. Their source of wealth is usually the large industries (Union Camp, of course, and Savannah Sugar) plus the Citizens and Southern Bank. Their traditional repository of public power has been the Chatham County Commission.

On the other side of the divide are the Elks Club rich, the insurance salesmen and real estate brokers who have made it big during Savannah's expansion. There are fewer of these people, and their aggregate economic

* MacLean was appointed mayor in 1960 when Mayor Lee Mingledorff resigned from office to run for the county commission. MacLean then won election to a four-year term in 1962.

strength is naturally less than that of the factories and the banks. They have also generally been left out whenever local political muscle was distributed. All that changed in 1966, however, when J. C. Lewis rode to power.

While Lewis is personally unobtrusive and apparently motivated more by purely acquisitive instinct than by an urge to become a titan of Chatham County, he has stretched his economic fingers into almost every corner of Savannah life. Without even realizing it, many Savannahians pass the major portion of their lives under the auspices of J. C. Lewis. Families live in J. C. Lewis houses (in the new "Habersham Woods" development, complete with English heraldic plaques on the street signs) and play at the neighborhood YMCA (built on J. C. Lewis land). They buy food at the J. C. Lewis supermarket or eat dinner at his Regency Room restaurant. Car buyers choose from several J. C. Lewis auto dealerships, or simply rent from his Avis franchise. Travelers stay at the J. C. Lewis Downtowner motel and watch shows on his WJCL television station. But no one can send his sewage to a J. C. Lewis treatment plant.

The firmly conservative viewpoint of the Lewis administration undoubtedly contributed somewhat to his delay in building the sewer system. So did the embarrassingly small amount of time he was able to spend being mayor. (While in office and while actively running his other enterprises, Lewis applied for and fought hard to get the local television license. In his application to the Federal Communications Commission, he pledged to devote his full time to the station—which may explain his often vague grasp of city programs.) Neither conservatism nor entrepreneurship, however, created as much havoc as the new government's profound naïveté in the art of governing. The mayor and his aldermen spent most of their first year trying to figure out how the government worked. This training period could not have come at a worse time for the sewage treatment program. In all their confusion and innocence, Lewis and his supporters found themselves in the middle of the most bizarre chapter of the entire sewage story—the Sewell-Wiedeman feud.

Dan Sewell, a local engineer who had hoped to get

the contract to design the city's sewage treatment system, found in December 1965, that he had been left out. Several days later, he began a campaign against the engineer the city had chosen—Theodore Wiedeman of the Atlanta engineering firm of Wiedeman and Singleton. Sewell began his attack in the press and then carried it to the state engineering board. Through an interminable set of hearings that kept at least two Savannah lawyers occupied for months, Sewell tried to prove that Wiedeman should lose his engineering license for assorted violations of professional ethics.

The truth about the case is buried somewhere in the 35-mile long transcript in the city files. Its impact on Savannah, however, is much easier to see. As soon as Lewis took office, he found himself with a sewage treatment plan that was undesirable on almost every count. It was expensive, it had no immediately apparent virtues, and the man who had designed it was being accused of incompetence. If the city government had had a more intense interest in getting the treatment system completed, Lewis might have found a way to press ahead with it, perhaps by getting an independent appraisal of its merits. But, realizing that quick progress on the sewage plan would automatically mean some kind of tax increase, Lewis thought it best just to wait.

The crisis came in September of 1967, when the engineering board finally decided to revoke Wiedeman's license. Wiedeman appealed, but in the meantime, Lewis had to do something about the sewers. The whole plan was tainted by accusations that suddenly had more substance than they had had before. Lewis' decision was to ask the state Water Board to review Wiedeman's sewage plan and tell the city what to do.

R. S. "Rock" Howard, head of the Georgia Water Quality Control Board, who was throughout this period in a constant state of anxiety about the city's delay, wasted no time in finishing his part of the job. In January 1968, his office released its terse review, which essentially endorsed everything Wiedeman had planned for Savannah. If Howard thought that was enough to get the city moving, however, he still had a lot to learn about the mayor. Through most of the rest of 1968, Lewis retained his aplomb in the face of constant irritation. His city manager, Picot Floyd, issued and reissued memoranda telling the city council that the time had come "where action on the part of the Mayor and Aldermen is needed." [4]

On March 29, 1968, a Superior Court judge restored Wiedeman's license, ruling that the engineering board hearing had been little more than a kangaroo court.* Still Lewis refused to budge. Deadlines came and passed for collecting Federal money to help with the project. Howard sent a stream of steadily more irritated letters to the city. For example, on April 30: "We have become very concerned over the City's hesitancy to move forward"; [5] on May 27: "I earnestly request that you give this matter your urgent attention and take the necessary action to accelerate Savannah's abatement program." [6]

Through it all, Lewis was imperturbable, answering Howard's letters with palliatives, such as, "I also recognize the desirability of moving along as rapidly as possible with these programs. The city administration has pledged its cooperation to your office in connection with these essential programs, and I wish to restate that pledge of cooperation at this time." [7] In frustration, Howard finally threatened to prosecute. He sent a telegram saying that the State Attorney General was reviewing Savannah's record "prior to taking appropriate enforcement action." [8]

In the face of this threat, Lewis—who had been out of town when Howard came calling earlier in the year—found it worthwhile to have a meeting with Howard. There he told Howard what had been on his mind: the city wanted another review of its program, this time by a California firm called Engineering Science. But Lewis promised that if Engineering Science also endorsed the

* The decision restored Wiedeman's license and went on to say that the hearings before the State Board of Registration for Professional Engineers and Land Surveyors had been:

"a) Arbitrary, capricious, and characterized by an abuse of discretion.

"b) Clearly erroneous in view of the reliable, probative, and substantial evidence on the whole record.

"c) Based on unlawful procedure.

"d) In violation of the constitutional and statutory provisions of the State of Georgia.

"e) Characterized by a clearly unwarranted exercise of discretion." (Source: Ruling in Fulton County Superior Court, Civil Actions B-31807 and B-33542; March 29, 1968) original sewer plan, the city would "proceed immediately to implement this particular program." [9]

However, the delays stretched into another whole year. Engineering Science released its report in November 1968 and, like every other review, it endorsed the original plan. After that, the city's resistance took a new approach. Early in 1969, the city government began to exploit the most politically unattractive element of the whole sewage system: separating the pipes that carried human sewage from those that carried storm water runoff. Like many other cities that built their sewers in the days before sewage treatment was a major civic concern, Savannah had combined these two sets of pipes throughout most of the older section of town. Separating them would not only be expensive but would also mean blocking off and digging up several downtown streets. The city's general political-economic resistance to the project got a boost from a consulting engineer, Joseph Hutton, who predicted that it would be impossible ever to get the two pipe systems completely separated.

But the state and Federal authorities were equally convinced that the combined sewer system had to go. In some cities, like New York or Atlanta or Cleveland, the cost of separation would be literally billions of dollars. There, the only practical approach is to treat the combined storm/sewer effluent and not worry about separating them. In Savannah, however, local circumstances made separation more logical: during the brief but torrential rains that fall almost daily during the summer, the combined pipe system backs up and spreads human sewage over the streets. To take care of this problem without separating the sewer systems, the city would either have to build a huge treatment plant, many times bigger than the one contemplated, or else resign itself to letting all sewage by-pass the treatment plant and run untreated into the river during the rains. Engineers, the Georgia Water Board, and the Federal Water Pollution Control Administration insisted that the cost of separate systems for Savannah was so small and the hazards of not separating were so large that the city had no other choice.

This, however, did not convince Lewis and the aldermen. Throughout the first half of 1969, they appealed again and again for a new kind of treatment system. Again and again they were turned down, and in July 1969, they decided at last to go ahead with the original plan.

At the time of the second Federal enforcement conference in October 1969, Howard had some caustic words about the city's stalling. In his castigation of the city (unjustly aimed, during the conference, at City Manager Floyd rather than at those who set the policy), Howard put his finger on the source of the problem:

> And I will tell you another thing, if we had had the same priority for getting this pollution cleaned up in the last five years almost as we have had for getting the civic center built, and for getting the historical homes restored, and for getting the [bridge to] Skidaway Island built, we would be almost finished. That is what I want to say. It is a matter of priority . . .[10]

"Priority," of course, is just another name for the heart of the problem: money. There are some things money cannot buy, but it would have gone a long way toward getting a high "priority" for Savannah's sewage program.

The order to build a sewage plant presented the elected officials with an extremely unappealing set of prospects. The costs were high—higher than any other single expense in the city's history, though not as high as the $30–40 million the mayor wanted to spend for a new local expressway. The advantages, while of general benefit to everyone, offered no great attraction to any special interest group. The general attitude seemed to be, well, we have lived with a dirty river this long. . . . One generation of Savannahians was in the position of shelling out the entire cost for correcting centuries of neglect.

A local government convinced that this had to be done, regardless of the obstacles, might have persuaded the people to support the project. Lewis, however, did the opposite. By repeatedly calling the project "financially distasteful" and emphasizing that the city was being forced to act by the state, he may have won a few votes as protector of city pocketbooks, but he effectively aborted any city enthusiasm for getting the plant built.

Lewis even managed to parley his theory into a whole plan for financing the sewage system. Under Public Law 660, which is designed to help towns in treating their sewage, the Federal government will pay up to 33 per cent of the cost of a treatment system. From the time of the earliest designs of Savannah's system, city officials had stressed, in private memoranda and public speeches, that Savannah would naturally have to pay the remaining 67 per cent. At the same time, the city was trying hard to get another large source of financial help. Under Public Law 660, the Federal government will pay up to 55 per cent of the total sewage cost—if the state government agrees to pay 25 per cent. As far as Savannah was concerned, the difference was huge: if the state government did not contribute any money, then the Federal government would pay only 33 percent, leaving Savannah with the remaining 67 per cent (about $8 million in the first versions of the plan; later up to $14–15 million). But if the state would cough up a mere 25 per cent, Federal money would cover 55 per cent, and Savannah would pay only 20 per cent of the cost.

The incentive was so great that it spurred even Lewis' city government into active lobbying with state legislators. But when the lobbying failed to make any dent in the thick crust of rural representatives encasing Georgia's legislature, the city government chose another course guaranteed to please the home-town voters. Lewis, and his main confidante on the city council, mayor *pro tempore* Benjamin Garfunkel, redefined the city's responsibility. They decided that 20 per cent of the total cost—the amount the city would have to pay if both the state and Federal governments came up with maximum grants—was Savannah's "proper share" of the sewage treatment cost. If the state (i.e., Howard) was so eager to get the system built, Lewis and Garfunkel told reporters and audiences, why didn't they pay their proper share, just like Savannah? As Garfunkel said at the 1969 conference:

I am real concerned over the fact that the city of Savannah, I think, has shown more than good faith in what has to be done in the programs that it has implemented, and I think that the city of Savannah of the three, considering the Federal Government, the State of Georgia, and the city of

Savannah, that the only one that can appear today with clean hands is the city of Savannah. In spite of the accusations that came from the Federal Government and from the State, the city of Savannah is prepared and is ready to implement the program and pay *their fair share* [i.e., 20 per cent].[11] (Emphasis added.)

The city seems finally to have found a solution, but it makes almost no one happy. For the next 20 years, Savannah's water users will be paying a 24½ per cent "pollution abatement surcharge" on their water and sewer bills. The surcharge has made some people angry because it is too high: people who live outside the city limits but still use Savannah water end up paying about twice as much per month as families inside the city. The state Water Board is also unhappy—because the surcharge is too low. The money the surcharge brings in will pay off the "revenue bonds" the city floated to finance the building of the sewage system. At its present level, the surcharge will only cover 20 per cent of the sewage system cost—Savannah's "fair share."

Nobody knows, however, if the state will kick in an additional 25 per cent. During his term as mayor, Lewis was never able to say what would happen if the state legislature continued to refuse Savannah a sewage grant. Perhaps the city will have to triple the surcharge; perhaps it will have to sell more General Obligation bonds. In any case, Lewis doesn't have to worry about it any more. His vigilant defense of the city tax dollars went unappreciated in the 1970 municipal elections. The new mayor, John Rousakis, is a more enthusiastic supporter of sewage treatment than Lewis. The important test for him, however, will be the same Lewis faced: whether he can convince the tax-paying voters that curbing the pollution is worth the dollars it will cost.

The irony of Vernonburg—the town that gleefully took Savannah to court but then refused to replace its own inadequate sewage system—points up the more general dilemma of Chatham County and similar areas. Water pollution is a regional problem; sewage does not stop at arbitrary state or county boundaries. Too many efforts aimed at curing pollution, however, are mired in the old concepts of city-by-city planning. So it is in

Chatham County. For reasons that have no basis in geographic or economic logic, the county is carved up into seven separate cities. Savannah is the giant, but it is rimmed by Thunderbolt, Vernonburg, Port Wentworth, Garden City, Pooler, and—at a respectable distance—Savannah Beach.

All of these are placid little towns, tenaciously happy with their own grassroots form of government. What these small citizens want, said Arthur Gilreath, mayor of Thunderbolt, is a government "close to the people, so that they don't have to write any damn letters to get attention for their individual problems." [12]

In an impersonal world, the homey touch is welcome. But when it comes to treating sewage, local autonomy causes many more problems than it solves. For years, the Metropolitan Planning Commission—the countywide planning body, which officials of each city usually regard with thinly veiled suspicion—has urged a coordinated county "Master Plan" for sewage treatment. This plan would not only save money by combining the sewage systems of several small areas into one more efficient plant but would also do something that the current plans will not be able to do in the foreseeable future: get all the county's sewage treated. The county health department, occasional members of the county commission, and even some Savannah officials have also realized that countywide treatment is the only way to clean the rivers of their sewage.

Because of undying opposition from towns eager to retain their sovereignty, pleas for coordination have so far been futile. Meanwhile, each town has inched ahead with its own version of a sewage system. In some cases, this has brought good results: Quinnie Roach, mayor of Pooler, found in 1962 that the town's septic tanks were beginning to act up. In the face of a county ban on any construction in Pooler until the situation improved, Roach and his town of 2,000 reacted in the best possible faith. They built an entirely adequate sewage treatment plant, complete with room for future growth.

Port Wentworth, which has refused to go along with Savannah and Garden City on joint treatment plans, may still make the best of its separate situation. It is now considering plans for building a large treatment plant for the combined wastes from the city and its two industries, Continental Can and Savannah Sugar. If the industries finally decide to join Port Wentworth, everyone involved will save money. From the river's point of view, the more important effect will be that one plant will get rid of not only Port Wentworth's trickle of sewage but also the large waste flows from the two mills.

But the city-by-city approach has its drawbacks, as the experiences of other towns show. Under the state's Water Quality Control Act, Howard can take action only against cities that are actually releasing sewage into a river. The septic tanks that Thunderbolt and Vernonburg use are unhealthy because of the county's poor soil conditions; but because they pollute the river only indirectly, there is nothing the state can do about them.

Occasionally a situation arises which serves as a living reminder of some abuse, and thereby argues more powerfully for its correction than any set of theories. In Chatham County, Savannah Beach performs this pitiful function. Its most immediate need is something as prosaic as countywide sewer planning; but by implication, more sweeping urban reforms are suggested.

The town is twenty miles downstream from Savannah, on a beach that is not classed as one of the east coast's best. Its problems are those of a city of 1,800 which must provide services for hordes of daytime tourists. The tourists come only in pleasant weather, but when they do, they are abundant: 10,000 on weekends in May, 30,000 on hot June and July weekends, a steady 20,000 throughout the summer.

Sewage treatment is the most expensive service the town provides. On summer weekends, the volume of sewage is so great that the city bypasses its treatment system and sends the sewage, after brief chlorination, straight to the sea. If the town's permanent residents cannot find some way to make the tourists bear part of the cost of the new treatment plant, each year-round citizen will have to pay about $800 for the plant. They are understandably irate, but have no idea of what to do.

The other municipal services—police, firemen, garbage collection, power, etc.—have their problems too. The irony of the situation is that the city has brought the problems on itself. Savannah Beach does what it can to attract tourists and make their stay comfortable; there are showers along the concrete boardwalk, lifeguards, and cookout facilities. But the tourists are generally poor and reluctant to spend money in Savannah Beach. "The kind of people we get here—we can't get anything out of them," said one city councilman during an interview. "They buy their lunches in some Savannah grocery store and eat them out of the trunks of the cars." [13]

The cost of the municipal services is not the end of the city's woes. The tourists who flock to the beach have no stake in its preservation; vandalism is a constant cost and worry. To keep trash off the beach, the city installed 50-gallon garbage cans at the end of each street leading to the beach. People stole them. The city sank metal posts by the cans. People turned the cans over and stomped their sides in. Tourists also rip the locks out of parking meters, have keys made, and come back the next day to steal all the quarters from the meters. When the city redesigned the meters, people chopped the tops off. Usually, the theft from the meters is quieter; as each summer season ends, the city files away $20,000 worth of unpaid parking tickets.

Why does the town seek these tourists, with their extra sewage, their small change, their destruction? "Because they are there," seems to be the only explanation. It seems inevitable that places like Savannah Beach exist, where many want services but few are willing to pay. As long as they do exist, however, the only way to protect them is to share expenses like sewage costs through large-scale planning.

4

The Lesser Evil: American Cyanamid

Before examining the many ways that paper mills in general and Union Camp in particular affect their towns, we should take a brief look at the other major industrial polluter of the Savannah, American Cyanamid.

Cyanamid is a relative newcomer to Savannah; by the time it arrived in the early 1950's, Union Camp, Savannah Sugar, and Continental Can had been in business for years. Since its arrival, Cyanamid has not tried to force its way into the general flow of Savannah life as have some of the other industries. Cyanamid's managers have decided that it is more important to impress corporate headquarters in New Jersey than the local populace. Also, many of the Cyanamid executives regard the Savannah plant as a way station on the road to promotions; the managerial staff is much more transient than the semipermanent dynasties that preside over some of the other local mills.

At its plant on the far east side of town, downstream from both Savannah and all the other industries, Cyanamid's 500 employees produce titanium dioxide, a white pigment used to write the m's on M&M candy, among other things. As a by-product of manufacturing the pigment, Cyanamid delivers some six million gallons of waste water to the Savannah every day.[1] Aside from its considerable volume (in terms of waste production per employee, Cyanamid's waste flow is about twice that of Union Camp), the effluent has two distinctly bad effects on the river.

The greatest danger is acid pollution. In 1965, investigators reported at the Federal enforcement conference that Cyanamid released 690,000 pounds of sulfuric acid daily. In a 1969 survey, the Georgia Water

Board found even higher totals, ranging between 831,000 and 1,005,000 pounds of acid daily.[2] Most forms of aquatic life are extremely sensitive to changes in the river's normal acid-alkaline balance caused by Cyanamid's waste flow; for example, slightly acid water with a pH of 6.5 * is enough to cut the respiration rate of oysters by 90 per cent.[3] The acid that comes from Cyanamid's outfalls is so concentrated that its pH is often in the 0.9–1.0 range.[4] As the acid flows down the river, it is gradually neutralized, but Cyanamid's own surveys show pockets of water with a pH factor as low as 4.0 in the marsh lands downstream of the plant.[5] Local shrimpers, who claim that there are widespread shrimp kills whenever Cyanamid opens up its acid pipes on the outgoing tide, report even lower pH readings.

Along with the acid, Cyanamid's waste also exerts a heavy oxygen demand on the river. Company officials put great stress on the fact that their pollution contains no Biological Oxygen Demand. While this is true, it is meaningless: the Chemical Oxygen Demand (COD) that Cyanamid's waste contains does just as effective a job of using up dissolved oxygen in the river. This COD comes from the large amounts of iron—between 50 and 130 tons daily—that flow out of Cyanamid's pipes. The soluble ferrous compounds react with the river's dissolved oxygen to form several different iron oxides. In the process, the waste draws somewhere between 25,000 and 35,000 pounds of dissolved oxygen from the river, exerting a heavier oxygen demand than all of Savannah's sewage.[6] After the iron has combined with the oxygen, it sinks to the bottom of the river and, in the words of the state Water Board, "contributes significantly to the sediment load." [7]

Apart from its day-to-day pollution, Cyanamid is also responsible for one of the worst disasters in the river's history. For several years, Cyanamid has used large holding ponds to store its wastes, because the company is only allowed to release acid on the outgoing tide. At best, the ponds are a very primitive form of treatment:

* "pH" is a measure of acidity or alkalinity. A pH of 7 is neutral; each decrease of 1 pH means a ten times greater concentration of acid. The concentrated sulfuric acid used in most laboratory experiments has a pH of 3.

some of the solids settle out, and the acid is slightly diluted by the company's other waste water. But no one appreciated the ponds' worst danger until July 17, 1968, when a torrential rainfall caused a 40–50 foot section of the earthen dike that lines the ponds to give way. Thirty million gallons of waste water, containing at least three and one-half million pounds of raw sulfuric acid, ran into the river.[8]

Fish died for miles down the river, not only in the Savannah near Cyanamid but also in the Wilmington River, although Cyanamid officials still insist their pollution never enters this tributary. In the understated prediction of the year, Howard had earlier pointed out the dangers of the stored acid: "Something of that size could get down the river on the ebb tide and hurt the shellfish and fish."[9]

Glen McBay of the state game and fish agency added another warning: "Acid could not only create an immediate fish kill, but could affect the fish spawning and nursery grounds in the back waters."[10]

In the days after the tragedy, investigators were not able to calculate the size of the fish kill, except to say that it was "sizable."[11] The long-term effects on spawning grounds were even harder to trace.

The steps Cyanamid has taken to guarantee against a repeat of the acid spill are not encouraging. Even before building the dikes around the ponds, the company knew that the land beneath was marshy and unstable.[12] Because the land could not bear heavy loads without settling, Cyanamid built the rest of its plant on special pilings. But since no one had bothered to put pilings underneath the dikes, when a heavy rain weakened the ground, the dike simply sank.

Cyanamid's remedy for the problem was to spend only $50,000 for a larger, broader dike.[13] While this new dike may spread the load over a larger portion of land, there is no way of being sure that another very heavy rainfall will not make this dike cave in, too.

Like the other industrial polluters on the river, Cyanamid is under a deadline for cleaning up its effluent. In late 1969, the state Water Board told the company to make three changes by the middle of 1972:

1. Reduce the quantity of acid discharge to a level that will not lower the river pH below 6.0 at any point in the river more than 1,000 feet downstream of the plant discharge.
2. Reduce the oxygen demand of the effluent by 25 per cent.
3. Reduce the suspended and settleable solids by 90 per cent.[14]

So far, Cyanamid has taken steps to correct only the acid concentration. It installed a new fixture on the end of its waste discharge pipe; this "diffusion header" was to spread out the acid in the river, instead of leaving it in concentrated pockets near the bank. Like many other corporate decisions, the selection of the header was a compromise between cost and efficiency. Although the company's engineers knew that extending the discharge pipe farther into the river would do a better job of dispersing the acid, the cost would have been high. So Cyanamid settled for the header.

The header was not enough, as the state Water Board found when it studied the system's performance. "The work done on May 20, 1969, indicated that the recently installed diffuser had not corrected the pH problem in the Savannah River at American Cyanamid, *especially in the South Channel and Wilmington River.*" [15] (Emphasis added.)

The mention of the South Channel and Wilmington River is crucial for two reasons. From a biological point of view, these two stretches are somewhat less contaminated than the main North Channel of the Savannah. Families along the Wilmington still like to think of it as a recreational stream where they can boat and fish. Acid contamination of the Wilmington, therefore, is even more destructive than in the main navigational channel of the Savannah, where there is little wildlife left to kill.

From a sociological-political point of view, the Water Board's report also says something about Cyanamid's corporate honesty. Cyanamid's officials, especially plant manager C. W. Sieber, realize that the public would prefer to think that all the acid is going into already fouled rivers rather than into recreational streams. And so, on three different occasions during the summer of

1970, Sieber told members of our project that *none* of the plant's acid went into the South Channel or the Wilmington River.

Given the stream configuration in this area and the position of Cyanamid's discharge pipes close to shore, it is difficult to imagine how Sieber's theory could be true. To avoid the South Channel, all of Cyanamid's wastes would have to surge straight across the river and reach the other side before the Savannah forked into the North and South Channels.

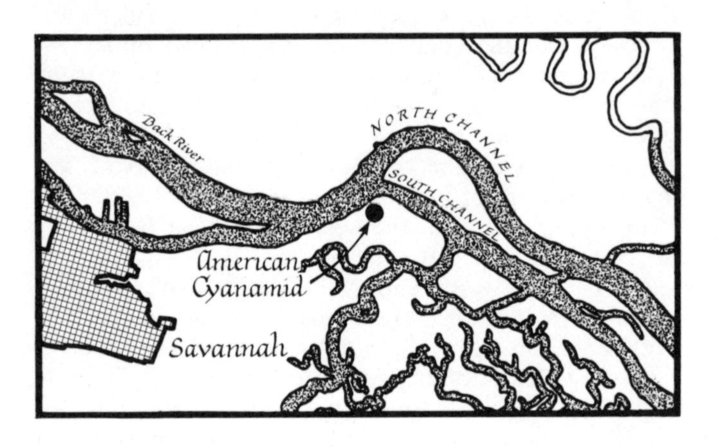

But Sieber had more than mere speculation working against his story. More than a year earlier, in May of 1969, Sieber and his staff had cooperated with the Georgia Water Board in its survey of the river, even going so far as to supply the boat used during the second day of testing. It is highly improbable that Sieber had overlooked the Water Board's report, which concluded:

> It is apparent that from field investigations conducted by the GWQCB's [Georgia Water Quality Control Board's] staff in 1968 and 1969 *and the results of the Company's survey* that the waste water leaving the Company's property is not mixed with the river flow. Past studies and reports have assumed that the acid waste was mixed with the flow in the Savannah River; consequently, it was assumed the buffering capacity of the River was available to neutralize the acid. *All data obtained in the field indicated that the waste never mixes with the River, but it is held to the south bank and*

most of it moves into the South Channel.[16] (Emphasis added.)

Even if he had somehow passed over this report, Sieber had Cyanamid's own biweekly river surveys to consult. In all, it seems impossible that Sieber believed what he told us in three separate interviews. This kind of dishonesty is bad enough when there are sources available, such as the Georgia Water Board's records, to disprove what the company says. The situation becomes even more dangerous when the public has no other choice but to "trust" the company story. After his plant had installed a new process for producing titanium dioxide, Sieber told one of our project members that the public had no right to know what was coming out of the company smokestacks—even though later investigation showed that it was deadly chlorine gas (see Chapter 9). At the time, the Chatham County Health Department knew nothing about the situation, and the state Air Quality Control Branch had seen the report but apparently forgotten about it.

In keeping with Cyanamid's generally tightlipped attitude, further details on its waste treatment plans are not yet available. When they are released, the Savannah public would do well to find someone besides Sieber to confirm that the systems are working.

5

Papering the Earth

Our civilization is wonderful, in certain spectacular and meretricious ways . . . wonderful in its spying out of the deep secrets of Nature and its vanquishment of their stubborn laws . . . wonderful in its hunger for money, and its indifference as to how it is acquired. . . . It is a civilization which has destroyed the simplicity and repose of life; replaced its contentment, its poetry, its soft romance-dreams and vision with the money-fever, sordid ideas, vulgar ambitions, and the sleep which does not refresh; it has invented a thousand useless luxuries and turned them into necessities; it has created a thousand vicious appetites and satisfied none of them.

Mark Twain, Letters From The Earth

One of the surest measures of a country's economic development and well-being is the amount of paper it consumes a year.

John E. Ray III, Executive Vice President, Union Camp Corporation

In hundreds of useful and useless and undetectable ways, the paper industry has made itself part of our lives. The pages of this book are paper and, if the reader fits the statistical average for Consuming America, they will be only part of the 1.6 pounds of paper he will use before the day is out. To reach his annual consumption of 576 pounds of paper, however, each American must surpass the old-fashioned uses of paper. Newspapers, writing tablets, and book paper are not enough any more; together, they make up less than one-fourth of our paper use.[1] We must create new paper needs now—toothpaste boxes, many-layered wrappings for rolls of film and sticks of gum, brown paper sacks, white disposable dresses, and finally the pinnacle of paperbound creativity, the Pillsbury Space Food Stick. The Pillsbury designers have attained a sort of modern ideal by swathing each one-third-ounce stick in equally heavy amounts of cardboard and tinfoil.

Few people choose to use this much paper. But even if the choice were ours rather than industry's, the price of extravagant consumption of paper products would still seem small. Enormous paper consumption has become such a fixture of American life that it is easy to forget where the paper came from, and at what cost. After all, the housewife might reason as she strips cardboard wrappings from her food, paper is so cheap. Why shouldn't we just throw it away?

Cities like New York are beginning to learn one answer to that question. As their garbage—60 per cent of it paper—threatens to reinvade from the sea, and as the bill for merely collecting the garbage rises above $90 million annually, New Yorkers are starting to think that perhaps simply putting their trash in the trash can is not as permanent a solution as they might have imagined.

High as that price may be, there is an even higher price—one that is usually invisible where paper is carelessly used and carelessly discarded. In Georgia—which produces more paper than any other state, and where paper mills do more polluting than any other industry—the cost is easier to remember. In reeking paper mill towns, it is hard to think of anything else.

The fact that the paper industry contributes about one-fourth of the nation's industrial water pollution[2] and inflicts terrible harm on the air is only one reason for examining the industry closely. Oddly enough, the paper industry is *potentially* one of the most environmentally safe in the country. Using available technology, it is possible virtually to eliminate the industry's three main offenses against nature: the ever expanding harvest of forest land, the air and water pollution that come from making the paper, and the mound of garbage left over when the paper is thrown away. With proper safeguards, the forests could be conserved, the air and water protected, and the garbage minimized. Obviously, too few of those steps are being taken. In tracing the path of the industry's current neglect, an important lesson about industrial priorities emerges. When natural resources appear on the balance sheet, then conservation becomes part of normal business practice. The mills, for example, must pay for the timber they use, and have therefore learned to replace what they take. But whenever resources are free—when a mill can fill a river with its deadly filth—then the public pays.

The paper industry, like every other, is out to make money. The briefest glance over its history shows that it has been amazingly successful. In 1925, when American paper tastes were still being developed, the industry produced about nine million tons of paper and cardboard; each American in those prosperous Coolidge days used about 180 pounds of paper each year. In less than twenty years, national paper use doubled. Shrugging off the Depression, the paper industry turned out 19 million tons of paper in 1944—319 pounds for every person in America. And ten years later, paper use was three times as high as in the twenties. In the middle of the affluent fifties, happiest days for the paper marketers, industrywide production hit 30 million tons and per capita consumption rose to 420 pounds. By 1969, production had risen almost 80 per cent, to 54 million tons, and consumption set another record at 576 pounds of paper for every man, woman, and child in America.

To see just what it means to consume 576 pounds of paper annually it helps to compare our performance with that of other countries. It is no secret that the United States is the "world leader" in production and consumption of paper, as the paper trade magazines proudly put it. But the paper-consumption gap between America and the rest of the world is so huge as to be embarrassing, and it instantly dispells the idea that our use of paper is in any way "necessary" for normal life.

There are 143 countries in the world where people use paper in measurable quantities. Of those, only the

United States' per capita consumption tops 500 pounds. When Sweden's consumption rose to 410 pounds in 1969, it became the second country ever to top 400. Only 25 countries use more than 100 pounds of paper per person annually, and there are 80 countries which use less than 20 pounds apiece. The three and one-half billion people who are not Americans average only 46 pounds of paper per year—less than one-twelfth the American consumption.

Although the United States is in a wholly different category from even the most highly industrialized nations of the rest of the world (Sweden, with its thick forests and numerous paper mills, still used less paper per person in 1969 than America did in 1944), the dividing line in paper use still comes between the developed Western countries and the undeveloped nations of Africa and Asia. Of the 44 countries of Africa, only South Africa annually uses more than 15 pounds per person. One ton of paper—which a large mill like Union Camp turns out about every 32 seconds—would supply an American's paper needs for three and a half years. The same amount would take care of an average Russian for thirty-six years, and would hold a resident of India, Red China, Indonesia, or Pakistan for many centuries. The 1.6 pounds of paper an American uses daily would supply a North Vietnamese for a year. The United States, with less than 6 per cent of the world's population, now uses almost 45 per cent of the world's paper.

This swollen American consumption is no accident. For the first few decades of its modern growth—starting during the twenties, moving through even the Depression thirties, and beginning to soar in the forties—the paper industry was in a state of constant expansion. As far as the manufacturers could tell, the American economy would absorb every scrap of paper placed in front of it.

By midcentury, however, the once bottomless paper market was beginning to fill up. So much freight was carried in cardboard boxes, so many businesses had a full supply of paper forms, so many housewives carted home their groceries in paper bags, that the industry was not sure where it could turn for future expansion. By 1955, the trend was clear: production increases had

TABLE 5–1
Per Capita Paper and Board Consumption of Countries (by rank)

	Population 1968 (000's)	*Per Capita Consumption in Pounds*				
		1956	*1960*	*1967*	*1968*	*1969*
1. United States	201,152	432	431	512.4	551	576
2. Sweden	7,925	208	265	377	370	410
3. Canada	20,700	280	280	348	368	393
4. Switzerland	6,000	163	195	283	294	317
5. Denmark	4,830	154	198	269	272	313
6. Netherlands	12,750	117	185	241	265	298
7. United Kingdom	55,068	180	236	258	270	282
8. West Germany	60,165	129	174	216	244	270
9. Australia	11,818	156	176	229	249	260
10. Norway	3,785	159	180	243	238	255
11. New Zealand	2,735	141	177	233	228	246
12. Japan	101,410	60	103	194	213	243
13. Belgium/Luxembourg	9,970	110	137	186	206	236
14. Finland	4,687	131	156	212	214	230
15. France	50,300	106	127	176.5	179	203
16. Ireland	2,910	81	90	145.4	148	173
17. Austria	7,350	72	103	135	146	161
18. Iceland	200	93	92	135	147	148
19. Italy	53,930	43	63	120.5	128	144
20. East Germany	17,100	82	92	134	135	143
World	*3,530,675*	*50.4*	*55*	*70*	*71.7*	
World except U.S.A.	*3,329,523*	*28.1*	*32*	*45.3*	*46.5*	

Source: *Pulp & Paper,* June 1969 and 1970.

settled down to a steady annual rate of 4.5 per cent—still respectable, but only a shadow of the booming old days. Per capita consumption grew only slightly, and during certain slow economic periods, it actually fell.

The largest paper companies, horrified at the idea of

a saturated market, saw the threat of what one company later called "the profitless prosperity." But there was no single response that was instantly recognized as the solution to the problem of the saturated market. One group of paper theorists had an attractively simple idea to bring in more money: simply jack up the prices. "During the last two years," one theorist said, "our mills have been working at or near capacity, and yet the improvement in prices for most grades has been picayune. With such a high level of demand, who are our marketers afraid of? Ninety-five per cent of our customers have no other product to turn to when they resent our price increases." [3]

But there was a problem with this approach. While other industries—notably automobiles and steel—had raised prices with impunity and success, the arrangement in the paper industry made this almost impossible. Unlike many other industries, paper is not dominated by a few giant companies. In 1968, about 79 per cent of the auto business went to General Motors, Ford, Chrysler, and American Motors; the four largest aircraft companies did 59 per cent of the aircraft business, and the four largest steel mills held 50 per cent of the market. By comparison, the paper industry swarms with "small" companies. The four largest companies—International Paper, Boise Cascade, U.S. Plywood-Champion, and Georgia-Pacific—control only about 25 per cent of the market. Even a company as far down the line as Union Camp, the eleventh largest paper company, can have a big, $400-million business. To add to the confusion, many large conglomerates like International Telephone & Telegraph or Continental Can have their own small paper operations.

The simple plan to raise paper prices was thwarted because of the number of competing companies. None of the bigger companies could be sure that the smaller ones would follow suit if it raised its prices. Even though the market was already flooded with more paper than it wanted, some companies, looking for a way out of the financial doldrums, thought to expand their operations in hopes of cornering a larger share of the total sales. But for the many medium-sized companies that make up the paper industry, any expansion would have

TABLE 5–2

Company	*Sales first half 1969*	*Earnings first half 1969*
1. International Paper	$853,888,000	$55,901,000
2. U.S. Plywood-Champion	709,961,000	36,399,000
3. Georgia-Pacific	588,830,000	52,110,000
4. Boise Cascade	588,140,000	30,580,000
5. Weyerhaueser	575,700,000	69,700,000
6. Crown Zellerbach	439,150,000	25,195,000
7. St. Regis Paper	433,069,000	18,924,000
8. Kimberly-Clark*		
9. Scott Paper	363,952,000	29,357,000
10. Diamond International*		
11. Union Camp	222,305,000	15,730,000

Source: *Pulp & Paper,* September 1969 and June 1970.
* Information not available.

to be mammoth—often a doubling in size—to bring in a profitable return. The costs of such expansion would be huge; the anticipated returns, at least in the short run, were small. So paper companies began expansions only reluctantly, but enough of them took the step so that the joint effect was to aggravate the industry's problem: paper companies found themselves even more "over-capacitated."

Financial reviews of the industry's growth reflect this plight. In its 1968 review of the paper industry the Chase Manhattan Bank said, "The rate of return for the last 10 years has been only 9.2 per cent. Now at least 26 major industries in the country have produced in the last decade a higher average rate of return than that."

Union Camp's president, Alexander Calder, Jr., told how the overcapacity had hurt prices for his company's main commodities: prices had dropped. "Margins for the paper industry have been down for the last fifteen years," he said in 1969. "As an example, the price per ton of 43-pound linerboard in 1956 was $127.50. In 1969, after a $15-per-ton increase the year before, it was $120 per ton. The story is the same for kraft paper and grocery sacks." [4]

As the president of the American Paper Institute summed up the problem in 1968: "In the last ten years, industry took an exceptionally large capacity expansion." But so far, it "has not yet paid off hoped-for levels of return." [5]

The lesson took. Instead of wildly turning out thousands of unwanted tons of the same old paper products, the industry would have to find new uses for paper. If the market for old-fashioned kinds of paper was saturated, the companies would produce new paper shapes and forms and carefully nurture consumer "demand" for these products. The whole approach depended on convincing the consumer that he really *did* want more paper, that he *needed* more paper, and that he actually had a duty to consume more paper. Modern living, the paper campaign implied, required that all modern livers use paper plates, wear paper clothes, and even sleep in paper houses.

There was an initial roadblock, of course: the American public did not yet realize that it needed all this new paper. As John Kenneth Galbraith put it, "Many of the desires of the individual are no longer even evident to him. They become so only as they are synthesized, elaborated, and nurtured by advertising and salesmanship." [6]

And so the paper marketers took up the task, putting all their intellectual might into the job of creating consumer demand. Union Camp, for example, set up a special endowment fund at New York's Parsons School of Design. Parsons' students were to "probe the range of paper shapes and characteristics with a view to adapting them to new uses in packaging and related areas." [7] The company also set up an in-house Ideation Group, in which engineers could "identify problems—and hence opportunities" for new paper products.[8]

The results of their studies became apparent in 1967, when Union Camp launched a massive national advertising campaign. Their point, hammered home in 25 full-page ads in *Time, Fortune,* and *Business Week,* was that paper had graduated from its old role as merely a vehicle for writing. Now paper had entered the space age ("Why on earth would they use *paper* to help launch a moon shot?" began an ad about paper-paneled rocket launchers); paper was part of modern medicine ("The surgical blade you don't have to sterilize."); paper was the solution to housing problems ("We bought our house at the Union Camp store."); and paper could modernize agricultural packing, with waterproof corrugated boxes ("A waterproof corrugated box?").

At the same time, Union Camp and other companies tried to convince the public that paper-making was "a progressive, diversified enterprise."[9] While the ads stressed new uses for paper, they also pointed out all the nonpaper pies in which paper companies had stuck their fingers. Union Camp released a series of ads about its plastic by-products, and another advertisement discussed its land development ventures. (See Chapter 11 for another side of Union Camp's land holdings.) The chemical by-products of paper-making, according to one lush Union Camp ad, made perfume and "all the ingredients for romance." (By the same logic, the paper industry seems to be missing a sure bet by not marketing the smell that comes from its mills as riot-dispersal gas.) Eventually the by-product ads moved into the area of clear deception. The sentiment expressed in ads like "We use all of the tree. Even the smell" is nice, but it is demonstrably untrue, as anyone knows who has seen mills pour tons of unused tree parts into nearby rivers. The advertising campaign finally abandoned the company's products entirely, concentrating instead on "image." "Buffalo Bill had it," Union Camp told the business public in a series of ads, "and we've got it on paper. Got what? Personality."

Different companies aimed at different markets. Weyerhaueser stressed its careful forest management; Hammermill advertised high-quality paper. But in nearly all the ads, an important theme appeared again and again. Like it or not, the industry's mainstay was still paper, not land or perfume. The goal of new uses for paper began to take shape as a coherent philosophy and eventually as its own industrial subgroup. The new theme, as advertisements told the buying public, was "disposables."

The theory behind "disposables" was that pottery plates or cloth dresses might be all right, but that cheap paper versions that could be used once and then made to vanish were much better. The idea was not entirely new, but its expression as a practical marketing approach began to pick up steam only in the sixties. By 1969, manufacturers of disposables had grown to the point where they considered themselves a separate industry. As they told themselves at a special conference in 1969 in Chicago, disposables had "the real opportunity to build for the future." [10] Consultant Arthur D. Little told the group that while normal paper use was leveling off, disposables were a "paper tiger" with a growth potential "among the highest." [11] The president of American Cyanamid, C. D. Siverd, told the disposable men that their products would be part of "the economy of tomorrow." [12] From its fledgling start during the late fifties, the industry was predicting runaway growth to $1.3 billion in 1975.[13]

The makers of disposables have their eyes on two major markets. First, they are trying to pump up their traditional markets of paper towels, cups, and plates. Scott Paper has dreams of opening a $1-billion wedge in this market with its new disposable diaper, the BabyScott. Already mothers around the country are using and disposing of BabyScotts and sewer operators are seeing the results in their already overloaded sewers.

The second disposable target will be harder to reach. Ideally, the manufacturers would like to supplant most of the cloth now used in this country. Instead of cotton dresses, women would wear paper; instead of sleeping on washable sheets, families would use throw-away paper. But customers have so far shown an unexpected reluctance to throw away a dress—even a paper dress—after wearing it just once. The Kendall Company may have found the way to solve the problem with its "wear-awhile" clothes. Kendall hopes these clothes, which can be worn three or four times and then thrown out, will soothe feelings of frugality and still guarantee a steady demand for more paper.

In fairness, the disposables industry has brought several advances in the quality of American life. Hospitals, for example, have found that some disposable medical supplies cut reinfection rates dramatically. But most of the other ways in which these products make their brief contact with our lives have potentially disastrous results. There is a central flaw in the logic of the disposables, and until it is exposed, the country faces a threat to its natural surroundings as serious as that posed by the aluminum can or the supersonic transport.

Taken on its own terms, the argument for disposables is reasonable enough: yes, it is cheaper to buy a paper sheet or dress than to spend time washing out the old ones. But that apparent economy is false, because of a gross miscalculation of costs. The price the customer pays for the paper dress or the BabyScott represents only a fraction of the total cost of each product. In addition to the relatively small purchase price, there is the price taken from the forests, the terrible price inflicted on the air and water where the paper is made, and the increasingly serious price of getting rid of the "disposables." Neither the manufacturer nor the customer has to pay these environmental costs directly; small wonder that disposables carry such bargain price tags.

Meanwhile the cost mounts up in different ledgers. The people of mill towns pay with the rivers they cannot fish in, the air they cannot breathe. City dwellers pay with littered streets and high taxes for garbage disposal. Until the nation decides that the paper industry—and ultimately, its customers—will have to pay the cost of repairing environmental damage, each disposable napkin or BabyScott will victimize the people whom fate has placed near a paper mill, and everyone who suffers from general environmental deterioration.

While the disposables industry is the newest frontier of paper marketing, it represents no spectacular change from the industry's general environmental philosophy. The dependable old brown grocery sack, friend of a million shoppers, is based on the same unjust distribution of costs as the newer disposables. To the grocery store manager and his patrons, the cost is virtually nothing. In Savannah and other bag towns, it is a different story.

The saga of the paper bag is especially important to Savannah, since the local Union Camp mill produces about 35 million bags a day—about one-fifth of all the bags used in the country. Union Camp also has a fatherly interest in the paper bag, for it introduced the bag to the world.

Back in the days before the Civil War, when housewives carried wicker baskets or mesh nets to market, a young man named Francis Wolle was hard at work on the first paper bag machine. By 1852, he had his first model working, and nine years later, with some financial backing, he was able to set up the Union Paper Bag Machine Company. As his bags spread out to blanket the country, Wolle's company grew and eventually changed its name to the Union Bag and Paper Company. For Wolle, the paper bag provided a comfortable retirement. For the rest of the country, the effect was—as Union Camp modestly puts it—to "revolutionize retailing and merchandising methods. Eventually, it changed the shopping habits of the nation." [14] In its nearly 35 years on the Savannah, one Union Camp plant has turned out an astounding 230 billion bags.

Wolle's business descendants realize the impact they have had on modern American living. "It's not too much to say," one of Union Camp's bulletins proclaims, "that we've been a major influence in shaping the food style of modern America." [15] A visit to any large supermarket shows that the company has, if anything, underestimated its importance, as these figures from one of Savannah's largest supermarkets show. In a month of normal operation, the store spends nearly $3,900 for paper bags and wrapping:

$2,531 for brown grocery bags
992 for meat wrappings, including the fiber trays under prepacked cuts
233 for separate bags to hold fruit and vegetables
117 for bakery wrappings

Some 40 billion bags—about 200 for every American—go out the doors of our supermarkets every year.

While some bags, especially those used for meat and baked goods, are probably necessary to keep the food clean, by far the biggest chunk of money goes for the least essential product—the big brown bags. Most stores would be happy to trade the money they now spend on those bags for a year's profit.

The bag companies are properly appreciative of the service supermarkets give them. "If Union Camp were to sit back and count its blessings," the company said in 1967, "the food industry would have to sit at the top. It's our biggest customer." [16] The amount of money that this biggest customer shells out just for paper bags is surprisingly large. A typical modern supermarket spends as much on paper bags every year as its entire profit.

But so what? Even if supermarkets, in an unlikely frenzy of belt-tightening, eliminated paper bags or made customers pay the 2½–5 cent cost per bag, what would it mean? Would the cost be enough to force shoppers into pre-Union Bag habits of bringing their own little baskets? Probably not. The savings involved would be so small—probably a 1 per cent reduction in food costs—that few would think it worth the considerable bother.

But again, as with paper dresses or BabyScotts, there is a false calculation of costs at work. While shoppers in Portland or Los Angeles or Topeka use cheap paper bags, residents of pulp towns from Savannah to Rumford, Maine, endure the side effects. If paper bags ever cost the shoppers as much as they now cost the pulp town dwellers, customers might suddenly find it worthwhile to tote baskets again.

Although paper companies do not like to use the word "pollution," they recognize that their product has three "side effects" on nature. There is, first, the drain on the forests, which give up 17 trees for each ton of paper that comes off the paper machines. Second, when the 17 trees emerge from the mill as paper, they leave behind from 10,000 to 150,000 gallons of polluted water, and incalculably large amounts of dirty air. Finally, once the ton has passed through the hands of its users and into the city dump, there is the problem of how to get rid of it.

The paper industry's response to these three problems has varied so wildly as to suggest that rival factions are at work, struggling for control of environmental policy. In dealing with the forests, the paper men have been extraordinarily careful; they seem to realize that their planning must extend beyond each day's output and take into account the long-term effects of production. But with the other problems, the industrial managers pretend not to know about anything that takes place outside the mill. The explanation for this curious schizophrenia may come from the different effects the three kinds of pollution have on the mill's yearly profit-and-loss statement. If a mill runs out of trees, it runs out of business. But if the streams get dirty or the garbage piles up, that is someone else's worry. The technical resources of the paper industry are formidable—nearly sufficient to solve the problem of dwindling forests. For the industry to turn its scientific arsenal against the other problems, the procedure is clear: the mills must be forced to pay for their dirty water and discarded garbage as well as for their trees.

Realizing from the start that its future was closely linked to the future of the forests, the paper industry has been careful in handling its woody resources. Industrial spokesmen proudly point to stands of pine growing in straight rows like so many stalks of tall corn that run through the red-dirt sweeps of Georgia and Alabama where, 30 years ago, there was only scrub brush. Signs all along Georgia's piney roads tell visitors which paper companies have planted 350 million trees in the last 20 years. Children in forest communities gather in 4-H groups to hear paper company agents explain that pine trees have replaced cotton as the South's staple.

Environmental skeptics are still not sure how sound the industry's foresting practices have been. The rows of trees that march across Georgia hillsides bear about as much resemblance to natural forests as chickens in mechanized coops do to flocks of wild herons. The qualities that make for a heavy pulp yield do not necessarily lead to a healthy balance of forest life: for example, forest managers like to grow their trees close enough together so that the top branches touch, forming a sunshade that gradually kills the lower branches. This saves time when the trees are ready to be cut, but it does not do much for the shrubby bottom growth that birds and small animals need for protection and food. The industry's practice of "clear-cutting"—gouging out every bit of wood from a tract of land, and then replanting all at once—may be more economical than the old habit of selectively cutting a few trees from one area, but it leaves horribly ugly scars on a countryside.* It also adds considerably to a forest state's air pollution problem when the loggers burn all the trees and shrubs too small to use.

When all the objections are tallied, however, it is still clear that the paper companies have been more careful with their forests than with any of their other resources. And they realize that they are going to have to be even more careful in the next few years. The current national demand for paper consumes about 80 million cords of forest wood; by 1990, the industry thinks it will need about 180 million cords.[17] As Union Camp's executive vice president, John E. Ray III, concisely put it, the demand will put "a tremendous strain on forest wood." [18]

Because their industrial welfare is at stake, the paper companies have been working hard to stave off the "tremendous strain." To ease the squeeze, several companies have even fought nature to develop a more compliant kind of tree. Union Camp geneticists are now at work breeding a new kind of tree, a Super Tree. The goal is to create a new forest crop, a tree packed full of usable cellulose, a tree that will shrug off normal tree disease, a tree that will grow more quickly and fall with everything but delight into the harvesting machines. "For more than a decade." Union Camp said in 1969, "we have been regenerating an increasing proportion of our forests with superior stock—those which grow more rapidly, have greater wood-fiber yield, and are more resistant to disease. We have pioneered in site preparing and space planting techniques, both initially important to optimizing growth." [19]

Other companies have similar plans, ranging from

* Visitors who drive through some of the more heavily logged areas may not notice the scars at all. Always sensitive to good public relations, the paper companies sometimes go to absurd lengths to put an attractive cover on their brutal forest work. In many areas, loggers leave a narrow strip of trees standing by the edge of the road, and then cut down every tree that lies beyond the motorists' sight. From the air, the effect is eerie: vast tracts of bare red earth are surrounded by a fringe of pine.

wholesale genetic engineering to modest improvements in harvesting technique. Interstate Paper, one of Union Camp's forest neighbors, has no plans for developing a "superior stock," but assures the men who sell it trees that it will replant their forests.

The ingenious vigor with which the industry has tackled the forestry problem makes its response to the paper garbage crisis look spectacularly torpid. Union Camp perfectly expressed the industry's insensitivity to the problem when it announced, with a note of pride, that "The number of bags made at the Savannah plant since it opened would reach, if laid end to end, from Earth to Venus and back with enough left over to *encircle both Earth and Venus almost 100 times.*"[20] (Emphasis added.) Remembering that the mill makes only one-fifth of all our paper bags, and that paper bags are less than one-fifth of total paper output, the outlines of the problem take frightening shape: the earth really is in danger of becoming encircled by its paper. More than 41 million tons of paper found uncomfortable homes in the nation's garbage dumps in 1966, and by 1976, the amount may reach 69 million tons.

The industry has expressed some formal concern about this "third pollution," but there have been no signs of any action by individual companies. When the paper industry's technical arm—the Technical Association of the Pulp and Paper Industry (TAPPI)—tried to hold a meeting on Secondary Fiber Re-Pulping (paper re-use) in 1969, fewer than 140 people bothered to come. The TAPPI organizers were disappointed. "With so much at stake," they said, "it is surprising how little attention was given."[21]

The industry has taken a few mincing steps toward thinking about the disposal problem. But so far, interest has been tepid at best. Even the Disposables Association—whose product is more directly responsible for inflaming the garbage problem than any other commodity—has maintained a complacent disinterest. As its president Wayne Hays said in 1970, "We're just beginning to explore the disposal problem. In spite of our name . . . we have not really been involved with the problems of waste and pollution up to this point."

The most satisfactory way out of the disposal dilemma would be to re-use the old paper for new products. Recycling the paper would not only cut down on trash but would also ease the strain on the forests. Even *Pulp and Paper* saw the opportunity when it said in 1969 that "much could be done to alleviate this cost problem; waste paper could be exploited to a far greater extent as a fiber source."[22] Unfortunately, the industry has approached paper re-use with the same dainty disdain with which it handles other ventures that do not offer immediate promise of profit. There is a small amount of paper recycling now: of the 42 million tons of paper produced in 1969 that were technically suited for recycling, the industry salvaged about 11.5 million tons—slightly more than 25 per cent. The remaining 31 million tons—which could have saved 527 million trees occupying thousands of acres of land—piled up instead in trash heaps.[23] In 1969 and early 1970, the paper trade press reported that the U.S. rate of recycling not only was the lowest since the start of the century, but also lagged far behind the performance of other countries.[24]

"Why shouldn't waste paper make up 47 per cent of our furnish, as in Germany, instead of the current 25 per cent?" Container Corporation's chairman, Leo Schoenhofen asked his colleagues in 1969. "Why not 75 per cent?"[25]

Victor Brown knows one of the answers to Mr. Schoenhofen's question. Six years ago, Brown, an independent Texas businessman, decided to set up what he considered a "progressive—and profitable—idea." He designed a processing plant to sort through garbage and separate it into glass, paper, metal, and other kinds of rubbish. Brown then planned to sell the salvageable trash back to the steel mills, glass factories, and paper mills for re-use.

But things have not gone quite as well as Brown had hoped. St. Regis and several other paper companies discovered that the reclaimed paper would cost more than raw pulp, and they quickly turned down Brown's offers. Now Brown's 200-ton-per-week output goes to the construction industry for use in buildings. And it goes at a loss of two dollars per ton. So far Brown's losses have cost him $2 million since his plant opened and he cannot afford the research necessary to cut the cost of recycling. As the vicious cycle continues, reclaimed paper continues to be "unprofitable."

Mr. Brown, as one of the paper spokesmen gently explained, is "slightly ahead of his time."

6

Polluting the Earth

They [the American family] picnic on exquisitely packaged food from a portable icebox by a polluted stream. . . . They may reflect vaguely on the curious unevenness of their blessing.

John Kenneth Galbraith,
The Affluent Society

Everyone knows that it takes wood to make paper. For the mills, however, wood is far less crucial than water. In a pinch, a mill can use straw, cotton, old paper, or almost anything fibrous to make paper. But water—pure water, and in huge volumes—is irreplaceable.

Visitors to a modern paper mill may not realize that this material in so many unusual colors and consistencies is actually water, but water it is, constantly accompanying the wood through its whole progression into paper. From the start of the process, when the logs slide down water-filled sluices to the chipping machines, until the end, when rolls of finished paper containing 6 per cent water leave the mill, water is part of each step. In the mill's evaporators, digesters, and condensers, water cooks and carries and washes the wood. The most lavish use of water is the final paper-making step, during which purified cellulose is dissolved in 100 times its volume of water, and then dripped out onto a fast-moving wire screen. The fiber that stays on top of the screen is soon dried into a fresh new roll of paper. The water that drains out the bottom joins other waste streams to become part of the mill's total discharge.

Anyone who has seen pure water flowing into the mill and the foamy, barely recognizable sludge coming out the other side might think that something sordid was going on inside. The paper industry, always on the alert to correct misimpressions, hastens to reassure us. In a recent flyer describing its projects, the Southern Pulpwood Conservation Association presents a comfortable domestic picture of water use: "A pulp and paper mill uses water for many of the same reasons a housewife does—for cooking, for washing, and for carrying away wastes. . . . Just as the housewife covers raw vegetables or meat with water and adds the right condiments in cooking the family meal, a pulp and paper mill cooks wood chips in a solution of water and chemicals." [1]

This comparison is as valid as saying that an Apollo rocket burns fuel in the same way as a small alcohol lamp. One medium-sized paper mill, turning out 1,000 tons of paper a day, uses as much water as all the housewives, businessmen, and children in a city of one million. Mills vary in their use of water—from a high of 184,000 gallons per ton for certain high-quality book paper to a rock-bottom low of 2,200 gallons per ton of paperboard.[2] Most mills use between 10,000 and 100,000 gallons per ton; kraft mills, like Union Camp and Continental Can, usually use 20,000–40,000 gallons per ton of paper.[3] All together, the mills use and contaminate so much water that they account for about 15 per cent of all industrial waste water and nearly 25 per cent of biological pollutants.[4]

In fairness to the paper industry, the last 20 years have seen a drop in water consumption by the papermakers. Although the mills now turn out twice as much pulp as they did in 1950, water use per ton has been cut in half, so the total drain on water resources has stayed about the same.[5] Reductions in water use, like the careful handling of the forests, show the magic power that profit has to inspire industrial creativity. As soon as mills realized that they were paying for each gallon of water they pumped in—even though the cost was abysmally small—and that valuable fibers were sneaking out into the river, they decided to tighten production methods. The effect on the rivers was as if the mills had launched an "environmental improvement" campaign, but the reasoning behind it was quite different.

The result of these changes in methods is that each drop of water now does many tasks on its trip through the mill. When the pure water first comes from the mill's wells or river supply, it goes to the boilers or other "clean" operations; as it becomes somewhat fouled, it moves to the paper machines. From there on, the trip through the mill's washers and digesters is progressively more contaminated. Finally, the aged water, so polluted that it is only good for floating logs, runs through the wood yard sluices and out into the river.

The kind and amount of pollutant that the water carries out with it depends mainly on the type of mill it comes from. The sulfite process, one of two major milling techniques, produces high-quality paper by cooking wood chips in an acid solution. As a glance at any river unfortunate enough to pass a sulfite mill will attest, this process does almost unbelievable harm to the water that receives its wastes. The waste from a small 500-ton-per-day mill sucks as much oxygen from a river as does the sewage of two million people.

Compared to the sulfite technique, the other main pulping process, which is used in kraft mills, seems almost benign. A kraft mill, which makes paper by cooking wood in a sulfur-base alkaline solution, produces only one-tenth as much waste as a sulfite plant of comparable size.[6] This waste still adds up to a sizable pollution problem that is becoming more and more serious as kraft takes a larger and larger chunk of the paper market. As the paper industry has placed more and more emphasis on boxes, packaging, and disposable products, durable kraft paper has become an increasingly valuable commodity. In 1942, only 35 per cent of the country's paper was kraft; by 1962, the figure was up to 60 per cent, and now it has risen to a full 90 per cent of paper output.[7]

Despite the placid housewife imagery of the paper propagandists, both kraft and sulfite mills contribute three very dangerous forms of pollution. The first is the most obvious: sedimentation of the bits of dirt and wood that leave the mill. A large mill like Union Camp puts out huge quantities of these "settleable solids"—up to half a million pounds on a bad day. Aside from clogging up the river and requiring extra dredging in harbors like Savannah, this sedimentation also exterminates whatever bottom-dwelling animals have managed to survive near the mill. This, however, is rarely a serious worry, since the other two forms of pollution get rid of the aquatic life even more effectively.

The second danger comes from the toxic by-products of the paper-making process. In a kraft mill, sulfur compounds used to reduce once firm wood to slush sometimes escape with waste materials. Mills try their best to keep sulfur losses down, since they must buy another pound of chemicals to replace each pound that goes into the river, but some loss is almost inevitable. When the compounds do escape, they are in dangerous forms. As they go through the kraft process, harmless sodium sulfate and other "cooking chemicals" join with the wood compounds to make a variety of potentially toxic materials: resin acids, methyl mercaptans (the same compound in its gaseous form gives a kraft mill its unmistakable stench), hydrogen sulfide, and thio-lignins.[8]

But these lethal chemicals seldom get a chance to attack the aquatic life of the river. By the time the oxygen-consuming wastes—the third and most important form of paper pollution—have done their job on the river, there is often nothing left for the chemicals or the sediment to kill.

As paper mill managers never tire of telling the public, these wastes are "nontoxic." Taken on the most superficial level, this is true. The wastes are mainly organic compounds—the 40 to 50 per cent of the original tree that cannot profitably be made into paper. These organic compounds consist of wood sugars, minute bits of cellulose, and lignin, the adhesive that held the tree together when it was still alive. In small amounts, they provide food for the aquatic population, as does any form of organic food; Union Camp's Savannah manager has maintained that they are actually good for fish. But when dumped into the river in the 100-ton quantities that many mills produce daily, their effect is as deadly as any poison.

Like most other organic matter, these wood by-products decompose in the river. In the process, the bacteria that work to break them down use some of the oxygen dissolved in the water. The amount of oxygen that this rotting process draws from the water is measured as Biological Oxygen Demand (BOD). Thirty pounds of BOD—the average waste produced in making one ton of kraft paper[9]—uses 30 pounds of the river's dissolved oxygen to break down. When the BOD climbs high enough, it seriously depletes the river's supply of dissolved oxygen. In moderate cases, this means simply that there is no oxygen left to support other forms of life; in the extreme, it leads to one of nature's most unpleasant phenomena, anerobic decomposition.

The amount of BOD that mills dump into their rivers varies considerably from plant to plant. On one of its bad days, Union Camp puts more than 240,000 pounds of BOD into the Savannah, using as much of the river's oxygen as would sewage from a town of over one million people. Even more staggering are the statistics for certain sulfite mills, which emit as much as 750 pounds of BOD for each ton of paper produced.[10] At the other extreme, a carefully managed plant like Interstate Paper's kraft mill in Riceboro, Georgia, has cut its BOD emission to *one pound* per ton of paper. In all the pulp towns across the nation, mills produce a total of 5.9 *billion* pounds of BOD, more than one-quarter of all the industrial BOD produced, and only slightly less than the BOD that flows from all the country's sewers.[11]

Pulp town residents may curse as they watch lethal mill water flow past, but few know the worst part of the paper pollution story: none of it is necessary. Paper mill pollution—with its mountains of sediment and its gross oxygen consumption—is a technical anachronism. Unlike nuclear wastes or nerve gas, paper by-products require no complicated systems for disposal. All the wastes require is time to settle and quietly decompose before being released into the river.

There are many different ways to reach this general goal. The first step that most mills must take is to install a "clarifier." In essence, this is simply a large cement tank in which waste water can sit for several hours after leaving the mill. In the clarifier, oils and other floating debris rise to the top, and settleable solids drift to the bottom. The top and bottom layers are skimmed and scraped, and the slightly cleaner water moves on.

Although a well-run clarifier can eliminate about 90 per cent of floating or solid particles, a truly effective system needs one further step—"secondary treatment" or "biological stabilization." Small organic pollutants, if left to themselves, will decompose anywhere—in a bucket as well as in a river. If the mill lets them break down in a holding pond instead of rushing them untreated to the river, they can finally enter the stream in relative harmony with the aquatic life cycles.

Biological treatment takes many forms, from the most primitive (a holding pond in which the water sits for several weeks) to the most technically elaborate (the ominously named Activated Sludge system). Most mills use one of two similar systems: the "retention pond" keeps waste water in a large holding lagoon in which the organic pollutants decompose as they would in any natural lake. Mechanical surface aerators are added to the pond for the second form of treatment—the "aerated stabilization basin." Retention ponds are the most common form of treatment, mostly because they are so cheap (land costs are all that is involved). But as water pollution laws slowly stiffen, more and more mills are turning toward aerated systems. While the aerators require slightly higher capital and operating costs, they allow holding ponds to treat 20 times as much waste water as before. Even more important, the water that leaves an adequate aerated system has had 90 per cent of its BOD removed and can safely enter a healthy stream.

Beyond these two basic systems lie the host of more exotic devices that make up "tertiary treatment." These sophisticated processes—ion exchangers, reverse osmosis membranes, and systems to remove the coffee-brown color of kraft mill wastes—all make the waste water technically purer than the water that comes in. In a world of ideal paper mills, each with its primary and secondary systems humming along smoothly, tertiary systems would be worth serious consideration. (If Americans ever begin to realize that a stream should not be altered simply because someone built a paper plant nearby all mills will use tertiary treatment.) But for the present, while so many mills still send seas of untreated wastes into our waters, tertiary treatment is like treating blisters on a man bleeding from the jugular—it is simply not the most urgent problem.

The retarded state of paper mill pollution control is most obvious in the sulfite mills. Figures for 1970 show that not one of these extravagantly polluting factories has installed secondary treatment, and that few have even a primary system.[12] The kraft picture is brighter—of 113 mills surveyed, 96 had some kind of treatment. But only 60 had clarifiers, and only 35—less than one-third—had secondary treatment.[13]

The reason for the paper industry's crawl toward pollution control is not hard to figure out: money. Even from the perspective of large-scale corporate finance, the amount required to control pollution is staggering. Of the $2.6–$4.6 billion that American manufacturers will have to spend on pollution control in the next three years, paper's share will be a healthy chunk between $320–$920 million.[14] This means costs ranging from $200,000 for small operations to as much as $10 million for large plants like Union Camp's Savannah operation. (Industrial financiers are now nervously calculating that air pollution control will cost much more than this—perhaps twice as much as the total water control expenditures.)

Rather than bear the heavy weight of pollution control spending, several companies have found a more comfortable way to solve the pollution problem. Most of the materials that now run out mill sewers have potential use as marketable products; but until now, there has not been any profit in reclaiming them. As the cost of cleaning up after the pollutants increases, however, mills are suddenly finding it worthwhile to save the lignins and wood sugars that have been running freely into the rivers. Paper companies took the first step in reclaiming wastes nearly 30 years ago, when they began recovering resinous "tall oil" to make chemical by-products. These chemicals brought in $50 million in 1968 and should earn twice that much in 1973.

Recently, the mills have found several equally promising profit-makers in their search through the effluent. Xylose, a wood sugar, may soon recapture overweight hearts still grieving from the loss of cyclamates. Xylose, which is still undergoing tests for safety, is powerfully sweet but contains few calories.[15] The tough, adhesive lignins may also yield marketable compounds. Experimental uses range from glue to medicines which will take advantage of lignin's ability to flow through cell membranes. A lignin derivative, dimethyl sulfoxide (DMSO), created medical excitement several years ago as an all-purpose treatment for burn wounds, painful joints, and nervous tension.[16]

However, until someone discovers a market for the other pollutants that now leave the mills, paper companies will have to take a more direct approach to pollution control. A few companies have already started, and industrywide spending for pollution controls rose from $149 million in 1969 to $189 million in 1970.[17] Such figures are at best a crude measure of improvement; at worst, they are vulnerable to misinterpretation and outright deception. When connected to other indicators, however, they give some measure of the efforts companies are making.

Georgia-Pacific, for example, says that it will spend about $20 million to clean up its many mills. And the industry titan, International Paper, recently announced in nationwide newspaper ads that it would spend $101 million in the next four years to take care of its awesome pollution problems. The company did not say how much of the budget went to full-page ads in papers running the ideological spectrum from the *Wall Street Journal* to the *Harvard Crimson*.

The picture is usually clearer as it applies to individual mills. In between stories on new coating machines and ads for production boosters, the paper trade literature of the last two years yields the following examples of companies that have taken long or expensive steps toward purifying their effluents:

1. Scott Paper Company is preparing to spend between $16–$20 million at its Winslow, Maine, mill. Although the mill is small—it produces 390 tons of paper per day and is less than one-seventh the size of Savannah's Union Camp—it spews out 35 million gallons of sulfite pollutant daily, almost as much as the country's largest mills.

2. The Thorold Paper Company of Thorold, Ontario, has already spent $5 million finishing a water treatment

plant for its small (840 tons per day), aging mill built in 1912. The company now plans to install the sophisticated ion exchangers to reduce its water's chloride content.

3. The Glatfelter Company runs an even smaller (500 tons per day), older (1860) mill in Spring Hill, Pennsylvania. But the company is spending $4 million to reduce its BOD output by 95 per cent.

4. Kimberly-Clark, at its new mill in Anderson, California, spent $2 million on a water purification system for a tiny 180-ton-per-day plant. The treatment system is dotted with alarms that go off in case of trouble, and the water that leaves the mill is now so clean that salmon fingerlings thrive in it.

5. American Can Company has built what may be the mill of the nonpolluting future at Halsey, Oregon. The mill has not only installed several aeration ponds to keep its liquid waste safe but has also eliminated the sickening smell that usually surrounds kraft mills. According to newspaper reports, the mill manager stuck his head into one of the smokestacks to show its safety. Similar exhibitions would lead to high managerial turnover at a mill like Union Camp.

6. The Masonite Corporation has cut the BOD of its Laurel, Mississippi, mill by 90 per cent, at a cost of $2 million.

7. Owens-Illinois has been using a series of seven treatment ponds at its Valdosta, Georgia, mill since 1954. Using almost no sophisticated equipment, the system removes 95 per cent of the mill's BOD.

Some companies have done more than shell out money: they have developed coherent theories about their responsibility to protect the environment. In some cases, the theories seem to be of the silver-lining school, which attempts to make the best of a bad thing. Speaking to a group of reluctant mill representatives in 1969, a paper spokesman said that antipollution laws might be a "blessing in disguise," since they would force the industry to find more inventive uses for its by-products.[18] Georgia-Pacific recently soothed its stockholders' doubts about pollution control investments by saying that "those who have delayed will have to do the job later at much higher costs, which will work to our advantage."[19]

Other companies have put forth the revolutionary suggestion that they *should* purify their effluent, not that it is just a dreary duty they must perform. In a remarkable speech in 1969, the president of the American Paper Institute, Edwin A. Locke, recommended that the government beef up and coordinate its antipollution efforts, saying, "that is essential if we are going to overcome the threats of water famine, epidemics of respiratory disease, and shortages of raw materials." [20] As one of the trade journals tartly noted, "Mr. Locke's proposal startled many industry men. . . . Historically, the industry has opposed strong federal pollution controls." [21]

Kimberly-Clark has drafted one of the most complete environmental programs, including in its six-plank plan ideas that are still strangers to many industrial minds: "the evils of pollution cannot be measured in dollars and cents"; "if pollution is to be controlled, industry must lead the way"; "the amount of money spent is nowhere near as good an indicator of effort as are the results obtained," etc.[22] But none of the American companies has matched the simplicity with which one Swedish mill expressed its sense of responsibility to the community. After the Skaghall mill had taken all the normal steps toward reducing its pollution, the manager inexplicably decided to spend several hundred thousand dollars more to get rid of the kraft mill smell. He admitted to incredulous questioners that he had no returns to show for his money. But, he said, "it would attract people to the mill and the community." [23]

Not all companies have been so cooperative, in either thought or deed. For each Skaghall or Kimberly-Clark, there is a Potlatch Forest or an ITT Rayonier. Early in 1970, Potlatch of Lewiston, Idaho, ran a series of ads in *Time* which were meant to impress the public with the mill's dedication. "It cost us a bundle," said the caption under a picture of a blue and wooded stream, "but the Clearwater River still runs clear." What the ad did not say was that the picture was not taken near the Potlatch plant in Lewiston, but about 50 miles upstream. A *Wall Street Journal* story describing the incident said, "Perhaps another reason the picture was taken upstream is that downstream the Clearwater isn't so clear. At least a dozen times a year it churns with a foul-smelling white foam that sometimes spurts high into the air, just a few yards from the intake for Lewiston's water supply." [24]

ITT Rayonier has resorted to even cruder levels of public persuasion. After station WJXT in Jacksonville, Florida, aired a news story saying that effluent from the Rayonier sulfite mill was destroying the region's oyster beds, the station suffered a rash of bomb threats. Finally, the mill's personnel manager, Devant Purvis, made explicit the threat that hangs over every pulp town: "We are a pulp mill operation," Purvis said, "with a tremendous amount of effluent disposal. If it becomes impossible to dispose of these wastes, people could logically draw the conclusion that there would be nothing left but to close the plant." [25]

7
Three Pulp Mill Towns

Three pulp mill towns—strung like uneven beads along the Georgia coast—tell the whole story of the paper industry's relation to its communities. The mills' treatment of their local environments ranges from good to horrible; their role in the towns that house them runs from respectful noninterference to complete domination.

In Riceboro, Georgia, the Interstate Paper Company shows how far government action and private cooperation can go toward attaining the goal of an environmentally safe paper mill. Savannah's Union Camp is a big mill in a town too big to be just a mill town; still, Union Camp shows how a company can use sheer size to justify behavior that is usually irresponsible and occasionally illegal. And in St. Mary's, the last little town before Georgia gives way to Florida, the Gilman Paper Company shows how completely a mill can dominate the townspeople and how cruelly it can abuse its natural setting.

Riceboro: Interstate Paper

Riceboro is less a mill town than a collection of buildings that happen to be near a paper plant. Forty miles south of Savannah on the piney coast highway, the town of 200 is easy to miss. Riceboro's civic leaders had dreams of an economic boom when they invited Interstate to build a mill there in 1965, but somehow, the boom has not materialized, and the town has retained its sleepy appearance. Downtown Riceboro consists of a Shanty-Burger, several grocery stores and trailer parks, and a forest of signs advertising attractions further south.

Lurking in one corner of Riceboro is the Interstate

mill. Given a kraft mill's normal tendency to foul the air for miles around with its unique smell, Interstate's relative invisibility is a technical victory. Although the "wet scrubbers" on the smokestacks sometimes release long white plumes of steam into the humid air, the gaseous pollutants—and the smell—are gone.

By using the most effective modern equipment, the mill has managed to eliminate the side effects that made kraft mills such loathsome neighbors in the past. And, as Interstate's managers are delighted to report, in spite of the high cost of some of the equipment, the mill still shows a profit.

Interstate's rendezvous with Riceboro began in the early sixties, when three northern box companies decided to build their own kraft paper mill.[1] Like most paper companies since the Depression, they decided to build in the South. Rural Liberty County, one of the more sadly impoverished counties in Georgia's poor coastal plain, was delighted when it heard that Interstate planned to build in Riceboro.

But before the county could sacrifice its vast natural resources to whatever demands the mill might make, the state Water Quality Control Board stepped in. Rock Howard and his staff were just setting up their office when the Interstate issue arose in 1965; their quick response not only protected a valuable estuary but also set the tone for the Water Board's future policy. In spite of weighty pressure from the Chamber of Commerce to lure the mill to Riceboro, Howard refused to okay the site unless the mill would adhere to an unprecedentedly rigid set of environmental standards. For example, Howard said the mill could only put 800 pounds of BOD into Riceboro Creek every day; this is about the amount produced by a mill like Union Camp every eight minutes. In the years since 1965, Interstate has become more sensitive to antipollution controls and now claims that protecting the valuable shellfish waters of Riceboro Creek and the North Newport River was its own idea. But in 1965, Howard had to turn the company down three times before it finally agreed to his terms.

Once the rules were established, Interstate built one of the most successful water treatment plants in the entire paper industry. The most gratifying aspects of the system are not only its effectiveness but its elegant simplicity as well. Managers of older paper mills complain that it is harder for them to install pollution controls than for managers of new mills. But the important conclusion from Interstate's operation is that the most essential treatment elements can be added to almost any mill, even an aging behemoth like Union Camp.

A trip with a bit of Interstate's effluent through the several treatment steps shows the main features of the system. As the five to six million gallons of water leave the mill every day, they hit the only sophisticated part of the whole treatment operation—a color removal tank. One of the conditions Howard imposed on Interstate was that the mill must remove the strange brown color that marked all kraft wastes. At that time, no paper mill in the country had a color removal system. Most companies—and most state water control agencies—agreed that the color was aesthetically obnoxious; but all things considered, it seemed one of the less harmful elements of the paper pollution problem, although no industry scientist was sure just what chemical compounds made up the "color bodies." The Georgia Water Board's request was aimed both at learning more about the color bodies and preventing any unknown damage they might do. As one of Howard's aides later explained, the Board wanted to make sure that the apparently harmless little bodies did not build up in the marsh and perhaps work some disastrous change in its life cycle 20 or 30 years later.

Interstate responded with a "lime flocculation" tank. When the mill waste, looking like strong, day-old coffee, runs out of the sewers, it spends 45 minutes in a large tank while lime percolates through it. The next step is the clarifier, where the lime gathers into clumps and sinks to the bottom of the clarification tank, taking with it most of the color.

Once the water has shed its color, it runs through systems that have been part of the industrial repertoire for years. The same clarifier that removes the clumps of colored lime also skims off the oil and drains away the settled solids. With all these preliminaries out of the way, the water finally enters the most dramatic part of the treatment system: Interstate's aeration pond.

Visitors driving to Interstate on the winding road from Riceboro pass what seems to be a large natural lake. In fact, it is the aeration pond where the final step in the mill's treatment system takes place. Technically, the job the lake has to do is to break down all the organic pollutants and fill the waste water back up with dissolved oxygen. It does these jobs well; by the time the water finishes its half-year trip through the pond and slips into Riceboro Creek, its dissolved oxygen content is usually higher than that of the natural river water.

The aeration pond is extraordinarily effective. Long and oval, it covers nearly one square mile of the mill's land. Long dikes protrude from alternate sides of the pond, forcing the water to zigzag up and down the lake on its trip to the creek. At the end of the first dike, there are already signs of life. A few fish break the water, but they are only a hint of what is ahead. By the middle of the pond, a complete aquatic life cycle is under way. Bass and other game fish breed in the water, attracting not only fishermen ("Fishing by Permit Only," say signs that are probably unique in the industry) but elegant American egrets and blue herons. Ducks paddle out to eat the fish and retreat to stands of marsh grass to raise their families. Here water birds do not face the common danger of death through pollution, but the water does hold another threat: Interstate officials swear that large alligators lumber into the pond from nearby marshes and gobble unsuspecting ducks.

Although the pond water is already capable of supporting life, it goes through one final treatment before entering Riceboro Creek. Since Interstate releases water only on the outgoing tide, the water waits several hours in a cement tank which has a furiously whipping mechanical aerator. Technical measurements show that the water entering the Riceboro Creek has about six parts per million of dissolved oxygen—one or two ppm more than creek water. The BOD has almost totally disappeared. Although the mill is allowed to put in 800 pounds of BOD per day, the pond usually removes all but 300 to 400 pounds—an immeasurably small amount.

"Our only worry," says Interstate manager William Verross, "is that the water we're putting in is too pure for the marsh. It's used to a heavier load of organic wastes."

Why is one company able to make such progress in pollution control while so many others merely crawl along? Part of the reason, of course, is the strict requirements the state Water Board imposed on Interstate. But an equally important explanation is the attitude that Interstate has taken toward the marshes and waters that surround it. As Verross and one of his technical directors, E. L. Hart, constantly point out, the mill has installed several safety features that the state Water Board never even asked for. For example, during the treatment process, the waste water passes through four emergency holding ponds, ready to catch any dangerous batch of effluent before it reaches the marsh. To avoid thermal pollution, the mill itself decided to build a one-and-a-half-mile cement cooling pipe.

To set up its color removal process, the only part of the system that demanded technical creativity, Interstate took advantage of a Federal program designed to encourage private research. The Federal Water Quality Control Administrator offers private companies up to 70 per cent of the cost of antipollution research, requiring only that the company make its results public. While some of the industry's leaders, including Union Camp, pat themselves on the back for not relying on Federal money, more progressive companies have found these grants an excellent way to publicize technical advances, and the paper industry in general is more receptive to the findings of one of their own companies than to university laboratory experiments.

"You take one of these projects done by some longhairs up at a university," Verross says. "A manager will look at it and say it's nice. But when he sees what we have and sees that it *works,* then he knows it's practical." There are more than a dozen of these Federal grant projects under way now, ranging from foam removal to joint treatment of municipal sewage and mill wastes.

Naturally Interstate has had to spend money. Closest estimates are that of the mill's total $27-million cost, 10 per cent went into pollution controls, with most of the money devoted to building the huge lake. Calculating from Interstate's production figures—the mill makes 500 tons of paper per day, slightly less than one-sixth of Union Camp's output—Union Camp would have to spend about $15 million to cure its Savannah pollution. Some economies of scale, however, could cut the cost drastically. Because Interstate had the luxury of a large tract of land, it could afford to build a simple pond without aerators or other mechanical frills. But with a few high-power aerators, the same pond would be able to handle up to 20 times as much waste water. Theoretically, Union Camp could get along with an aerated pond one-third the size of Interstate's. Such a pond would fit nicely on the golf course the company has built in its front yard.

Representatives of Union Camp and other "old" mills object to comparison with the new plants. They say that it is much harder to install pollution controls for their creaking old machinery than for the new models. They feel, too, that the dirt from their mills is somehow more excusable than that from the new plants. Their reasoning is partly true: Interstate knew from the start that it could not get away with unloading tons of filth into the creek, and it therefore made several design changes. But the complaint of the mills does not ring true because of two other facts. First, the large old mills are putting more than negligible amounts of pollutants into their streams. Union Camp, the most notable example, regularly dumps 100 to 200 times as much BOD pollutant into the Savannah as Interstate is allowed legally. Second, any mill that was serious about curbing pollution could easily add the most important part of Interstate's treatment system: the holding pond.

The story of the second pulp town shows how a mill can avoid even this easy step.

Savannah: Union Camp

> *For 30 years, Union Camp has used billions and billions and billions of gallons of fresh water, and they never spent a penny for pollution control until they were made to do it. They sat down there for 30 years and*

> *discharged billions of gallons of waste into the Savannah River—and that stuff's not feeding the fish, brother. After all this time, they ought to say, "I'm happy to pay Nature back for what I took." . . . They ought to have sense enough to know that it's a different ball game today.*
>
> *Rock Howard, Georgia Water Quality Control Board*

> *The Name of the Game: Profit-Ability*
>
> *Union Camp's 1970 Slogan*

This is a big mill, the biggest kraft paper plant in the world. The mill squats on the river outside Savannah's limits but still it thinks of itself as the social and moral leader of the city. Reading corporate publicity and counting up the Union Camp scholarships and charities, one would think this was a mill that took pride in its city and cared for its people.

If any mill could take the lead in ending pollution, this is it. With its massive production, Union Camp could absorb the costs more easily than its fledgling brothers. As the industrial giant of the lower Savannah, it could encourage other industries on the river to follow its lead. As the largest paper producer in the Southeast, it could help change the pattern of environmental neglect in the whole region.

But the bad example Union Camp has set appeals to the most recalcitrant elements of the paper industry. Faced with a set of legal requirements that were politely mild, Union Camp has made only the most grudging progress in cleaning the river. In the last five years, the company has consistently violated even the undemanding standards set by the state water control agency. Meanwhile, company representatives purport to be "concerned generally as responsible citizens with all aspects of the Savannah harbor pollution" [2] and they bristle at the suggestion that their mill is not doing its best.

From the time Union Camp set up business in 1936 until the Federal government held a pollution control conference in Savannah in 1965, the company had taken few steps toward controlling its liquid filth. It had put screens over some of its outfalls to catch pieces of bark and undigested wood, and it had tried to eliminate the smelly white foam that sailed down the river from the mill. Like most other paper companies, Union Camp saw a dollar sign on the horizon of its efforts. Each wood fiber they caught in a "save-all" filter was a fiber they could turn into paper; each gallon of water they reused was another gallon they would not have to pump from the ground. From the river's point of view, these self-interested improvements did just as much good as if they had been part of a formal antipollution campaign. The problem was that the company could see no further than profit; Union Camp stopped making the improvements when the improvements stopped making money.

When the enforcement conference came to town in 1965, Union Camp was the main attraction. Federal researchers discovered that this one mill produced 70 per cent of the combined industrial and municipal pollution in the lower Savannah and accounted for 80 per cent of the industrial total. The 135,000 pounds of oxygen-consuming pollutant (BOD) that Union Camp released daily was eight times greater than that which came from Savannah's sewers, and consumed as much oxygen as would sewage from a town the size of Cincinnati.[3]

The conference took place in the days when companies still made public their irritation and annoyance over their antipollution responsibilities. In this spirit, Union Camp manager James Lientz gave a brave if slightly off-target defense of his mill's performance. He told the conference how many people the mill employed and how much money it had brought to Savannah; for example, ". . . other economic contributions made by the plant to Savannah and the area in 1964 included pulpwood purchases of over $18,000,000 . . ."[4] Lientz warned that raising the river's dissolved oxygen level might impair one of its "major assets": its "ability to assimilate waste."[5] And he reminded the conference that mill pollutants were not really dangerous: "They do not constitute a health hazard. In proper quantities they contribute food to the small organisms which provide food for fish."[6]

This last statement did not get past Murray Stein, the Federal official in charge of the conference, who said, "Now, there is one curious statement that I have been reading. . . . You talk about your waste. You say in proper quantities they contribute food . . . I guess they will make it good for fish. I don't know if this happens in the laboratory, but really I don't know of any plant operating that the contention has been made that this is good, really good for the fish."

Lientz replied, "Well, Mr. Stein, I have to fall back on our technical staff as a source for that information. . . . I will put it this way: we are not in the market of recovering waste to feed fish. . . ."

"As far as I understand it, no one . . . as far as I know, has ever selected a place downstream from a pulp and paper mill to really start and really build fish, . . . and really, I have not singled that out as the ideal situation," retorted Stein.

Herbert Rogers, who represented the Department of Health, Education and Welfare at the conference said, "If you haven't got the oxygen, how is the fish going to live? I think that is the real question."

Lientz answered Rogers: "The statement was merely put in this report to emphasize the facts that we are talking about a material that is certainly not harmful, nonpoisonous." [7]

The verdict of the conference was that each industry on the river would have to cut the BOD of its effluent by 25 per cent and reduce the amount of settleable solids by a full 90 per cent. The deadline for making these changes was the end of 1967. In view of the industries' later performance, it is important to remember just how lenient the conference's timetable was. There was no technical reason why the paper mills should not have been required to install complete treatment systems immediately. As Rock Howard later pointed out in a letter to Lientz, Federal authorities had originally demanded that the mills build complete secondary treatment systems right away. But the state decided to make the schedule more "reasonable," apparently to ease payment problems.

Even this major concession, however, was not enough to spur Union Camp to effective action; the company still cut its performance as close as possible. Company engineers went to work on a treatment system and emerged with plans for a 300-foot clarifier, which they hoped would do what the state wanted. Early in 1967, the company broke ground for the clarifier and got out $3.5 million to pay for it. But the clarifier was plagued with complications from the very beginning. A series of construction delays and other problems kept it from operating until July, 1968—more than half a year over the deadline set at the enforcement conference. Then Union Camp found that the clarifier simply could not do what it was supposed to. While it removed a respectable portion of settleable solids, it hardly reduced the BOD at all. The mill's response was to make a few changes in the mill processes, which reduced the BOD slightly, and which it could have done years earlier. Meanwhile, Union Camp clung to its limping clarifier.

Early in 1969, it became clear that the clarifier was failing to do even its most basic job. In a letter to Howard on January 7, Lientz admitted that some sludge—the thick, dark, sticky sediment that collects at the bottom of the clarifier—was escaping into the river. "Any disturbance such as a high sludge load, need for maintenance, poor sludge characteristics, etc. now leaves us without enough capacity to handle all of the sludge." As a faintly cheering promise, he added, "We will do everything we can to keep as much primary sludge out of the river as is practical with the equipment now in operation." [8]

Howard thought as little of that explanation as Stein had of Lientz' "good for fish" remark. On January 8, he gave Union Camp his blunt reply:

> We are extremely disappointed in the progress Union Camp Corporation had made to date. We feel that your accomplishments have not been commensurate with:
>
> 1. The tremendous pollutional load discharged to the Lower Savannah River by Union Camp for over 30 years.
> 2. Union Camp's position as the principal polluter of the Savannah.
> 3. The State's initial reasonable requirements for treatment as against the Federal agency's demands for immediate installation of secondary treatment.

4. Union Camp's great demands on the water resources of the State.
5. Union Camp's overall industrial and technical competency.[9]

In the next nine months, between this exchange of letters and the second Federal enforcement conference in October, Union Camp inched ahead. Testifying before the conference on October 29, 1969, Lientz reported that things were looking up for the clarifier: since April, it was meeting legal standards by removing 91 per cent of the settleable solids, and it was coming closer to the requirements by removing 21 per cent of BOD. During September and October of 1969, Lientz told the conference, the BOD removal rate had been 27 per cent—a full 2 per cent better than the standards set down four years earlier.

From other perspectives, the picture did not look so bright. At the same 1969 conference, Charles Starling, the Georgia Water Board's industrial specialist, reported on his tests of the Union Camp effluent. Leaving aside one questionable reading, Starling's three days of tests showed that Union Camp's BOD rate was only 14 per cent below its 1965 level—a clear violation of the 25-per-cent reduction requirement. The mill had done a better job in treating its settleable solids; figures from both Starling and Union Camp confirmed an 85–90 per cent reduction.

Starling's report, however, was not the last nor worst word about Union Camp's performance. In a similar situation, a private citizen who was still violating a state order four years after it was given might be inspired to correct his misdeeds in a hurry, breathing a small sigh of relief for escaping prosecution. If Union Camp's emission rates for the next few months are any guide, the company did not feel a similar fear.

The table on page 87 tells the story. Each month, Union Camp and other Georgia industries send reports to the state Water Board on their pollution output. The charts on which Union Camp records this information are so detailed that the mill has a good idea at all times of what it is putting into the river. The forms record not only the total amount of water and pollutant going out of the mill but also give a complete breakdown of the source and treatment of each of the waste streams. No one at the state board checks regularly to make sure that the mills are sending in true figures, but comparisons of the readings Union Camp makes with the charts sent to the state board show there has been no alteration.

The table shows how much pollutant Union Camp put into the Savannah during eight months between August 1969 and July 1970.* The first group of columns gives the mill's output of settleable solids; the second covers BOD. For each pollutant, the table shows not only the average number of pounds dumped each day but also the maximum amount of pollutant that came from the mill on the worst day of the month. These maximum figures are at least as important as the monthly averages. The highest pollution output rather than the average determines how much damage an industry does to the fish and microorganisms in the river (see Chapter 13). As the Union Camp chart clearly shows, the difference between average and maximum output can be enormous. In July 1970, for example, the mill's highest output of settleable solids was 1600 per cent of the monthly average.

The third set of columns shows the BOD and solids emissions as percentages of the 1965 levels. This comparison is important because Union Camp's current BOD output should be only 75 per cent of what it was in 1965, according to the ruling handed down at the 1965 enforcement conference. Solids should be a mere 10 per cent of the 1965 total. As these figures unmistakably show, Union Camp's performance bears no resemblance to the legal requirements. In all but two months of the eight, the mill's BOD level was significantly higher than the 75 per cent rate it should have been. During three months, Union Camp actually put out more BOD than it had in 1965. Averaged over the whole period, the mill has cut its BOD pollution by only 9 per cent since 1965. In 1970, two and a half years after the deadline for re-

* These readings were chosen at random from reports in the state water board files on August 19, 1970. Reports for the rest of the year were not in the file that day; however, it is unlikely that they would greatly change the statistical conclusions.

TABLE 7–1

Month	*Settleable solids lbs/day* *Average*	*Max.*	*BOD lbs/day* *Average*	*Max.*	*Per cent of 1965 levels* *solids*	*BOD*
August 1969	11,000	66,000	115,000	188,000	13%	85%
October 1969	8,000	28,000	103,000	187,000	9	76
November 1969	12,000	57,000	139,000	188,000	14	103
December 1969	41,000	295,000	138,000	245,000	47	102
January 1970	9,000	77,000	135,000	192,000	10	100
February 1970	15,000	73,000	156,000	241,000	17	115
May 1970	9,000	47,000	108,000	170,000	10	80
July 1970*	30,000	496,000	92,000	213,000	34	68
Maximum:	*496,000*		*245,000*			
Average:	*16,900*		*123,000*		*19.4%*	*91.3%*

Source: Figures submitted by Union Camp to Georgia Water Quality Control Board.

* The mill was shut down for the first six days of July 1970. When the mill was in operation, the averages were: BOD—101,000 lbs/day (75 per cent of 1965 level); solids—34,000 lbs/day (39 per cent of 1965 level).

ducing BOD by 25 per cent, this is hardly an adequate or legal showing.

Union Camp's clarifier had slightly better luck in its fight against the settleable solids. In four of the eight months, solids reduction was close to that demanded by the state board, but the average for the whole period was still far too high. During the eight months, Union Camp spilled out twice as much solid material as it legally should have—almost 20 per cent of the 1965

TABLE 7–2

Union Camp, Savannah, Georgia

Date	*Water discharged, in millions of gallons/day*	*Settleable solids discharged to river, in pounds*	*BOD discharged, in pounds*
May 1, 1970	38.2	7000	111,000
May 2, 1970	39.4	6000	150,000
May 3, 1970	37.7	5000	131,000
May 4, 1970	37.0	8000	112,000
May 5, 1970	33.1	6000	89,000
May 6, 1970	36.7	1000	124,000
May 7, 1970	36.0	4000	170,000
Average for week:	*36.9*	*5286*	*126,714*
May 8, 1970	40.2	47,000	150,000
May 9, 1970	40.8	25,000	155,000
May 10, 1970	38.8	17,000	109,000
May 11, 1970	37.2	23,000	102,000
May 12, 1970	36.9	5000	77,000
May 13, 1970	36.8	4000	89,000
May 14, 1970	36.6	0	93,000
Average for week:	*38.2*	*17,286*	*110,714*
May 15, 1970	34.8	2000	73,000
May 16, 1970	35.1	2000	98,000
May 17, 1970	30.5	1000	86,000
May 18, 1970	37.0	1000	94,000
May 19, 1970	37.7	2000	98,000
May 20, 1970	34.3	5000	91,000
May 21, 1970	42.0	1000	83,000
Average for week:	*35.8*	*2000*	*89,000*
Average for three weeks:	*37.0*	*8190*	*104,048*

Source: Reports filed with Georgia Water Quality Control Board, May 1970.

TABLE 7–3

Interstate Paper, Riceboro, Georgia

Day	*Water discharged, in million gallons*	*BOD discharged, in pounds*
August 3, 1970	7.46	187
August 4	3.63	91
August 5	7.91	198
August 6	7.73	194
August 7	6.20	155
August 8	7.35	184
August 9	7.0	175
Average for week:	*6.75*	*167*
Average for preceding week:	*6.95*	*283*

Source: Reports filed with Georgia Water Quality Control Board, August 1970.

total, instead of the 10 per cent required by the state Water Board.

Tables 7–2 and 7–3, taken from reports filed with the Georgia Water Quality Control Board, show the difference that good pollution controls can make. Interstate Paper has good control; Union Camp does not.

As Union Camp months go, May was a good one; the mill's monthly averages for BOD and solids were both reasonably close to the levels set by the state board. Other months were considerably worse (see Table 7–1). The figures shown here are for the first three weeks of May 1970 and, if anything, they present the company in an unusually favorable light; the average figures for both settleable solids and BOD discharged to the river in this three-week period are lower than the averages for the month as a whole. Yet the benign averages conceal dangerous day-to-day fluctuations. During the first 11 days of the month, the mill had an almost uninterrupted series of extremely high BOD levels. While the less polluted days during the week of May 15 gave the river a chance to recover, they could not undo the damage to aquatic life caused during the first two weeks—any more than a brief spell in the freezer could restore a melted candle to its original shape. Any fish with the bad luck to choose one of these days as the time to head upstream would make it no farther than the belt of oxygenless water before suffocating. These variations are not confined to May; as Table 7–1 shows, they are the rule rather than the exception.

The week of August 3, 1970, was chosen at random to show Interstate Paper's pollution control, but the figures for that week are by no means atypical. There are no figures for settleable solids discharged, because they disappear so completely during the treatment process that they are not even measured. But the figures for BOD output are revealing: on the average, Union Camp produces 2,812 pounds of BOD for each million gallons of water it uses; Interstate Paper produces less than 25 pounds per million gallons. Measured in terms of BOD, Union Camp is more than 100 times more offensive than Interstate Paper—and Union Camp produces settleable solids to boot. Because the amount of BOD discharged by Interstate Paper is extremely low, day-to-day fluctuations are not likely to cause damage to aquatic life around the Interstate plant, as they do in the case of Union Camp.

July 14, 1970, marked a record day for Union Camp's output of settleable solids. On that day, the mill put half a million pounds of settleable solids into the river —16 times the monthly average, and more than 60 times greater than the standard set by the 1965 enforcement conference. The catastrophe happened because something went wrong with the clarifier, and the plant engineers decided to send the waste straight to the river. Blunders like this, which take an incalculable but undoubtedly large toll on the river, need never happen. An emergency holding pond in which the mill could store its waste until the clarifier returned to action would prevent such disasters. In its normal paper-making operation, a mill makes sure to have efficient back-up systems to avoid production disasters, but Union Camp has never bothered to show the same concern about pollution disasters.

Although the July 14 incident brought the river an unusually large amount of raw effluent, Union Camp has a more systematic way of getting untreated pollutants into the Savannah. From a casual glance at the company's publicity, most readers would assume that the mill sends all waste water through its expensive new clarifier. In fact, only about 55–65 per cent of the mill's total effluent ever goes near the clarifier. The rest—usually over 15 million gallons per day—runs directly into the river, carrying its full burden of original pollution.

As Table 7–4 shows, the amount of untreated pollutants is considerable. The figures are for July 22, 1970,

TABLE 7–4

Untreated Waste to River, Union Camp

	Wood Yard Flume	*#60 Sewer Sump*	*Paper Mill Sewer Sump*	*#1 Pulp Mill Sewer*	*#8 Pulp Mill Sewer*
Flow, gallons/min.	694	108	—	7633	6458
Solids, lbs/day	26,263	605	—	—	—
BOD, lbs/day	—	6189	10,646	9694	1443

Source: Reports filed with Georgia Water Quality Control Board, 1970.

when the wood yard flume water carried out 26,000 pounds of settleable solids, and other untreated sewers bore nearly 30,000 pounds of BOD to the river. It is unclear whether Union Camp leaves these wastes untreated by preference or whether its clarifier is simply too small to treat them all. Either way, the gallons of raw mill sewage make one unmistakable point about the company's priorities: Union Camp will do only what it is forced to, and sometimes not even that.

> *We're hearing hysterical "Doom's Day" predictions from ecologists and now political candidates are even trying to get onto the bandwagon with it.*
> *People get extremely emotional about losing a species, but animals have been dying out every year clear back to the dinosaur, and in most cases man had nothing to do with it. For that matter, it probably won't hurt mankind a whole hell of a lot in the*

long run if the whooping crane doesn't quite make it.

Glenn Kimble, Union Camp director of Air and Water Protection

Most large corporations today are shrewd enough to dilute their harsh environmental effects with soothing public words; companies that have mastered the soft-soap technique would never allow a man like Kimble within a mile of a newspaper reporter. But it is more than simple corporate artlessness that permitted Kimble to become Union Camp's environmental protector; he is also a poetically just guide to the philosophy that lies deep in Union Camp's heart. The lackluster performance of the Savannah mill perfectly expresses Union Camp's general attitude toward streams, fish, and other non-marketable commodities.

Not all Union Camp executives are public relations roughriders like Kimble. President Alexander Calder, Jr., and chairman Hugh D. Camp showed in the company's annual report for 1969 that they, too, realized it was a good time to be concerned about pollution. They said,

> The seriousness of the problem of mill waste disposal is not a matter of sudden awareness with us.* In the last ten years the company has spent over $10,000,000 in the application of the best current technology and equipment to control air and water pollution. We are continuing our efforts to further refine anti-pollution procedures at each of our major facilities. And, of course, we are cooperating closely with all appropriate government agencies.[10]

Unfortunately, Calder's and Camp's statement does not quite jibe with the facts. By the company's own calculations, the amount of money spent on pollution controls is ridiculously small. The $10 million Union Camp has measured out in the last ten years is about one-third of 1 per cent of the company's $2.99 billion revenue during the same period. That means that about 29 hours' worth of revenue per year has gone into paying for

* Quite true: as early as 1937, Union Camp forced Savannah to protect it from antipollution suits. See Chapter 10.

chronic mistreatment of natural resources. Union Camp is not a poor corporation that might quickly succumb under the burden of higher pollution control expenses. In the same ten-year period, the company's total revenue more than doubled, from $217 million in 1960 to $457 million in 1969. Clear profit rose by more than 65 per cent, from $18.6 million in 1960 to $30.4 million in 1969. The trend continued unimpeded into 1970; during the first half of the year, Union Camp once more broke all records for sales and profit. Meanwhile, the corporation has been able to afford a large series of expansions. The most recent, at the Franklin, Virginia, mill, cost $57 million—more than five times the ten-year pollution control budget.

After $3.5 million was spent for Savannah's clarifier, only $6.5 million was left to be spread thinly among the company's 40 other installations. And if the bumbling Savannah clarifier is any sign of what "the best current technology and equipment" have to offer, the other mills should not get their hopes up about controlling their pollution. (Fortunately, the experience of the Interstate mill in Riceboro shows that the best equipment *can* do the job.) It is also worth remembering that while Union Camp "of course" cooperates with government agencies, its largest and worst polluting plant still chronically violates state water standards.

Union Camp's local statesmen generally spend less time on pledges of good faith than its New York managers do. But when the men of Savannah speak, the inconsistencies in their stories are formidable. In the summer of 1970, in a news story announcing the mill's upcoming antipollution plans, Union Camp manager James Lientz gave this description of company philosophy: "Union Camp recognizes the desirability and necessity of operating its facilities in a manner compatible with the interests of its own employees and the reasonable use and enjoyment by others of the lands, water, and air in the vicinity of its plants." [11]

When Lientz said "reasonable," he was echoing the sentiment he had expressed three years earlier in a hearing before the state Water Board. The board was then deciding what water quality standards to apply to the river. Lientz urged a "balanced" use of the Savannah:

"We must do a very careful job in balancing our needs for the various uses of the river and for making multiple uses of the river in a manner assuring maximum benefit to all interests which the harbor and river serve." [12]

But Lientz' "all interests" did not seem to include fishermen (or for that matter, fish), swimmers, or anyone concerned about restoring the river. In almost the same breath as that declaration, Lientz went on to oppose the only measure capable of bringing life back into the Savannah—mandatory secondary treatment facilities for all polluters on the river. "It seems to us that this provision destroys the value of water classifications as far as industry is concerned," he said. "It puts a heavy economic burden on existing industry . . . by requiring treatment *which produces no benefits* and which is not needed for a waterway to serve its designated use." [13] (Emphasis added.) No company—at least not in the 1970's—would oppose child labor laws because they "put a heavy economic burden on existing industry." But too many industrialists have not yet learned that environmental protection, which benefits everyone, is the same kind of responsibility that companies must assume as part of the cost of doing business.

In day-to-day life on the Savannah, Union Camp rarely faces direct questions about its environmental policy or its antipollution performance. The Savannahians who have learned to live with Union Camp's smoke, their dead water, and the company pay resigned themselves years ago to the mill's constant presence. Many of them claim not to notice even the smell, grossest evidence of Union Camp's existence. Because the people are resigned, they question the mill even less frequently than they question the skies that bring them heat and rain. This attitude naturally works to the mill's advantage; it spares Union Camp the need to develop a presentable, coherent policy on pollution control. Instead, mill officials learn a few phrases to insert in newspaper articles, and then they act on more deeply held beliefs.

In a series of interviews with members of our project during the summer of 1970, Union Camp executives explained these beliefs. An examination of their statements helps explain the current state of the Savannah River. In one remarkable interview on July 16, 1970, a cluster of local and corporate executives showed with brutal clarity the indifference their company feels toward its natural setting.

According to Calder and Camp's 1969 annual report, Union Camp has known for years about the "seriousness" of paper-mill pollution. But in practice, that meant to James Lientz that "until these [water control] laws were passed, we really didn't consider this a problem." Both Lientz and technical director Richard Chase admitted that the mill has only the faintest curiosity about the damage it is doing; both said that Union Camp has never studied the river to figure out what its pollutants are doing to the water life.

The highest-ranking corporate executive at the interview was John E. Ray III, a tough-minded Southerner who is now Union Camp's executive vice president, reportedly on his way to the presidency. With a few brief comments, Ray fleshed out all the worst implications of what Lientz and Chase had said. Union Camp will do as much to control pollution as it is required to by law, Ray said (and, as the record shows, sometimes not even that much). But it will not go further; it will not extend the creativity it shows in finding new uses for paper bags to discovering the most efficient way to curb its pollution. "We are not going to spend our stockholders' money foolishly," he explained.

Vice president Ray and manager Lientz are both empowered to make decisions that can preserve or destroy thousands of acres of land and many miles of stream. We asked them what they were doing about Savannah's supply of drinkable ground water (see Chapter 8). What will happen, we asked Lientz, if heavy industrial pumping dries up the city's wells?

"I don't know," he answered. "I won't be here."

Later, in discussion with Ray, another project member explored the legal subtleties of the pollution issue. He asked Ray if there were any restrictions that Union Camp felt it could not abridge as it continued to deplete the ground water.

Ray was right on top of the problem: "I had my lawyers in Virginia research that," he said, "and they told us that we could suck the state of Virginia out through a hole in the ground, and there was nothing anyone could do about it."

As daylight was beginning to fade on the afternoon of May 8, 1970, a Coast Guard boat on a routine patrol of the Savannah harbor discovered large patches of oil floating down the river. The events that began that night and continued for the next three months offer the most disturbing testimony of all about Union Camp's concern for the river, about its respect for law, and even about its corporate honesty.

Eleven days before, Union Camp lawyers had spent a brief day in Federal court. On April 27, 1970, the company faced charges of violating a Federal antipollution law by spilling oil into the river. This first violation had taken place on June 30, 1969; the Federal prosecutors claimed that the spill violated the Refuse Act of 1899. The Refuse Act was passed by a Congress that was mainly interested in keeping the waters open for navigation. When the Act came to the public's attention in 1969, government officials and reports in the press made it sound like something only recently discovered after decades of dormancy. It had in fact been used occasionally to control industrial pollution, and has been for years the legislative authority under which the Coast Guard has assumed the duty of regulating oil discharges in the nation's rivers and harbors. They use the Refuse Act, rather than the more specifically applicable Oil Pollution Act (33 United States Code § 1001), because of its administrative simplicity and because it does not require proof of intent to violate the statute.

Indeed, the Refuse Act remains the strictest anti-pollution law on Federal books. With almost Biblical simplicity it outlaws the dumping of *any* refuse (with the one exception of municipal sewage) into *any* navigable stream. It does not matter whether the dumping is accidental or intentional, nor whether there is any proven harm to the river's life cycle or fitness for navigation. There need only be proof that some person, ship, or land-based operation let some form of pollutant, liquid or solid, into the water without a permit from the Corps of Engineers. Under regulations developed by the Coast

Guard, a spill of anything more than one quart of oil may constitute a violation.

In its April trial, Union Camp pleaded *nolo contendere* and was convicted of the violation by Federal District Judge Alexander A. Lawrence. Instead of imposing the $500 to $2,500 fine possible under the Act, Lawrence gave Union Camp a suspended sentence and placed the company on one year's probation.

Before even two weeks of probation were up, however, the Coast Guard found the second oil spill.* Firsthand reports of the incident suggest that this spill, like the first, was of large proportions—certainly more than one quart of oil. Randall B. Guidry, one of the Coast Guard members who sighted the spill, said in his official report that "the spill stretched from American Oil Co. to Savannah Machine and Foundry"—about one mile of the river front.

A cluster of Coast Guard men gathered to find the source of the oil. After tracing the spill to a Union Camp drainage ditch, Coast Guardsman Jimmy Johns followed the oil-laden ditch along its winding course through Union Camp property. Neither Johns nor the investigating officer who joined him, Ensign Denny Dobbs, ever found the exact point in the mill that had discharged the oil. But they had no doubt that it came from somewhere in Union Camp's vast tract. The Coast Guard took samples of the oil and began its regular procedure of reporting possible violations of antipollution laws.

Early on the morning of May 9, two Union Camp representatives appeared at the Coast Guard's Savannah headquarters. According to several Coast Guard members who witnessed the visit, the company's main complaint was that the Coast Guard had come barging into private mill property without getting permission. Legally, the objection was hollow; while searching for the source of a spill, the Coast Guard may legally enter private

* A violation of the Refuse Act is a criminal offense. Since as of this printing no action has been taken by the U. S. Attorney on the alleged spill, the reader is cautioned that the following events are merely the findings of a preliminary Coast Guard report and of the investigation by the members of the Project. Though we have presented our evidence to the U. S. Attorney in the good faith belief that it warrants prosecution, the guilt of the corporation and its officials should be determined by a federal court and not by the Coast Guard, the U. S. Attorney, nor by the authors.

property. Union Camp's visit did not prevent the Coast Guard from sending the oil spill report off on its elaborate bureaucratic journey that eventually leads to prosecution. Under normal circumstances, the report must make many stops in many different offices before it can ever come to suit: from the Savannah office, it goes first to Miami (District Coast Guard headquarters), then back to Savannah (Corps of Engineers District office), to Washington (Chief Engineer of the Corps of Engineers' office), and finally back to Savannah. There, the U.S. Attorney gets the report and decides that he should either prosecute—as he did in the case of the first spill—or not.

During the course of our summer study, we had heard vague, rumored accounts of a "second Union Camp oil spill." Without factual evidence to support the rumors, we simply asked Union Camp officials whether or not it was true. No, Mr. Lientz assured us at the July 16 interview. There had been no repetition of the June 30, 1969, oil spill. Was it possible that somehow the mill had spilled oil and Lientz did not know about it? No, Lientz repeated. Very unlikely.

The rumors persisted, some of them coming from Union Camp employees. And so on July 23, at our second meeting with Lientz, we asked once more. This time Lientz was far more assertive. No, he said, there had definitely been no second oil spill.

Perplexed by the gap between the private reports and the official denial, we made a routine study of Coast Guard files and other possible sources of information. Finally, in early August, we found what we thought we had been looking for: the official Coast Guard report of the spill, complete with statements from four eyewitnesses.

We made our last visit to Union Camp on August 12, 1970. Once more, we asked Mr. Lientz whether his mill had spilled oil into the river since the original June 1969 incident. "No," he said. "What are you getting at?" We showed him the Coast Guard report and explained that that was what we were getting at.

Lientz and his mill technical director, Everett Harriman, then began to remember some of the details of the "reported 'oil spill.' " The reason he had not linked that incident with our repeated questions about oil spills, Lientz said, was that technically it was not "oil" and it did not "spill." The gooey matter the Coast Guard found floating on the water was not "oil" in its normal petroleum sense, but "tall oil," a wood by-product. Legally, the distinction is meaningless. The Refuse Act applies to tall oil as completely as it does to Arabian petroleum. And most people who do not earn their living in a paper-mill laboratory—for example, the Coast Guard—would have a difficult time telling "tall oil" from the "oil" Lientz assumed we were asking about.

The "spill" distinction was equally fine. Lientz said that there had not been any sudden discharge (i.e., "spill") of oil into the river; rather, tall oil that built up on the sides of an old drainage ditch had been washed out into the river. This semantic difference was also too small to escape the Refuse Act, which prohibits even placing refuse on a bank where it is likely to be washed into a river.*

Lientz then launched into an attack on the Coast Guard for infringing on Union Camp's property rights. He began by saying repeatedly that the Coast Guard "does not have the authority" to enter the plant territory. The law, however, does not recognize Lientz' definition of property rights. The Coast Guard, as Lientz finally conceded, has every legal right to go into the plant in hot pursuit of an oil spill. The only "authority" they lacked was clearance under the mill's normal procedure for letting visitors on the property. "The procedure is well known," Lientz said. "During working hours, these agencies [the Coast Guard, the local police, etc.] are supposed to report to the main receptionist. After hours, they go to the main gate. . . . We have a right to know they were there. We have a right as owners of property to keep trespassers off until we are satisfied that they are properly authorized to be there."[14]

* Although Lientz went so far as to admit that "tall oil" had been washed into the river, his superior, John E. Ray III, does not acknowledge even that. In a speech in Savannah on October 19, 1970, which is reproduced in Appendix 1, executive vice president Ray said, "As to oil, we had an accidental spill of oil in June, 1969. This incident has been disposed of to the court's satisfaction in April, 1970. We can't guarantee that accidents won't happen again, but I can assure you that extensive additional safeguards have been established to prevent them." Apparently the safeguards failed.

These words come from a man whose mill, by all reports, broke a Federal law while still on probation for violating the same law. There are parts of this nation where men accused of repeat violations can be clapped in jail for "preventive detention," even before they are tried. Only the manager of a large company could get away with complaints about his property rights while ignoring the essential complaint—his company had, once more, broken the law.

At the second Federal enforcement conference in 1969, Union Camp and the other industries on the Savannah were ordered to take the step they had long been avoiding. Under state and Federal order, they had to reduce the BOD of their effluent by 85 per cent; for most industries, that meant building a secondary treatment system.

The details of Union Camp's treatment plan are not entirely clear. It will probably involve a holding pond or aeration lagoon, and it will probably cost about $10 million. If Union Camp carries out the plan as vigorously as it does its marketing campaigns, the people of Savannah can look forward to a measurable improvement in the health of their river. But the record of the last 30 years presents a clear warning: Union Camp has avoided pressure from the government and it has distorted the picture it presents to the public. Eternal vigilance, as a modern Thomas Jefferson might say, is the price of clean water.

St. Mary's: Gilman Paper Company

According to signs along the long, dead-end road into town, St. Mary's is the second oldest settlement in the country. Local historians say that the Spanish explorers who prowled through Florida looking for the Fountain of Youth made a brief stop in this southeastern corner of Georgia. Whether or not the stories are true, the town now bears little mark of its pre-1940 past. Instead of commemorating the explorers, St. Mary's now stands as a particularly grim monument to an American phenomenon: the company town.

The social and economic structure of St. Mary's is no

different from that of Savannah or any other city with one large mill. The mill here is the Gilman Paper Company, like Union Camp, a maker of bags and boxes. Also like Union Camp, Gilman destroys its surroundings, manipulates its community, and deludes its townspeople, all in the glorious name of free enterprise. What is different in St. Mary's is the extent of the paper company's influence and control. None of the buffering factors—the many small businesses, the aura of history and culture, the thousands of families who do not work at the mill—that dilute Union Camp's influence in Savannah are present in St. Mary's. All that is left is the mill and the men who must work there. The town has boiled away the superfluities; St. Mary's shows the relationship of mill company to mill town distilled to its most brutal essence. Some of the abuses Gilman has perpetrated make Union Camp and other mills look benevolent by comparison. In addition, the situation in St. Mary's raises alarming questions about what other companies might be doing if they had the chance.

Gilman's relation with St. Mary's began in the late Depression years. Charles Gilman—whose father had built the original Gilman mill at Gilman, Vermont, in the 1870's—watched the national pilgrimage of paper mills toward the pines and cheap labor of the South during the 1930's. He decided that he should follow suit, and in 1941 he opened the St. Mary's mill. Twenty-six years later, when his two surviving sons sold the Vermont mill to another paper company, only St. Mary's remained of the Gilman chain. The two Gilman brothers, Howard and Charles, Jr., now preside as New York-based absentee owners of a wholly Southern operation. In the years since its opening, the St. Mary's mill has grown almost as quickly as Union Camp. After the most recent in a long series of expansions, it now produces 1,000 tons of paper per day—nine times its original capacity.

Like most other kraft mills, Gilman has few hesitations about letting the local landscape absorb all the by-products of paper-making. But even by the paper industry's lenient standards, Gilman dumps an extraordinarily heavy load of effluent into the nearby rivers and marshes. According to the state Water Board's record, Gilman discharges into the North River about 100,000 pounds per day of BOD—as much as Union Camp produces, with a mill nearly three times Gilman's size. Along with the BOD, each day's effluent carries another 100,000 pounds of settleable solids—many times more than Union Camp's total.

North River is only a small tidal stream, with a much lower absorption capacity than the Savannah. The effect of Gilman's waste load on such a vulnerable body of receiving water has been predictably devastating. Throughout the North River, dissolved oxygen levels hover around one or two parts per million. (Four ppm is the usual minimum for supporting fish.) In occasional deadly patches, the dissolved oxygen content is absolutely zero.

Before there was a mill, there were fishermen in St. Mary's, shrimpers and crabbers. Many of them still remember the days before the mill, when North River was one of the lusher fishing spots on the Atlantic Coast. Now, they ruefully send their boats far out to sea to bring in a dwindling catch.

"You take a crab, and you throw him in the river," said one shrimper, pointing to the cloudy North River water beneath his dock. "You know what he'll do? Number one, he'll crawl right out of the water. And number two, he'll die."

As early as 1955, the Georgia Public Health Department had records on the mill's effect on local fishermen. In response to "numerous complaints" about Gilman's pollution of North River, St. Mary's River, and the Cumberland Sound, the Health Department sent investigators to St. Mary's. After talking with George W. Brumley, then as now manager of the mill, the Health Department researcher, Frank T. Knapp, filed the following report:

. . . A bleaching process was installed in 1954 which increased the problem of foaming and also added an acid effluent to the waters. To decrease the foam in the various processes, kerosene is used. The amount of kerosene used varies from ½ to 1 gallon per ton of pulp or paper produced. At the upper figure of 1 gallon per ton, this would mean that 465 gallons would be used per day at peak production. (This figure is exceedingly low compared with the hearsay reports of the oil-truck drivers who make deliveries to the mill. . . .)

Note: an unnamed operator from the plant informs me that the pump used to transfer the acid effluent to the river must have parts of it replaced every three days because of the action of the acid. This, if true, indicates a much stronger acid condition of the effluent than indicated by Mr. Brumley. . . .

Mr. Brumley said that St. Mary's Kraft was always concerned about keeping pollution as low as possible. I then asked him if there was any provision for holding back the effluent at low or slack tide and he answered "no." I further asked him what the total daily discharge of effluent was and he stated he did not know but that the variation in amount from day to day was slight. On summing up this part of the discussion, I pointed out that dilution factors based on average values are meaningless and that if the [Gilman] Corporation were truly concerned they would not release much effluent at slack tide levels. . . .

As a matter of policy, Mr. Brumley stated that even though the St. Mary's Kraft Corp. was a major factor in the economy of the St. Mary's area it did not consider that it had any right to hurt other industries. This was in answer to a statement by Mr. Miller that his fishing industry had been destroyed completely. He can no longer catch shrimp in the area and any fish caught from Cumberland Sound, St. Mary's River, or adjacent areas are unsalable and unpalatable because of a "turpentine" or "kerosene" flavor. His business was sustained last year by shrimp from the Gulf of Mexico, but he has been operating at a serious loss for the last six months. These conditions are forcing him to contemplate closing his business at the end of the year. Note: the "last six months" correspond closely with the inclusion of a bleaching process by St. Mary's Kraft. Mr. Brumley then stated that his corporation stands ready to cooperate with the State in reducing pollution to the lowest possible level.[15]

Even the air in St. Mary's is poisoned. The graceful gray-green moss that drips from trees in other Georgia towns is gone from St. Mary's. So is the chrome from cars that have been too often exposed to the air. Most townspeople have learned to store their cars in garages and to keep any "good" cars as far away from the mill as possible. But these measures offer little real protection. When the wind brings down plumes of caustic smoke, walls and windows are not enough. Gilman's smoke seeped into one man's garage and ate away the chrome window frames on his car. This same smoke settles on all the houses in town, and enters all the lungs. Parents report that often they cannot see their children playing across the yard, for the air is too opaque.

"Hell," said one man, returning from a shift at the mill. "You know this can't be good."

One of the tragedies of paper mill pollution is that in their quest for wood and water the mills usually damage areas of great natural beauty. Like other mills on the Georgia coast, Gilman is flanked on one side by marshes and on the other by pine forests. But beyond the marshes and across a narrow sound from Gilman lies one of Georgia's most valuable natural treasures: Cumberland Island.

Cumberland is the wildest and most spectacular of Georgia's chain of coastal islands. Long and narrow, the island contains within its 40 square miles a harmonious balance of scenery and wildlife. Flat beach stretches for 15 miles, wide, white, and unspoiled. In the island's interior, herds of cattle, horses, and pigs—all left over from the earliest settlers—run wild through stands of pine and live oak. The many forms of animal life and vegetation on the island are sustained in a rare ecological balance. The same palmettos and flowering bushes that keep Cumberland's sand dunes in place also provide food for several animals and shelter for the wild birds. Dozens of inlets snake their way through the island's fertile marshes, supporting a complete aquatic population, where they are not polluted.

Cumberland has had human inhabitants since at least 4000 B.C. White explorers found Timucua Indians there in the mid-sixteenth century and evidence of an Indian culture dating back thousands of years. Spanish priests built missions on the island in the late seventeenth century, and the wife of Thomas Morrison Carnegie (Andrew's brother) built the first of several family resort mansions there in the late eighteen hundreds.

Most of the homes are in ruins now, although the old families still hold land and come down for occasional weekends. The island has reclaimed almost all of its natural peace since its social zenith in the nineteen twenties. But at every turn the opulent splendor of the ruins is powerful enough, even in the midst of one of the most serene islands in the world, to evoke the expectation of the sound of jazzy parties and loud, laughing car rides, reminiscent of Gatsby and his age. Behind some of the oldest houses lie the automotive relics of the pleasant lost days; ancient Fords and Packards lie wheelless in the sand and gray lizards sit in the same seats that once held wealthy children.

Now the bushes and animals that have reclaimed the island face the threat of a different invasion. Waves of white mill foam and invisible but more deadly pollutants flow directly out of the North River and St. Mary's River into the Cumberland Sound, which washes the island's marshes and beaches. Even at the center of the island, it is frequently impossible to escape the thick pulp mill odor.

The pollution of St. Mary's and Cumberland Island is, of course, no more necessary than the pollution of Savannah. By cleaning its mill wastes, Gilman could have protected the surrounding area from such large-scale degradation. But the slightest effort at pollution control is more than the mill's managers have been willing to make. Despite steady pressure from the state Water Board, Gilman managed to fall nearly two years behind schedule in its plans to build a primary treatment system. As of late 1970, Gilman's wastes receive *no* treatment before they flow to the river.[16] Rock Howard of the Georgia Water Quality Control Board has decided to by-pass the intermediate timetable for building a primary treatment system. He has given Gilman a choice: finish a secondary treatment system, consisting of holding ponds and other equipment to reduce the BOD by 85 per cent, by the end of 1972, or "be prepared to suspend operations at that time."[17]

Howard had good reason for taking a firm stand with the Gilman mill. In 1967 mill manager Brumley testified before a panel from the state water board and opposed its high standards for waste treatment. Like Lientz of Union Camp, Brumley began his presentation with a long catalogue of the economic benefits his mill had brought to St. Mary's.

We presently employ 1625, with an annual payroll in excess of $10,000,000. We produce an average of 900 tons of paper per day, utilizing 1350 cords of wood per day. . . . Gilman Paper Company is the only major Georgia industry south of Brunswick and east of Waycross. It can be safely stated that not less than 75 per cent of the economy of Camden County is directly dependant on Gilman Paper Company. . . .[18]

With Gilman's benefits established, Brumley moved on to his major point: the "very major expenditure" required to clean up the river "will contribute virtually nothing to any segment of the population." [19] Brumley was not satisfied to let his argument rest on the economic difficulty of installing treatment plants. No, he said, the whole idea of even trying to clean the river was "illogical."

"A waste treatment system could not be designed with current knowledge *which would surpass the service North River performs in waste treatment and assimilation,*" Brumley told the uncomfortable panelists from the water board. "These functions are natural and logical stream uses. . . . The current and potential value of North River *lies solely in waste treatment and limited navigational use.*" [20] (Emphasis added.)

When he has not been arguing against curbing pollution, Brumley has found other ways to obscure his mill's record. In early 1970, for example, newspapers in the area carried stories about an ambitious new $10 million pollution treatment project at Gilman. About $4 million of that would go for the water-treatment system that Gilman had been ordered to build, but the heart of the story was the $6.5 million project which would "control all areas of the plant's emission of air pollution, including the lime kiln and recovery boiler areas." [21] What the articles did not mention, but what close readers of the paper trade journals knew, was that the $6.5 million "air pollution control" was actually a huge new recovery boiler, designed to aid mill production of more paper for less money. The new boiler will, coincidentally, cut the air pollution slightly, but hardly enough to change life in St. Mary's or justify the disproportionate publicity. Nor was it enough to justify the exemption from state sales tax which Georgia law provides for pollution control devices. The company's request for approval of the exemption was denied in a curt letter from the Water Board, which specifically noted that the primary purpose of the boiler was to improve internal efficiency and profit.

The people who live in the mill's shadow are naturally unhappy about pollution, but their anger flares only when something unusually bad happens—a fishing trip to Cumberland finds an aquatic wasteland, the mill's normal rotten-egg stench becomes even worse, the corrosive fly ash from the mill's stacks eats the paint off their houses. The townspeople realize that most of their chronic complaints—from bad working conditions to political intimidation to smoky air—are due to Gilman's undisputed domination of its company town. When nearly every pay check comes from one company purse, the lines of local influence and control are not hard to trace.

In St. Mary's, the lines lead to two men who exercise the power that Gilman represents. One is mill manager Brumley, who determines the economic futures of 1,800 employees; the other is his lawyer ally, Robert Harrison. The importance of Brumley's position is to be expected, but the concentration of power that Harrison has achieved is more unusual. In a town with competing economic forces, Harrison would never have become so influential. His position in St. Mary's, however, demonstrates how easily economic interests can spill over to warp political and legal processes.

For a start, Harrison has been the district representative to the Georgia legislature. He is also attorney for Camden County (whose largest town is St. Mary's), for St. Mary's and Folkston, for the local tax board, for the hospital authority, and for almost every other governmental body in the area. But none of these duties take as much effort, or get as much loving care, as Harrison's service for his most important client, the Gilman Paper Company. Since Gilman is the largest taxpayer and landowner in the county, almost any action Harrison takes as county attorney or state legislator raises the danger of conflict of interest. Harrison's record, especially his performance in the legislature, suggests that he has lost little sleep over the problem.

Georgia's legislature has for many years continued

the old-fashioned tradition of local legislation—special acts which apply to only one city or county. Under this unwieldy system, it is not only natural but essential that a legislator become a lobbyist for parochial local interests. In Harrison's case, however, the local interest he protects has more often been the mill than the electorate. In his years in the legislature, Harrison has sponsored several bills aimed at improving Gilman's general economic health. One bill gave the mill special tax concessions, another forced St. Mary's to turn over some city streets to Gilman. But by far the most flagrant example of Harrison's conflicting interests came in early 1969 with the introduction of Georgia Resolution #688.

On the surface, Harrison's bill would have done nothing more than create an innocuous-sounding Camden County Recreation Authority. But the clauses listing the Authority's powers contained some strange provisions. The Authority was to have a 99-year life span, and its two Camden County representatives were to be Brumley and one of his old cronies. As members of the Authority, they would have the power to condemn land up and down the Georgia coast and sell it off to the highest bidder. It soon became clear that the Authority was aimed at one special target: Cumberland Island. The private interest that stood to profit from the bill was not the mill but another of Harrison's clients, millionaire land developer Charles Fraser.

Fraser, the man who turned South Carolina's Hilton Head Island into a retirement paradise for rich old Yankees,* had the same fate in mind for Cumberland. His theory was that undeveloped patches of beach and forest might be all right, but resorts with golf courses, jetports, and tasteful landscaping were infinitely better. As he later told a legislative committee investigating Harrison's bill, Fraser thought Cumberland should be open for use by "the largest segment of our population . . . those persons earning $10,000 a year and over." [22]

Not everyone agreed with Fraser about Cumberland's ideal use. In 1955, the National Park Service had called the island "one of the two most outstanding undeveloped

* In an ironic reversal of his position on Cumberland, Fraser led the fight to keep the notorious German chemical company, BASF, from bringing its plant and pollution to Hilton Head.

seashore areas remaining along the Atlantic and Gulf Coasts." Cape Cod was the other, and in 1961 Congress made it a National Seashore. Progress was slower on Cumberland, although many of the island's landowners joined local conservation groups in asking the Park Service to buy the wild land.

Fraser, meanwhile, was hurrying to outbuy the Park Service. By the beginning of 1969, he had bought nearly 3,500 acres on Cumberland—about 15 per cent of the island's territory. Later in the year, his bulldozers began clearing three "firebreaks" on the island. Had they been completed, they would have been the only paved firebreaks in the world. The largest strip was 200 feet wide and 5,000 feet long—big enough to handle most jets. Construction crews freely admitted that they were building two access roads and a jet runway.

Just at this time when Fraser was having trouble prying loose the remainder of the island from its owners, Harrison filed his Camden Recreation bill. Even the normally tolerant Georgia legislature objected when it discovered that Fraser was Harrison's client, and that the vice president of Fraser's development company was the son of George Brumley, who was, of course, to be a member of the Recreation Authority. Resistance to Fraser's project grew throughout late 1969; in early 1970 conservation groups circulated petitions and held rallies to ask protection for Cumberland. Whether in response to this pressure or to a reported Federal Aviation Administration rejection of an airport permit for Cumberland, Fraser finally gave in. In August 1970, amid great public relations fanfare, he gave the Park Service an option on the island.

Fraser's capitulation came just as two other cracks were opening in St. Mary's power structure. The first challenge was aimed at Harrison, who for the first time faced serious competition in his campaign for re-election to the legislature. Physician Carl Drury, one of the few St. Mary's residents with no ties to Gilman, decided to run against Harrison and the "special interests" behind him. Drury's decision was important because he made public issues of complaints that had been whispered for years. The campaign was a dirty one, at least on Harrison's side; several mill employees, St. Mary's townspeople, and even one county commissioner reported confidentially that they had been told to vote for Harrison or lose Gilman's patronage. The local newspaper, edited by Harrison's brother, refused to carry Drury's advertising. In a front-page announcement, Kenneth Harrison said:

> After examination, this particular advertising copy was not accepted by me as Editor of the *Camden County Tribune* because, in my opinion the insinuations, half truths and misleading remarks were contrary to my sense of fair play.
>
> The copy in question was not refused by me because it was in opposition to my brother, who is also a candidate for public office (we have published advertisements for his political opponents on many occasions). . . .
>
> For further information of the public, a news story announcing that a candidate to oppose my brother as State Representative had qualified against him was not published for the simple reason that such information was not submitted to this newspaper and was obviously given to another weekly newspaper, because the news story was carried in that paper which was printed on the very day, and possibly prior, to the actual time the opposing candidate had qualified.
>
> This newspaper, its editor and family has served the people of this county to the very best of our ability in a reasonable, fair and impartial manner for the past twenty years, and we expect and intend to continue to do so.[23]

Drury's "insinuations, half truths, and misleading remarks" that Harrison complained about were comments such as: "Unlike my opponent, my hands are not tied by special interests," and "I believe that a representative of the people must be free of associations which might put controls over his freedom to represent all of the people impartially and fairly. His representation certainly should not be self-serving or weighted toward the special interests of any individual or group. If these conditions were found in our present representative, I would support, rather than oppose, him for re-election."

In the Democratic primary of 1970—which, as in many other parts of Georgia, is the election—Drury lost to Harrison in St. Mary's but pulled enough votes from surrounding areas to win the seat in the legislature. But Drury's troubles with the local power structure were not yet over. Ten days before he was to be seated in the legislature, Drury was called by the only other physician in town, the Gilman mill's doctor Barker. Barker told him that a Mr. Bloodworth (a salaried employee of the mill) was planning to bring rape charges against Drury, but that if Drury left the state Barker could be persuaded to hold off. After having Barker call back and repeat his offer while Drury's lawyers listened in, Drury refused to leave. A few days later, three women signed affidavits charging Drury with rape and assault.

One of the three was Bloodworth's sixteen-year-old daughter, who claimed that Drury had tried to rape her while she was convalescing from a tonsillectomy in the Gilman Hospital. Another was Miss Bloodworth's hospital roommate, who said she had witnessed the attempt. (Bloodworth himself claimed that Drury had *actually* raped his daughter, a discrepancy that did not go unnoticed in court.) Drury denied the charges, claiming that they were politically motivated.

Drury's medical license was suspended and a grand jury was convened. On February 6, 1971, shortly after Drury had been sworn in as a legislator, the jury issued its report. The charges were dropped because Miss Bloodworth's roommate denied in court having seen the rape attempt. She added that she had been taken to Harrison's office by Bloodworth and forced under various threats to sign an affidavit that Harrison wrote and that she had not read. Benjamin Martin, the county juvenile judge, told reporters "a majority of the people in this county think this was a framed-up political deal."[24]

The second change in St. Mary's came at about the same time. On August 1, 1970, for the first time in Gilman's history, its workers went out on strike. For years, the only countervailing force in St. Mary's has been the strong labor unions. This year, after many near misses, the Pulp and Sulfite workers voted to walk off the job. Their main grievance was the mill's pension plan; according to union leaders, it gave some 25-year veterans less than $50 per month in retirement pay. The strike was crippled from the start because Gilman had planned all along to shut down the mill for two or three weeks during the summer to work on its new recovery boiler. Coming when it did, the strike gave Gilman just the opportunity it needed.

But despite their frustrations, the men who walked out had learned several important lessons by the time the strike ended in late August. The unions are considering, for example, taking legal action against the mill for shady pressure tactics it exerted during the strike. Gilman locked out members of nonstriking unions and shut down the local bag plant, both in apparent violation of labor law. It is unlikely that the unions would have considered suing five years ago. Moreover, men who had always relied on Gilman for pay checks discovered during the strike that other jobs were available, in factories in neighboring Georgia counties or across the river in Florida.

"You used to think that Gilman was the only thing in the world," said one locked-out maintenance man midway through the strike. "Now I think things will be a little different."

But these minor steps have not appreciably changed the bitter flavor of life in St. Mary's. Besides the mill, there is virtually nothing here: a few dismal dry goods stores, a barbershop, and Larry's Café, where a televised Jackie Gleason competes with the juke box for the attention of Saturday night diners. People who have lived in St. Mary's for ten years or more, families whose children were born under the pall of a Gilman sky, still say they are "from" somewhere else—from Vidalia, from Waycross, from one of the other spots on the South Georgia map, but never from St. Mary's.

"Nobody calls this place home," a veteran union official said. "This is where the people who work at the mill sleep."

8

Union Camp's Divining Rod

I had my lawyers in Virginia research the question, and they told us that we could suck the state of Virginia out through that hole in the ground and there was nothing anyone could do about it.

John E. Ray III, Executive Vice President of Union Camp, July 16, 1970

On a clear, mid-March day in 1968, scientists at Georgia's Marine Institute on Sapelo Island began what seemed to be another normal work day. Many years before, tobacco tycoon R. J. Reynolds had donated his estate on the island to the University of Georgia. Today, in the stables where Reynolds once raised race horses, scientists have set up laboratories for the study of marine life.

As students walked past one of the fountains Reynolds had built, however, a strange thing happened. The fountains, which had run for years on natural artesian water pressure, suddenly dried up. Several miles away in Riceboro, the Interstate Paper Company had turned on its huge underground pumps for the first time. The silence on Sapelo, according to Georgia's respected ecologist Eugene Odum, was "deafening."

What happened that day at Sapelo differs in two ways from what is now happening to much of coastal Georgia: it was more sudden, and it did relatively little harm. The supply of ground water that disappeared in one day from Sapelo is undergoing similar but more devastating attacks throughout coastal Georgia and in many other parts of the country. If there is one natural resource which we have more systematically mismanaged than our surface water, it is the invisible water system that runs beneath the ground. The same chronic shortsightedness, the same single-minded quest for profit, and the same refusal to think of consequences that have polluted our rivers and lakes now also threaten the ground water with great potential disaster.

Although ground water has not yet entered the standard vocabulary of environmental concern, it is one of our most important—and most threatened—resources. From a scientific viewpoint, it is impossible to think of ground water separately from the total network of rivers, lakes, and oceans that make up the world's water supply. Ground water is an integral part of the constant circulation of water through the air and ground; it is the subsurface reflection of the rivers that run above ground.

Ground water also has a crucial practical importance in daily water use. In 1960, for example, ground water accounted for about 20 per cent of the water used in America;[1] but it accounted for a disproportionately large share of the kinds of water Americans rely on. One-fourth of all private industrial water, one-half of all municipal water, and more than 90 per cent of all water for rural homes was supplied by ground water.[2] To fill these demands, ground water use rose from 30–35 billion gallons per day (bgd) in 1950 to 46 bgd in 1960—an increase of 35–50 per cent. If current predictions of population growth and water use hold true, this country will draw an astounding 280 bgd from its ground water supplies in 1980, and ground water will account for half of all water use by then.[3] As supplies of surface water become more heavily polluted and reach their limit as producers of usable water, we will turn more and more to the ground to find water.

Since we will continue to depend more and more heavily on ground water, the universal neglect with which we have treated our supply is all the more tragic. Ground water use in Savannah, for example, clearly shows this indifferent and gluttonous attitude. In the Georgia coastal area, where the ground water supply is uniquely plentiful, Savannah would seem to have all the water it could possibly need for centuries to come. But because of insufficient information, nonexistent regulations, and poor understanding, farms, industries, and towns in the area all face the threat of a water famine.

In theory, the coastal plains of Georgia have such a huge supply of surface water—a phenomenal 25.7 billion gallons flow through their rivers every day [4]—that the region should not need a drop of ground water. Its rivers have long been polluted, however, that the region relies on ground water for nearly all its water needs. Fortunately, the available ground water is in plentiful supply; only the Pacific Northwest has more underground water. But the supply has not been enough to withstand the heavy loads that industrial pumps have put on it. The water level in the whole coastal plain region has dropped drastically since the beginning of the twentieth century. In several areas, the ultimate threat has come true: salt water has oozed in from the sea to contaminate ground water supplies. This is not a purely Southern problem; between 80 and 90 regions on the Atlantic, Pacific, and Gulf coasts have all experienced the same disaster.[5] But its appearance in the water-rich Georgia coastal plain is more troubling than in most other areas.

Ground water depletion is not a new problem that rushed upon the region before anyone could plan for it. Even in Savannah, a city that has been chronically slow to recognize environmental problems, the ground water depletion threat is well known. As early as 1943, the Chatham County Commissioners—never a group prone to hysteria about natural resources—announced:

> . . . it has come to the attention of the Commissioners and Ex-officio Judges of Chatham County, Georgia, that the water supply in and around the County is being seriously affected by the boring of additional artesian wells in said county, and . . .
>
> The County Authorities have been notified by many residents in the County that the flow of water in their wells has stopped and the water-head has sunk to such a depth that it is impossible for the wells to be pumped. . . .
>
> The County Authorities have also been notified by the Town of Pooler that the water-head in the waterworks well of that Town has sunken to a dangerous point and it appears

that for the general welfare of the citizens of Chatham County, protection of the public health, and safety required that the County Authorities pass a rule, regulation and ordinance preventing the further boring of artesian water wells in the County, except on permission especially granted by the Commissioners . . .[6]

In spite of the concerned tone of the Commissioners, the ordinance has had virtually no effect. Most of the damage had already been done; Union Camp and other local industries had already drilled large-bore wells. The permit system that evolved from the ordinance amounts in practice to what one well company official called "a smile, five dollars, and a handshake."

The supply of ground water that the regulation was designed to protect had, only a short time before, been plentiful. When Savannah sunk its first well in 1885, water gushed out to an elevation 40 feet above sea level and 18 inches above the land surface. The tremendous pressure upon the water came from its underground source, the principal artesian aquifer. The aquifer, a rock structure made of porous limestone, soaks up water in the highland portions of South Carolina and Georgia, where the limestone is near the surface and the water can seep in. As the aquifer moves east and south through Georgia, the limestone dips farther beneath the surface; since impenetrable rock formations lie above the limestone, the water cannot escape. Finally, the aquifer passes under Georgia's Coastal Plain and, in former times, the fresh water flowed out into the sea. At almost any point before it leaves the aquifer, however, the water will flow up through a well if given the chance.

But a few years of heavy pumping have changed the aquifer. The naturally flowing wells have been gone for years from Savannah. Instead, the heavy, constant drain from a few deep wells has drastically lowered the water level, thereby reducing the artesian pressure. Maps which show the amount of water decline leave no doubt about the cause. On the maps, rings describe areas where the decline has been the same, i.e., where the water level has fallen 10, 20, or 30 feet. All these rings center around one bull's-eye; directly below the Union Camp well field, the water has dropped to its deepest point. There, in what geologists call a "cone of depression," the water level has fallen 150 feet since 1880, to 120 feet below sea level. Even 15 miles away from the Union Camp wells, the water level has dropped 50 feet.[7] The influence of the Savannah pumping stretches for miles, through many Georgia counties and up into South Carolina.

To satisfy the voracious industrial demand for water, many small consumers have paid the price of lower water levels. Hundreds of farmers in rural areas surrounding Savannah have found that as the water level has dropped, they have had to install bigger and bigger pumps to bring the water to the surface. Farmers with the bad fortune to live near Riceboro have learned how quickly the water level can drop. Within the first 18 months of Interstate Paper's operation, which began in 1965, private well owners five miles south of the plant watched the water level drop a full eight feet.[8]

The decline in the water levels of these small private wells is only a signal of the more serious damage to come. As Union Camp and other industrial pumpers continue to draw from the cone of depression, they work a fundamental change in the aquifer. The fresh water in the aquifer used to flow steadily out to sea. Now, because of the steady suction from one small area, the direction of the flow has reversed and water flows from all directions toward the pumping point. From the seaward edges, salt water begins to move in. The salt water can come from two major sources: water from the sea water may flow into the limestone that used to emit fresh water, or "connate" water—pockets of salt water deposited in previous geologic ages—may move laterally toward the pumping point. When salt water from either source enters the aquifer under a well, the result is catastrophic and practically irreversible. The well water becomes salty and unusable, and the well owner must go elsewhere for his water.

Already, the massive pull Savannah exerts on the aquifer has drawn salt water into wells less than 50 miles away. Both Parris Island and Beaufort in South Carolina have had to abandon their now salty wells. The cost of finding new water has been painfully high; for Beaufort, a town much smaller than Savannah, the price of a new

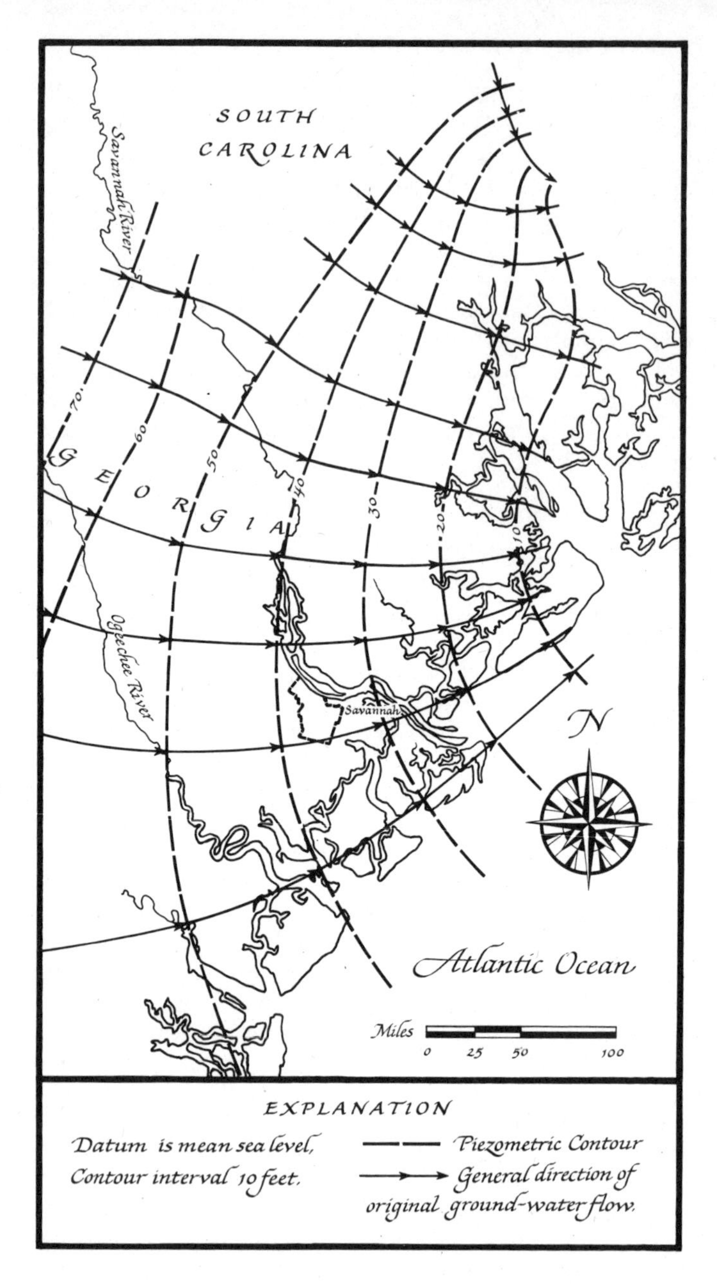

Source: United States Department of the Interior Geological Survey.

Map showing piezometric surface of artesian aquifer in Savannah area about 1880.

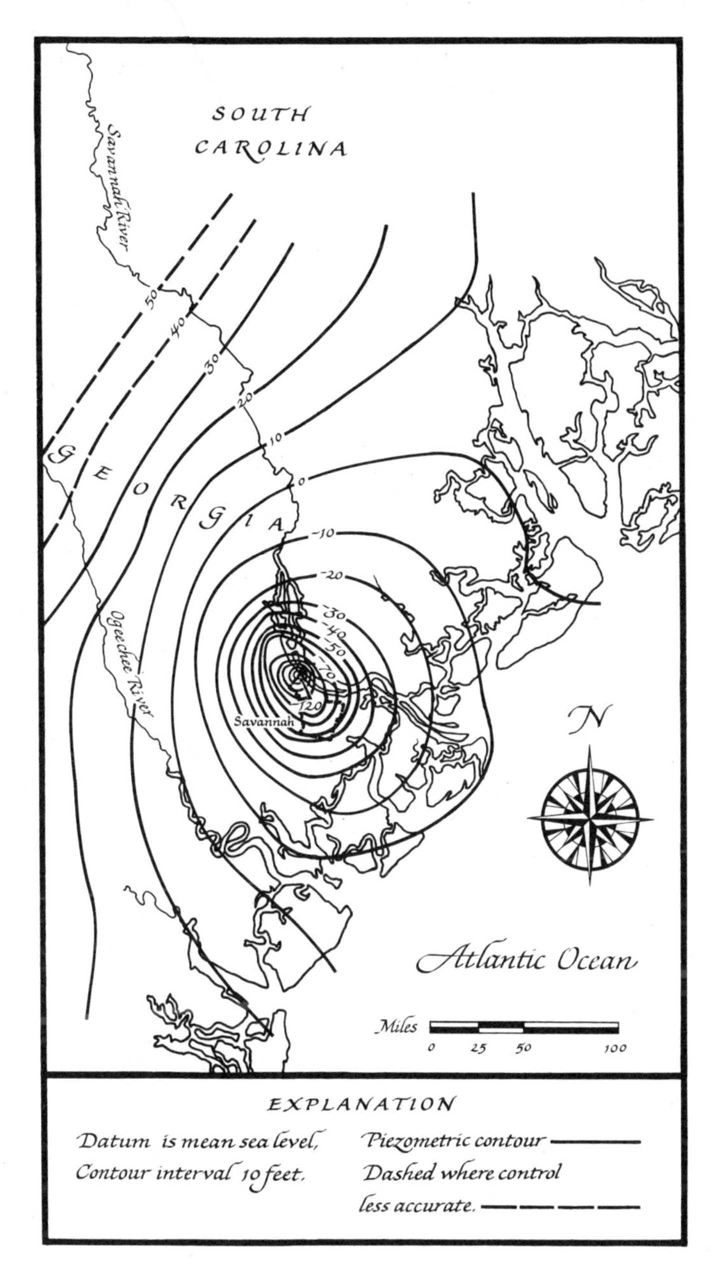

Source: United States Department of the Interior Geological Survey.

Map showing piezometric surface of artesian aquifer in Savannah area in December 1961.

water system was six million dollars. Eighty miles south of Savannah, Brunswick is having ground water problems of its own. In response to pumping by the city and its paper mills, connate salt water has entered the aquifer and contaminated water supplies.

Savannah faces three threats of salt water encroachment. Ocean water could flow in from the Parris Island–Beaufort area to the north; connate salt water could move in from the same area; or a large pocket of connate salt water which sits just below the aquifer could move up toward the pumping point. Hydrologists are not sure how long it will take the salt water to move under Savannah; some predict that the city has only ten years left, while others think supplies may hold out for 50 years or more. Nearly all agree, however, that salt water is on its way, and that if pumping continues at its current irrational rate, the city's wells will surely draw salt.

The day that happens, the city will start to pay a heavy price for its improvidence. With the ground water gone, the only other source of water will be the filthy Savannah.

In volume, the river could take care of a city many times the size of Savannah. But purity is another question. In order to make the river fit for domestic faucets or industrial water mains, the city would have to treat the water extensively. The technology needed to do that is already available; Savannah's industrial and domestic water supply system now takes 46 million gallons of water out of the Savannah every day and cleans it for industrial use.[9] But water purification treatment carries a high price tag. The plant of the Industrial and Domestic Water Supply Commission cost $3.5 million when it was built 30 years ago, and it would take a plant at least four times as big to serve Savannah if the wells went salty. In addition, most engineers predict that the city would have to re-lay much of its water main system to handle water from the treatment plant. All told, the cost could easily come to more than $20 million.

Even at that cost, Savannah would be more fortunate than the many coastal plains towns without large nearby rivers. Many rural residents who now depend wholly on artesian water would find themselves as waterless as if they were stranded in central Nevada. Their only choice would be to pay the high price of piping treated water from one of the large rivers.

If the ground water goes, who will be to blame? It does not take long to see that a few voracious industries now use most of the ground water. Throughout the whole coastal plain region of Georgia, industries take 65 per cent of the total 300 million gallons that come from the ground daily.[10] In the ten counties that now have major cones of depression, industry uses an even larger share —197 of the 279 million gallons per day (mgd), or more than 70 per cent.[11] In Brunswick, which has had salt water problems since the late 1950's, industries use the vast majority of the 127.6 mgd of ground water pumped there.[12] Savannah has more people and therefore does more domestic pumping than any other part of the coastal plain. Still the city's industries use more water than Savannah itself; industrial pumping makes up 60 per cent of the total.[13]

And in effect, "industrial pumping" in Savannah means Union Camp pumping. Union Camp's one mill uses three times as much water as all the other city industries put together. It also uses more water to make its 2,800 daily tons of paper than all 120,000 Savannahians use to live. Savannah's domestic pumping comes to 22 mgd, while Union Camp's five wells suck out 27.6 mgd, almost 40 per cent of all Savannah area pumping.[14] Partly because of this extraordinarily heavy load, and partly because Union Camp's wells are concentrated in a dangerously small area, the Savannah cone of depression has its absolute center under Union Camp's plant.

Of all the abuses it heaps on Savannah, Union Camp's arrogant assumption that it can use unlimited amounts of ground water is probably the worst. There is no good reason why Union Camp should take 27 mgd from the fragile aquifer. The Savannah River could supply huge amounts of treatable water and the cost of treatment would not be so great if Union Camp did not so grossly pollute it. But to minds shaped by Union Camp's annual slogan for the year 1970—The Name of the Game: PROFIT-ABILITY—it is easier and cheaper to use ground water. By continuing to draw on the ground water, the mill saves about $500,000 per year.*

When all these values are toted up on the company balance sheet, the conclusion is obvious: take the ground water now, and worry about the consequences later. The $500,000 that Union Camp saves this way is a tiny drop in the corporate bucket—about one-tenth of 1 per cent of Union Camp's annual revenue. To get this last ounce of profit, the mill endangers the water supply of an entire region. But Union Camp has little to fear from salt water encroachment. When the ground water is finally depleted, it will have to use treated water, but since its machines can get along with water less pure than people need, its treatment costs would be far below those of Savannah.

It is not ignorance that keeps the Union Camp wells pumping. The mill managers know what they are doing. In 1953, when the new American Cyanamid plant asked permission to sink wells into the aquifer, Union Camp raised a vigorous protest in the unaccustomed name of municipal well-being. Plant officials wrote to the County Commission and warned that Cyanamid's pumping could lower the water table and lead to salt water encroachment.[15] Since then, Union Camp's fears have apparently been soothed, for the mill has increased its own pumping rate by the same amount (6 mgd) Cyanamid proposed.[16]

John E. Ray III, Union Camp's executive vice president, has apparently forgotten his company's fight against American Cyanamid. On October 19, 1970, he told the Savannah Rotary Club that, for all Union Camp's enormous pumping, the aquifer "has not even been strained." Rock Howard disagreed, calling Ray's statement "ridiculous," and he added, "I think it's about time we stopped all this smart, clever talk and started exercising some old-fashioned honesty."[17]

Unfortunately, Union Camp's attitude is not unique.

* Pumping ground water is the cheapest possible way to get water; it probably costs Union Camp less than $10 to pump each million gallons out of the ground. Treated river water, while still inexpensive, costs slightly more; at current I&D rates, Union Camp would have to pay about $1,700 daily to buy the water it now pumps. Over the course of a year, the difference between $1,700 and pumping costs for 27 mgd would come to about $500,000.

Before its plans to locate in Beaufort were thwarted, the infamous German chemical company, BASF, had dreams of pumping at least 48 mgd from the aquifer which would have added 80 per cent to the total drain on the aquifer [18]—an extra load it could ill bear. Special Assistant to the National Director of the U.S. Geological Survey, Albert N. Cameron, pointed out the danger the area faces. "We don't know how much more pumpage the aquifer can stand," he said, "but we certainly don't recommend much more in there." [19]

American Cyanamid had even more dangerous plans in mind. In 1969, as a cheap way to get rid of its tons of acid waste, Cyanamid thought to drill a deep hole and pour in the acid. Although the company did not plan to inject acid directly into the aquifer, the dangers of dumping sulfuric acid anywhere near the porous limestone are obvious. The state water board managed to convince Cyanamid to find a different disposal plan.[20] But it is more difficult to convince Cyanamid or Union Camp or the other industrial polluters to take stock of their responsibilities and begin to conserve rather than waste valuable natural resources.

To protect their irreplaceable resources, water users of Georgia rely on the United States Geological Survey, which theoretically has great potential as an environmental defender. The agency collects information on where and how fast the ground water is moving and releases recommendations which could cut back ground water use before serious damage is done. In practice, however, the attitudes of the USGS are only slightly more restrained than those of Union Camp and Cyanamid, and they pose an almost equally great threat to domestic water supplies.

In Georgia, the USGS also has an institutional handicap. Its monitoring programs in the coastal plain are all carried out under the auspices of Georgia's notorious Department of Mines, Mining, and Geology. Originally set up to expand commercial use of Georgia's natural resources, the department has scrupulously followed the theory that what is good for large mining companies is good for the state. Intentionally or not, this attitude may seep through to the USGS, as its record in Brunswick illustrates.

Shortly after Brunswick's water supplies began to suffer salt water contamination in 1959, the USGS set up a monitoring program. Since then, the USGS has poured more money into the project and stepped up its monitoring. Instead of urging Brunswick to cut back its pumping, the USGS has watched as ground water withdrawals rose 35 per cent—from 94 mgd in 1959 to 127.6 mgd in the summer of 1970.[21] Predictably enough, the salt water has also spread to contaminate a larger area. Dean Gregg, local director of the USGS in Brunswick, thinks that the area's industries are doing their best to prevent further contamination. They have steadily increased their pumping, but Gregg feels this is all right. "Industry must grow to exist," he explains.[22] For corporate directors planning new mergers, this theory is probably true, but when applied to the use of ground water and other limited natural resources, it means that soon there will be no room for anyone but industry.

In Brunswick, as in Savannah and elsewhere, the problem of ground water depletion has an easy solution. The large industrial water users could turn to the abundant surface waters. Instead of recommending the use of surface waters, the USGS has taken the incredible position that the industries should use the ground water while they can. "If using a resource [artesian water] heavily for 20 years meant that it would be destroyed thereafter," one USGS employee in Brunswick said, "then *this course would be preferable to not using the resource at all.*" [23] (Emphasis added.) This is the reasoning of an Alaskan gold prospector, or of someone who faces the choice between draining the aquifer or having no water at all. Coming as it does from the agency in charge of protecting ground water resources, this statement almost amounts to criminal neglect.

The monitoring program the USGS conducts in Savannah also has as its purpose the prevention of salt water contamination of the city's water supplies. According to geologists from the University of Georgia and the South Carolina Water Resources Commission, the program is inadequate to do the job.[24] The retired Coast Guardsman who is locally in charge of the project freely admits that he often lacks the time to gather and evaluate essential data about the water level.[25] To make its predictions about Savannah area pumping rates, the USGS must rely on information from the city and local industries.

Because its drinking future depends on protecting the ground water, the city has every reason to cooperate with the USGS and its state ground water director, Harland Counts. Even so, Savannah's data are incomplete because the city government has no way of metering the many large private wells that pump throughout the city.[26] Although Savannah makes large withdrawals from the aquifer, there are several good reasons why the city can continue its ground water use. The 22 mgd that Savannah draws from the ground is not enough to threaten the aquifer. It would also be much more expensive for Savannah to use treated river water than for the industries. If either the city or its industries must give up ground water use, the city has a firmer claim to the resource which it uses to keep its citizens alive; the industries use it only to cut production costs. By allowing unlimited use of the aquifer, Savannahians are subsidizing cheap paper bags for nationwide customers.

The USGS can be even less confident of its information from the industries. Union Camp and the other large companies report their pumping rates to Director Harland Counts, but he has no way of confirming them. As Richard Chase, Union Camp's Division Technical Director for Unbleached Products, has said, "Counts only knows what we tell him." [27] Counts himself admits that "We [USGS] have to scrounge for everything we can get." [28] Perhaps the difficulty Counts has in getting the information explains his dogged refusal to share it with the public. As members of our project discovered, Counts will release pumping figures only after repeated requests and only after giving the source of the data a chance to veto disclosure. Despite obvious flaws in his monitoring program, Counts still claims that it is accurate enough to predict the future of the aquifer.[29]

Counts' insistence on the accuracy of his program is misleading because few people realize what slim evidence the predictions rest on. In its several studies of Savannah—two of them co-authored by Counts—the USGS has given heavy industrial pumping only passing mention. The reports have practically ignored the most obvious needs—for more carefully planned water use and for the steady weaning of the industries away from their deep artesian wells. Instead, the USGS continues to present pacifying pictures of the water situation and deliver promises of more and more water for the future.[30] While this information is soothing to heavy ground water users, it does not guard the resource.

The local industries need only turn to the river for a supply of up to one billion gallons per day.[31] They will not use river water until the public, through laws and informal pressure, forces them. But strong public pressure cannot develop without an adequate source of information. The essential first step in improving the ground water situation is therefore to gather the accurate hydrologic data now missing. With its current limitations, the USGS has at best secondhand and incomplete information. If it is ever to perform the information-collecting function it has theoretically, the USGS needs not only a new attitude but also new legal powers.

Other states consider the preservation of natural resources too important to leave in the hands of one group. In North Carolina, for example, universities and state agencies work closely with the USGS to get the most complete data possible. This, unfortunately, is the exception rather than the national rule; too many states lack both the information and the enforcement power necessary to do the job. Once states have a clearer idea of what is happening underneath their soil, their next step is legislation; as most states have bitterly learned, nothing short of strict legal sanctions will stop industrial polluters.

With proper management and regulation, quick progress is possible. Some water experts have said that a more prudent arrangement of wells (spreading them out farther to avoid concentrated cones of depression, for example) could enable the aquifer to bear much heavier pumping loads with less danger of salt water intrusion. This is not a long-term solution but a valuable stopgap that should have been taken years ago. Industries have known this for years but have not been willing to spend extra dollars to drill safer wells.

California has enacted legislation that can serve as a guide to the rest of the nation. Its "correlative" doctrine of ground water law forces industries to share ground water rights with other users. Whenever excessive industrial pumping begins to restrict the water rights of another user, the industry has to get along with less ground water. Before other states find themselves "sucked out through a hole in the ground," they must take similar scientific and legal steps.

9
The Smell of Money

When a [Union Camp] paper mill was constructed in a little Alabama town some 20 miles from Montgomery, it tinged even the Capitol's corridors, on especially muggy mornings, with a vague reek. Wallace, who was then Governor, would note on such mornings, "Yeah, that's the smell of money. She does smell sweet, don't it?"

Marshall Frady, Harper's, *May 1970*

Some visitors to Savannah are first impressed by the city's gracious Southern charm, by its cobblestone roads and its tress dripping Spanish moss. Others first notice the graceful restored town houses with their wrought-iron railings and the potted flowers tumbling over them. The people of Savannah still own the charm, but the mood of Savannah is only one thing; the atmosphere is another. Union Camp and American Cyanamid, in their grim pursuit of profit at the city's expense, have taken away the ground water and the river, but their thievery does not stop there. They have taken the air.

Still other visitors are quite literally assaulted by Savannah's air pollution. On October 31, 1966, the captain of the freighter *Louisiana Brimstone* found out just how bad the air could be. As he sailed down the Savannah past Union Camp, the ship suddenly smashed into the leg of a railroad bridge. The captain later explained that he had lost his way in a heavy "fog" just as he passed the factory.

Early in 1970, drivers on Savannah's new Interstate

highway had a similiar experience. Union Camp had been burning wood on a plot of land it was clearing. The smoke settled on the highway, and drivers panicked when they could not see past their hoods. One lady got a few feet into the smoke before deciding to get out. And so, on the middle of an Interstate highway, she began to back out of the cloud. After the crash and subsequent lawsuit, Union Camp settled out of court for $30,000.

Local pilots suffer the most chronic annoyance of all. Airport maps list Union Camp as the number one smoke source near the municipal airport, Travis Field. The pilots become livid as they tell about having to use radar to get through the clouds of smoke covering the field. The Federal Aviation Administration requires radar whenever smoke from the mill cuts visibility to less than three miles. So far, use of radar has managed to spare the airplanes from accidents like the *Brimstone*'s.

If opacity were the worst part of the pollution, Savannahians would feel more comfortable about the air they breathe. As matters stand, however, the people who percolate the air through their lungs 24 hours a day are paying a heavy price. Although many American cities are plagued with foul air, there are relatively few where *smell* is an important part of the pollution. Savannah and the other towns that harbor kraft mills know that the distinctive stench—and the accompanying economic and physiological damage done by kraft pollution—are normal features of daily life.

It is difficult to describe the smell of a kraft mill to people lucky enough never to have been near one. The human nose is more sensitive to the two chemicals—hydrogen sulfide and methyl mercaptans—that make up the smell than to almost any other substances. It can detect these chemicals in the air in concentrations of two to three parts per billion. Scientists have speculated that the reason is evolutionary: long before there were paper mills, cave men learned to tell if meat was fresh or rotten by sniffing it for hydrogen sulfide. Whether or not the theory is true, it gives some idea of how repulsive the mill smell is.

The damage is more than merely aesthetic; it includes numerous hazards to property and health. At a 1966 conference on kraft pulping emissions, two scientists summed up the ways in which kraft pollution is harmful. According to R. L. Stockman of the Washington State Department of Health, and Donald Anderson of the University of British Columbia, the most likely immediate effects of kraft pollution are "odor, visibility reduction, corrosion of metals, damage to painted surfaces, physiologic, [and] general dirtiness and soiling of surfaces." [1]

The results of these immediate effects, the scientists said, are:

1. Reduced desirability of the community as a place in which to live;
2. Reduced attraction to the community for other new industries and commercial enterprises;
3. Reduced attraction to hotels, motels, and resorts for the traveling business and touring public;
4. Depreciation in property values and rentals in summer-home areas;
5. Hazard or inconvenience to travelers because of reduced visibility, e.g., in marine navigation, highway and freeway travel, and conceivably in airplane landing and takeoff.[2]

Savannah has suffered all five results of kraft pollution, from hazardous travel to vacant tourist motels. Perhaps worst of all are the complex miseries so coolly summed up as "reduced desirability of the community as a place in which to live." Some of the ways kraft mills in other towns have attacked the "desirability" of living are the following:

1. government employees in one kraft mill area get a 60 per cent bonus in their mileage payments to help them replace the chrome and paint corroded by the air;
2. an Oregon court awarded damages to a home owner who claimed that kraft pollution was corroding his metal, damaging his paint, and sickening his trees and shrubs;
3. in Washington, a businessman charged that kraft pollution was increasing his expenses for cleaning and painting his place of business. The court upheld his claim, awarding him $2,500 in damages plus $300 for personal discomfort;

4. property owners in an affluent suburban district successfully tried to get their property assessments lowered because of constant kraft odor.[3]

The most complete list of kraft pollution dangers is from a government conference studying pollution in Vermont and upstate New York. Families who had lived for years in the shadow of International Paper's Ticonderoga, New York, mill came in with the following complaints:

> upset stomach, nausea, headache, eye and respiratory irritation, aggravation of illness conditions, interference with sleep, reduction in appetite, offensive odors, discouragement to tourist trade, reduction in property rentals and loss of tenants, decrease in property values and sales of resort property, interference with comfortable enjoyment of property, damage to the community's reputation, and distraction to the conduct of school classes.[4]

A resident of Lewiston, Idaho, where the Potlatch Forest mill makes its home, put the complex problems as simply as possible when he said, "I believe the horrible, rotten stench coming from the smokestacks of the Potlatch Pulp Mill here in Lewiston is killing me; I am afraid to remain here; I don't want my family or myself to die premature deaths." [5]

Sociologists have long known that pulp towns often house broken-spirited people who assume they can never expect anything other than the smell and smoke. Scientists now are concerned that the mills may be doing more insidious damage to the town's spirit; there is worry that kraft odor may affect mental health, learning capacity, and general productivity.[6]

There is already compelling evidence to show the dangers of hydrogen sulfide, which both Union Camp and Continental Can release in Savannah, in amounts they refuse to specify. A report prepared by Litton Industries for the National Air Pollution Control Administration says,

> Hydrogen sulfide is highly toxic to humans, and at [high] concentrations . . . quickly causes death by paralysis of the respiratory system. At lower concentrations, hydrogen sulfide may cause conjunctivitis with reddening and lachrymal secretion, respiratory tract irritation, psychic changes, pulmonary edema, damaged heart muscle, disrupted equilib-

rium, nerve paralysis, spasms, unconsciousness, and circulatory collapse.[7]

It is emotionally simple but scientifically very difficult to establish the direct relation between poisons in the air and victims on the ground. The casualties of air pollution appear slowly and undramatically. The human cost of a heavy day of kraft pulping may not show up for years, until a family loses its father sooner than normal, or when young men and women retire to sedentary lives years before they should. For many substances that fill the air, we still have no definite idea of the possible dangers. No scientist has yet had the time to see what 20-year exposure to contaminated air does to human bodies. All of us living now are serving as laboratory rats for a grim experiment, which no one is watching.

The closest definition of the air pollution level in most cities is confined simply to listing which contaminants are in the air. Chatham County drew up an "Air Pollution Emissions Inventory" in 1968. Although the inventory was based on crude, indirect systems for measur-

TABLE 9–1

Pollutants in Savannah's Air

Compound	*Amount (tons/year)*
Carbon monoxide	96,155.2
Hydrocarbons	16,397.5
Particulates	10,133.5
Nitrogen oxides	7,219.3
Sulfur oxides	3,022.6
Hydrogen fluorides	1,480
Organic acids	628.5
Aldehydes	422.8
Ammonia	13
Chlorine gas	?
Hydrogen sulfide	?
Methyl mercaptans	?
Dimethyl sulfides	?
Calcium sulfides	?
Calcium carbonate	?
Sodium sulfate	?
Sodium carbonate	?
Titanium dioxide	?

Source: Chatham County Air Pollution Inventory, 1968.

ing pollution and its figures are hopelessly inaccurate, and it admittedly ignored 15 per cent of the local industries, at least it shows how many different kinds of chemical pollutants are regularly part of Savannah's air.

For some of these pollutants, health hazard is an established fact. The chlorine gas that comes from American Cyanamid is obviously lethal, although the company claims that ground level concentrations are still within "safe" limits. When the chlorine comes from the stacks, however, it is so concentrated that it would quickly kill anyone who breathed it.

The major pollutant in Savannah, as in most other cities, is carbon monoxide, one of the most common and potentially most dangerous airborne poisons. Since carbon monoxide combines with the hemoglobin in human blood much more easily than oxygen does, it can effectively suffocate a person by preventing his blood from carrying essential oxygen throughout the body. In small concentrations, such as are often reached in heavy city traffic, it can cause dull headaches. As the concentrations increase, carbon monoxide can lead to nausea, severe headaches, loss of muscular coordination, dizziness, unconsciousness, and eventually death.[8] Hydrocarbons have been tentatively linked with lung cancer, and many of the other elements in Savannah's air have at least potential health hazards.

The large amounts of carbon monoxide and hydrocarbons which circulate above Savannah come mainly from cars and trucks; the dangers Savannahians face because of them are essentially the same as those Americans endure in almost every city. But there are at least two additional hazards which Savannahians get courtesy of their large industries.

Savannah's most measurably disturbing pollution problem is the disproportionately high amount of particulates in the air. Particulates are tiny bits of matter, never more than .0005 meters in diameter. Chemists have succeeded in determining only about 40 per cent of particulate composition. From what is known, however, it is clear that particulates inflict damage in two ways. The particles themselves lodge in the delicate linings of the lungs and respiratory tract, causing irritation and inflammation. The substances attached to the particulates are an additional danger. The particulates may combine with and carry sulfur oxides, various aerosols, insecticides like DDT, radioactive isotopes, or the obnoxious odor elements from various sources. By carrying these other compounds and releasing them inside human lungs, particulates greatly magnify the health hazards from other kinds of pollutants.

From studies of several heavily polluted cities, researchers have established cutoff points at which particulates become a serious danger. The figures probably underestimate the problem; until last year, the commonly accepted standards labeled air with less than 50 micrograms/cubic meter of particulates as "clean"; between 50 and 100 as "light"; 100 to 150 as "moderate"; and levels above 150 as "heavy." After the Public Health Service reviewed the evidence in 1969, however, the

TABLE 9–2

Particulate Levels

A. Top 30 cities with particulate pollution, released by Public Health Service in 1966, based on 1961–65 readings

Town	*Milli-grams/ cubic meter*	*Town*	*Milli-grams/ cubic meter*
1. Chattanooga	180	17. York, Pennsylvania	140
2. Chicago	177	18. New York	138
3. Philadelphia	170	19. Akron	134
4. St. Louis	168	20. Boston	134
5. Canton, Ohio	165	21. Cleveland	134
6. Pittsburgh	163	22. Cincinnati	133
7. Indianapolis	158	23. Milwaukee	133
8. Wilmington, Delaware	154	24. Grand Rapids	131
9. Louisville	152	25. Nashville	128
10. Youngstown	148	26. Syracuse	127
11. Denver	147	27. Buffalo	126
12. Los Angeles Co. area	145	28. Reading, Pennsylvania	126
13. Detroit	143	29. Dayton	123
14. Baltimore	141	30. Allentown-Bethlehem	120
15. Birmingham	141		
16. Kansas City	140		

Source: Public Health Service, 1966.

B. Savannah particulate readings

Date	*Lathrop Ave. (Union Camp)* Average	*Lathrop Ave. (Union Camp)* High	*City Hall* Average	*City Hall* High
July–December 1967	143	405	139	464
January–June 1968	190	431	157	412
July–December 1968	178	399	96	220
January–June 1969	207	358	122	426
July–December 1969	168	442	66	127
January–June 1970	161	508	80	132

Source: Chatham County Health Department.

C. Particulate readings from national air sampling network (Public Health Service, Department of Health, Education and Welfare; based on 1966 readings)

City	*Particulate average mg/m³*	*Maximum*
Savannah	139	529
New York	134	252
Chicago	124	273
Los Angeles	119	233
Atlanta	97	189
Newark, New Jersey	96	179
Cleveland	116	227
Seattle	76	181
Steubenville, Ohio	254	602
Charleston, West Virginia	226	684

Source: *Air Quality Data,* Department of Health, Education and Welfare, Public Health Service, 1966 edition.

limits were drastically lowered. The Public Health Service now warns that in its study areas, "adverse health effects were noted when the annual mean level of particulate matter exceeded 80 micrograms/cubic meter." [9]

Readings from a national air pollution survey show that Savannah's particulate level is in the running for the worst in the nation. Savannah constantly edges out such notoriously foul cities as New York and Los Angeles in its particulate pollution readings. Only towns like Steubenville, Ohio, or Charleston, West Virginia, with large, particulate-spewing mills nearby surpass Savannah.

The way Savannah's air hovers on the boundary between unsafe and lethal particulate concentrations is especially disturbing. Particulate levels in the poor, black housing developments near Union Camp are consistently twice as high as the Public Health Service's danger level. Data from British and American studies have shown that particulate levels much lower than those which usually prevail near Union Camp cause or aggravate many kinds of diseases.[10] In downtown Savannah, the concentration is still well above the danger level. It is only in some of the newly developed, mainly white residential areas on Savannah's outskirts that particulate concentration reaches acceptable levels.

Most people who live near Union Camp realize that their area is aesthetically less pleasant than the suburbs, but few of them know that they may be sacrificing their lives to the mill. A University of California scientist studied the effect that varying particulate rates had on vital statistics in different parts of the same town. He found that mortality rates for white males between the ages of 50 and 69 were twice as high in parts of the city where particulate levels were 135 mg/m^3 as in areas where the level was below 80 mg/m^3. For the same group, deaths from respiratory diseases were three times higher in the more polluted areas than in the cleaner sections.[11]

TABLE 9–3

Particulate pollution levels in Savannah, January–June 1970

Station	*Average mg/m^3*	*Maximum*
City Hall (downtown)	80	132
West Lathrope & Augusta (near Union Camp; black low-income neighborhood)	161	508
Abercorn & Columbus (white residential neighborhood)	70	119
Windsor Forest (affluent white neighborhood)	35	45

Source: Chatham County Health Department.

In Savannah one group regularly endures particulate levels above 150 mg/m^3, while in another part of town particulates rarely exceed 35 mg/m^3. Savannah knows the danger its particulate pollution presents, but it can only speculate about the hazards of the other major kraft mill pollutant—sulfur oxides. The problem is not that the sulfur compounds of sulfur dioxide and sulfur trioxide are any less dangerous, but only that the systems for measuring them are completely inadequate.

Accompanied by particulate pollution—as they so obviously are in Savannah—sulfur oxides can become dangerous at very low levels. At levels of .11 parts per million, sulfur dioxide may aggravate respiratory diseases; at concentrations above .19 parts per million, mortality rates increase. At times of extremely high particulate pollution (750 mg/m^3), sulfur dioxide levels as low as .25 parts per million may lead to increased daily death rates.[12] Sulfur dioxide (SO_2) also oxidizes into the more toxic sulfur trioxide (SO_3) that, in turn, often changes to sulfuric acid (H_2SO_4) in humid weather.

According to readings taken by the Chatham County Health Department, sulfur oxide levels in Savannah have not yet reached the danger point. From August 1969 to July 1970, the Health Department's highest sulfur dioxide reading, taken at the sampling station near Union Camp, was .025 parts per million. To obtain its readings, the Health Department visits its five sampling stations monthly. From the chemicals trapped in its "lead peroxide candle" sampler, the department calculates the total amount of sulfur dioxide sampled in the month. The figures it then releases are the calculated averages for each month, and do not reflect maximum levels.

That is fine as far as it goes, but it is about as useful for determining health hazards as an average monthly temperature reading would be for predicting daily weather. Like many other pollutants, sulfur oxides do their damage in brief periods. Exposure to levels of .1 or .2 parts per million for as long as 24 hours can be disastrous, whether or not there is any sulfur oxide in the air during the rest of the month. The Health Department's readings are therefore almost meaningless, because the important factor is the peak sulfur oxide concentration rather than the average monthly concentration.

The assault on Savannah's air mirrors the degradation of Savannah's waters except for the complicating factor introduced by gasoline-powered cars that emit hundreds of tons of carbon monoxides and hydrocarbons. The number of cars—and the level of automotive pollution—continues to rise. Like other American cities, Savannah is virtually helpless to change the situation alone. The cities cannot hope for relief until public pressure forces auto makers to produce the nonpolluting engines they have known about for years.

When Savannah's share of that national problem is put aside, the air pollution problem follows with depressing fidelity the pattern set by industrial water polluters. When a profit-making corporation finds that it can save money by pouring its filth into the air, it will do just that. The lesson that has proved true for controlling water pollution also applies to the air pollution problem: public outrage and legislative pressure are the only ways to change corporate minds. Some of the chemical contaminants have different names, and the physical state in which they escape is gaseous instead of liquid. But these superficial differences do not conceal the fact that air and water pollution are two phases of the same problem.

Savannah's major air polluters are the familiar top three of the water pollution charts. Union Camp, Continental Can, and American Cyanamid together produce an overwhelming proportion of the air's daily burden. Exact figures on their pollution output are difficult to find, both because of technical limitations and some cases of deliberate corporate secrecy. But by most calculations, the big three produced about ten times more pollution than all the other nonautomotive polluters in the county combined.

The figures that are available on these industries' output are unhappily impressive. American Cyanamid puts out daily about 26 tons of sulfur dioxide, more than three tons of sulfur trioxide, and smaller amounts of chlorine gas, titanium dioxide and hydrochloric acid. Continental Can produces about three tons of particulates per day plus unspecified but large amounts of sulfur dioxide, methyl mercaptans, hydrogen sulfides, and other sulfur compounds. Union Camp releases no figures on its output; however, extrapolation from Continental Can's emissions and use of the Public Health Service's emission factors for kraft mills suggest that Union Camp produces at least 15 tons per day of particulates, plus all the other kraft mill gases in quantities about five times larger than Continental Can's.[13]

As disturbing as the airborne pollution is the mills' assumption that their emission figures are a private corporate affair. As soon as the pollutants leave the company smokestack and pass into the public air, however, they cease to be private corporate concerns. Instantly they are matters of urgent public interest; the public must breathe the polluted air, and it has a right to know what it is breathing. Clinging to a social philosophy developed during the 1890's, many mill managers still insist that the public has neither need nor right to know what chemicals are seeping into its air. As long as the townspeople know that the horrible odors are "the smell of money," they don't need to know anything more.

A spectacular illustration of this total disregard for public welfare came from Union Camp. Under Georgia's new and by no means strict Air Quality Act, industries throughout the state were to file registration forms with the state's Air Quality Control Branch. The forms asked what products the industries made, what kind of fuel they used, what pollutants they sent into the air, and what they were trying to do about it. Given the congenital weakness of the Georgia Air Quality Branch, industries had little to fear if they sent in incomplete or even distorted forms. Nevertheless, most industries in the state—and all but one in Chatham County—filed the forms in relatively good faith. Most companies near Savannah, such as Continental Can whose form follows in Table 9–4, described what polluting compounds were released and how many pounds of pollutants were released per day.

Union Camp was the one Chatham County industry that did not submit a completed form. Perhaps Union Camp's environmental specialist Glenn Kimble felt that since he had presented the state legislature in 1966 with a proposed bill which, in effect, became the Air Quality Act, he had a right to interpret the Act in any way he wanted; perhaps the company had a special reason for refusing to cooperate. In any case, the result was a slap in the public face. Union Camp did include on its form information about the height of its smokestacks and

TABLE 9–4

REGISTRATION REPORT (Continued)

VII. MANUFACTURING ACTIVITIES (Continued)

B. PROCESS EMISSIONS

Operations Which Are Exhausted Or Release Contaminants To Outside Air (List Separately) (1)	Materials Used During Operation (2)	Rate of Exhaust From Operation (3)	Control Equipment Used And Removal Efficiency (4)	Compounds Handled By Control Device (5)	Uncontrolled Compounds Released To Outside Air (6)	Height Of Outlet Above Ground (7)	Size of Outlet (8)
CALCINING - Rotary Lime Kiln	Feed- Calcium Carbonate at 60% solids Product -Dry Calcium Oxide	36,500 CFM Saturated	Spray Chamber and wet scrubber, 95-98% eff.	Calcium Oxide and Calcium Carbonate	0.5 - 1.2 TPD tons/day	52 ft.	4.5 ft.
Black Liquor Recovery Furnace (2)	62,500 pounds of solids per hour sulfur Gases	220,000 CFM W.B.180°F D.B.280°F	Electrostatic Precipitators -90% Eff.	Sodium Sulfate & Sodium Carbonate	3 - 5 TPD	250 ft.	14 ft.
Batch Pulp Digesters (9) Relief and Blow Gases	Wood Chips, Cooking Liquor (Na_2S, NaOH) & Blk. Liquor Dilutent	Unknown	Tubular and Jet Condensers	Turpentine, Mercaptans, H_2S	Non-Condensable Sulfur Comp.	Relief- 73 ft. Blow- 60ft.	Relief-0.7 ft. Blow-1.2 ft.
Black Liquor Evaporator Non-Condensable Gases (2)	Weak Black Liq. (13%) Evaporated to 50% solids	Unknown	Partial removal with one wetscrubber	H_2S, SO_2 & other sulfur compounds	Unknown	40 ft.	0.7 ft.
Tall Oil Acidulation	Soap Skimmings and Sulfuric Acid	Unknown	None	H_2s, SO_2	Unknown	22 ft.	1.6 ft.

EXAMPLES:

(1) Casting cleaning, spray painting, degreasing, iron-molding cupola, screening, drying, mixing, acidulation, digesting, etc.

(2) Identify specific compounds and amounts per day.

(3) Cubic feet per minute. Specify conditions of gas stream (temperature, humidity, etc.).

(4) Baghouse, electrostatic precipitators, cyclone, settling chamber, wet scrubber, etc. Give operating efficiency, if available.

(5) Iron oxide and dusts, trichlorethylene, formaldehyde, sulfur dioxide, etc.

(6) Pounds per day, tons per month, or other convenient units if known. Give quantity of each identified compound contained in exhausted mixture.

(7) Give height in feet.

(8) Give inside dimensions.

NOTE: *If you cannot complete all portions of the above table, fill out as many portions as possible and give explanation. Use extra sheets where needed. Indicate in the space under remarks the basis used for the estimates given above-assumption, material balance etc. If sampling was done, please give method. If compounds are not released continuously, specify the number of hours.*

the number of corrugated boxes it made. All that was missing was the most important information: what the mill was putting into the air. Column #5 ("Compounds handled by control device") and #6 ("Uncontrolled compounds released to outside air") are both perfectly blank throughout the entire nine-page Union Camp form. By way of feeble explanation, Kimble noted on the bottom of one page: "We have some emission test data, largely spot tests, but because of the many variations in analytical method, operating conditions, etc., these are not suitable for tabulation." This meant that Union Camp either did not know what was coming from its stacks—an unlikely possibility for an industry obsessed with profitable recovery of by-products—or that it had absolutely no intention of telling anyone.

The question marks in columns five and six of Union Camp's form were written in by hand, presumably by an Air Branch staff member who never bothered to find out the answers. It is hard to decide which is worse: Union Camp's arrogant disregard for the public right to know or the state Air Quality Branch's meek decision to accept and "validate" the mill's hollow report.

American Cyanamid dutifully filled out its registration forms; in less blatant ways, however, Cyanamid has also shown its contempt for the public's right to know what is in the air. Early in 1970, Cyanamid put the finishing touches on a new system that would produce titanium dioxide through the "chloride process," which has sometimes led to discharges of deadly chlorine gas when used in other mills.

Because we felt that the possible danger of chlorine poisoning was a serious public health concern, our project tried to find out whether Cyanamid's process would release chlorine gas. The Chatham County Health Department was little help; its staff said that it did not even know that Cyanamid was using a new process. When a member of our project tried to get an appointment in the summer of 1970 to see C. W. Sieber, American Cyanamid's plant manager, he told her that she had "no right to know about it." She replied that she, like the other residents of Savannah, had a basic right to know whether she might be breathing dangerous substances. Sieber stood firm, saying that he might agree to a meet-

TABLE 9–5

REGISTRATION REPORT (Continued)

VII. MANUFACTURING ACTIVITIES (Continued)
B. PROCESS EMISSIONS

Estimated

Operations Which Are Exhausted Or Release Contaminants To Outside Air (List Separately) (1)	Materials Used During Operation (2)	Rate of Exhaust From Operation (3)	Control Equipment Used And Removal Efficiency (4)	Compounds Handled By Control Device (5)	Uncontrolled Compounds Released To Outside Air (6)	Height Of Outlet Above Ground (7)	Size of Outlet (8)
No. 8 Smelt Dissolving Tank Vent	88 tons/day smelt	4100	Mesh pad			99	3'-0" Ø
No. 9 " " " "	88 " " "	4100	" "			99	3'-0" Ø
No. 10 " " " "	142 " " "	6600	" "			112	4'-0" Ø
No. 11 " " " "	142 " " "	6600	" "			112	4'-0" Ø
No. 12 " " " "	267 " " "	15,300	" "			132 1/2	5'-0" Ø
No. 13 " " " "	267 " " "	15,300	" "			132 1/2	5'-0" Ø

EXAMPLES:

(1) Casting cleaning, spray painting, degreasing, iron-molding cupola, screening, drying, mixing, acidulation, digesting, etc.
(2) Identify specific compounds and amounts per day.
(3) Cubic feet per minute. Specify conditions of gas stream (temperature, humidity, etc.). 158°F, 40% moist.
(4) Baghouse, electrostatic precipitators, cyclone, settling chamber, wet scrubber, etc. Give operating efficiency, if available.
(5) Iron oxide and dusts, trichlorethylene, formaldehyde, sulfur dioxide, etc.
(6) Pounds per day, tons per month, or other convenient units if known. Give quantity of each identified compound contained in exhausted mixture.
(7) Give height in feet.
(8) Give inside dimensions.

NOTE: *If you cannot complete all portions of the above table, fill out as many portions as possible and give explanation. Use extra sheets where needed. Indicate in the space under remarks the basis used for the estimates given above-assumption, material balance etc. If sampling was done, please give method. If compounds are not released continuously, specify the number of hours.*

TABLE 9–6

REGISTRATION REPORT (Continued)

VII. MANUFACTURING ACTIVITIES (Continued)

B. PROCESS EMISSIONS

Operations Which Are Exhausted Or Release Contaminants To Outside Air (List Separately) (1)	Materials Used During Operation (2)	Rate of Exhaust From Operation (3)	Control Equipment Used And Removal Efficiency (4)	Compounds Handled By Control Device (5)	Uncontrolled Compounds Released To Outside Air (6)	Height Of Outlet Above Ground (7)	Size of Outlet (8)
Recovery Furnace 8 & 9	430 Tons/Day Black Liquor Solids	138,000 (A)	Electrostatic Precipitator	?	?	195	20'-0" Ø
" " 10	345 " "	128,000 (B)	90% "			150 1/2	11'-0" Ø
" " 11	345 " "	128,000 (B)	"			150 1/2	11'-0" Ø
" " 12	650 " "	178,000 (B)	90-95% Eff.			177	11'-0" Ø
" " 13	650 " "	178,000 (B)	"			177	11'-0" Ø

EXAMPLES:

(1) Casting cleaning, spray painting, degreasing, iron-molding cupola, screening, drying, mixing, acidulation, digesting, etc.

(2) Identify specific compounds and amounts per day.

(3) Cubic feet per minute. Specify conditions of gas stream (temperature, humidity, etc.). A-150°F, 25% moist. ; B-220°F, 35% moist.

(4) Baghouse, electrostatic precipitators, cyclone, settling chamber, wet scrubber, etc. Give operating efficiency, if available.

(5) Iron oxide and dusts, trichlorethylene, formaldehyde, sulfur dioxide, etc.

(6) Pounds per day, tons per month, or other convenient units if known. Give quantity of each identified compound contained in exhausted mixture.

(7) Give height in feet.

(8) Give inside dimensions.

NOTE: *If you cannot complete all portions of the above table, fill out as many portions as possible and give explanation. Use extra sheets where needed. Indicate in the space under remarks the basis used for the estimates given above-assumption, material balance etc. If sampling was done, please give method. If compounds are not released continuously, specify the number of hours.*

ing but that he would "only talk in generalities—nothing specific." [14]

Our next appeal was to Cyanamid corporate headquarters. Since Cyanamid's president, C. D. Siverd, had recently joined President Nixon's National Industrial Pollution Control Council, charged with encouraging "the business and industrial community to improve the quality of the environment," we thought this would be an ideal opportunity for Siverd to demonstrate his own company's concern. We asked him whether the Savannah plant was sending chlorine gas into the air.

The reply, from Pigments Division Manager J. Ludden, told us that "extensive efforts were made to incorporate into the design of this plant all of the features required to assure good air quality control," and that the control system was recommended by "an eminently qualified air pollution control engineer." [15]

Ludden did not mention chlorine, suggesting only that we visit the Air Branch and inspect the registration form. We had, in fact, checked the Air Branch several weeks earlier, and were told by one of the agency's officers that the registration form could not be found.

Late in August 1970, we visited the Air Branch again, and the agency's Mr. Lowrey found the Cyanamid chloride registration. Why yes, he said, the company is putting out chlorine gas, and several other contaminants as well. According to the registration, Cyanamid planned to discharge 7,000 cubic feet of gas per minute, containing:

500 parts per million of chlorine gas
50 parts per million of titanium dioxide
5 parts per million of hydrochloric acid
133 moles * per hour of carbon monoxide. [16]

By itself, the pure emission was concentrated enough to kill anyone who breathed it, but Cyanamid had told the Air Branch that by the time the gas wafted down from the 200-foot smokestack, it would be diluted enough to be safe. Ground level concentrations, Cyanamid had said, would be at most:

* One mole of any gas occupies 22.4 liters at 0° Centigrade at sea level.

0.2 parts per million of chlorine gas
0.5 parts per million of hydrochloric acid
0.3 micrograms per cubic meter of titanium dioxide
30 parts per million of carbon monoxide.[17]

If Cyanamid's figures are reliable, then the chlorine may not pose an immediate danger. Cyanamid's estimate of 0.2 parts per million is about one-fifth the level at which chlorine gas begins to produce irritating effects. The carbon monoxide emission is another story. Air quality boards from California to Sweden have set 30 parts per million as the absolute maximum that humans can tolerate for a period of eight hours without serious harm.[18] If, for even a brief period, the company's prediction is too low, the plant employees may pay a heavy price for the miscalculation.

Cleaning the air often takes more technical ingenuity than that required to build the simple holding ponds and activated sludge chambers that can solve industrial water pollution. But the technical obstacles are hardly insurmountable; the same wonderful creative spirit that has given us paper dresses and titanium-dioxide coated M&M's has also developed ways of controlling dirty air. Even the kraft paper mills, long thought to be permanently cursed with their unique smell, can now take hope. A series of new systems—"wet scrubbers," electrostatic precipitators, and various internal process changes—are now capable of greatly reducing mill smell and pollution. By most estimates, effective equipment would cost between $3–5 million for Union Camp, and about one-third as much for Continental Can.[19]

This money will never leave the corporate treasuries until it has to. Corporate managers, who face dividend-hungry stockholders each quarter, cannot see the sense of spending the money until strong laws force them to. Although coughing citizens may reserve a special rancor for the mills that brought the pollution, the real target for pressure is the government. If a government agency forces companies to install pollution control, the costs become a normal part of doing business; if the agency looks the other way, the smoke keeps rolling out.

In Georgia, it does not take long to learn which way

the state Air Quality Control Branch has looked. Most Georgians do not even know that the Branch exists; if they did, they might suppose it had some influence over air pollution. That, as the record shows, would be a sad mistake.

In fairness to the men who staff the Air Branch, many of their woes are not of their own making. In 1966, one Georgia legislator tried to introduce an air pollution law that would actually do something about pollution. (It began by saying that the state's firm policy should be "to preserve, protect and improve the air quality of this State so as to safeguard the public health, safety and welfare of the people of the State." Not a very radical set of statements, but much different from what came later.) After that potentially costly and embarrassing bill succumbed in committee, Union Camp's Glenn Kimble appeared before the Air Pollution Study Committee on December 9, 1966, with another proposal. Appearing, as he put it, "in behalf of all Georgia Industry," he presented a model air pollution law designed to bring cheer to every industrialist in Georgia. "It is a firm law which can be enforced," Kimble said, showing how easily words can be detached from their normal meanings, "yet it provides the safeguards and flexibility which are essential to prevent the crippling of segments of our economy by trying to reach Utopia too fast." *

* Kimble's presentation is such a classic exposition of his company's philosophy that it deserves further exposure. Appearing before the Air Pollution Study Committee on December 9, 1966, Kimble said: [20]

I am Glenn Kimble, and I am Technical Director for Union Camp Corporation in Savannah. However, I am appearing today in behalf of all Georgia Industry, as Chairman of the Associated Industries of Georgia Air and Water Resources Committee. . . .

An air pollution control bill was introduced into the Georgia Senate last January, but in view of the tremendous economic and social impact of air pollution legislation the Assembly decided that further study was warranted. A resolution establishing your committee was passed, and a group of interested industrial people agreed to work with the Health Department to develop a bill which would be acceptable to the Health Department and to Industry, and which would do the job that needs to be done for citizens of our state. We have done so, and are pleased to report the results to you.

We were fortunate in having a very competent and experienced group for our bill drafting committee. We started with several very good Georgia technical and business men from the Associated Industries of Georgia Air and Water Resources Council. To this nucleus we added representatives of other Georgia industrial groups inter-

After making a few almost imperceptible changes, the Georgia legislature made Kimble's dream into law. It is hardly surprising that Union Camp's Savannah manager James Lientz has said that he thinks the air law is "a very good one." [21]

The excessively moderate flavor of the Air Quality Act is clear from the start. In its opening paragraphs, the Act says that its policy is "to preserve, protect, and improve the air quality of this State so as to safeguard the public health, safety, and welfare of the people of the State *consistent with providing for maximum employment and the full industrial development of the State*." [22] (Emphasis added.) This philosophy is elaborated in the rest of the law whose general purpose is to make sure the state does no more enforcing than is comfortable for industry. It does the job well:

1. the Air Quality Branch may not forbid burning of forest land—an important consideration to the state's many paper companies, but a disturbing concession for citizens who live near the smoke; [23]

2. in setting its standards the Air Branch must consider other matters than human health and damage to property; it must also solicitously guard industrial interests by considering:

a. "The predominant character of development of the area of the State, such as residential, highly developed industrial area, commercial, or other characteristics"; [24] in other words, the intolerable pollution levels in housing areas near Union Camp may be judged acceptable for a "highly developed industrial area";

---

ested in air pollution, such as Mr. Holmes of the Petroleum Council. We were able to enlist the help of legal and technical experts with nationwide experience. The services of such men were provided to us by Mead Paper Corporation, Hercules Powder Company, the Petroleum Council, the Manufacturing Chemists Association, and others. We retained as consultants Dr. E. R. Hendrickson of the University of Florida, nationally known as an authority on air pollution control and the administration of air pollution law, and Mr. George Williams, a well-known Georgia lawyer who is a senior partner in Bouhan, Lawrence, Williams, and Levy [historically Union Camp's law firm].

It is a firm law which can be enforced, yet it provides the safeguards and flexibility which are essential to prevent the crippling of segments of our economy by trying to reach Utopia too fast.

b. "Effect on efficiencies of industrial operation resulting from use of air-cleaning devices"; [25]

c. "The economic and industrial development of the State and the social and economic value of the source of air contaminants"; [26]

3. If a law-enforcement decision somehow survives all these debilitating clauses, there is one final barrier. The Branch may exempt any industry from the state's air standards if "it finds that strict compliance with such rule, regulation, or general order is inappropriate . . . because of special circumstances which would render strict compliance unreasonable, unduly burdensome, or impractical . . . or because strict compliance would result in substantial curtailment or closing down of one or more businesses." [27]

In addition to the ineffectual act empowering the Air Branch, it must also stagger along with other legal loopholes, a ridiculously small staff, a low budget, and officers extraordinarily conscious of the limits of their power. Because they are not able to do many of the things they should, members of the Air Branch take consolation in the few things they can do. Visitors to the air office in Atlanta emerge clutching the one pathetic symbol of the agency's action: an aluminum beer can labeled "A Breath of Clean Air Imported from Georgia's Mountain Country." The Air Branch has the cans sitting on shelves all over its office and considers them a nice public-relations touch.

It would have been even nicer if the cans had never been made. Whoever thought them up apparently forgot to look in the agency's own technical books, which show that the processes used to make each can—manufacturing aluminum and paper, trucking the cans to the office, and finally disposing of the aluminum garbage—contaminate many times more air than the few ounces inside.

The Chatham County Health Department is the local arm of Georgia's air pollution "control" system. While the state staff concedes that there is little it can do, engineers of the Health Department react with outrage to any suggestion that they lack the legal power or technical tools to handle air pollution control. In truth, however, their operation is riddled with legal and technical holes.

The Health Department's problems begin with its most important function: taking air quality samples. Because local pollution levels always border on and often cross over into dangerous concentrations, accurate readings are imperative, but the systems used to measure pollution levels simply cannot do the job. Like most other local health agencies across the country, Chatham officials use three clumsy and inaccurate measurement devices: the high-volume sampler, the Ringleman Scale, and the lead peroxide candle.

Because the health of so many communities depends on these systems, it is worth describing their failings in detail.

The high-volume sampler, most efficient of the three, measures particulate pollution by recording the amount of particulates that have fallen onto a filter pad in a given period of time. In judging particulate pollution, it is most important to know the maximum ground level concentration of the particulates; since the sampler is stationary, it is only by mere coincidence that it ever measures the air with maximum concentration. Investigators in Texas said,

> [The sampler is placed] at the point of maximum ground level concentration. . . . The point of maximum concentration, however, is about as constant as the wind and a good deal less predictable. Presumably control officials are expected to go chasing about with their samplers, looking for the magic point. When they find it—how they are to know when they find it is an interesting question—they take their measurements, hoping all the time that the wind speed, the wind direction, and the half dozen other factors that determine pollution concentrations and dispersion will remain unchanged.[28]

The Ringleman Scale is a far more primitive way of measuring industrial emissions. The user need only find a smokestack, hold the scale up against the sky, and compare the color of the smoke with colors on the scale. In its pamphlet, *Air Quality Criteria for Particulate Matter,* the Department of Health, Education and Welfare flatly rejects the Ringleman Scale, saying,

> It is not possible to determine the mass emitted per unit of time from a smokestack solely on the basis of visually per-

ceived light scatter or absorption. The mass per unit time emitted from the stack, and not the appearance or optical properties of the plume is pertinent to the eventual air composition, even though appearance may be aesthetically objectionable.[29]

The lead peroxide candle purports to measure sulfur oxide concentrations. As discussed earlier, the candle has one debilitating flaw: it measures only *average* concentrations over long periods of time, instead of any instantaneous reading or daily peak. Because the crucial health factor of sulfur oxides is peak concentration rather than a long-term average, the system is virtually useless. Its attractions are that it requires only monthly attention and it is cheap. There are other systems which record useful readings at low cost. The Department of Health, Education and Welfare recommends the West-Gaeke system, which can take daily or hourly readings for the extremely small investment of $50–$100.

To most people concerned about air pollution, the fact that inaccurate systems are used throughout the nation is cause for serious dismay. But in the Chatham County Health Department, the reasoning is opposite; if the systems are used elsewhere, then they must be all right. It is not the Health Department's fault that it still uses these systems; hundreds of other smalltime public health agencies suffer the same economic and technical roadblocks. The real danger is the Board's single-minded refusal to acknowledge its problems. By clinging desperately to the idea that its pollution readings are absolutely accurate, the Health Department spreads a comforting but unjustified feeling of safety throughout the county. It is not hard to imagine the grisly circumstances in which this myth might die. Some day, when the particulate load is heavy, the sulfur oxides level will briefly hit the danger point and drive people to the hospital. But the Chatham County Health Department, seeing that its monthly average readings show no danger, will refuse to believe that any of it is taking place.

One step toward effective pollution control is knowing what is in the air; another step is finding out where the emission came from. The Health Department has made commendable attempts to trace the sources of Savannah's air pollution, but again the results have been spotty and without practical use. In 1968, the Health Department decided to draw up an "Air Pollution Emissions Inventory" by sending out questionnaires to local industries (see Table 9–1). The plan ran off course at the start. Fifteen per cent of the industries never bothered to send the forms back, and the forms that did return did not yield much practical information. The questionnaire asked each factory what its final products were rather than asking what pollutants it emitted. Then, using conversion charts developed on national averages for various industries, the Health Department tried to calculate the individual pollutant emissions. This indirect approach might have been justified as a last resort to get around factories that do not know or will not tell what they put into the air. There was no justification for using it as the first and only line of questioning, other than the Health Department's usual reply that the conversion charts are used "nationwide."

As if to vindicate its reputation, the Health Department points proudly to its enforcement record. Their files, county officials say, teem with examples of vigorous Health Department action. County Engineer Harbison and his colleagues recall the 1968 clampdown on open burning, which brought the full wrath of the Health Department down on the heads of small junk yard owners and scrap metal dealers. There have also been the two classic cases in which they tamed industries: the routing of Kaiser Chemicals, and the reformation of Southern States Phosphate and Fertilizer.

The Health Department says that it "forced the [Kaiser Chemicals] plant to shut down" instead of continuing its gross pollution of an island directly across the river from City Hall. According to Kaiser records, the creaky old mill was already scheduled for destruction before the Health Department made its suggestions.

According to the Health Department, Southern States installed pollution control systems in response to its unremitting pressure. Actually, the mill managers had installed a new process with a more efficient recovery system because they were losing money with each pound of chemicals that escaped from their stack. One mill official was unaware that the Health Department had ever applied pressure on him.

As with its sulfur oxide readings and pollution inventory, the Health Department is more the victim than the villain in its enforcement failures. It lacks the legal power to do anything effective about the county's considerable air pollution problems. Someday, the Health Department may admit its weaknesses, thereby convincing the public that more effective laws are needed. As long as the Health Department persists in maintaining its façade, it destroys the possibility that Savannahians will realize the dangers they face.

"The county doesn't need anyone to tell it its problems when it is run efficiently like the Chatham County Health Department is run," Harbison still says. "We're part of the statewide program, and we're respected."[30]

10

The Making of a Company Town

I: A Present for Mr. Calder

Be it further resolved that expressions of warm welcome be extended to the personnel of the Union Bag and Paper Corporation with an expression of appreciation for the confidence its officers have shown in the city of Savannah.

Resolution by the mayor and aldermen of Savannah, May 29, 1935

The people of Savannah live closely with their history. The lessons Savannah learned in withstanding cotton, General Sherman, mosquitoes, and the Depression have left their mark on the modern outlook of the city.

One historical lesson has especially influenced Savannah's relation to its major industry. This lesson is more subtle than the other major psychological element in the Savannah-Union Camp relation—the mill's constant reminders that it puts the food on 5000 dinner tables every night. But it is equally persuasive—perhaps more so, because it is the unspoken and therefore unarguable background to every decision the town makes about its mill.

The theory is briefly this: before Union Camp came to Savannah, the town was on the verge of complete economic collapse. But after the mill brought its prestige and its jobs, Savannah revived. While its economic state today could be better, there is no telling how bad it would have been without Union Camp. The conclusion of this lesson is that because Union Camp saved Savannah, Savannah owes a powerful and perpetual debt to the company. Together with the threat that 5000 company jobs might disappear overnight, this feeling of indebtedness has done an extraordinarily effective job of blunting all criticism of Union Camp. It does not matter if the grievances have no logical connection with the town's economic history; all complaints—about hiring practices, the mill's heavy-handed meddling in local politics, and environmental pollution—run into a psychological brick wall.

From ledgers of the Union Bag and Paper Company and from musty city files comes a different twist to the old myth. The paper company undoubtedly injected fresh economic blood into the city's veins; but whatever it did for Savannah, Savannah did more for Union Bag. Instead of reminding themselves how fortunate they are to have attracted the mill, Savannahians might start asking Union Camp to pay back its 35-year debt.

Contrary to current lore, the city's economic lot at the start of the twentieth century was not all bad. The economy centered on the river, as it had since the days of Oglethorpe. In 1923, after the legislature passed a state constitutional amendment permitting city-owned port terminals, the Savannah Port Authority was formally set up as a full-fledged "department of municipal government." The twenties saw increasingly heavy river traffic as ships carrying passengers and freight steamed out of the harbor to ports around the world. The cargo alone handled in an average year was worth more than $500 million. The rising economic tide continued until 1930, when all-time records for port activity were set.

Then things changed for Savannah. Along with the Depression paralysis it shared with the rest of the nation, several of the city's traditional economic supports were suffering their own special problems. Both cotton and naval stores—for many years the major commodities that rode in and out of Savannah's harbor—were nearing the bottom of a long decline. On its long trip eastward, the boll weevil had cut Georgia's cotton production drastically. While the region still could produce naval stores

—pitch, turpentine, and tar—the old markets were no longer interested.

It is hard to measure the toll the Depression took in Savannah. City records show that port activity dropped, unemployment rose sharply, city salaries fell, and relief lines grew. Many surviving witnesses insist that the Depression dealt Chatham County only an indirect blow; Savannah, they say, avoided this national trend as it had so many others. While the port might have seen the last of cotton and naval stores, whatever the Southeast's new commodity would be after the Depression, Savannah would be ready to export it.

Long-range consolations, however, did little to ease the immediate panic. Most planners thought that the best way out of their current economic troubles was to attract an industry to Savannah. To that end, in October 1933 a group of anxious citizens and uneasy businessmen formed the Industrial Committee of Savannah to find an industry for the town. Savannah was glad to offer whatever help it could. On September 19, 1934, the mayor and aldermen empowered the Port Authority to buy land and offer it to industries as plant sites. Savannah's businessmen realized they had many other things besides cheap Port Authority land to offer an industry. The city had a commercially strategic location; its natural resources were abundant and unspoiled; its work force was large and eager. Savannah's excellent port gave it a special bargaining edge over other Southern towns at a time when many industries were migrating toward the cheap land and labor of the South.

"The combination of abundant free water, water travel on the river or by sea, plus all the railroads and highways serving us, makes this area a natural for many kinds of business and industry," said Savannah Mayor Lee Mingledorff 20 years after the Depression.[1] The view Mingledorff took in the comfortable fifties was harder to put faith in during the thirties, as Savannah's agreement with Union Bag shows. The provision of the agreement show fear for the city's future that led Savannah to barter away many of the town's most valuable assets.

One of the quirks of the Union Camp myth that shows the company as Savannah's economic savior is its strange unevenness of detail. While it deals fully with Savannah's financial plight, it pays no attention to Union Bag's economic history. This omission from the myth is crucial, for Union Bag's balance sheets show not a booming financial venture but a frail company rapidly weakening that rushed to Savannah in a frantic race to escape economic doom.

Union Bag and Paper Corporation was 65 years old when it came to look at Savannah in 1934. It was born in Pennsylvania in 1869 as the Union Paper Bag Machine Company; after two reorganizations, in 1899 and again in 1911, it emerged as Union Bag and Paper. The company's original business was distributing patents on bag-making machines, but by the 1920's that market no longer provided a good living. Blaming the problem mainly on poor management, a later review of the company's history said, "During the roaring twenties, almost every corporation made money. One of the few exceptions was Union Bag and Paper." [2]

At the end of the twenties, a large management shake-up left Alexander Calder, father of Union Camp's current president, sitting in the president's chair. Although "Sandy" Calder later proved to be the company's financial Moses, when he took over the presidency no one thought the job would last more than a year or two. The company was showing no improvement over its 1920's record, and the long, profitless years had left it too weak to endure many more problems. The company's woes stemmed from two main problems, Calder said later: "First, we had high-cost obsolete mills in the North; second, our supply of pulpwood in northern New York state had become exhausted." [3]

In 1932, Union Bag ended the year with a net loss of nearly $260,000. The next year, workers at Union Bag's only pulp-making mill walked out on strike; after they left, the mill never turned out another pound of pulp. By the end of 1933, Union Bag's outlook was dismal. Its five paper-making mills were full of obsolete equipment and they had to turn either to rival companies or unreliable independent dealers for raw pulp. With no reason to expect an upswing, Union Camp's life expectancy seemed short.

Calder's solution to escape bankruptcy was to go

South, where labor was cheap and land cheaper, where the company could build a new, modern mill. Calder picked three cities which had the life-restoring qualities he was looking for: Jacksonville, Florida; Charleston, South Carolina; and Savannah, Georgia. The only problem was money. No investment banker would consider lending the company the $4 million it needed to build a mill. It was at this point that Union Bag opened negotiations with Savannah.

The ideal solution to the joint problems of Union Bag and Savannah came in March 1935, when Savannahians were finally able to dig up money for the factory. Mills B. Lane, president of the Citizens and Southern (C&S) National Bank, agreed to a five-year loan of $1 million at low interest; he also offered to put up another $1.5 million if Union Bag could raise $1.5 million through sale of common stock. The local investment firm of Johnson, Lane, Space, and Co., said that it would find the additional $1.5 million. "It was," senior partner Tom Johnson recalled later, "the hardest money that I've ever had to raise." [4]

With the sudden appearance of $4 million, Union Bag found a new lease on life. Of course the loans were only available if Union Bag were to come to Savannah, bringing its expected bounty of jobs, but the offer of the Savannah bankers was too good to pass up. As Calder said later, although the company paid some attention to Savannah's port location, the cheap land, and other considerations, it was the available money that was "the most important" reason. "I would like to reiterate," Calder said, "the City of Savannah and Union Bag and Paper Corporation are greatly indebted to the C&S National Bank and Johnson, Lane, Space, and Co. for helping us finance this first unit." [5]

Having narrowly escaped financial death, it seemed likely that Union Bag would accept whatever contract terms Savannah offered. But during the contract negotiations, the company dictated terms and demanded concessions. City representatives, overly eager to have their hands on an industry, put up little resistance. The result was an economic plum for Union Bag.

The company's main obligation was to start construction of an integrated bag factory, including a 125-ton-per-day pulp mill, a 125 ton-per-day paper mill, and a paper bag factory. The mill was to be ready to turn out its first paper bag by early 1936. In return, the Port Authority leased 440 acres of prime river front land to Union Bag for extremely low rates. The lease would run 99 years, and Union Bag would have the option to buy the land at any time. The rent would gradually increase the longer Union Bag held the lease:

Year	*Rent*
1–5	$300/year
6–15	$500/year
16–35	$1,000/year
June 1, 1970–May 30, 2034	$10,500

Three years before the payments were to jump to a level reasonably consistent with the land's value, Union Camp exercised its option and in 1967 bought the land for $250,000. At the time, according to several real estate experts, the land was worth between $2–$4 million.

In the contract, Savannah further agreed to build a road to the mill; lay railroad tracks "not to exceed two miles in length" (it eventually laid three miles); and spend up to $35,000 for a terminal wood dock. All told, these fringe benefits cost the city $80,000 Depression-value dollars; including the cost of the land, the total cost of bringing Union Bag to Savannah was nearly $400,000—as much as the city's projected tax revenue for 1936. With such heavy subsidies going from the city treasury to Union Camp, it is hardly surprising that a New York consultant reported in a 1937 review that the city's finances were "fundamentally sound but temporarily . . . the cause of serious embarrassment" because of a "distressing shortage of cash" brought on by "overspending." [6]

Even with judgments dampened by the Depression, some Savannahians thought the city was trying too hard to make Union Bag happy. Newspapers hinted that what caused the most unhappiness was the company's annual $300 rental for land that cost the city $12,000 annually in principal and interest payments. The low rental might have been an acceptable incentive for a fledgling industry, critics argued, but there was no good reason to extend the protection for 35 years.

If civic watchdogs found the rent clause worth attacking, their reaction, had they seen the full set of agreements, would have been apoplectic. Near the end of the contract, an innocuous paragraph opened the door to some potentially costly concessions for the city. The paragraph referred to a separate "agreement" signed by the city and Union Bag. The terms of the agreement were not listed in the contract.

Copies of the agreement are retained only in city and, presumably, Union Camp files. When one of our project members found the city copy, it was dusty and obviously not used to inspection. Beneath the dust were several terms.

> 6. As a part of this agreement, it is understood that neither of the parties hereto nor any of its associates will solicit the location of a similar sulphate and pulp and paper and bag plant during the term [99 years] of this lease.
>
> 7. The parties hereto agree to use their best efforts to secure the necessary action and if possible legislation on the part of the governmental bodies concerned, *to protect and save you* [*Union Bag*] *harmless from any claims, demands, or suits for the pollution of air or water caused by the operation of the plant.*
>
> It is agreed that *in case litigation arises or suits are brought against you on account of odors and/or flowage from the proposed plant that the Industrial Committee of Savannah will pay all expenses of defending such suits up to a total amount of $5,000* . . .
>
> 15. There is, as we have explained to you, a bill in the State Senate which will, when if passed by a vote of the people of the State of Georgia in the next General Election, exempt pulp and paper mills and bag factories from taxes for a period of 15 years. We pledge to you our support of this bill. We shall use our best efforts to have pledged to you in support of this bill the leading newspapers of the State, and you may rely on our support and cooperation in this behalf.[7] (Emphasis added.)

Over and above the terms of the contract, this loaded agreement saddled the citizens of Savannah with still more obligations to Union Bag. The agreement effectively prevented the city from trying to attract other paper plants, committed the city to lobbying for special interests in the state legislature (lobbying for measures that would constrict an already inadequate tax income), and gave the industry license to ignore the environmental welfare of the people of Savannah. Since the Industrial Committee got a large share of its funds from the city, the terms of clause #7 could force Savannah to use citizens' funds to defend the industry against citizens' lawsuits.

It is hard to understand what was going on in the city negotiators' minds when they handed away such a large chunk of their constituents' rights. Partly, they were eager to end Savannah's financial difficulties by attracting Union Bag, though the facts suggest that Union Bag might have come anyway. Some of the men may have been personally involved in protecting Union Bag's welfare; Robert Groves, chairman of the complaint Industrial Committee, went on to become a director of Union Bag, as did William Murphy, another prominent Savannahian who helped bring the mill to town. Perhaps the negotiators believed that the townspeople would go to any lengths to attract Calder and his company.

In an attempt to put a permanent stop to scattered criticism about the contract, Mayor Gamble wrote an article for the Savannah newspapers on December 3, 1936, in which he listed "all" the terms of the city's contract with Union Bag and defended them on grounds of competitive necessity. He carefully avoided any discussion of the "agreement" or its terms. As far as our project was able to tell, the citizens have never been told how much their city actually gave away.

Because of the contract and the agreement, Union Bag had retreated from the brink of disaster to obtain an ideal situation. It now had a prime plant site at virtually no cost; low-cost financing; a guaranteed lack of local competition; and protection from complaints about its pollution. The company had also taken the first long step toward psychological indenture of the people of Savannah. Having built an empire on bluff, Alexander Calder and his company convinced the city that *it* was the lucky one.

Fifteen years later, the *Savannah Morning News* carried an item that had first appeared in *Investor's Reader* and that gave a new perspective on Calder's empire. Without the Savannah mill, the story said, "Union Baggers agree that the company would have gone bankrupt."[8] By the time the story appeared, however, it was too late to make a difference.

With its Savannah beachhead firmly established, Union Bag moved into a period of profit and growth. A few months after the first paper-making machine was finished, the management announced plans for a second; before the second was done, a third was under way. Expansion continued so rapidly that, in 1955, the *Journal of Commerce* reported that "the company is said to have today what is considered the world's largest and probably the lowest-cost completely integrated pulp and paper mill, in Savannah, Georgia."[9] By 1960, the Savannah plant held seven paper-making machines, one of the industry's largest pulping mills, a refinery for tall oil and other chemical by-products, a paper bag factory, and a corrugated box factory.

The heavy investments in the Savannah plant paid off lushly from the start; company sales jumped 47 per cent in 1937, and another 65 per cent in 1938. In 1937 Calder reported:

> Net profits for 1937 reflect the improvement resulting from the new Savannah plant. . . . Despite the general business recession of the last quarter of 1937, it is significant that the final net profit for the year shows an increase of $345,471 over . . . profits for the first nine months.[10]

The company was now able to get the long-term credit it needed to grow. During the second half of the thirties, according to Wall Street reports, Union Bag was growing three and a half times as fast as the whole rapidly expanding paper industry.[11] When its third machine started making paper in Savannah, the company became entirely independent of outside sources of pulp and paper.

With its pulp mill, paper machines, and bag and box makers all nesting under one plant roof, the company was able to cut costs dramatically. The $3 million it had saved by moving operations to Savannah was reflected in a tripling of profits between 1936 and 1937. Exactly how much income the Savannah plant represented is hard to tell, since the company refused to break its profit down by individual plant. Union Bag's 1938 balance sheet gives a rough idea of the Savannah plant's contribution: in January, when the mill was shut down for ten days, the company brought in $1,317 in profit. In February, with the mill in full operation, profit was almost $40,000, and by March it was up to $113,000.*

By the late 1950's, the company was growing at a rate that made its 1930's expansion look pale. Union Bag was then measuring its growth in companies acquired, not in paper machines added. In July 1956, Union Bag merged with a major Eastern competitor, the Camp Manufacturing Company, to form the Union Bag-Camp Paper Corporation (later simply Union Camp Corporation). In quick succession, the newly formed Union-Camp coalition gathered controlling interests in four other large Eastern competing companies—Universal Paper Bag Company, Highland Container Corporation, Eastern Box Company, and Allied Container Corporation.

In 1960, however, the Federal Trade Commission began to have doubts about this concentration of bag-making power. On October 11, 1960, the FTC charged Union Bag-Camp Paper with five counts of violating the Clayton Anti-Trust Act, including hampering competition and creating a monopoly in Eastern and Southern paper markets. The subsequent "consent" order † required Union Bag-Camp to get rid of six of its factories. With this as its biggest worry, Calder's company had come a long way since the precarious days of the Depression.

* Although the company still refuses to break down its profits, there are approximate measures of the Savannah mill's share. In 1966, when the corporation sold a total of 1,325,306 tons of paper products, the Savannah plant processed 1 million of those tons, about 75 per cent of the total. Since the recent opening of the Montgomery, Alabama, plant, Savannah's share has dropped; in 1969, the Savannah plant still turned out between one-half and two-thirds of the corporation's 1,556,983 tons of paper products. Of the corporation's 15,000 employees, more than one-third work in Savannah.

† A consent order is a legal device which allows the company to save face by claiming it is not guilty of an offense, but it still pays a fine and must promise not to repeat the offense.

> *I think perhaps the true enemy of preservation of our environment is our own system of government, and by that I mean that the local governments and the county government which is entirely dependent on the property tax and the increase of its payroll structure is the true enemy of conservation today. It may be that we must revise the entire structure of the United States as to taxes, that conservation can never be accomplished so long as a local government must as a means of its financial survival get a new tax base, new development, and payrolls into its boundaries.*
>
> *Congressman Paul D. McCloskey, Jr.*[12]

Union Camp does not need to discuss its history; the story of how Union Bag saved Savannah is a quietly accepted part of local mythology. The company has another psychological truncheon that it exhibits frequently in newspapers, in private conversations, and in the general flow of Savannah thought and conversation to get its message across: Union Camp has the biggest payroll in town.

Mill officials seize every opportunity to drive the message home. Through constant repetition, the mill's employment statistics have become a kind of magic panacea. No longer limited to describing how many people work at the mill, the employment figures serve as all-purpose answers to any complaint about the mill. In testimonies before state and Federal antipollution agencies, Union Camp vice president and Savannah plant manager James Lientz regularly begins by counting the dollars the company has brought to Savannah. For example, at the 1965 Federal conference, Lientz said:

> Mr. Chairman, my name is James R. Lientz and I am Vice President of the Union Bag-Camp Paper Corporation.
>
> The Savannah plant of Union Bag-Camp Paper Corporation, which produces pulp, paper, linerboard, bags, corrugated shipping containers, and chemicals, is the largest operation of its kind in the world.

The plant began operations in 1936. Its daily rated productive capacity at that time was 120 tons of paper. The plant employed approximately 500 persons, whose total annual wages approximated $1,000,000.

Today the plant produces 2,500 tons of paper and paperboard daily, and employs 5,000 persons, whose annual wages total $33,800,000.

Other economic contributions made by the plant to Savannah and the area in 1964, included pulpwood purchases of over $18,000,000, and freight payments totaling over $17,000,000. Inbound and outbound freight cars total 90,000 annually, representing 40 per cent of all rail cars handled in the metropolitan Savannah area.

Union Bag-Camp Paper Corporation's 1964 payroll to residents of South Carolina, which includes the employees of the company's Spartanburg box plant supplied with paperboard from Savannah, totaled $1,100,000, and the company purchased pulpwood in 1964 in the amount of $2,700,000 from South Carolina tree growers.

Occupying the position we do in the Savannah community, we are deeply concerned with any conditions in the Savannah Harbor which might adversely affect the health and economic welfare of anyone in this area. . . .[13]

There is no logical connection between the Union Camp payroll and the company's failure to fulfill its social and legal obligations. The mill does pay out many millions of dollars, but it uses them to buy the hard days of work its employees put in. And the fact that it has paid for that commodity does not give it any special right to shortchange its way out of other deals. Union Camp buys trees from many Georgia farms. But that does not give it the right to break Georgia laws or run its lumbertrucks without licenses. Applying the company's payroll logic to private behavior, any patient who paid his doctor bill could then set up camp in the doctor's office, rub his feet over the furniture, and maybe take the doctor's wife out on a date. It is difficult to think about the payroll with icy detachment when the payroll is putting clothes on the children and food in the stomach. Many Savannahians feel a vague threat that what the mill has given, the mill might take away. Complaints about Union Camp quickly boil down to the inescapable problem: the mill hires 5,000 people, and what would they do without Union Camp? On the surface, the threat is plausible. But in fact, the threat is a bluff. The plant is no more likely to leave Savannah than the river.

The first problem would be to find another site that would offer both Savannah's geographical virtues and tolerance. As national awareness of environmental problems grows, no mill can expect to get away with the abuses Union Camp has practiced in Savannah. Interstate Paper's experience in Riceboro shows that new factories will have to be much cleaner than the creaky monsters of the past.

Even if Union Camp did find a town ready to sacrifice itself, the sheer cost of moving would almost certainly stop the company. Although the company refuses to discuss exactly how much money it has buried in the Savannah plant, several experts in the industry have estimated that it would cost between $350–500 million to replace the mill.* If the main local problem was pollution which would cost only about $10 million to control, chances are that the company would build a holding pond and stay a while longer in Savannah. The company would not have to replace the Savannah mill, of course, but it would be difficult to find another dependable source of a million tons of paper yearly. The company would have an even harder time explaining to its stockholders why it had abandoned its traditional money-maker. In light of these arguments, it is safe to assume that it would take a lot more than complaints about pollution to drive Union Camp away.

Aside from jobs, what have they brought, these mills that flocked to Georgia during the thirties and forties? They like to think they have brought prosperity. In a publication put out by their regional association, the Southern paper mills give their version of the economic history of the South:

* The cost of building a modern kraft paper mill is about $71,000 for each ton of daily capacity. Since Union Camp's Savannah mill produces more than 2,800 tons per day, a new mill would cost nearly $200 million. In addition, the Savannah plant includes a $50-million tall oil plant, a $50-million box and bag operation, inventory worth $40–50 million, plus office buildings, docks, land, and other improvements. (These estimates come from experts within the paper industry who have asked to remain anonymous.)

> In the 1930's, for example, the South was described as "The Nation's No. 1 Economic PROBLEM." But, a decade later, the region and its people were demonstrating such startling vitality, endeavor, and development that the area was referred to by business and industrial leaders as "The Nation's No. 1 Economic OPPORTUNITY."
>
> Like a sleeping princess, or more like a slumbering giant, the South had awakened. . . .
>
> Part and parcel of all this, and a most important part, is the pulp and paper industry.[14]

But the No. 1 Economic OPPORTUNITY has not turned out quite as the mills describe. The paper plants provide work, but paper has not brought prosperity to the Southeast. Parts of the South have boomed, but their strength has usually rested on something besides pulp. Savannah and the surrounding region are a clear example of the mixed blessings paper mills have brought.

Savannah is in the middle of a densely concentrated belt of paper mills. Along the Southeastern Coastal Plain, running from lower South Carolina through Georgia to the northern tip of Florida, are more than a dozen paper mills capable of producing over 13,000 tons of paper per day. In Georgia alone, the mills on the coastal plain have a daily capacity of 8,250 tons of which Union Camp accounts for more than one-third.[15] All these mills—from veterans like Union Camp to Interstate, newest of the group—have done well in their years in the South. Union Camp's growth within 25 years from a one-machine mill to the world's largest is only one example of the general pattern of steady profit and constant expansion.

The mills have not shared their affluence with the region. Black-belt Alabama and certain parts of the Mississippi Delta have lower per capita income averages, but they are virtually the only regions more depressed than the Southeastern Coastal Plain. In 1967, researchers from the Georgia Institute of Technology found that the North Carolina-Georgia coastal region—called "Cretacia" because of its geologic origins in the Upper Cretaceous period—was poorer by almost every measure than Appalachia. For example, in Cretacia, half the families live on annual incomes of $3,000 or less. In

Appalachia, only one-third of the families are below this "poverty line" income; and in the rest of the country, only one family in five lives on less than $3,000.[16]

Poverty is especially acute in the Georgia stretch of Cretacia (roughly the southern half of the state) where more families have yearly incomes below $3,000 and more adults have less than five years of schooling than

TABLE 10–1

Income Distribution

Per cent of families with income

Area	*Less than $3,000*	*More than $10,000*
Appalachia	30.7 per cent	8.7 per cent
Cretacia	46.8	6.1
Georgia portion of Cretacia	47.2	5.9
United States	20.5	15.6

Source: Georgia Institute of Technology Report, Engineering Experiment Station, Project A-787, 1967.

in the other coastal states. The region immediately surrounding Savannah is one of the most depressed areas. In the 11 counties that ring Savannah, the average income is about one-half the national average. Savannah is more comfortable than the poor rural areas of the coastal plain, but when compared to the nine other metropolitan

TABLE 10–2

Per Capita Buying Income

Area	*Average buying income per capita*	*Percentage of national average*
Standard Metropolitan Statistical Areas (SMSAs) in Appalachia	$2,381	95
SMSAs in Cretacian Coastal Plain	2,231	81
Savannah Metropolitan Area (SMSA)	2,156	80
Savannah Trade Area (11 surrounding counties)	1,511	56

Source: Georgia Institute of Technology Report, Engineering Experiment Station, Project A-787, 1967.

areas, Savannah is one of the most depressed in the coastal plain. Even with its knot of industries, the town's average buying income is lower and its proportion of poor families is higher than in nearby cities like Charleston or Brunswick.

Industry has not brought poverty to Savannah any more than it has brought prosperity. But in return for even the meager bounty from industry, the Georgia coast may have sold its most important chance for permanent economic recovery. Traditionally, towns like Savannah have turned to the old god Industry to boost their economies. However, *the mills that Savannah has attracted since 1935 now seriously cut its chances for ever getting new industries.* With its industrially depleted water supply, its manipulated tax system (See Chapter 11), and its polluted air and water, Savannah has much less to offer now than it did when it was courting Union Bag.

In the last five years, many Southerners have gradually realized that there is another course open to them. The rest of the country has the heavy industry the South has so long sought; and the rest of the country is beginning to get tired of it. As Northern cities become more crowded, more filthy, and generally less inhabitable, the South grows steadily more attractive to heavy industry because it is less developed, there are fewer large cities, and more open space and clear water—natural commodities that become rarer every day. As they do, their value increases. It is somewhat debasing to put any economic price tag on the fertile coastal marshes or stretches of pure river; but even from a purely fiscal point of view, the South has many good reasons for protecting its natural heritage; a whole economic system can grow from an unpolluted estuary. Industries from shrimping to tourism can build a stable financial base and offer greater promise for economic salvation than the mills.

This new kind of economic base has special importance in Savannah. For most of this century, the town quietly hid most of its considerable historic treasure behind the dingy façades of Depression architecture. The squares and spired churches were all here, but the city stayed, as local culture puts it, the "nation's best kept secret." But by the mid-1960's, the town realized just how much it had to offer. The appeal of historic Savannah is no manufactured tourist sham. By restoring row after row of its old town houses, by replanting its downtown squares, and polishing up its fountains, Savannah has created one of the few downtown districts in America that is a pleasure just to walk through. A study by the Georgia Institute of Technology pointed out in 1965 that tourism was the town's single most promising economic prospect.[17]

Savannah has had a harder time restoring its historic area than it would have had 35 years ago. The industries that have moved to town since then have done serious damage to Savannah's centuries-old attractions. Factor's Walk, home of the old cotton exchanges, runs along the river front; two old forts, Jackson and Pulaski, sit over the river as they did when guarding against English and Yankee ships. But the river, natural focus of old Savannah, is a jolting contrast to its buildings. Raw sewage rushes into the river right below Factor's Walk. The city's plans to build a riverside park fell through when everyone realized that few visitors would picnic next to a stinking river. Even the parts of Savannah far from the river's vapors lose their historic charm when the heavy reek of kraft pulping settles down.

Savannah has learned to live with these handicaps; it may even learn to disguise them well enough so that the river front is once more presentable. But industry may yet take an even heavier toll of the city's natural and historic resources in the next few years. According to most economic predictions, the major industries along the Savannah will not hire many more people in 1975 than they do today. Federal researchers say that five years from now, paper mills and other heavy industries on the Savannah will hire only 4 per cent more people than they do today—53,000 instead of the current 51,000. After that, rapidly increasing mill automation will probably cause employment to level off or possibly even to decline. At the same time, the industries expect to increase production—and, therefore, pollution discharge. By 1975, heavy industrial production along the Savannah will be 26 per cent greater than it is today. Unless the industries change their processes drastically, the pollution poured into the river will also rise by 26 per cent.[18] The mills, which have grown rich in the South and given the area so little in return, may complete their domination by crushing the region's chances for finding another kind of wealth.

11

The Making of a Company Town

II: Representation Without Taxation

> *[The property tax] puts a premium on dishonesty and debauches the public conscience; it reduces deception to a system and makes a science of knavery; it presses hardest on those least able to pay; it imposes double taxation on one man and grants entire immunity to the next.*
>
> *Edward Seligman,* Essays in Taxation

Local tax systems often rival local sewers for the title of most complicated and least comprehensible phase of municipal life. Taxpayers may not know exactly how the system works, but they know something is wrong as they watch their tax bills rise out of sight. They respond to spiraling taxes in the only way they know; howeowners fight to get property taxes cut, and voters elect politicians who promise to keep public expenses to a minimum. This backlash may be inevitable, but it inflicts heavy damage; not only does it cripple public services, but also perpetuates the injustices of the tax system. While citizens fight small battles and win minor victories on the tax front, they often overlook the heart of the problem, the tax imbalance. As small taxpayers stagger under steadily increasing loads, the largest property owners—corporations and industries—escape with ridiculously low taxes.

With the possible exception of its air pollution, there is no way in which an industry can more directly harm its townspeople than through manipulation of the local tax system. By right, large industries that demand extra services should pay a large share of the local tax bill; their trucks roll over public roads, their property requires police and fire protection, their employees expand the need for municipal services. Towns are willing to put up with the unpleasant aspects of nearby industries because, in theory, the companies add to the tax base. In practice, however, the companies pay only a small share of the cost they impose on a city. The result shows up at tax collection time, when homeowners wonder how their bills could ever have risen so high.

In Chatham County and Savannah over the last decade, taxes have risen so sharply that they are now considered the major local problem. As taxes have gone up, the people have tried to cut corners; within the last year, voters turned down a bond issue to pave county roads, and the County Commission refused to match Federal funds for a new mental health center. Countless other projects, particularly improvements in the school system, will have to endure another year of postponements and delays. Savannah's five-year delay in building a sewage treatment system presents the most dramatic example of the harm that tax shortages can do to a city's general public welfare.

Meanwhile, Savannah's taxpayers have practically been subsidizing the large industries. By most calculations, the largest landowner, Union Camp, shortchanges Chatham County by a $3–$4 million dollars every year, a lot of money in a county whose annual budget is $11 million. This money would be enough to solve many of the school problems, to build new roads and pave old ones, to pay for Savannah's sewage system over three or four years, or even to build a water treatment plant for Union Camp over two or three years.

Chatham County's bitter experience is far from unique; industrial abuse of local tax systems is more the American rule than the exception. The many-layered system that Chatham County industries, led by Union

Camp, have developed to guarantee their position is particularly ingenious, and offers a special chance to study the influence of corporate power on small-scale government.

The foundation of the industrial tax system, the "industrial zones," has by now taken on a smooth veneer of age and respectability. The genesis of the zones, however, was less respectable, and for many years the whole arrangement had the well-deserved smell of impropriety.

Although Savannah's industries now claim that life would be impossible without the zones, things went along quite nicely without them until 1948, when newly elected mayor, John G. Kennedy, found his city budget heavily in the red. Kennedy did what any city official would have done in the same predicament: he tried to expand the tax base. Looking past the city limits to Union Camp and further upstream to the other mills, none of whom paid a fair share for the city services they received, Kennedy decided that the city should expand its borders and annex the industries. Since Savannah was already providing municipal services, it would cost the city no more to annex the areas, but the plan looked very, very bad to the industries. Their city tax bill would jump from zero to many hundred thousand dollars. When Kennedy presented his plan to the state legislature, Chatham County's industries therefore did everything they could to fight it. Since Kennedy had already convinced most of the county representatives to support his plan, under the normal pleasant conventions of Georgia lawmaking, their endorsement would have insured automatic passage of the bill. But the industrial lobby was strong enough to kill the annexation bill in committee.

Having come so close to tragedy, the industries wasted no time in making sure it would not happen again. In 1949, Huguenin Thomas, chairman of the Chamber of Commerce City Limits Extension Committee, suggested that the county form several "industrial zones." With the unanimous and grateful support of Savannah's industries, the zones were amended to the state constitution; by 1950, the state legislature had passed the amendment and the voters of Chatham County had ratified it. The first industrial zones included Union Camp, the present site of American Cyanamid, and Hutchinson Island, in the middle of the Savannah. In 1956, a similar constitutional amendment added three more zones that neatly protected the remaining large industries, Savannah Sugar, Continental Can, and Southern Nitrogen.

The stated purpose of these zones was "to sustain a natural growth and . . . to encourage the progress of Savannah and Chatham County and to increase the prosperity of its people." In practice, only the prosperity of the industries increased; they now had a permanent tax shelter within the industrial zones. The most important provision of this legislation stated that the industries could never be annexed to the city; they would therefore never face the problem of paying city taxes. As a sop to the Savannah treasury, the industries would pay a small fire protection tax, amounting to 5 mills per dollar of calculated value, less than one-fifth of the 26-mill tax the industries would have had to pay as full-fledged taxpayers.*

Savannah is far from the only city in the country to give industrial tax breaks; however, most cities, mainly interested in attracting new industry offer tax advantages limited to the first few years of an industry's operation. After that, it is assumed that the companies will pay their fair share of the tax load. In cities similar to Savannah along the southeastern coast—Charleston, Jacksonville, St. Petersburg, and Mobile—industries can get cut-rate taxes, but only for their first five or ten years in town. Savannah is virtually alone in giving its industries a permanent free ride.

While the zones have "sustained a natural growth" by attracting a few minor industries, their most important effect has been to give a large financial present to industries that had come to the county several decades earlier. The industrial zones have a further bad effect on everyone who is not a stockholder of the companies involved. Although Union Camp, Cyanamid, and the others are outside the city limits, they affect the people of Savannah in many important ways. They pollute the air that Sa-

* The property tax system is quite complicated. To compute the tax, one first multiplies the appraised value of the property by a percentage, currently 40 per cent. Then, one applies the millage to the product; Union Camp, therefore, pays five mills tax for 40 per cent of every dollar of assessed property value.

vannahians breathe, they foul the water that runs past Savannah, and endanger the ground water supplies Savannah depends on. Since they are permanently free from Savannah's jurisdiction, the city is completely powerless to regulate their air and water pollution or their ground water use. The city's only recourse is the Chatham County Commission, which has historically been most sympathetic to the industrial cause.

It might be expected that the companies would be grateful for the windfall of the industrial zones. Instead, their attitude imples that Savannah owes them the zones, and much more as well. In 1966, when the city made a brief attempt to get the zone setup changed, industrial leaders reacted indignantly to the presumption that they should pay city taxes. This campaign has been the most recent attempt to repeal the industrial zone legislation. The administration of J. C. Lewis figured out just how badly the zones were hurting the city, and mayor *pro tempore* Ben Garfunkel openly asked that the zones be abolished to enable Savannah to annex the industries. In response to Garfunkel's proposal, Arthur Funk, a Savannah representative to the state legislature, held an open meeting to discuss the question. John Rousakis, then a county commissioner, said that industries normally looked for other things besides a permanent tax break when choosing a city—good school systems, adequate recreation, and efficient transportation, for example. Civic organizations and several politicians opposed the zones; labor organizations pointed out that two major employers, Grumman Aircraft and K-Mart, got along well without the crutch of industrial zones. Even the normally timid *Savannah News-Press* hinted that permanent tax exemptions might be a bad idea.

But no objection could withstand the industrial torrent. Representatives from Union Camp, Savannah Sugar, and the Savannah Port Authority painted a dark picture of Savannah's economic future if the zones were taken away. Convinced, Funk said that zone repeal could be considered dead unless Mayor Lewis formally asked him to do something more. Given Lewis' customary indecision, it was no great surprise that the campaign soon ended.

In interviews with our project members, Union Camp

officials repeatedly stressed that the zones were part of the city's "bargain." "It is a contract," plant manager James R. Lientz said.[1] "The community has an obligation to live with this agreement," the hard-nosed executive vice president, John E. Ray III, added. "We would react adversely to proposals to change it." [2] What this reasoning ignores is the historical fact that the zones were a gift not a "bargain" or "agreement." So far, this twisted reasoning has been enough to preserve the industries' favored cases.

Within the industrial zones, companies still pay a 29-mill county tax and a five-mill fire fee to the city of Savannah. Since those payments vary with the assessed value of each factory, the managers are naturally interested in keeping their assessed value as low as possible. With the help of county "laws," of dubious legality, the three or four largest companies bilk the other county taxpayers of several million dollars yearly.

The story of the current tax hoax begins in 1965, when Chatham County and Savannah were reorganizing their tax systems. With the advice of several consultants —the Hunnicutt tax appraisal firm, and Atlanta consultant Louis Hohenstein—county attorney John Sognier devised a new system for assessing "business personal property," which includes machines, furniture, fixtures, and other nonpermanent equipment. Under Georgia law, this property must be placed on the tax books at "fair market value." Chatham County's new law, however, had a different way of assessing the property. Businesses were told to:

> Attach schedule showing date of purchase, cost new or used. Depreciation shall be computed on a straight line method based on asset life as determined in the Internal Revenue Service procedure 62-21. Asset life of furniture and fixtures and machinery and equipment used in general business is ten years. A 10 per cent depreciation per year is therefore applicable, figured from the date of purchase off the new cost. Maximum depreciation allowable is seven years or 70 per cent.

The importance of this paragraph does not become clear until it is compared with section 92-5701 of the Georgia Code. All property—including business personal property—must be "returned for taxation at its fair market value." The law defines "fair market value" as "what the property and subjects would bring at cash sale when sold in the manner in which such property and subjects are usually sold."

This means that the assessed value of the property—and therefore, the taxes paid on it—should rise or fall with the market value of the property. For some goods, the market value may rise over time as the goods become scarce; other equipment, especially the large machines used in heavy industry, may retain their value over many years if kept in good working condition. Under Chatham County's peculiar laws, however, the value of all business machines falls by an inescapable 10 per cent every year until it hits the base of 30 per cent of original value.

Tax experts have unambiguously condemned the system of cost minus depreciation as a way of figuring out fair market value. Referring specifically to Chatham County's arrangement, former Savannah Finance Director, Herb O'Keefe said, "Cost and value are synonymous only at the point of exchange, and even then only if both buyer and seller are willing and knowledgeable. Depreciation has absolutely no relation whatsoever to value. There is no methodological way to arrive at value based on age and cost." [3]

In a letter to the former chairman of the Savannah-Chatham Joint Tax Board, financial consultant and tax expert from Maryland, Alex K. Hancock, had this to say about Chatham County's tax system:

> Cost less depreciation, the usual book value for fixed assets . . . obviously has little or no relationship to market value, so that its use for assessment purposes is of doubtful legality in many if not most cases. . . . In cases where the establishment of true market value of installed machinery and equipment is impossible or extremely difficult, replacement value might be considered, or, better still, value the plant as estate appraisers often do. Disregard the actual physical assets and value the plant, exclusive of real estate, on the basis of annual gross business. This is usually the most important factor to a purchaser and is therefore often the best indication of market value.[4]

When translated into dollars, the difference among the varying tax theories is stupendous. Members of our project asked officials from several paper companies to calculate the "value" of Union Camp's Savannah plant. Estimates of "fair market value"—that is, what it would cost to build a similar plant or to buy this plant—covered a wide range, between $375–550 million. One detailed breakdown offered this appraisal:

Paper mill—2,800 tons per day	$212,000,000
Bag plant	40,000,000
Box plant	20,000,000
Tall oil factory	40,000,000
Inventories	40,000,000
Unimproved real estate (30,000 acres in Chatham County)	70,000,000
Improvements	10,000,000
Total	*$432,000,000*

While the actual value may be closer to $400 million or even as high as $500 million, this estimated value is many times higher than the $80–$90 million values on which Union Camp has based its county taxes over the last several years. At its current assessment, the company pays about $1.4 million in county taxes. If its value were raised to even $300 million, the tax bill would jump to $5.1 million, supplying an additional $3.7 million in county revenues.

The depreciation system takes one extra ounce of blood for the other citizens of the county. Although Savannah's goal is to attract new industries, this tax loophole helps to drive them away. Instead of giving tax shelter to fledgling industries, this law subsidizes the older, established companies. By now, nearly all the equipment of Union Camp and Savannah Sugar has been reduced to 30 per cent of original value, and their taxes, based on these depreciated values, are extremely low. A new industry would pay much heavier taxes for at least its first seven years in Savannah.

County tax assessor G. Miner Peagler has an arsenal of unpersuasive defenses for the tax system, most of which stress that this system is the closest anyone can come to guessing fair market value. Even if examples like Union Camp did not make that contention patently ridiculous, the county would be left with a system that violates all state tax laws. Conveniently, the system does not force any business filing a tax return to break the law. At the bottom of each tax form is an oath attesting that the corporation has followed the county's tax rules: "I do solemnly swear or affirm that the above declarations are a full and correct statement *as shown on the books of account* of the taxpayer . . ." (Emphasis added.) Since most businesses carry the depreciated value on their "books of account," this form allows them to follow the county's regulations.

The oath, however, is in clear violation of the state law. Section 92-6216 of the Georgia Code says:

> The oath to be administered to all persons making returns of taxable property . . . *shall be as follows:* "I do solemnly swear that I have carefully read (or have heard read) and have duly considered the questions propounded in the foregoing tax lists, and that the value placed by me on the property returned, as shown by said list, *is the true market value thereof* . . ." (Emphasis added.)

Even if the county officials could not figure out themselves that their oath contradicts the state law, there have been more direct reminders. In response to a letter from Richard Heard, then chairman of the Chatham-Savannah Board of Tax Assessors, the state attorney general's office said flatly that the tax oath was illegal:

> Ga. Code 92-6216 [the prescribed tax oath] . . . recognizes no discretion in county officials to vary the law. This conclusion is buttressed by Ga. Code Ann. 92-6217 (1935). . . . Your oath requires the taxpayer to swear that he valued the property at its book value. Clearly book value and fair market value are not synonymous. . . . This deviation from the requirements of 92-6216 renders the oath presently given unauthorized.[5]

When Heard publicized this letter, county officials responded with their customary play-dumb approach that has so successfully obscured the tax system. "If we have the wrong form we may have to get another one," said Robert F. Lovett, chairman of the County Commission. "It doesn't seem to be such a big matter. It is up to our lawyers and the chief tax assessor to decide on the form."[6]

In addition to the industrial zones and the Chatham

County tax system, there is a third form of tax manipulation in the county. Less complicated than the other two and without their coating of pseudolegality, it consists of routine and large-scale underassessment of raw land. Since the corporations are often the large landholders, this tax bunco provides them one more subsidy. Chatham County is not, of course, the only part of the United States that has land-assessment problems, but in this, as in many of its other inequities, it demonstrates the problem in spectacular ways.

Peagler's office argues quite reasonably that it is impossible to keep track of all the plots in the whole county. True, the value of land rises and falls quickly, and an undermanned assessment office simply cannot keep up with the fluctuations in the entire county, but helpful guides do exist. The value of similar pieces of property offers some clues, for example; construction plans usually raise property values; and the purchase price gives the assessor a fairly good indication of what the "fair market value" of the property is.

The tax assessors of Chatham County have ignored these guideposts. They have conscientiously raised assessments on private homes, meanwhile leaving huge plots of land with assessments that would have seemed reasonable in the nineteenth century. Like the depreciated business tax, underassessment makes a serious dent in the county's tax income.

In June 1970, Chatham County tax records showed the assessments on property that had recently changed hands. (See opposite page.)

In each case, the buyer did not even have to bother making out a tax form; Peagler willingly carried forward the old values on the tax books. There might be an excuse for such an oversight if Peagler had not heard about the new high-price sales, but in each of these cases, Peagler had records of the sales on his tax cards. In each case, he ignored them and gave the owners another year's grace with the ridiculously low values. Families who bought a new house for ten or twenty times its assessed value might wonder how long they would get such favored treatment.

The master of this game is, predictably, the Union Camp Corporation. For several years, the company has

TABLE 11–1
Chatham County Tax Assessments

Property identification number	Owner	Date bought	Sale price	1970 tax value	Value as percentage of sale price
158-01-07	Crumpacker	2/12/70	$108,000	$15,000	14
015-45-09	Hewson (agent)	2/11/69	28,000	5,830	21
611-01-46	Skytest Inc.	1/ 7/70	150,000	1,170	1.3
611-01-45	Skytest Inc.	12/29/69	26,500	4,690	18
293-02-16	Friedman, Haslem. Weiner (agent)	10/13/69	390,000	38,950	10
290-01-01	"	10/10/69	880,000	24,720	3.7
289-01-01	"	10/10/69	402,000	43,390	11
159-03-11	Abercorn Trust	7/29/69	200,000	25,100	12.5
168-02-01	Chrysler	9/18/69	200,000	27,330	14

Source: Chatham County tax records, 1970.

owned more than 7,200 acres on Skidaway Island, a marshy region southeast of Savannah destined for the city's next suburb. Since the island was inaccessible except by ferry, most of the land remained unused. In 1967, the Georgia Parks Department offered to build a park on the island if the county would pay for a bridge to Skidaway. Later that year, county voters approved a $3.6 million bond issue for the bridge, making Union Camp's development plans look better and better. The situation brightened even more when the location of the bridge was announced. Instead of building it on the north end of the island, closest to the city and the state research institute on Skidaway, county planners put it at the south end. That meant that the access road to the research institute would run for nearly ten miles through Union Camp territory.

All this time, Union Camp's island holdings had been assessed at less than $20 per acre. They were still at that level in early 1969, when the state asked to buy 109 acres of high land for the park at whatever price an independent assessor would place on the land. The total appraisal was $212,500 for the 109 acres, about $2,000 per acre. "I know it's high," said State Parks Director John Gordon, "but what can you do?" [7]

Even after the sale to the state, Peagler's office continued to assess Union Camp's remaining Skidaway land at less than $20 per acre, about 1 per cent of what the state had to pay. County Administrator Joseph Lambright ridiculed the theory that the value of the land had risen because the county was building a bridge to the island. "What if the bridge never gets built because we run out of money or it falls down or something?" he asked. "Then what would the property be worth?" [8] The answer, of course, is that if one of those catastrophes happened, then the property value could be lowered again, to reflect the altered value of the land. Using Lambright's reasoning, homeowners could come to Peagler and say, "What if my house gets hit by lightning and burned up? What will it be worth then?"—and ask that it be assessed at the worth of a burned-up house.

By any reasonable theory of property value, however, the potential worth of each acre on Skidaway rose as soon as the county decided to build a bridge. That is why the state paid so high a price for the land; that is why Union Camp is already figuring out the best use for its remaining acres. As Union Camp told its stockholders in the 1969 Annual Report:

Our new subsidiary is now working with the Resource Development Department on the final evaluation of the company's 3300 acres on Skidaway Island. [Union Camp still owns over 7,000 acres on the island.] "Skidaway" is eight miles from downtown Savannah and a bridge-causeway connecting it to the mainland is scheduled for completion by the end of 1970. Preliminary land use planning and cost have been completed.[9]

If buyers and owners take the bridge into account when figuring the value of Skidaway acreage, so should the tax assessor. It is more likely that the land will never be fairly asssessed until it is split up irto small lots and sold to the public.

The annals of Savannah include another example of underassessment of valuable land. Franjo, Incorporated, a subsidiary of the Kerr-McGee Company, came to Savannah in the late sixties looking for a site for phosphate mines. In 1967, Franjo bought Cabbage Island and Little Tybee Island for a total price of $2.2 million, $1.6 million for Little Tybee and $.6 million for Cabbage. At the time, Little Tybee was on the tax books at $8,830 and Cabbage Island at $1,135. When the county tax office tried to raise the assessment on Cabbage Island to $260,000, Franjo filed suit to block the increase. Franjo argued that the islands should have the same assessment as the other coastal islands, regardless of their phosphate content, because a county ordinance forbade mining there. The company would not have bought the islands had it thought the ordinance would stick, but the argument held off the new assessment. In August 1970, Little Tybee was still assessed at $8,830, and Peagler said that he was "not aware" that the islands had been sold since 1955.[10]

Part of the reason for Chatham County's chronic tax problems is that the assessors are inexperienced, underpaid, and overworked. Before entering the world of taxes eight years ago, county assessor Peagler had been a used car salesman. His current salary of $12,000 is barely enough to lure him away from the used car business; it comes nowhere near what is needed to hire an experienced assessor. Peagler tries to squelch criticism by pointing out that he has had ten courses in tax appraisal at the University of Georgia; what he does not say is that each "course" lasted only three days.

Even if Peagler and his minute staff were well trained and enthusiastic, they could never keep up with all the day-to-day property changes in the county. This does not mean that Peagler is now doing the best he can; there is no reason why his office should not do routine reassessments once every year or two. And there is certainly no excuse for scandals like Skidaway. But criticism of the tax system is less properly aimed at Peagler than at the men who run him. As Peagler neatly pointed out in court in the summer of 1970, he is the "low man on the totem pole." [11] "I take my orders from the County Commission," he said on another occasion.[12] With that sentence, Peagler put his finger on the problem. Ideally a function as important as tax assessment should be protected from political pressure and private interests. Like most local governments, Chatham County makes no effort to provide this protection. Indeed, the tax assessment office has become another long arm of a county government which is largely the tool of private interests.

From their earliest days in Savannah, the large industries, led by Union Camp, realized the importance of getting a foothold in local government. Very soon their foothold became a strangle hold. During parts of the 1940's and 1950's, a crew of Union Bag cronies and political bosses, led by lawyer John Bouhan, had Chatham County politics tightly under their control. Several "reform" governments have come and gone since then, but the county government still bears clear marks of industrial influence.

In 1970, the chairman of the Chatham County Commission was Robert F. Lovett, vice president of the Citizens and Southern Bank. In the 35 years since the bank gave Union Bag the money to build a plant in Savannah, the two firms have been inseparable business allies. Union Camp president Alexander Calder used to serve on the bank's board of directors; when he was asked to leave because of poor attendance, Union Camp's Savannah manager, James Lientz, took his place. Another member of the Commission was Remer Y. Lane,* nephew of the bank's president, Mills B. Lane, Jr. Still another Commissioner, Pete Clifton, is an old business partner of Lovett's; Lovett is a director of Clifton's construction company, and they have been partners on several real estate ventures.

All in all, the Commissioners are a friendly little group. Even the token black member, the aging Reverend Scott Stell, is so palatable that he rarely disagrees seriously with the other Commissioners. The fraternity-like atmosphere of the weekly meetings gives the impression that the Commission is a benevolent, harmless group. But at least one Commissioner, William McNeal, exemplifies the blatant and dangerous industrial influence that permeates the Commission. As Commissioner in charge of finance, McNeal oversees the county's income and expense; as an executive of Union Camp, McNeal knows that his company pays the largest single share of any county expense. It does not take long to see the conflict of interest. Each budget recommendation McNeal makes means Union Camp dollars saved or spent, and his instructions to Peagler's office ("I take my orders from the County Commission") can save Union Camp literally millions of dollars.

It was no quirk or Act of God that planted a Union Camp official on the Commission. McNeal got his seat in 1965, when he replaced Tex Kelly, another Union Camp executive. McNeal was out of town when he was invited to join the Commission and, according to the local newspaper, "It could not be learned whether or not he will accept. *It is presumed that he will, however, because the firm has been consulted and has given consent.*" [13] (Emphasis added.)

When asked about his employees' vigorous political activity, Union Camp manager Lientz said that the company "encourages its employees to take an active part

* Lane was appointed rather than elected to the Commission in the spring of 1970, when John Rousakis resigned to begin his successful mayoralty campaign. Since less than half of the four-year term had expired when Lane was appointed, he had to run for his seat in the 1970 elections. He lost by a healthy margin to Robert McCorkle, a local baker who promised to represent "the people" rather than any unnamed special interests.

in their community."[14] This is an honorable attitude that finds practical and honorable expression in Joe Battle, a Union Camp electrician who is also a state legislator. When the company's managers and executives are involved in local politics, it is a different story. Most companies admit that their top officials cannot separate their personal interests from the company's; an executive has both a psychological and an economic stake in his company's success. At Continental Can, for example, company policy permits employees to become involved in politics, but executives may not run for office. Although the company allows McNeal to serve as finance director for the County Commission, it is unlikely that Union Camp thinks he can act as a free, impartial protector of the public interest. Union Camp's decision reflects either its disregard of a conflict of interest, or else its commitment to a damn-the-public attitude.

As long as the County Commission stands guard, opponents of the tax system realize that they have no chance of reforming it. So they have chosen the only two courses open to them: publicity and the courts. Leading the publicity battle has been Richard Heard, a Savannah businessman who has spent most of the last four years investigating and exposing the tax abuses. In his brief spell as chairman of the joint city-county board of tax assessors,* Heard used the office as a forum for attacks on the tax assessments. Since they cannot answer Heard's arguments, county officials have attacked Heard himself. On at least two occasions, County Administrator Joe Lambright has described Heard as "paranoid, senile, irrational and mentally deranged."[15]—terms that might better be applied to the tax system.

Now that Heard has severed his official connection

* After the 1965 rearrangement of the city and county tax systems, Savannah and Chatham County combined their tax assessing offices. As part of this new system, a six-member city-county board of tax assessors took office in September, 1967, with Heard as its chairman. Very shortly afterward, the county tax assessor's office—Peagler—claimed that it still had the power to set city and county assessments; the new tax board said that it should have that power. After a year and a half of arguing, Savannah voted to withdraw from the board, effective after the mandatory one-year waiting period. Since then there have been several legal challenges to the whole joint assessing arrangement, leaving most officials unclear about where they stand. For practical purposes, however, the city still uses the county assessments, and therefore suffers from the same assessment problems.

with the tax system, he has jumped into the legal battle as well, joining two Savannah lawyers—Ogden Doremus, the manager of several environmental suits in the area, and Aaron Kravitch, a pessimist in his seventies.

For the first legal attack, Doremus and Kravitch filed separate suits challenging the legislation that had set up the joint city-county tax assessment system. Superior Court Judge Edwin McWhorter, a man who believes in the old way of doing things in Savannah, turned down both suits, adding that since the city had already decided to withdraw from the agreement, the city-county tax system was out of business anyway.*

After that defeat, Doremus, Kravitch, and Heard attacked again, this time challenging the very heart of the county's tax system. In their suit, Doremus and Kravitch asked for an injunction to keep the county from sending its "tax digest" (the list of all taxable county property) to the state capital. Using the letter from the attorney general's office (see page 179), they argued that the system used for assessing "business personal property" was illegal.

The two-day trial was one of those affairs that make prospects for American justice look bleak.

Midway through the court proceedings, Judge McWhorter leaned down and said, "I'm going to rule that the digest is going to Atlanta." When Kravitch asked if this meant he should simply give up on the spot, the judge replied, "I just indicated how I'm going to rule. If I announce my verdict now, you'll say I had my mind already made up." [17] To no one's surprise, McWhorter ruled nine days later that the digest would go to Atlanta. The trial, however, was not a complete loss, since McWhorter ordered the county to "strictly comply" with state law in making up next year's digest. While he said nothing specific about the tax form, his ruling may provide the groundwork for future legal action.

From a public relations point of view, the trial was a huge success. Using the examples Heard had discovered

* After McWhorter issued his ruling, the county appointed its own three-man board of tax assessors, consisting of Peagler and his two assistants, whose job was to review Peagler's assessments. The move was so blatant that even Savannah Mayor J. Curtis Lewis said that the arrangement put tax assessment "right under the thumb of county authority."[16]

of grotesque underassessments (Table 11–1), the lawyers forced Peagler to admit that all the figures were correct. In the week between the end of the trial and the day the judge released his decision, Peagler hurriedly raised the assessments on many pieces of property, including most of those mentioned at the trial. The force of publicity was even enough to make him raise the assessment of Union Camp's Skidaway land—from about $20 to more than $400 per acre.

County Commissioner and Union Camp executive Billy McNeal put the final touch on the whole affair. Posing as a tireless crusader who had once more helped the public interest, McNeal announced the increased assessments that would increase the county tax digest by $2.5 million to bring in an extra $100,000 in revenue. This money, he proudly announced, would go to the public schools.[18]

If anyone could convince McNeal of the benefits of certain other increases in the county tax base—the multimillion dollar increase that would come from fair business assessments, for example, or the somewhat smaller increase from realistic land assessments—Chatham County might stand a chance of equalizing the tax burden. Until that unlikely moment, however, the companies will continue to profit and the homeowners will continue to pay.

12

Bringing Down the Law

You can do anything you want, you can be anything you want to be, just as long as you don't hurt nobody. And remember, kids, I am your friend.

Hair

"Sic utere tuo ut alienum non laedas," said an English judge in *Fletcher v. Rylands* in the nineteenth century, and the Golden Rule became part of the common law pertaining to water rights: use your own property so as not to hurt that of another. Over the years, the rule acquired the expected trappings of judicial construction and reduction, to make it appear more complicated than it really was and to keep the Crown's barristers busy. But in the English common law, it retained much of its common sense fairness.

The New World, however, had an industrial revolution to get under way. In the face of pressing industrial demands, some judges not only wavered in applying the Golden Rule of water rights but actually doubted its validity, as a Pennsylvania farmer found out in 1886.

J. Gardner Sanderson and his wife Eliza owned a farm on top of some of the richest coal veins in the nation. When a coal company moved in nearby, the stream that ran through Sanderson's farm quickly became contaminated. The cows would not drink the water, and the crops did not do well, so the Sandersons sued the Pennsylvania Coal Company. The presiding judge was not impressed by their case. In his opinion, Judge Clark told the Sandersons:

> The plaintiff's grievance is for a mere personal inconvenience; and we are of opinion that mere private personal

inconveniences, arising in this way and under such circumstances, must yield to the necessities of a great public industry, which, although in the hands of a private corporation, subserves a great public interest.[1]

In a much quoted statement, he continued: "To encourage the development of the great natural resources of a country trifling inconveniences to particular persons must sometimes give way to the necessities of a great community." [2]

There is hardly a student essay or law review article on water rights that does not begin by criticizing *Sanderson.* In its own way, however, the opinion is economically and legally sophisticated. The judge gave the real reasons for his decision—the coal mining potential of the region, the proper allocation of natural resources, the technical problems involved in stopping the pollution, and the logical expectations of the parties. The Sandersons, he reasoned, might have been expected to know that local streams would be susceptible to mine waste pollution.

Other courts of the same generation analyzed water pollution problems differently. Future generations of environmentalists will someday recognize that the Union Camp Corporation was the source of one of the truly great legacies to the cause of environmental protection. The company stayed in New York long enough to lose a water pollution case; in doing so, it let a smart judge write one of those timeless, resonant opinions, which manages to keep its tone through the decades and then ring out when society really starts to need it.

Mr. Whalen, the plaintiff in this case, was a New York state farmer whose 255-acre farm was downstream from a $1 million paper mill. Like many of its successors, this Union Bag mill discharged "large quantities of a liquid effluent containing sulphurous acid, lime, sulphur, and waste materials consisting of pulpwood, sawdust, slivers, knots, gums, resins, and fiber" into the water.

The trial court found in favor of Mr. Whalen and would have granted him an injunction against Union Bag, but the Appellate Division reversed on the issue of damages. Its suggested solution was to let the mill keep polluting but pay Mr. Whalen $100 annually for damages. When the case came before the Court of Appeals, its decision upheld the trial court.

> Although the damage to the plaintiff may be slight as compared with the defendant's expense of abating the condition, that is not a good reason for refusing an injunction. Neither courts of equity nor law can be guided by such a rule, for if followed to its logical conclusion it would deprive the poor litigant of his little property by giving it to those already rich.[3]

Two decades later, Union Bag moved to Savannah, where "mere private personal inconvenience" still yields "to the necessities of a great public industry."

The two cases of *Sanderson* and *Whalen* are often discussed in contrast with each other; but the lesson that should be drawn is not that one judge saw the dangers of pollution and the other did not, for both show how cases may be won on common law principles in modern courts.

Many legal experts casually dismiss the usefulness of private suits in the battle against water pollution. Instead they discuss new constitutional rights to a clean environment, or possible legislative remedies. This despair about private action is probably no longer justified; both *Sanderson* and *Whalen* contain the seeds of legal theories that may increase the chances of victory for the private citizen in the courts.

In *Sanderson,* the court considered the issue of *expectations,* and ruled against the farmer. Today, the expectations have changed; judges—who, like other people, read the newspapers and watch ecology specials on TV and notice, at last, that at least one Justice of the Supreme Court takes hikes along the C&O barge canal every year—cannot remain blind to them. They will not shut down a huge factory without warning; but the judges know *that the factories know* they are supposed to be making some progress. With those new expectations, the courts can shape their decision to make the factories move somewhat faster toward control of their environmental pollution.

In *Sanderson,* the judge also considered the "necessity" for the pollution and the technical difficulty of controlling it. Today, as pollution control systems continue their rapid development, fewer attacks on the environment can reasonably be called industrial "necessities." In making this point before a court, a citizen will get a better hearing if he comes prepared with expert testimony about the practical alternatives to continued pollution.

As the concept of internalized costs (the theory that industries must pay for the damage they inflict on the air and water) becomes more widely accepted, courts will begin to view pollution control demands on industry as "reasonable." Concern over our polluted environment will mount as more and better evidence becomes available to justify the concern; courts will realize that the "great public interest" which must be served is the preservation of our natural environment, not unlimited industrial expansion which the judge in *Sanderson* had in mind.

The implications of the *Whalen* decision are infinite. Courts are now more receptive to "equal protection" arguments; any situation that makes wealth or capital investment a condition for enjoying fundamental liberties will undergo increasingly close scrutiny.

There is a mill town in Virginia, nestled in a windless valley where industrial air pollution is so bad that house paint corrodes from mere contact with the atmosphere. The industry responds by painting the houses every few years. If exposure to the smoke peels off paint, there can be little doubt about what is happening to the lungs of these house owners. A situation like this, in which basic rights to health and safety are traded for small payoffs, is particularly vulnerable to attack by the *Whalen* view.

Our society has long understood that some values are so important, so fundamental to the goals and purposes of our lives, that any attempt to define them in economic terms is debasing and invalid. No court would allow a little town to bar a religious order if it paid the preacher a little money for each Sunday he was not allowed to preach. Neither could a town ban a newspaper as long as it paid the ousted printer. Values like freedom of speech and the right to privacy are so dear to us that they may not be quantified. We live to enjoy their existence.

As the *Whalen* court recognized in 1913, questions of environmental rights are also too important to be reckoned in purely economic terms. The important issue is that part of the *quality* of an individual's life is being altered against his will. The person's income, the value of his property, and his economic contribution to the community all fade in importance when compared to the loss of one of his important rights. Various legal theories have evolved to express the concept of a fundamental right to a nondegraded environment. In part, the issue may be seen as a facet of the right to privacy. For example, Union Camp's sulphur dioxide in Savannah's backyards and bedrooms and lungs can be seen as an invasion of the townspeople's privacy—a right gaining increasing legal protection in our crowded times.[4]

Another constitutional approach is suggested by the Ninth Amendment, which says in part that "the enumeration in the Constitution, of certain rights, shall not be construed to deny or disparage others retained by the people." The most obvious interpretation is that there are other liberties that deserve the same protection as those mentioned in the Bill of Rights. Certainly enjoyment of clean, safe air and water and the right to live in an uncorrupted environment can be included in these rights.[5]

A final approach citizens may use against polluters comes from a re-examination of the principles of eminent domain—the power to condemn property and buy it from the owner without his permission. When a citizen loses a nuisance suit, the decision can be seen as amounting to the unlawful taking of property without just compensation. When decided in favor of the polluter, the decision can be interpreted as taking property without due process of law. The right of eminent domain is carefully limited to Federal and state governments only. When the court ruled against the Sandersons in 1886, it was, in effect, condemning their land for the benefit of a private user. Even if the polluter is forced to pay damages, the result is still the condemnation of one person's land for the benefit of another private interest, an interest which has no legal power of eminent domain.

This analysis of nuisance suits may seem ridiculous to tradition-bound practitioners and law professors who know that the courts have always decided nuisance cases without fretting over unjust use of eminent domain. But as our knowledge of land use becomes more sophisticated, and as the complex urban interactions among land users require more regulation, the courts will necessarily recognize that there are many ways land can be "taken" from its owners without affecting the formal title to the land. Destruction of the air or water that surrounds a piece of land may soon be considered "taking" the land from its owner.

In a vigorous dissent in a recent New York Court of Appeals case, the judge discussed the question of private condemnation. After the majority of the court decided that the polluter should pay damages rather than halt pollution, the judge dissented for two sound reasons. First, he said, once the polluter makes a payment for permanent damages, he has no further incentive to eliminate the problem. Further, the majority opinion was, in effect, licensing a continuing wrong. He called this a kind of "inverse condemnation" which "may not be invoked by a private person or corporation for private gain or advantage." [6]

The foregoing theories, predicated on the Constitution, can only be used against government actions, or in situations in which the state is responsible for the violation. The legal arguments by which these theories can eventually be turned against private polluters are too technical to discuss here. The purpose of exploring these theories even briefly is not to outline a brief for the private litigant but rather to alert citizens to the legal frontiers on which these theories are evolving.

Citizens preparing private actions should study state and Federal standards for air and water pollution. As these laws become more specific and stringent, they may be used as illustrations of "reasonable" demands upon a polluter. Private litigants should also consider asking courts to shape their rulings to conform to state or Federal pollution abatement plans. The ruling may make no immediate change in the pollution, but it can add the threat of contempt of court penalties to the usually weak provisions for enforcing abatement schedules.[7]

The law relating to environmental quality control is changing rapidly, and constantly growing more complex. Any individual or citizens group with an environmental grievance should consult expert legal advice before rejecting litigation. Some of the traditional barriers to private suits are dropping away in ways and areas that only the up-to-date specialist will be familiar with. Probably the largest barrier to citizen legal action is not inadequate laws so much as inadequate legal resources. The problems of finding an interested, competent lawyer and paying for his time are serious enough. Beyond that, litigants face the further expensive and uncertain tasks of proving a legal "harm," demonstrating a danger to life and health, showing that the pollution actually exceeds legal limits, finding the exact sources of the pollution, and considering the technically feasible control systems. The practical effect of these obstacles is to tip the legal balance heavily in favor of the large corporate polluters who can afford both the legal help and the technical "expertise" they need to defend themselves in court. The longer the case drags on, the greater their advantage becomes over citizen groups with limited legal budgets.

The fiscal magnitude of the problem was shown clearly in one of the environmentalists' first great court stands: *Scenic Hudson Preservation Conference v. Federal Power Commission* [354 F.2d 608 (2d Cir. 1965) cert. denied, 384 US 941 (1966)]. The Preservation Conference was eventually successful in its campaign to block a large hydroelectric project which would have destroyed the natural and ecological environment of New York State's Storm King Mountain. But by the time the case reached its second rehearing, the conservationists had already spent $250,000. It was not clear how much longer they could have held out, and it is certain that most nonprofit conservation groups would have had to drop out, impoverished, much earlier.

Statutory Law

One of the reasons we chose to study Savannah was the outstanding example it offered of how the government fights pollution. Officials in Washington and the local members of county government have had their say; the Federal Water Quality Administration, the United States

Coast Guard and Army Corps of Engineers, the Georgia Water Quality Administration, and the fact-finding committees of the Chatham County Grand Jury have all taken official note of the river's pollution.

By seeing how efforts at pollution control had succeeded and why they had misfired, we hoped to understand some of the obstacles to effective pollution control. At the start, we had several hunches about the results; the Federal government, we thought, would certainly be the brightest spot in the grim landscape. In 1965 and again in 1969, the Federal interstate enforcement conference had come to Savannah, interrogated the major polluters of the region, listened to their evidence, and had left town with ominous warnings about "deadlines" and "enforcement schedules." By comparing these dramatic efforts with what we expected to be the weak flailings of a captive state government, we hoped to understand the difference between successful government action and futility.

There was a comparison to be made, but not in the way we had anticipated. On one hand, we found Federal agencies making the least of already flimsy laws; on the other, we saw the Georgia bureaucrats—a group as potentially vulnerable to local political pressure as any in the country—straining at the limits of their laws, stretching and innovating until they won victories that Federal agents would hardly dare attempt. Given the normal priorities of Southern state governments, it would have been easy for the Georgia Water Quality Control Board to become a clique of industrial boosters. The Water Board is largely the creation of Governor Carl Sanders, who lost the 1970 elections mainly because the voters felt he was too friendly with large industrial interests; and it has the bad example of Georgia's ineffectual and overly influenced Mines and Mining Department to follow. Nevertheless, the principled and dedicated men of the Water Board and their director Rock Howard have resisted. Over the last five years, they have demonstrated one of the ageless lessons of governments: while laws make a difference and bad laws can lead to tyranny or corruption, the integrity of the men who execute the laws can often make more difference than the laws themselves.

The root of the Federal failure lies in its uncertain pollution control laws. The newest, the National Environmental Policy Act of 1970, has not yet shown its effect; an old and often overlooked law, the Refuse Act of 1899, has recently been called into new and unusual forms of service. Until one of these acts steers Federal policy in a new direction, however, the base for most Federal action will remain Section 10 of the Federal Water Pollution Control Act.

Section 10 is sometimes murky and ambiguous, but its application goes far toward explaining the simple Federal philosophy about curbing river pollution. Its most important provision is the creation of Federal "enforcement conferences." These nationwide conferences are theoretically the first part in a three-step progression toward genuine enforcement. When the Federal government, acting on complaints from local groups or on its own initiative, decides that a particular river or lake deserves special scrutiny, a formal conference is called, and representatives from the state water agencies join Federal representatives as presiding "conferees."

To discover firsthand the problems of cleaning the water, the conferees "invite" industrial and municipal representatives. The invitation is not a subpoena and cannot force a reluctant factory manager to appear, but Federal conferees make it clear that their hearts may be softened by industrial cooperation. At the end of Savannah's second enforcement conference, in October 1969, Murray Stein, who, as Assistant Commissioner for Enforcement of the Federal Water Pollution Control Administration has been involved in nearly all the enforcement conferences, stated:

> I think the cities and the industries that we have heard today have presented as always their situation and their cases with candor. If other cities and other industries don't avail themselves of this opportunity, and we don't have the full record, I would hope they would bear in mind when they raise the question of why they might have been selected in some future cases when the industries that came forward and participated here were not.[8]

The City of Savannah, Union Camp, and Continental Can were at the conference; American Cyanamid was not.

Once the talking is over, the conferees draw up a list of remedial recommendations that they leave with the state water agency to enforce. (In Savannah, this agency is the Georgia Water Quality Control Board.) The industries and cities are given a minimum of six months in which to carry out the suggestions.

If, as frequently happens, six months pass and the changes do not come, the Federal government may take the second step by calling a public hearing before a board of Federal and state agents. The board reviews the evidence once again, decides on new recommendations, and tells the polluters what they must do. There follows another grace period of at least six months before the industries or cities again face a "deadline." When that deadline comes, a polluter who has ignored the Federal orders may feel the bite of Federal power. The Secretary of the Interior may ask the United States Attorney General to file court action.

The process is complicated and time-consuming. Including the time required for conferences, hearings, and tedious court action, the absolute minimum required to curb even the most flagrant offenses is likely to be a year and a half. At each step, there is a serious danger that enforcement will disappear in the sodden channels of bureaucracy. Already, there are proposals before Congress to reform the system—mainly by abbreviating the mandatory waiting periods and combining the conference and hearing stages into one preliminary step.

These theoretical criticisms, however, do not explain the actual workings of the cumbersome Federal enforcement system nor the virtual absence of significant Federal action. In spite of the more than 30 enforcement conferences held so far, only once—did the government decide to take the second step of holding a public hearing—in 1960, the city of St. Joseph, Missouri, was called to account for its sluggish sewage program. There have been no repetitions of public hearings and, needless to say, the Federal government has never filed a suit against the polluters who continue to degrade our waters. The problem does not lie entirely with the law, although it certainly needs to be strengthened; the men who refuse to use the tools the law has given them are also culpable.

Perhaps to make up for their lack of more stringent

measures, Federal agents have turned with wild enthusiasm to the gentlest device: the increasingly popular enforcement conference. The Colorado River has had six conferences so far; Lake Erie has had four; and the Hudson and Potomac Rivers have each watched as on three separate occasions officials deliberated their fate. The history of the conferences on the Potomac shows how proceedings can drag on interminably.

The first conference was back in the days of Sputnik and Eisenhower, in August, 1957. Acting with unaccustomed vigor, in February, 1958, the Federal conferees called another meeting—not a public hearing to see how the orders of the first conference had been carried out, but a *second* enforcement conference. Eleven years passed. Then, in May, 1969, the government sprung into action once more. Instead of a public hearing, instead of lawsuits, there was a *third* enforcement conference, which one official tactfully labeled "session 3" of the 1957 conference. The 1960 St. Joseph, Missouri, hearing was an exception; in the other conference cities the inconclusive pattern is the same—if things get bad enough, there will be a second conference. If they stay bad, perhaps a third or fourth session, but not much more.

It would be wrong to dismiss the conferences as totally ineffective smoke screens. Aside from the criticism that there should have been other action as well, the conferences have had at least limited success in cajoling or bullying some cities and factories into cleaning their effluent. Savannah's conferences are a good example; while few of the industries met the timetable set in 1965, most began some restrained progress toward the goal. It is unlikely that Union Camp would have built its clarifier or that the city of Savannah would have even mouthed concern about a sewage system if the 1965 and 1969 conferences had not goaded them along. David Zwick, who has been studying the Federal Water Quality Administration, had this to say in hearings before a Senate committee in the summer of 1970:

> Persons familiar with the history of the Federal water pollution control program thus far are virtually unanimous in their agreement that enforcement proceedings initiated by the Federal government have been directly or indirectly re-

sponsible for most of the tangible progress that has been made against water pollution to date.[9]

This is damning with very faint praise; the "tangible progress that has been made against water pollution to date" is a distressingly small measure of achievement.

The men of the Federal Water Quality Administration are not corrupt men, nor are they eager to abuse the law or see their rivers killed. They are bureaucrats, who have learned which requests will provoke cries of pain from businessmen, which concessions will make conservation lobbyists suspicious. Walking a tightrope among the various interest groups, they give in most often to the side that pushes hardest; the history of enforcement conferences shows that the strongest shoves always come from industry. The relationship between the Federal government and industry has an "ecological balance" all its own. When upset, it yields an earthquake, as the wounded protests following Walter Hickel's stern action against oil companies with leaking wells showed.

The exchange between Murray Stein, head Federal conferee, and Senator Muskie before a Senate committee illustrates this business-political aspect of environmental policy-making:

SENATOR MUSKIE: Now, with respect to the decision-making, what factors must you submit to justify an enforcement action?

MR. STEIN: Well, I think the factors are: one, the situation of pollution; and secondly, what we would determine would be the reaction of the State water pollution control officials. . . .

MUSKIE: So you really supply them with two sets of facts—one of the merits of the case, and two, on the political climate?

STEIN: Yes—in the broad sense—yes sir.[10]

If the Federal government is so vulnerable to political pressures, it is easy to imagine how much more intense the pressure can be on state and local officials. As the story of towns like Savannah and St. Mary's illustrates, the closer a government gets to an industry, the more deference it must show. An industry's threat to pick up its payroll and leave weighs more heavily on a local mayor or state governor than on the Secretary of the Interior.

Against this background, the actions of the Georgia Water Quality Control Board are all the more exceptional. Before our project went to Savannah in the summer of 1970, our only introduction to the Board and its director was a blast Howard fired after Ralph Nader first announced the project:

> I would suggest that if Mr. Nader's interest is honest and serious and if it goes beyond the exhibitionist and publicity seeking, he need stray no further than his own Washington, D.C., to find a much more critical pollution clean-up job. I'm referring to the sewer called the Potomac. On the other hand, if he'd like to organize some volunteers or volunteer himself to climb in and out of some of our manholes and outfall sewers and help us collect some samples or measure flows, we'd be glad to direct such activities after a brief training course.

Shades of the civil rights movement: warnings against "outside agitators" who abandon their own problems to come make fun of the South. We therefore expected to find a water board proud and jealous of its power, secretive and reluctant to share its secrets with outsiders. We were wrong.

Instead we found a group of men that could serve as a model for other administrators. Proud men, yes; but theirs was a pride with reason. Howard was jealous, too, understandably irritated with the outsider who captured headlines with one announcement, while *he* had spent five years on the cause. Howard was impatient as well and very likely scornful of the instant ecologists descending on him. While these could easily be the traits of a petty bureaucrat trying to anchor an insecure position, in Howard, they were reflections of the uncompromising personal morality that he has retained as director of the Board.

Howard is a curious figure who embodies intangible qualities like perseverance and honesty, dedication and energy. He is a mixture of down-country roughness and urban sophistication. He is moving quickly toward retirement age, but he still has the vigor and caustic good humor of a man 30 years younger. Howard has mastered the different poses necessary for the arenas in which he must perform; before a Georgia audience he is a master of cracker language; before a legislative committee, he is an articulate, urbane spokesman for environmental protection. Howard's dislike for legislative appearances, however, is reflected in his characteristic uncompromisingly blunt speech.

The Georgia Water Board is an equally uncommon bureaucracy in which each staff member feels a personal commitment; in which the hours are as long as the job requires. It is an agency that takes pride in its victories and regrets its defeats. The obstacles the Board faces are formidable: a lackluster law to work with, and a shortsighted state legislature that provides little support and less money. The Board's impressive achievement has been to milk every last bit of power from the law it was given to administer, and to use an inventive array of informal tactics to plug gaps in the law. One of the Act's clauses, for example, empowers the Water Board to set water quality standards for different categories of streams. That is obviously an essential power, but it is relatively ineffective without a complementary one: the power to set specific effluent limits for each of the pipes that dumps into a stream. Lacking any direct authority to set effluent standards, the Water Board simply assumed the authority.

Much of the Water Board's impact comes from its sheer assertion of its presence in situations where a meeker body might never intrude. When new industries get ready to move to Georgia, Howard makes it clear from the start that the Water Board will be paying close attention. The Interstate Paper mill at Riceboro, which would have been a catastrophe had the Board not insisted on effluent standards of unprecedented strictness, is just one example of the Board's policy toward industrial development. With existing offenders, too, the Board makes its presence felt by tirelessly exerting constant pressure on both city and industrial polluters. Following Savannah's two enforcement conferences, hardly a month passed in which Savannah's city manager did not get a prodding letter from Howard; at the same time, Union Camp, too, was building a file of Howard's recommendations and orders. When the situation justified stronger words, Howard was always ready to speak them. When Savannah slumbered over its sewer plans,

Howard provoked the city to action by threatening court action. When Union Camp tried glibly to explain that its clarifier was not working properly, Howard replied with his standard "We are very disappointed . . ." letter. While this constant attention has obviously not built a sewer or saved the river from industrial filth, whatever progress there has been may be largely attributed to the Water Board's diligence. When a manager or mayor—in Savannah or in any other Georgia city—knows that he can expect words of reprimand and the threat of harsher action, he is not likely to ignore the Board's suggestions. Like the stockholders or the voters, the Water Board becomes a pressure group that must be appeased.

The relative success of the Board's informal persuasion is also important for another reason: Howard and his staff must realize that if negotiation failed and they had to rely on their raw statutory powers, they would be on much weaker ground. The Board's ultimate power is to take the action it threatened in Savannah—to turn the case over to the courts. While this sounds tough and effective, it is in practice the least successful way to clean the river. Court action can come only at the end of a long, slow process. First the Board must issue an order for a certain polluter to abate his pollution. Even before the order can be issued, the Board must give the polluter technical help and allow him reasonable time to solve the problem. After the order, the polluter can ask for a hearing, which also involves a mandatory waiting period. If the hearing upholds the order, the polluter can appeal to the courts where he is given a *de novo* hearing, in which the issues are thrashed out again and all the original arguments are reconsidered.

Because of the huge practical problems involved, it is no criticism to point out that in the Board's five-year history it has carried only two cases in court. Legal action is both slow and costly, and the Board has neither time nor money to spare. During fiscal year 1969, for example, the Board's operating funds were only $526,269; in fiscal 1970 they were about $600,000. Avoiding courtroom time and expense leaves Howard with men and money to use out of court; there he can use them very well. Interstate Paper, for example, complied without any hearings or suits. If Howard's staff had been tied up in litigation when Interstate was drafting plans, the mill might well have escaped his pressures.

Even outside his official function, Howard has applied consistent pressure for sane use of the state's waters. The victory that gives him most satisfaction was won in an unofficial skirmish, by which the Kerr-McGee Corporation was kept out of Savannah's finest marsh land. Kerr-McGee had planned to mine phosphates—which already glutted the market—from the marsh lands. To do that, it coolly proposed to strip off the top few feet of marsh and soil from most of the estuarine area around Savannah. The result would have been total destruction of the vital marsh life cycle. Despite the enthusiasm of Governor Lester Maddox, a concerted effort by naturalists, biologists, and anxious citizens thwarted the plan, with the help of Howard's timely intervention:

It all changed on May 17, 1968—when R. S. "Rock" Howard, Jr. got a late afternoon call from a friend in the State Game and Fish Commission advising him that the State Mineral Leasing Commission, inactive for years, was meeting to consider advertising for bids on a large lease of off-shore land to the Oklahoma-based firm of Kerr-McGee Corporation for the mining of phosphates.

Howard obtained permission from Governor Lester Maddox's executive secretary to sit in on the meeting. When he'd taken a seat he looked up to hear Charles Gowen, an Atlanta attorney representing the corporation, tell the commission, "We'll use that [ten feet of material overlaying the phosphate deposit] to fill up the marshes."

"I jumped about ten feet in the air," he recalled.

He blasted the proposal to lease 25,000 acres of marsh. Lacking specific facts, he warned the commission of general dangers of dredging and filling the marshes. . . .

Howard urged that the commission delay any action until public hearings could be conducted. The commission agreed.

"That was the turning point," Howard said, "when the governor had to have public hearings before any decisions were made about the lease. If we hadn't been there it would have eased through." [11]

The Refuse Act

Beyond the inclusion of certain minimal powers of investigation and enforcement, such as those absent from the Georgia air law, the formal structure of an environmental protection law loses its importance in the face of how the law is administered. The critical questions then become what kind of men are being appointed to responsible positions, what staff and appropriations they are allotted, and what kind of support they receive from elected officials and the public.

There is one exception to this general scheme; when the law allows for citizen actions, by granting them standing in court, or allowing them to use agency data, for example—there will be some protection of the environment regardless of the propensities of the administrators. The outstanding example of a law that, by allowing citizen actions, can be an important tool for environmental quality control is the Refuse Act of 1899 (33 U. S. Code 407).

In its provisions outlawing pollution, the Act says, "It shall not be lawful to . . . discharge . . . any refuse matter of any kind or description whatever. . . ." The sole exemption is refuse "flowing from streets and sewers and passing therefrom in a liquid state," which courts have interpreted as municipal sewage. For those who violate the Act, the penalty may be a misdemeanor conviction and a fine of between $500 and $2,500, or a prison term of between 30 days and one year. One of the Act's most significant clauses says that anyone who gives "information which shall lead to conviction" is entitled to half the fine imposed on the violator.

Environmentalists thought this provision especially important because it could give citizens an unusually strong position in court. The Supreme Court has ruled that when a law allows citizens to collect a "bounty" for reporting violations, then they may act in the name of the government and file suit against the violator if the government does not prosecute. Generally it is impossible to file a suit in which a private citizen acts against a polluter for creating a general public nuisance; the government does not want its citizens to act as private attorneys general. Unless a citizen can prove that he has some special interest in stopping a public nuisance, the courts usually deny him the legal standing necessary to file suit against the nuisance-maker. In some cases, the courts have ruled that just because a citizen lives closest to the source of the nuisance, or because he performs activities which are affected by the nuisance, he still may not have legal standing to file suit. The decisions in these cases conflict, of course, but the problem of legal standing has always been a serious barrier to private legal actions.

This "bounty" provision of the Refuse Act provides one way to achieve legal standing. Under similar provisions, the possible right to bounty has given the citizen enough special interest in the case to afford him standing before the court. A number of suits have been filed across the county against polluters by private citizens using the Refuse Act. They argued that if a citizen reports a possible violation to the government, and the government does not then prosecute, the citizen may file a *qui tam* suit—an action in the name of the government. This form of suit has its roots in ancient common law and has been specifically authorized by the United States Government since its inception.[12]

Modern courts have not accepted the theory so readily, however. Four recent federal cases, including one filed by Congressman Henry Reuss, have held that the bounty provision of the Refuse Act does not give an individual the right to maintain a *qui tam* action after the government fails to prosecute. Though more cases are expected to be filed under the Act by private citizens, and the cases referred to will undoubtedly be appealed, the decisions are a severe limitation to the effectiveness of the strongest anti-pollution law on the books.

For several decades, the Refuse Act has been the standard statutory authority for prosecuting both ships and industries that fouled the waters. Through U.S. Attorneys, agencies like the U.S. Coast Guard relied upon the Refuse Act for authority to prosecute oil spills.

It was often argued that the Act had as its single, narrow purpose to keep the water clear for navigation. In 1960, the Supreme Court specifically rejected that interpretation. Writing with his characteristic common sense vision, Mr. Justice Douglas made it clear that the Act could protect more than a river's navigational function: "We read the 1899 Act charitably in light of the purpose to be served. The philosophy of the statement of Mr. Justice Holmes that 'A river is more than an amenity, it is a treasure' forbids a narrow, cramped reading. . . ." [13]

So, a decade ago, Justice Douglas proved what will always be true, in the law as elsewhere: that when it comes to a question of whether or not something gets done, the attitudes and concerns of the people involved are far more important than the formal structure of laws. If responsible government officials had wanted to use the Refuse Act during its long dormancy, they could have, before this decision and especially after it. As the Act has become a more common part of public knowledge, government agencies must now justify their refusal to use it against major polluters. The confused rush of the Departments of Justice, Interior, and the Army (whose Corps of Engineers may issue permits under the Act) to explain the Act back into a state of archeological quaintness offers an insightful study of what can go wrong with abstract organizations and the swamp-footed men who run them. Like sheriffs in a Western movie, living in a town dominated by the ferocious bad guys, these enforcers do not know what to do when they are suddenly handed the cold goods on a modern Black Bart. They shuttle the information along through endless and circular paths of organizational charts, crying out that direct, forceful action is not the way things are supposed to be.

Even discovering what decision the enforcers have come to can be a task in itself. On June 15, 1970, the Department of Justice sent to all its U.S. Attorneys a memorandum entitled "Guidelines for Litigation Under the Refuse Act (33 USC 407)," which was supposed to explain where the Justice Department's responsibility ended and Interior's began in enforcing the Act. In its most important section, the memo outlined several categories of cases which local U.S. Attorneys could not bring without first getting approval from the Justice Department.

Several weeks afterwards, members of our project asked the assistant U.S. Attorney in Savannah for a copy of the memo. Although the memo had been widely and thoroughly reported in the press (though not, admittedly, the Savannah press), the attorney was not convinced that this was a matter of public information. "You have to understand these *documents,*" he said. He called the memo a "policy statement," not a matter of national security, of course, "but a matter of confidence between our office and *Washington*—not something we'd like a defendant to get hold of—you understand."

The attorney called his superior, long distance, and found to his relief that his caution was vindicated. At that point, we were stymied, for we knew that he could not go over his superior's head and call Washington. A few minutes later, when we returned to our office and called the Justice Department in Washington, the secretary who answered sent us a copy of the memorandum.

When the memo finally arrived, it was itself an abstract construction, unconnected to well-established court interpretations or the statute. The jargon touched on reality only glancingly, only as reality fit departmental dreams. These are dreams in which organizational charts and categories become more important than the goals, long forgotten, for which they were first created: dreams in which administrative decisions exist in a world free from public or judicial opinion.

The Justice Department was not to use the Act "in competition with the Federal Water Pollution Control Act or with State pollution abatement procedures." [14] Industries which were following some state or Federal timetable for pollution abatement would therefore be safe, regardless of how many thousands of tons of refuse they discharged daily. (For example, the Department could apparently take no action against Union Camp for unloading half a million pounds of solids into the Savannah on one disastrous day in 1970.) The Justice Department would, however, bring "appropriate actions either to punish the occasional or recalcitrant polluter" or to stop pollution which had not been "subjected to a proceeding conducted by the Federal Water Quality Administration or by a State." [15] In other words, once an industry had been "subjected" to state or Federal proceedings, it was safe unless it "failed to comply" with the orders.

Environmentalists reacted with vigorous criticism when the policy was announced, charging that the Department had abdicated the use of a forceful antipollution weapon. Several weeks later, however, when it was discovered that mercury in rivers and lakes might be poisonous, the Justice Department announced that several major mercury polluters were about to face suits under the Refuse Act. This self-contradictory behavior is unfortunately typical of several present Federal policies. While the problem of mercury poisoning was one that no responsible government official could ignore, the conservationists have asked for something more than this one-time response. What is needed is leadership and a sense of urgency from the national government; what we have gotten, from the Refuse Act squabble to the Administration's water quality legislation, is considerably less substantial and effective. As an example, one need only compare the Administration's water quality proposal, S. 3471, to the more vigorous bill introduced by Senators Muskie, Bayh, Eagleton, Randolph, and Spong.

The Administration version retains the mandatory delay period of the present water quality act, whereas the Senate bill makes it possible to order a polluter to stop his violation immediately. Mandatory review and upgrading of water quality standards are integral provisions of the Senate bill, and discretionary in the Administration version. In contrast to the Administration bill, the Senate bill makes the issuance of abatement orders mandatory. The Senate bill contains such other important provisions as the requirement that new industries use the latest pollution control techniques. While neither is faultless, the Senate version is a much clearer statement of national commitment than the Administration bill.

The broad problems of protecting the environment cannot be solved by limited, case-by-case litigation. There will be no substantial cooperation from the industries until they learn to expect stringent, precise enforcement of all environmental standards. The *ad hoc* prosecutions of the mercury polluters do not forecast a new enforcement era; Mitchell's department went only half as far as it could have. In the amounts discharged by many industries, mercury can render its victims blind, speechless, and insane. In the face of similar threats to the public health from rioters or bombers, the Justice Department has asked for rigid new penalties. For the mercury polluters, Attorney General Mitchell authorized only civil suits, although under the Refuse Act, he had complete authority to approve criminal actions as well. In view of the terrifying seriousness of the problem, the Department's gentle diplomacy seems misplaced at best.

The Justice Department and the Federal Water Quality Administration must tailor their public policies to the grim reality that scientists and citizens are now discovering—degradation of the environment is a serious crime against society, an act deserving sober moral judgment, a crime that can be far more dangerous than violence in the streets. And yet, irresponsible government officials refuse to use the tools the law has given them to help end the destruction.

There are several steps the concerned citizen can take to fight the problem on his own. The Refuse Act, handled so timidly by the Justice Department, offers many opportunities to the private citizen. The business-minded Congress that passed the Act in 1899 was probably only concerned with protecting the nation's shipping business. Since then, however, Federal courts have rejected this shortsighted reading of the law.[16] Under judicial rulings, the Act applies to "all foreign substances and pollutants," whether valuable (oil) or worthless (industrial wastes), deliberate or accidental. In keeping with the more widespread understanding of the dangers of thermal pollution, a court in Florida recently decided that dumping hot water can also constitute a violation of the Act.[17]

One of the most recent Federal court rulings on the Refuse Act may open the way to even broader interpretations. The central issue in the case was whether one clause of the Rivers and Harbors Act of 1899, which gave the Army Corps of Engineers the authority to issue permits for dredge and fill operations, would allow the Corps to judge ecological factors in granting or denying permits. The result was a decision the court was obviously proud of (it began, "It is the destiny of the Fifth Circuit to be in the middle of great, oftentimes explosive issues of spectacular public importance. . . ."

In affirming the claim that the Corps could weigh the ecological impact of projects, the court said:

> The establishment [the Secretary of the Army and the Chief of Engineers] was entitled, if not required, to consider ecological factors and, being persuaded by them, to deny that which might have been granted routinely five, ten, or fifteen years ago before man's explosive increase made all, including Congress, aware of civilization's potential destruction from breathing its own polluted air and drinking its own infected water and the immeasurable loss from a silent-spring-like disturbance of nature's economy.[18]

From this decision, we may conclude that the anti-refuse provisions of the same act should be judged on the same common sense ecological provisions. With this broad legal field mapped out, citizens interested in putting the Act to work have several places to start. One of the most important first steps is to find out whether the suspected polluter is one of the rare industries which has legal authority to dump its wastes. Under the Refuse Act, the Corps of Engineers may give permits for kinds of pollution that would otherwise be illegal; so far, however, there have been very few of these permits. A recent Conservation Foundation *News Letter* reported that there are no permits for industrial discharges in 23 states, and only a total of 266 permits in the rest of the country.[19]

Words into Action

Midway through our summer's research, we discovered that we might have a chance to test our theories about the Refuse Act. If the evidence we had collected of a "second oil spill" from the Union Camp site were true, it would mean that the company had committed a second violation of the law. If the dates were right, they would place the violation only two weeks after Union Camp had been convicted of breaking the same law (see Chapter 7).

We decided to take the information to court. Our decision came not (as many Savannahians suspected) from malice or a desire to "punish" Union Camp. In fact, it was only a coincidence—even though a coincidence hardly surprising in light of Savannah's history—that Union Camp was the company involved. We were interested in the law, not the violator; we wanted to see how far a group without special legal, political, or financial support could get in seeking law enforcement. Would the fine, tough pronouncements of the Refuse Act fall apart when aimed against the biggest private interest in the area? Could citizen groups really count on the law, or would delays and legal complications thwart them? Would the Refuse Act be useful only in rare, isolated situations or would it have the sweeping applicability we hoped for? We hoped our test would show some of the answers.

As of April 1971, the results are not yet clear. We presented our complaint to the U.S. Attorney for Savannah, R. Jackson B. Smith, Jr., a young man appointed under Nixon. He quickly promised to investigate our evidence and take "appropriate action." The delay since then is probably due to our inclusion of the Coast Guard report in our complaint. Seeing it, the U.S. Attorney deduced that at some point the government might have considered prosecuting the case, as it had with Union Camp's first oil spill.

Smith had to first find out whether the complaint was still alive somewhere in the bureaucratic channels. This meant tracing the Coast Guard report along the tortuous route to a criminal prosecution, from Savannah to Coast Guard District Headquarters in Miami, then back to Savannah care of the local Corps of Engineers Office. After studying the report, the Corps sends it via the Corps of Engineers Divisional Office to the Chief Engineer in Washington; if the Chief Engineer thinks that the report warrants criminal prosecution, he eventually sends it back to Savannah and the U.S. Attorney.

The perils of such a journey are obvious. When we made our complaint, we had no way of knowing whether the original report had vanished, or if it was still in some corner of Coast Guard or Corps headquarters. It ultimately turned up at Coast Guard District Headquarters in Miami. When U.S. Attorney Smith found that the report was still nominally "active," he decided to wait and let normal bureaucratic processes digest the

Coast Guard report. If the recommendations that finally come to him look ripe for prosecution, he will take Union Camp to court. "It is the intention of the Government to prosecute," he said in a letter, "if said prosecution is warranted by the Corps of Engineers report." What criteria he will use to decide whether prosecution is warranted are not clear, but at some point, either the government will begin prosecution or give us a chance to do it ourselves.

Whatever the outcome of our test, the difficulties that plagued us are not likely to be common problems; in most cases, the information that leads to filing a complaint will not be an exhumed government report. More usually, citizens will file a complaint because they have seen factory flumes opened at night or watched a dump truck unloading especially foul wastes. Boaters have frequent chances to detect suspicious patches of refuse, and factory workers can often get a firsthand look at suspicious practices. With any of this direct evidence, the path that leads to justice is much more direct than the one we had to follow.

Considering the huge amount of legal machinery it can set into motion, the citizen's task in filing a complaint is surprisingly simple. It is important to remember that the "complaint" is not as formal or legalistic as it sounds; it simply requires reporting to the U.S. Attorney that a violation has been made. Drafting a full legal case that can stand up in court is the job for the U.S. Attorney who will investigate the claim and prosecute if necessary. The only legal preparation the citizen must make is to learn what the law covers, and one or two readings of the Refuse Act make it clear that almost any kind of dumping can amount to a violation.

This report of the violation should be as convincing as possible. The complaint should explain why a crime is suspected and should include all important evidence—events the citizen has seen, conversations he has had, documents he has read. There is an additional practical reason for making a detailed report; under the "bounty" provisions of the Act, citizens who file complaints are eligible for half the fine levied—but only if the information they gave led to the conviction. If a complaint is sketchy and forces the Government to prowl around on its own, it is much less likely to win a "bounty" payment, than one that has all the relevant information.

In our complaint, we included evidence from three sources: the Coast Guard reports, interviews with Coast Guard officials, and an interview with Union Camp manager James Lientz. Little of this evidence would be admissible in a court case, but our information had made us suspect a violation, and all the complaint required was to report it to the Attorney. Without using special legal form or language, we simply summarized what we knew and asked the Attorney to look further.

The best concise guide to drafting a successful complaint comes from Congressman Henry Reuss. In his packet of information on the Refuse Act, available on request from his office, Reuss gives a nine-point check list for a citizen complaint:

1. the nature of the refuse material discharged;
2. the source and method of discharge;
3. the location, name, and address of the person or persons causing or contributing to the discharge;
4. the name of waterway into which the discharge occurred;
5. each date on which the discharge occurred;
6. the names and addresses of all persons known to you, including yourself, who saw or know about the discharges and could testify about them if necessary;
7. a statement that the discharge is not authorized by Corps permit, or, if a permit was granted, facts showing that the alleged violator is not complying with any condition of the permit;
8. if the waterway into which the discharge occurred is not commonly known as navigable, or as a tributary to a navigable waterway, facts to show such status;
9. where possible, photographs and samples of the pollutant or foreign substances collected in a clean jar which is then sealed and labeled with information showing who took the photograph or sample, where, when, and how, and who retained custody of the film or jar.

In Appendix 3 we have reproduced the complaint that we filed.

Once all this information is collected and handed over to the Attorney, there is another group to keep in mind: the news media, and through it the public. Legal cases are serious matters, especially ones like this involving criminal offenses, and it is a disruption of justice to try accused violators in the press. Nevertheless, it is possible to show examples of the kind of action the public may take; articles in the news media can also effect influential changes in public opinion. Changes in public opinion may also influence governmental minds; punishing big business used to be an unpopular pastime, but mounting public concern about big business damages might encourage the Justice Department to be more enthusiastic about the Refuse Act.

The unaccustomed glare of public attention can also have a miraculous effect on the speed of government action. Within days after we filed our complaint, the Coast Guard report which had been forgotten for months was suddenly dancing along the official channels. No administrator wants to be the one the public looks to for answers. The problem is to keep the attention focused, for as soon as interest dies, an official may simply let the complaint sit. To speed a complaint all along, there are several possible steps. One is to find out which offices will be handling the complaint; in our case, this meant five separate stops. A letter to each potential snag, asking to know when the complaint was received and when it will be passed on gives the impression that someone is watching. A note at the bottom of the letter, saying that copies have been sent to a congressman, a senator, the local chamber of commerce—someone Important—may persuade an administrator to work on the complaint promptly.

Above all, it is important to retain a perspective on what the law is and what action is being sought. As delays pile up and the memory of the damage blurs, despair and apathy are two easy alternatives. Excuses begin to sound plausible; a citizen may hear, as we did from Mr. Lientz, that what had happened was not really a violation. At this stage, it is possible to think that maybe the polluter's good intentions make a difference; perhaps he is not responsible because the pollution was accidental. The Refuse Act, however, does not recognize these distinctions; it does not recognize Lientz' argument that the "tall oil" was not an "oil spill." In its magnificent simplicity, the Act includes them all. As Mr. Justice Douglas put it in *United States v. Standard Oil Company*, "Oil is oil. . . ." [20]

13
Bringing Back the Water

How long will the land mourn
and the grass of every field wither?
For the wickedness of those who dwell in it
the beast and the bird are swept away.

Jeremiah 12:4

A house has a garbage can; Savannah has a river. Spoken or unspoken, rubbish-heap philosophy has long underlain America's use of its natural resources. Land and air are there to be filled with factories and roads; with fumes and soot.

The blighted American landscape along the freeways of Los Angeles, past the mills of Gary, and on the streets of New York shows the full, devastating effect of our environmental neglect. If there were some menacing foreign enemy, some secret internal conspiracy to which we could turn with accusing fingers, much of our frustration might escape. But there is no one else to blame; we all share the painful knowledge that our landscape, like our social instability, is the true testament to our way of life.

Over the years, we have developed a peculiar schizophrenia in our ideas about property. Each of us defends what is his, but the air and water we own in common gets protection from none of us. Meanwhile, cities open their sewers into the common lakes and rivers, and factories send their stacks into the common skies. The simple force of corporate balance sheets leaves the landscape little hope. It is cheaper to "dispose" of waste into the public domain than to treat and detoxify it. The common land will continue to be used as a trash can until we demand that it serve other purposes.

Our attitudes are beginning to change now that we are feeling the pinch. When the frontier closed, we learned not to waste land; now, as the air literally closes down upon us, we must learn to preserve our atmosphere. The temptation remains strong to hide behind the old philosophy of isolation, to assume that what goes out of sewers and stacks is gone forever.

This outmoded temptation is almost irresistible in places like Savannah, where environmental crowding has not yet become an inescapable fact of daily life. Surrounded by marshes, rivers, and inlets, it is difficult for Savannahians to believe that one polluted river can make any difference. From time to time the city has worried about its river, but by a curious twist of logic, the town has evolved a theory that has turned its use of the river into a virtue. We are protecting our resources in the wisest way, we pour our filth into the Savannah and thereby save the marshes and small creeks where we swim and fish; this is efficient use of nature.

Unfortunately, this comfortable theory is simply not true. In this sense, Savannah's tragedy is instructive for all of us. For the moment, we may be able to concentrate our garbage in city dumps and send our sewage to cesspools, but we delude ourselves by trying to carve natural surroundings into neat compartments. It should come as no surprise when pesticides used on farms somehow show up in our water and in our cells, or when the air pollution from city factories turns up in our suburbs.

It may soothe Savannah's conscience to believe that the nearby marshes and creeks are safe from the river's filth, but a reasonable man, looking at Savannah for even the first time, would have a hard time embracing the town's faith.

A glance at the map shows that the river is no more separable from its surrounding creeks than one part of the sea is from another. As the Savannah runs down from the west, it splits into a dozen channels and inlets. At its mouth the river forms a wandering delta, sweeping past the city and snaking with many fingers to the sea. The line between river and sea is blurred and uncertain; it changes with the tides. When the water is high, islands with names like Cabbage and Ossabaw stand surrounded by water; at low tide, the departing water reveals flat marshy plains. This is the bed into which the Savannah discharges its load of sewage and pulp waste. Without even considering how necessary Savannah's pollution might be, it is clear that the consequences of destroying the marsh, for whatever reason, are unacceptable. There are parts of nature, unique creations like the palisades of the Hudson or the Grand Canyon, whose disappearance or degradation leaves us all poorer. The life cycle of the estuarine marshes deserves that high status.

The marshes that line Savannah's creeks and islands are part of a long belt running from the Carolinas down through Florida. The marshes are ubiquitous and surprisingly extensive; in the 115 miles that separate Savannah from St. Mary's are some 2,344 miles of shoreline, most of it covered by marsh. Tourists may simply be impressed by the romantic mystery of the marshes: the white herons swooping down through acres of green spartina grass, the blue water rising and falling under the moon. Inside there is much more. Looking into the life systems of a marsh is like pulling the cover from a watch. Under the blank exterior, all is motion, everything has a place. From the algae and plankton at the bottom of the biological pyramid to the fish and birds at the top, each part of the marsh system is in precise balance with the others. Millennia of evolutionary specialization have brought about this balance; the right minerals are trapped in the marsh, the right temperature nurses its creatures, the right mixture of salt and fresh water bathes it from the estuary. As a result, more life goes on in an acre of marsh land than in any other acre of the earth's surface.

One acre of healthy marsh land will produce about ten tons of dry organic matter in a year's time; this includes the plants, the algae, and all other forms of life.[1] By contrast, an acre of open sea, on which we have long relied for food, produces only one-twentieth as much life as the marsh; green alfalfa fields are only one-seventh as productive. Normal stretches of wooded land are not even in the running, and the summit of man's agricultural technology—the intensely cultivated corn field—creates only half the organic matter of a salt marsh.[2]

If all the growth on one acre of marsh could be transformed into food, it would yield something like 32 million calories, enough to feed 2,000 people for a year.[3] Marsh life is no more easily convertible into food, than are the stalks and leaves in a corn field, but it is theoretically possible to harvest about 10 per cent of the marsh's production without damaging its life systems. Using this 10 per cent conversion factor, marsh farmers could probably extract 2,000 pounds of usable food per acre each year from intensely managed areas and 200 pounds per acre over wider regions.[4] Experimental cultivation of South Carolina marsh ponds has produced huge yields: 250 pounds of fish, 300–400 pounds of shrimp, and 100 pounds of crab from each acre yearly.[5] The marshes also serve a more immediate practical function; almost every kind of commercially important fish in the Southeast spends some portion of its life within the coastal marsh.

Important as these features may be, there is another reason to preserve these marshes. We have seen in too many other cases the subtle, intricate ways in which environmental disruptions can spread. We did not know that spraying our crops with DDT would kill our eagles or that overreliance on cars would begin to ravage the pine forests of the Southern California mountains. If we have learned anything at all from those lessons, it is that we must approach the precarious marshes with apprehensive caution. Here, where living beings react with each other in unparalleled intensity, small tears in the natural fabric can have unimaginable consequences. Simply because they are unimaginable now, we cannot assume that the consequences will stay away. By the time we see them, the damage may be done.

> *No one hears their death cries, as their graves are measured and dug by the cubic yard. In the remaining vacuum few will detect the absence of so many tiny lives—snails, mud worms, phytoplankton, and algae, killifish, silversides, anchovies, and mullet. Suddenly, however, the bass, bluefish, and flounder, the terns, herons, and grebes, loons and mergansers, the crabs and the terrapins, and ultimately the mammals will be seen to disappear if the bottom of the*

> *food chain is destroyed. All these tiny lives depend on the salt marsh for survival.*
>
> Nancy Butler, *The Islander*

But it is the river that is filled with pollution, not the marshes. The marshes are miles from the factories. What, Savannahians have asked, is the connection?

There are rivers on this planet which run ram-rod straight into the sea; places where geology and tide combine to keep the water from meandering. If this were Savannah's situation, the marshes would be out of immediate danger; we could wait until the sea itself began to stink and fill up. But this is not the case, and the city is left with an immediate problem. As the Savannah, carrying millions of gallons of sewage, kraft waste, and acid, moves down past the city and toward the sea, it takes its deliberate Southern time. It dawdles and sprawls, and spreads its toxins to the area that can least endure it: the surrounding marsh.

Evidence of this deadly dispersal is easy to find. One of the most familiar signs is the Condemned Oyster map found in health department offices. Ever since the late forties, many thousands of Savannah's best oyster-producing acres have been closed; between 25 and 30 per cent of Georgia's entire oyster area has suffered similar condemnation.[6] In almost every case, the reason was the same; bacteria from human sewage had contaminated the water near the oysters. Because of their special ability to build up enormous concentrations of impurities, the oysters were soon filled with bacteria that had recently been part of human bowel movements. When concentrations of *Escherichia coli,* a fecal coliform, reach a critical level, health officials condemn the affected oyster beds to keep the oysters off the market. This coliform itself poses little threat, either to the oysters or to humans. But where there are large colonies of coliform, it is reasonable to expect that there are also other fecal bacteria, some of which cause hepatitis or typhoid fever.

As long as health departments do their job and fishermen obey the orders, the tainted oysters do not immediately threaten the towns that pour sewage on them. The real importance of the oyster map is what it suggests about other problems in the marine life cycle. It takes no great imagination to deduce that the fecal bacteria that pile up in oysters came from human sewage; the sewage that pollutes the oysters comes from the sewage outfalls that pour into the Savannah River. The black area on the map on page 223 illustrates more than just the area of sewage contamination; it also gives a rough idea of where the Savannah's water goes after the river meets the sea. (Since fecal coliform perish more quickly in salt water than do some other kinds of bacteria and mineral pollutants, even larger areas of marsh and inlet may actually be suffering from Savannah's contamination.)

Several years ago, the Army Corps of Engineers made detailed studies of the Savannah's flow. The Corps went to Vicksburg, Mississippi, and built a model Savannah basin in a laboratory. The experimental model was rigged to duplicate all the natural forces acting on the Savannah: rainstorms, tide, even Corps dredging projects. In one test, the Corps used dye studies to see where the river water goes after reaching the mouth of the stream. The results offer scant consolation to those who hope that the marshes are safe.

Soon after it passes the city and ten miles before it reaches the ocean, the Savannah splits into the North and South Channels. The North Channel is the heavy industrial highway which, in an ideal system of "efficient pollution," would carry all the river's dirt. The less traveled South Channel is more vulnerable to pollution primarily because it feeds into the Wilmington River and the network of small tidal creeks south of Savannah. In its tests, the Corps found that the alarmingly high amount of the total river flow—30 per cent—feeds into the South Channel (and, as later evidence will show, nearly all of the river's acid pollution goes directly into the South Channel and on to the marsh lands). From the South Channel, at least 5 per cent of the Savannah's initial flow turns up in the Wilmington River, which feeds into the southern marsh lands and fishing creeks.

North of the river, things were no better. The Corps studies confirmed what should have been obvious from the oyster map; the Savannah reaches out to infect South Carolina's marshes as well as Georgia's. After releasing

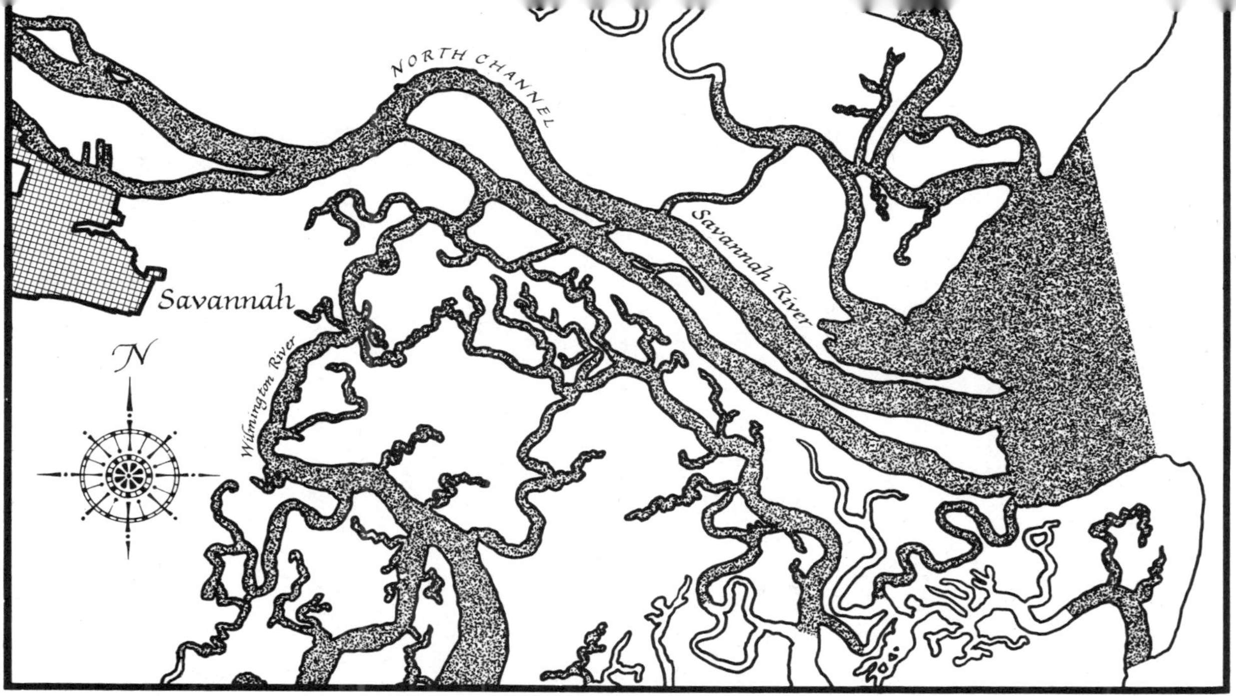

Condemned Oyster Beds at Mouth of Savannah River

Source: Chatham County Health Department.

dye into its model river to simulate sewage discharge, the Corps tested dye concentrations up and down its miniature coast. By the time the Savannah reached its mouth, the dye concentration was somewhere between 12 and 20 per cent of the original concentration. But instead of immediately disappearing into the wide ocean, the dye showed a perverse tendency to hug the coast. In the Wright and New Rivers on the South Carolina coast, the dye was still at 2 to 5 per cent of its original concentration. The exact percentage makes little difference; what the figures mean is that the South Carolina marshes are enduring millions of gallons of sewage and paper mill pollution daily.[7]

In light of other evidence, these results seem almost too cheery. American Cyanamid's reluctance to admit where its acid goes (see Chapter 4) is a frightening sign of damage in the marsh. Most of Cyanamid's 700,000 pound daily acid output goes straight down the South Channel, resulting in acid concentrations of pH 4 in the downstream marsh lands [8] and pH 6 three miles away from the plant.[9] The direct impact of industrial pollution on raw marsh land is obvious; the later effect numbs the imagination.

It is easy to list the names and amounts of these waterborne pollutants—690,000 pounds of acid per day; 36 million gallons of kraft mill waste; sewage from more than 100,000 people, the by-products of sugar-making, pulp cooking, urban life. Determining the results of the effluent is much more difficult; we have a pitifully scant supply of information about our waters and air. Now, as we realize how desperately we need the data, we can often only snatch in frustration at the strands that are available. During the summer, each of the score of scientists we interviewed said, yes, something bad is happening to the marsh land. But they do not know what it is, nor how bad it has become; there are too many areas we have not studied, too many holes that need to be filled. It may be many years before we see the worst of it; consequences we never imagined may turn up in a generation. For now, we do not know.

Using what patches of clarity do exist, we can at least outline the possible consequences. One sure measure is that of "dissolved oxygen"—the familiar by-product of

Biological Oxygen Demand (BOD) pollutants. The importance of dissolved oxygen is perfectly simple; fish, like humans, need oxygen. Unlike humans, they breathe it from the water rather than the air. When there is not enough oxygen, the fish die. Most fish populations need between four and eight parts per million (ppm) of dissolved oxygen in the water. Four ppm is the minimum for long-term exposure; some experts recommend at least five ppm for 16 hours a day, with never even a brief dip below two ppm.[10] Federal agents recommend that "for a healthy warm water fish population, it would appear from a review of the literature that dissolved oxygen levels should not be below 5 ppm."[11] Below these levels, even minor variations can have catastrophic results. At three ppm, the fish slowly begin to die. Eggs hatch less frequently, and the young fish that do hatch are likely to die. Those that live are small and weak, and many of them are deformed. Adult fish cannot metabolize their food normally; they grow slowly and are easy victims to other hardships.[12]

When whole populations are deprived of oxygen, the biological machinery begins to fall apart on a large scale. As Georgia's respected ecologist Dr. Eugene Odum said,

> Many parts of the estuarine system are normally operating at full capacity with regard to oxygen. There isn't much leeway here. Since most types of pollution, both domestic and industrial, have a high oxygen demand, a relatively small added input can cause the system to go anerobic, which means that it becomes, biologically speaking, useless.[13]

Apart from compassion for the fish, humans should have a great interest in maintaining a river's dissolved oxygen content; when anerobic bacteria take over the job of decomposition, the stench rivals that of the worst factories.

It is helpful to keep these numbers—four to five ppm for healthy fish, three ppm for monstrosities and torpor—in mind when reviewing Savannah's situation. Perhaps in an attempt to legalize the pollution it has not yet been able to correct, the Georgia Water Quality Control Board has divided the state's waterways into different classes, depending on their water quality. The best streams are classified as "fishing" or "recreation"; the worst, as "industrial" or "navigation." Along its course, one river may change from class to class, as it moves from the pure headwaters into sordid urban areas.

The Water Board recognized reality when it classified the Savannah. Seventeen miles of the Savannah, running from River Mile 22, upstream of the large industries, to River Mile 5, past the last large outfall, are relegated to "industrial" or "navigation" status. This means that the water must be able to float ships or carry off waste. Technically, these low-class waters must contain an average dissolved oxygen level of three ppm, and the DO must never fall below 2.5 ppm.

Along this "industrial" stretch of the river, oxygen levels are too low for normal aquatic life. Apart from immediate damage to local fish, the 17 mile slug of dead water can have a more insidious effect. Every year, schools of anadromous fish—species like shad or striped bass, which swim from the ocean to the inland fresh waters to lay their eggs—begin their trip up the Savannah, passing through the long, lethal industrial zone before they reach the spawning grounds. Regardless of higher oxygen levels further upstream, the industrial zone can effectively plug up the river when its oxygen dwindles. It is hard to know exactly how many bass have died on the trip, how many have been turned away and prevented from laying their eggs. Whether the toll is measured in tons or individuals, the connection between low oxygen and sparse fish is clear.

But all these criticisms of the current standards are slightly futile, since the river often fails to meet even the minimal "industrial zone" standards. Over the last six years, a series of government agencies have monitored the oxygen level in the river; their results are shown in Table 12–1. In 1963, oxygen readings were constantly below levels which would support normal life; on one memorable day in August, the river came within .1 ppm of losing all its oxygen and going anaerobic. If the readings by the Corps of Engineers are reliable, the situation has since improved. The industrial clarifiers, holding ponds, and other internal devices installed since 1963 have had some effect. The overall oxygen demand on the river has fallen by almost 20 per cent (see Table

TABLE 12–1

Lower Savannah River

DISSOLVED OXYGEN (D.O. in ppm)

River mile*	August 1963† No. of Samples	Avg.	Min.	August 1968‡ No. of Samples	Avg.	Min.	1968§ No. of Samples	Avg.	Min.	1969§ No. of Samples	Avg.	Min.
S–2	71	3.6	*1.8*	16	3.2	*2.1*	20	5.3	*2.7*	19	5.6	*1.8*
S–5	71	2.8	*1.1*	16	2.7	*1.7*	20	4.7	*2.4*	22	5.2	*1.4*
S–10	81	1.8	*0.5*	15	1.7	*1.1*	18	3.9	*1.9*	22	4.7	*0.7*
S–11.5	70	1.8	*0.1*	18	2.3	*1.1*	20	4.5	*2.0*	22	4.8	*1.1*
S–14	77	2.1	*0.3*	16	2.4	*0.4*	20	4.5	*1.7*	22	4.7	*1.5*
S–16	75	3.0	*0.7*	15	3.2	*0.8*	20	5.0	*1.5*	22	5.0	*2.0*
S–19	31	5.3	*2.5*	15	4.7	*2.0*	20	6.0	*2.2*	22	5.8	*2.5*
S–22	28	6.3	*5.3*	16	5.5	*2.6*	20	7.1	*4.9*	21	6.7	*3.7*

* River miles are measured inland from the mouth of the river. S–2 indicates a sample taken from the Water Quality Sampling Station at river mile 2, etc.

† *U.S. Public Health Service Savannah River Pollution Report*, November 1964.

‡ *Water Quality Data—Lower Savannah River*, Georgia Water Quality Control Board. These samples were taken and analyzed during the period of August 12–22, 1968, by GWQCB personnel.

§ These were samples taken periodically during 1968 and 1969 by the Corps of Engineers, Savannah district and analyzed by laboratory personnel of the Chatham County Health Department. The data were listed in the *Water Quality Data-Lower Savannah River* as individual samples. We compiled the average and minimum figures from their listings.

12–2), and the river has begun to rally. In light of this improvement, new sewers and further industrial controls are especially important. Just because things are improving, there is no reason to rest now; further work may push the river over the top and make it healthy again.

TABLE 12–2

Lower Savannah River Biological Oxygen Demand per day in terms of Population Equivalents

Source	*1965 level*	*1969 level*	*Reduction in percentage*
American Cyanamid	†	†	
Certain-Teed Products	50,000	14,000	72
Continental Can	130,200	80,000	38
GAF Corporation (Ruberoid)	33,000	18,650	44
Hercules, Inc.	20,400	17,900	12
Hunt-Wesson Foods, Inc.	25,000	13,000	48
Meddin Packing Co.	1,740	420	
Savannah Sugar Refinery	37,500	29,850	20
Union Camp Corporation	810,000	696,000*	14*
Industrial subtotal	1,107,840‡	869,820	21
Port Wentworth	3,700		
Travis Field	640		
Garden City	5,200		
Chatham City	1,200		
Savannah	108,000		
Savannah Beach (summer)	16,700		
Total	*1,243,000*	*1,006,000*	

* This figure is based on a questionable sample not counted in the Georgia Water Quality Control Board's 1969 survey of Union Camp. However, later figures show Union Camp's success at BOD reduction to be even less. Their percentage reduction of BOD may be as little as 9 per cent of the 1965 level, which would put their BOD/day PE at about 736,000 PE.

† It has been determined that American Cyanamid's effluent exerts a significant chemical oxygen demand because of the oxidation of iron in its waste. The 1969 Conference gave an admittedly rough estimate of the oxygen demand in terms of a PE of between 150,000 and 200,000. However, this is only an order of magnitude estimate as Chemical Oxygen Demand and Biological Oxygen Demand measure two separate reactions that occur in the receiving stream.

‡ These figures were set as the base from which a 25 per cent reduction in BOD was to have been achieved between 1965 and the end of 1967.

In a superficial sense, Table 12-1 offers some good news: the 1969 tests show average levels well above the industrial zone standard of three ppm, and usually well into the four–five ppm "healthy" range. Unfortunately, these are *averages,* which simply do not tell the important story about dissolved oxygen. An "average" annual temperature of 75 degrees means little if half the year the temperature was below freezing and the other half was intolerably hot. The important factor is not the average oxygen level, although that too may be important if below endurable limits; it is the low points that set the limits. It makes little difference to the fish near river mile ten that the average oxygen level is now up to 4.7 ppm. That average cannot help them when the minimum, 0.7 ppm, hits. Whatever progress the upper river may have seen makes little difference in the marsh. At river mile two—more than twelve miles past the worst sources of pollution—the oxygen still sinks to disastrously low levels: 1.8 ppm. By the time the water reaches river mile two, it is on the lip of the outer marshes. By that time, much of the river water has already washed out to Georgia and South Carolina marshes through the Wilmington River and Fields Cut. The levels in the marshes themselves have not been measured yet. But all evidence suggests that they too have suffered seriously. In the marsh or the river, even a day of extremely low oxygen can do permanent harm. As a federal publication concluded, "Possibly there is as much damage to fish exposed to only occasionally minimum dissolved oxygen levels as those in a constant level of the lowered concentration."[14] Keeping in mind the effects of three ppm oxygen levels, we can imagine what 0.7 or 1.1 ppm levels do to striped bass or shrimp.

The contrast between the relatively innocuous yearly averages (columns three and four) and the plummeting August readings (columns one and two) points to the most acute danger. In the exasperations of our day-to-day lives, we have been forced to learn the meaning of "peak demand periods." During balmy springs, the average supply of electricity may be just fine; but in the summer, and especially when every family starts cooking its dinners and turning on its air conditioners, the system cannot endure. One need only watch the changes in traffic conditions between midnight and 8:30 in the morning to see what can happen when everyone uses a resource at once. The cycle of oxygen use in a river follows a similar pattern. August is the cruellest month. With its unremitting heat, it brings the river to its absolutely worst point. Like a bottle of Coke, a river holds more dissolved gases when it is cold than when it is hot. There are rarely serious DO problems in the middle of winter, but the summer concentrates every danger. Even if the pollution levels stayed the same the river would contain less oxygen. But the levels are not the same, for factories often step up production. At the same time, the monsoon rains of Savannah wash larger amounts of organic waste into the river. The river, which must struggle hard to handle its normal load of pollution and sewage, inevitably begins to lose, and the oxygen level sinks.

All this comes at just the time then the creatures in the river and the marsh can afford it least. All the year's crop of young fish has been born, so the aquatic population is unusually high. The marsh cycle moves into its highest gear. When the desperate August levels settle on this thriving life, the effect of low oxygen levels is multiplied. It is as if the whole life system were on the run. A man sitting quietly at his desk has no trouble breathing through one nostril; but if he is forced to run, the same meager stream of air will not keep him alive. On the *average* the summer crisis may be cancelled out by the fat times of winter, but many fish do not survive to enjoy the good side of the average. And we need only look at Union Camp's discharge table charting its erratic dumping of BOD to suspect how much the daily oxygen levels vary from the "average."

It would be more scientifically precise to "declare" rather than "imagine" or "suspect." Ideally, we would count up the bodies to compute the exact damage pollution has done to the food chain. The scantiness of the information is frustrating and dangerous; we may not know the total effects of low levels of oxygen in the Savannah River, but we cannot assume that there is no problem.

The same implications—ominous but indefinite—leer out from several of the other known measurements of the river's filth. Acid is a good example. For humans it has always been easier to become upset about acid than about BOD, kraft waste, or other tame-sounding toxins. Acid burns flesh.

But it is rarely possible to imagine how devastating its effect is. If there is one biological system that can least afford to absorb huge acid discharges, it is the estuarine marshland. The creatures there are used to a gentle saline environment. Since the sea is usually available in large enough quantities to buffer any acid that might enter the marsh, the salt-water animals have remarkably little tolerance to any unusual acid conditions. Normally, the marsh water is very close to pH 7, the neutral point in acid-base concentrations. When the pH descends as the acid becomes more concentrated, mammoth disruption of all vital processes begins. At pH 6.5, oysters decrease their normal functions by 90 per cent; [15] other species undergo similar, if less dramatic, havoc. By the time the pH reaches 4.8 or 5, most of the fish are dead.[16] Because of the great potential destruction, Federal officials recommend that "Materials that extend normal ranges of pH by *more than* $\mp$*0.1 pH units* should not be introduced into salt water portions of tidal tributaries or coastal waters. At no time should the introduction of foreign materials cause the pH to be less than 6.7 or greater than 8.5." [17]

Shrimpers who once worked the Wilmington River and the creeks south of Savannah say that clouds of dead shrimp rise on the waters when American Cyanamid discharges its acid every day. With a measured pH of 4 in the marsh land and 6 several miles from the plant, it is little wonder. The real question is how long there will be shrimp there to kill.

The river also carries human sewage and the leftovers from paper-making; both have predictably bad effects on the fish and marsh life. When sewage enters the water, the heavy material sinks and coats the bottom of the river with a dense layer of sludge that eventually kills the bottom organisms. When oysters drift to the sludge bed and attach themselves, they soon begin to sink out of sight and finally suffocate under a layer of sludge.

Studies in New York found that sewage could affect even animals more mobile than the oyster. When lobsters and crabs were exposed to sewage, their shells began to erode away and the animals broke out in infections. Sewage sludge, the researchers concluded, was "incompatible with most normal biological phenomena." [18]

As for the paper mill wastes, they usually escape with far less than their proper share of responsibility. The mills' main contribution is the staggering amounts of BOD released—100,000 pounds daily from Union Camp alone. Mixed in with the lignins and wood sugars, relatively harmless wood residues, are a number of more dangerous compounds. Most of them are sulfur compounds, left over from the "sulfate" paper-making process. During the "cooking" stage, the mill mixes the wood with a sulfate solution that digests the wood into a mushy solution. The mills try to recover as much of the sulfate mixture as they can for re-use, but inevitably some of the sulfurs wash out into the river. The most stable of these compounds, resins and fatty acid soaps, can be directly toxic to fish.[19] For a variety of reasons, the toxicity can vary greatly from mill to mill. Experimenters in California found that kraft waste could kill fish at dilutions ranging between 1:2 and 1:2000.[20]

We were not able to get a sample of raw Union Camp waste to test its toxicity, but the amount of waste the mill dumps into the river is well within the danger zone. Union Camp's executive vice president John E. Ray III told the Savannah Rotary Club in October 1970, "Union Camp discharges less than 40 million gallons a day of process water. . . . I think this is five-tenths of one per cent of the average flow of the river. It seems to us that the dynamic flow and diluting effect of the Savannah River itself is the best safeguard against putting it beyond redemption." [21] In light of the California studies, the "dynamic flow and diluting effect" are not quite enough. If Ray's figures are accurate, the entire river is filled with Union Camp waste at a 1:200 dilution. Because no one has yet bothered to find out whether or not the sulfur is concentrated enough to kill marsh life, the discharges go on.

The river's natural systems work a cruel multiplication with the different pollutants. In an orderly, logical Nature, it would be possible to trace the effect of each pollutant. Acid kills at *x* concentration, and there is *y* amount in the river; heavy metals are lethal at this level, and there is only that amount present now. Going through the hazards one by one, it might seem that no one of them was a serious danger. But in the delicate world of real natural systems, it is impossible to separate things so neatly. As one pollutant enters the water, it often makes the river more vulnerable to the attack of other pollutants. This "synergistic" effect means that the total impact is far greater than the sum of the individual pollutants.

There are several good examples in the Savannah. Along with its acid, American Cyanamid also discharges between 50 and 130 tons of iron compounds every day. As a system for killing marine life, it would be hard to find a more effective combination. A high acid concentration affects the level at which other toxins are dispersed in the marine system. With iron, the interaction is especially acute. In one series of experiments, fish were able to endure a pH level as low as 4.8 for limited periods, as long as there was no iron in the water. As soon as the iron concentration rose to .9 ppm, the fish died unless the acid was diluted to a pH of 5.5.[22] Cyanamid certainly did not have this effect in mind when it started releasing iron and acid into the river, but it could have found few quicker ways to destroy the marsh.

Union Camp's effluent also contains elements of the same kind of double-danger. When fish are simply faced with enduring a period of low dissolved oxygen, they can stand short periods of 2 ppm, if they do not have to fight other poisons simultaneously. But the results of one experiment showed that when a solution of kraft mill waste was added to the water, the fish needed three times as much oxygen—5.9 ppm—to stay alive.[23] The effect of the Savannah's oxygen shortage is bound to be worse because of the kraft wastes.

These details about the acid and the oxygen, the sewage and the sulfur do not come close to describing what is actually going on in the river. For each of the pollutants we can measure and study, there are probably dozens whose presence no one suspects and whose effect no one can imagine. The unpredictable results of mixing acid with iron or kraft waste with low oxygen show how dangerous it is to predict the final influence that a soup of different compounds can have on a marsh. We know that a few identifiable poisons are undoubtedly hurting the marsh, and we can make rough guesses at their toll. Beyond that, there is pitifully little to go on.

In interviews with more than 20 scientists during the summer of 1970, we collected endless lists of vital research topics that demand immediate investigation if we hope to learn about the estuarine life in time to save it. Every aspect of the river's biota, from the marsh land's productivity to the effect of modern insecticides, need more data, more analysis, more conclusions. The detailed explanations of each research priority would amount to another book, a book that is urgently needed. Because they apply not only to the Savannah but to nearly every river in the country, a few research areas demand general mention.

The area around the Savannah is not one of the more heavily farmed parts of the country, but many biologists worry that there may be substantial pesticide contamination in the river. Shrimpers say that they can predict a good shrimping season by the weather; when heavy rains wash DDT and other pesticides from the fields into the water, the shrimpers expect dismal harvests. Many questions arise from the observations of the shrimpers. How much pesticide goes into the river? What animals are building up dangerous concentrations? What have long-lasting pesticides done to the fish, the marsh, the water birds? Are humans endangered by eating fish from the river? Southerners generally carry more DDT in their bodies than other Americans because of the constant blanket of pesticides on their land; is it any different in Savannah? Why does the government continue its pesticide war on the fire ant by dropping Mirex from airplanes? Is there evidence to support claims that Mirex exterminates crabs instead of fire ants?

In the summer of 1970, mercury pollution became the latest in a series of environmental panics to seize the nation. While the dangers of mercury poisoning had been known and ignored for decades, it was only when a Canadian graduate student pointed out the extent of the existing pollution that the government began its frenzied attempts at control. Within a few weeks, rivers were condemned, factories were warned, and the public was left with another gnawing worry. The danger of such lightning action is that the sense of concern may pass as quickly as it came; with our great faith in the ability of *action* to control events, we expect that the problem is taken care of. But a hazard that has been established over long years of obscurity does not disappear quickly. For example, the entire stretch of the river between Augusta and Savannah was condemned because of a mercury leak from the Olin factory in Augusta. Now that the mercury is in the mud, the plants, and the animals of the river, cheerless biologists say it may take dozens of years to work itself out of the food chain. The lesson to be learned from the mercury tragedy is that we cannot afford to wait until subtle natural imbalances show themselves to become concerned about them; by that time, it may be too late. Rivers like the Savannah may already be suffering other kinds of metal pollution, probably more widespread and possibly more dangerous than mercury. Some scientists have repeatedly urged the government to sponsor research on heavy metal deposits in the Savannah. In 1969, when Dr. Herbert Windom of the Institute of Oceanography on Skidaway Island asked the Federal Water Pollution Control Agency to support a study of several heavy metals, including mercury, in the major estuaries along the Georgia coast, his application was rejected. When someone finally manages to trace the copper, lead, cadmium, and zinc in the marsh lands, we can only hope that the cost of the delay will not be as high as it was in the case of mercury.

The few available examples of how a pollutant affects species of marine life (e.g., acid of pH 6.5 cuts oyster activity rate by 90 per cent) are not enough to yield intelligent conclusions about the problems of our plant and animal life. Many scientists we interviewed recommended a hugely increased program of bio-assays to determine the effect of environmental conditions on certain species.

Like increasing numbers of American rivers, the Savannah has a nuclear generating plant on its banks. In the upstream reaches of the river, near Aiken, South

Carolina, the Atomic Energy Commission's plant takes in huge quantities of Savannah water each day to cool its generators and the heated water is then discharged into the river. What is this flood of warm water doing to the fish? Is anything besides water escaping from the plant and loading the riverbed with radioactive isotopes? Information available is too sketchy for any safe conclusions.

Many of the most basic facts about the condition of the Savannah are still hazily defined. Exactly how far do contaminated waters spread into the marsh? What foreign elements are they likely to bring with them? What is the probable effect? If the pollution were stopped, how long would it take the river to return to "normal"? Is the river past redemption? The lack of information that plagues Georgia scientists is a plight duplicated across the country. But the public, the scientists, and the government will all be culpable unless the necessary research starts soon.

"Them paper bag people is fiddlin' with our livelihood. . . . What's more important, a damn paper bag or us keepin' our livin'?"

Shrimpers at Savannah's Thunderbolt Dock

For more than a thousand years, archaeologists say, human families have fed from the rivers and marsh of Savannah. Native tribes who lived along the coast took fish and oysters from creeks where motor boats now roar. When Oglethorpe and his colonists followed, they, too, relied on this easiest source of food. For a town as closely wed to the water as Savannah, it was only natural that fishing should become a central part of economic life.

What was natural, however, was not lasting. As Savannah has clawed its way into modern life and new industrial wealth, fragments of the old life have been left behind. One of the saddest casualties has been fishing. The decline of Savannah's fisheries from the boom times of the early 1900's points up many basic changes in the Southern way of life that are too well known to need discussion. But the fishing story also provides a chronicle of the river's environmental history. The fish that men harvest are only the top of the food chain; at best, they are sketchy indicators of what goes on beneath them. But the unremitting fall of Savannah's fisheries adds another kind of evidence—evidence of direct economic importance—to the story of the river's degradation.

The idyllic good old days of fishing were the late nineteenth and early twentieth centuries, when the economy was recovering but the industries had not yet come. Wizened veterans in Savannah still reminisce over the days when they came back from a visit to the oyster man with a quart pail for a nickel. It is more than fuzzy memories or inflated prices that make those prices seem so low. In 1908, the prize year of Georgia's oystermen, there were more than 50 times as many oysters available as there are today.[24] Not every harvest has plummeted as drastically as the oyster catch, but the general trend is identical. As Table 12–3 shows, all commercial fish harvests have fallen off heavily since the start of the century.

Although it is hard to draw conclusions from slight changes in year-to-year harvests, it is more difficult to avoid the conclusion suggested by Table 12–3. In most cases, the catch has fallen to less than 10 per cent of its preindustrial peak. Red snapper and oysters are at 2 per cent of their 1908 peak; sturgeon, mullet, bluefish, and trout are all reduced to 1 per cent of their maximum level; and menhaden and blue crabs, two species that once had great commercial importance were simply not harvested in 1968. Other species have borne up better; shrimp, for example, was at 52 per cent of its peak and 1968 shad catches were at 43 per cent of the 1908 maximum. For others, such as flounder and blue crabs, the peak catch was actually several years after industry had come to the Savannah.

One cannot infer from the figures that the population of each species declined proportionately to the dwindling catch; but it is obvious that commercial fish are less plentiful, and perhaps less healthy, than they used to be. Whatever the complete explanation, it seems certain that industrial pollution has played a large part in the de-

TABLE 12–3
1880–1968
Georgia Fish Landings
Commercial Harvests

Species	*Maximum harvest in pounds*	*Year*	*Present harvest in pounds*	*Year*	*Percentage of maximum*
Alewives	125,000	1880	0	1968	0
Bluefish	50,000	1928	less than 500	1968	<1
Catfish	289,000	1902	66,000	1968	23
Croaker	46,000	1908	0	1968	0
Flounder	307,000	1945	23,163	1968	8
Grouper	160,000	1908	17,141	1968	11
King whiting	464,000	1955	123,421	1968	27
Menhaden	34,102,000	1927	0	1968	0
Mullet	194,000	1908	200	1968	<1
Sea trout	144,000	1890	2,134	1968	>1

Shad	1,333,000	1908	568,908	1968	43
Red snapper	880,000	1908	17,482	1968	2
Spot	103,000	1955	1,976	1968	2
Sturgeon	354,000	1880	544	1968	<1
Hard clams	43,000	1908	0	1968	0
Blue crabs	15,766,000	1960	3,668,832	1968	23
Oysters	8,070,000	1908	190,741	1968	>2
Shrimp	16,392,000	1945	8,535,688	1968	52
Total	*47,458,000 lbs.*	*1927*	*14,337,813 lbs.*	*1968*	*30*

Average total catch, 1918–68	22,190,000 lbs.
Total catch, 1968	14,338,000 lbs.
1968 catch as percentage of 50-year average	64.8

Source: South Atlantic Fisheries Historical Catch Statistics.

cline of the harvest. Since most of these fish come from the sea rather than the river, it is not at first apparent why the pollution should work such serious damage. The reason is that most of the fish are drawn to the marsh at some period in their lives. Either because of incubation periods in the marsh or feeding expeditions for marsh animals, 98 per cent of all the commercially important fish on the coast depend directly on the marsh for survival.[25] "The stability of the state's crab crop, shrimp harvest, and oyster production rests squarely on marshlands," experts from South Carolina's Bears Bluff Laboratory have said. "Unwise exploitation of the marshlands must be stopped." [26]

The crucial role of the estuary and marsh is not a phenomenon peculiar to the Southeast. Five of the nation's six most important commercial fish are either permanent or temporary residents of the estuary. These five estuarine species—crab, shrimp, menhaden, salmon, and oysters—together make up half the country's total fish catch every year.[27]

To see how a dirty marsh can damage its fish, we can examine the life cycle of the shrimp, the tiny crustacean that makes up 80 per cent of Georgia's fish sales.[28] After young shrimp hatch at sea, they return to the protective marshes for the first months of their lives. Only when they have grown to a decent size do they leave the marshes for the ocean and the shrimpers' nets. Since shrimp rarely live for more than a year, each year's catch depends on the crop that nursed in the marsh during the previous winter. During that period, if conditions in the marsh are poor, the young shrimp die, and there is no catch. Put in scientific terms:

> Majority opinion is that the fertile estuary constitutes an irreplaceable factor in the survival strategy of major shrimp resources and that the perpetuation of such resources at commercial levels, apart from their continued existence per se, will be contingent upon our ability to minimize the disturbance of the shrimp estuarine habitat.[29]

If we had more data, we could see exactly how many shrimp die when the acid and low-oxygen waters seep into the marsh; as it is, we can only be sure there is a danger.

The haggard oysters—victims of fecal bacteria, sinking into sludge beds, and acid-induced paralysis—depend on the marshes in much the same way as shrimp. Before they grow their shells, larval oysters drift through the estuarine waters. They are especially weak and vulnerable at this stage, and if the marsh should contain patches of acid or kraft waste, an entire crop of oysters may disappear.

Attacks on the marsh claim human victims as well. As the river gets dirtier and the fish become scarcer, many small fishermen and independent shrimpers who used to work out of ports up and down the Georgia coast find themselves out of a job. Some are able to get work in the factories that have taken over their rivers, but others do not want or cannot get new jobs. For those not raised in the poorer districts of this country, it is often hard to understand what the loss of a fishing stream can mean. In the quiet, desperate counties near Savannah, there are hundreds of families who catch fish not for fun or business but for their own food. This is perhaps the most socially reprehensible face of industrial pollution; those who run the companies and have jobs there do not suffer, but for their profit they close a last escape valve for the hungry human leftovers. In other parts of the country, this might be melodramatic, but not in coastal Georgia.

Big fishermen can survive where the small ones fail, and they react to the changed conditions with characteristic business sense. If the fish are harder to get, it costs more to get them; and the customer eventually pays exorbitant prices for formerly cheap fish. On the surface, this attitude is nothing more than the free market place at work, but it is worth examining more closely. The fish are disappearing mainly because some manufacturers are saving money by not cleaning up their effluent. There may be some slight consolation in the fact that consequently paper bags are cheap. But this is an artificial kind of cheapness, attained by forcing fishermen to endure costs that the mills should pay, and it is a cheapness that leaves the consumer no choice. Perhaps the American public would prefer to go home from the grocery store with less expensive fish inside a slightly more expensive paper bag. Until we decide that a corporate balance sheet cannot set the standards for our lives, we will endure these enforced choices and we will live in a landscape that looks like the one we now see around us.

JACKSON, S.C.—Arthur Ruffin can't spell the word "pollution," but he can define it. "It stinks and it's dirty and it gets on my trout lines and in my fish traps and it costs me a heap of money," said the 67-year-old fisherman.

Arthur Ruffin has derived a good part of his meager income by fishing the Savannah River for most of his adult life. He sells catfish, mudfish, carp, suckers, and shad to friends and neighbors.

"Sold 'em for forty cent a pound and made a right good livin' . . . but they won't lemme fish now and I can't hardly see my way clear," Arthur Ruffin said.

Ruffin and hundreds, perhaps thousands, of others have been cut off from part or all of their income since August 9, when the authorities in South Carolina slapped a ban on fishing in the Savannah after it was found that the Olin Corporation at Augusta was discharging mercury into the river. . . .

"Smell the air," he said. "That smell right to you? And look at that water out there . . . oily ain't it?" Ruffin estimates that the fishing ban will cost him nearly $1000 a year if the ban lasts that long. Even without the ban, he figures he is in trouble because some of his customers have complained about the fish he sells them.

"Some people told me that my fishes is bad. They say, 'Arthur, them fishes is real bad; they tastes oily.' And then I can't sell 'em no more fishes," he complained. Ruffin showed the visitor a couple of catfishes he hauled from the muddy and oily river. The fish were covered with festering sores.

"Can't hardly sell fishes like this," he said. "Them sores is right disgustful . . . awful lookin' things, they is."

Ruffin says he can't understand the deterioration of the Savannah in recent years. He remembers the river when it "looked pretty good, smelled good, and was chock full of all kinds of fishes."

"Why, I even used to drink that river water . . . thought nothing of it," he said. "Now the cows got more sense than to drink from that stinkin' river." . . .

He was told that the authorities are working on the problem.

"Sure wish they would hurry it up," Ruffin said. "I got to get back to fishin' again . . . real quick." [30]

In Savannah and Beyond Savannah: Conclusions

. . . all experience hath shewn, that mankind are more disposed to suffer, while evils are sufferable, than to right themselves by abolishing the forms to which they are accustomed. But when a long train of abuses and usurpations, pursuing invariably the same Object evinces a design to reduce them under absolute Despotism, it is their right, it is their duty . . . to provide new Guards for their future security.

The Declaration of Independence.

The only thing necessary for the triumph of evil is for good men to do nothing.

Edmund Burke

What is happening in Savannah is happening all over the United States. When Ralph Nader selected the city as the site of our project, he did so almost arbitrarily, as if he had pulled the name out of a hat. Four considerations affected his choice: we wanted a southern city, since industry is a newcomer to much of the South and its effects are less entrenched and easier to change, and since the South, always conscious of the beauty of its environment, might be more disposed to respond to criticism effectively and firmly; the Savannah River was known to be heavily polluted; there was extensive, readily available documentation of the amount and causes of the pollution and of governmental efforts to combat it; and Savannah's relatively small size made it easier to study than a giant metropolis. But with enough time and resources, what we have done in Savannah could have been done in New York or Cleveland or Los Angeles.

Neither the citizens of Savannah (who have known about their environmental problems for years) nor

Ralph Nader nor least of all we suspected that our study would find us thumbing through old city files and county tax records. But to have avoided seemingly unrelated topics would have been to renege on our commitment to a thorough report. Even so, we have only touched upon some important topics, such as the relationship between poverty and environmental discomfort. All five of Savannah's housing projects are located in areas where air pollution is unusually high. As with so many other issues, the poor suffer most and—since by definition the poor do not run industries and by custom the poor have little voice in government—can do least about it. If we had been examining air pollution in Los Angeles, we would have had to discuss much more than the effect of automobile exhaust fumes on pine trees; city planning philosophies, meteorology, land use, the policies of Detroit, and many other topics are important as well.

All of which is to say that human ecology, like natural ecology, is a seamless web. A decision made in one sector will affect others. If industries stop polluting the Savannah River, they will be able to use river water instead of the disappearing ground water. At the same time, fishing and its revenue would increase. If Union Camp and the other industries nestled in their tax shelters paid their fair share of taxes, Savannah would easily have been able to afford its sewer system long ago. If the air were free of kraft odors and the river free of raw sewage, Savannah's efforts to attract tourists and other industries would pay off.

The obvious question, in Savannah and beyond Savannah, is how to start the ecological snowball rolling. A great deal is at stake. Our country tends to respond to problems only when they reach crisis proportions, but our ability to inflict environmental damage is so much greater than our ability to rectify it quickly that we must begin work now. If we wait until men die it will be too late. Savannah can help lead the way out of the environmental morass. The suggested actions we offer here cannot claim to be definitive, and they will not be accepted without argument. This is as it should be. For too long Savannahians and other Americans have not argued as their environment was systematically torn apart; putting it back together will be too complicated a task and affect too many people in too many ways to be accomplished by fiat.

But in Savannah the problems, formidable as they are, are simpler than in some other areas where the environment has become almost inextricably tangled and fouled. New York City has decided to build a new subway line that might reduce, slightly, the number of cars in Manhattan—but at the expense of tearing up a large patch of Central Park. Partly because of its smaller size, partly because its environmental problems are of more recent and obvious origin, Savannah's choices will be easier:

1. Strengthening the Georgia air and water quality laws.

The State of Georgia owes a debt of gratitude to Rock Howard and his staff at the State Water Quality Control Board. What progress has been made in the last five years toward cleaning up the Savannah—and there will be more as pollution controls that are under construction come into use—has been of Howard's doing. He has had little help either from the federal government or from the state law he has had to work with. The most profound way the people of his state can express their gratitude is to give him a better, stronger law.

Three statutory adjustments could significantly improve the effectiveness of the Water Quality Control Act:

(*a*) *Citizen Participation.* Because of the threat which exists toward any regulatory body of becoming the captive of the industry it is supposed to regulate, and because citizen participation infinitely increases the protective resources available, and because private citizens are often most sensitive to the need for environmental quality protection at the local level, some effort should be made to involve private citizens in the state mechanism for control. The present law forbids the admissibility of state records (for the air and water agencies) in private court actions. The need to establish independent scientific data and the high legal costs that accompany any legal action combine to make private legal action prohibitive to any but the wealthiest citizens or citizens groups. The state law could meet this problem in several ways:

—allow that state records be admissible in private suits;
—establish that, once a private litigant has established a *prima facie* case of environmental degradation, the defendant has the burden of proof to justify his action;
—declare a citizen's right to a clean environment.

(*b*) *Remedies.* The present air and water laws do not provide an adequate range of remedies to meet the innumerable possible threats to our environment. Only criminal sanctions are available at the present time, though the public is not willing to accept the idea of calling corporate executives criminals. High standards of proof must be met to justify a criminal sentence constitutionally, and actual intent must be shown, when many serious ecological disasters can be rationalized as accidental. A new law should provide for:

—civil penalties, in the form of fines or actual compensation for damage done;
—injunctions, to compel polluters to take positive preventative measures;
—mandamus (an order to a public official to do his duty), to compel cities and counties to meet their environmental responsibilities.

(*c*) *Enforcement.* Given the present limited budgets of the air and water agencies, the present system of securing compliance with its orders is so cumbersome and drawn out that neither agency can afford to take many of its cases to court. Both agencies should, after an administrative hearing which allows due process for all parties concerned, be able to take an order to the court and then treat the order as an order of the court. This system of enforcement would streamline the legal process of state environmental quality control, and consequently place the agencies in a much sounder bargaining position with recalcitrant industries.

(*d*) *Standards.* The Water Board and the Air Board currently have power only to set standards for the general quality of the air and water—so-called "receiving stream" and "ambient air" standards. While these powers are essential, the boards should also have power to set effluent and emission standards for particular industries and other polluters.

2. Monitoring and regulating ground water use.

One of the most disturbing features of the ecological crisis in Savannah is that pollution of surface waters has made the area dependent on ground water for virtually all its water supply. The heavy Savannah pumping has unquestionably lowered the level of the artesian aquifer dramatically—a fact that is alarming in itself, but even more alarming because no one seems to be doing anything about it. Thus, years after fighting American Cyanamid's plans to pump 6 mgd from the aquifer, Union Camp increased its own pumping by the same amount. And Union Camp Vice President James E. Ray III, responding to an article about depletion of ground water in the Savannah *News-Press,* claimed that the aquifer had not even been strained by the heavy industrial pumping. This time Rock Howard did squawk, but he is powerless to do more. So there are two problems: monitoring the use of ground water, and making sure that no one uses too much.

Since ground water use is an interstate problem—the Carolinas and Georgia and Florida, for example, use the same aquifer—it is not illogical that the USGS currently watches over it. But the USGS is not doing its job well. In Savannah, it is unable even to obtain figures on ground water pumping from local industry unless the industry wants to talk, and it is in any case unable to verify the figures it gets. It is odd to entrust conservation of a vital natural resource to an agency that has shown no interest in conserving it—an agency that has confidently predicted that more and more ground water will be available, one of whose employees actually claims that "if using [artesian water] heavily for twenty years meant that it would be destroyed for the future, then this course would be preferable to not using the resource at all." It would seem that, at the least, authority over ground water should be vested in a federal agency, such as the Environmental Protection Agency. As Mr. William Ruckelshaus takes on his duties as the nation's environmental watchdog, we strongly urge that a study of ground water use and legislation for its regulation be one of his highest priorities.

There is no reason ever to run out of ground water.

All that need be done is to assure that no more water is taken out of the aquifer than is put in. This means, immediately, that efforts must be made to find out how much pumping the Savannah and other aquifers can bear. The ticklish problem then becomes deciding who can use the available water. Obviously, individual human beings, who require pure drinking water and lack the resources to purify what is polluted, should have priority over industries, who need water less pure and can usually afford to clean up what they need. (Especially if they did not pollute surface waters so badly, the cost would not be high.)

As Georgia's air quality law clearly demonstrates, the purpose of a law is often as important as its specific provisions. The purpose of any ground water control law should be to assure the availability of drinking water by assuring that no user or class of user is able to prevent its use by others. A law regulating ground water use should require:

—that all users of ground water report the amount they use to the regulatory agency;
—that those figures be made public;
—that the agency be given power to force users to curtail use if the agency deems it proper or necessary;
—that the agency be made responsible for assuring that ground water will be available for private use in areas where it exists;
—that citizens be given standing in court to sue either the regulatory agency or (if culpability can be assigned to one user) a ground water user if the citizen is forced to turn to another source of water because of abuse of the aquifer.

The study of ground water resources and the implementation of regulations for its use will take time, and, in Savannah and elsewhere, time is short. Until federal regulation comes into being, state and local governments must fill the gap. Chatham County, Georgia, which requires permits before new wells are drilled, should go two steps further and order, first, that new and existing wells be spaced further apart, and second, that pumping by industries in the county be immediately and significantly reduced. It is the only prudent course if the county wishes to avoid spending tens of millions of dollars looking for a new source of drinking water for its people.

3. Speeding construction of sewage treatment plants throughout Chatham County.

There is no more obnoxious affront to the Savannah environment than the feces boiling in front of city hall. Five years ago we would have strongly urged the six other cities in Chatham County to join in a regional sewage treatment plan, but the problem is urgent and the delays have been too long. There is no excuse for delay by those who (for some incomprehensible reason) prefer their sewage raw. The other cities, which have not for the most part bothered with their sewage, might consider one of two alternatives: banding together in twos or threes for joint sewage treatment, or working together with local industry. Port Wentworth, for example, is home to both Savannah Sugar and Continental Can, and could join forces with them to clean all wastes.

For Savannah, which has many more people and therefore much more sewage than the other cities, the problem is money. The money so far budgeted for sewage treatment will cover only as much as the city would have to pay if it were assisted by both state and federal governments, and the Georgia legislature has so far been unwilling to help out its seaboard citizens. This is, to say the least, unimaginative and shortsighted. Oysters are the earliest casualty of untreated feces, and oysters used to bring a lot of taxable income into the state.

If the state government cannot bring itself to do its share, the city will have to do it. Hiding from that fact will help no one. The money will have to be found, and the easiest way to find it is by broadening the tax base.

4. Reforming the tax structure of Chatham County.

If the state of Georgia will not help finance the sewer system, it will have to help with the tax problem. The quickest and most equitable way to raise enough tax money to pay for sewage treatment would be to incorporate the industrial tax shelters into the city of

Savannah. (Merely raising taxes in the zones to a level commensurate with those in the city would not solve the problem, since the revenue so generated would go to Chatham County and not to the city. On the other hand, if the Georgia legislature does pay part of the sewer costs, the money might better be given to the county to help its air pollution work.) The zones that have sheltered Union Camp and other industries were created by an amendment to the state Constitution and can be abolished only by another amendment. The state has a choice: either it should come up with the cash for the sewer system or it should let Savannah annex the zones so that the city can come up with the cash itself.

In any case industry should be made to pay its fair share of taxes, and the Chatham County tax system should be removed, insofar as possible, from political influence. One way to do this would be to establish standards that the county tax assessor must meet, through examinations, licenses, and the like.

5. Insisting on quarterly progress reports from Savannah's pollutors.

The impact of popular opinion or of a report like this tends to be, unfortunately, short-lived. The public mind wanders, public concern dies down. If they wish to avoid repeating the errors of the past, Savannahians must not let this happen. Union Camp is already years behind schedule in building pollution controls, and may fall behind again if the public allows it. The day before the press conference at which this report was released to Savannahians, Union Camp announced a pollution control system that it pledged would remove 85 per cent of BOD in time for the state deadline in 1972. Savannahians should insist that Union Camp make public reports of its progress toward this goal every three months. And, if and when Union Camp achieves the 85 per cent goal, they should start asking about the remaining 15 per cent. There is no longer any excuse for paper mill pollution.

Nor should full quarterly disclosure of anti-pollution efforts be the responsibility of Union Camp alone. American Cyanimid should do the same, as should the other industrial pollutors and the city of Savannah itself, which, after so long a delay, owes its citizens some facts about progress toward sewage treatment. Nationwide, too, consumers should press for full quarterly disclosure of industry's pollution and efforts to control it. No businessman wants the public to see what his company is doing to the environment, and publicity may be one of the best spurs to effective action against pollution.

Needless to say, the people of Savannah should not be content with glowing press releases that skirt the facts. Union Camp and others tell the Water Board the exact statistics on BOD and other wastes sent to the river, and the people directly affected by the filth should expect no less.

6. Requesting a third Federal Enforcement Conference in Savannah.

One way to keep the pollution of the Savannah River before the public until it is cleaned up is to call a third Federal Enforcement Conference. This conference should, in addition to evaluating progress made so far by pollutors, make use of its prestige to put pressure behind the city and industry to move ahead with its pollution controls quickly. It can do this by publically establishing interim deadlines to be met in the construction of pollution controls. These deadlines, which the FWQA would have power to enforce, would declare what construction stage the pollutor must have reached at a given point in time, if it is to meet the final, 1972, deadline.

7. Building citizen commitment to a clean environment.

The release of this report made big news in Savannah, with front-page headlines in the Savannah *News-Press,* comments by public and corporate figures, and an expression of concern from the mayor, who fears that this book will blacken the name of the city. An editorial in the *News-Press* responded to the mayor far better than we can:

> Mayor Rousakis said the report has made "the name Savannah synonymous with pollution." If that is true, of course, proper steps by the community and an impressive, concerted effort to move the city vigorously forward will

not only offset that temporary stigma but make our accomplishments all the more momentous.

For if people elsewhere regard Savannah as the city where Ralph Nader came to cite shortcomings, it can also be known as the city which overcame them and in doing so demonstrated that Savannah is a place where things get done and where people and businesses would be wise to stake their future. In fact, if we deal with our problems, the publicity from the Nader Report could turn out to be an asset because it would make our accomplishments that much more sensational as far as the outside observer is concerned.

Uniquely blessed by history and environment, typically cursed by degradation of that environment, Savannah can be a model to the nation. Most of its problems—with the important exception of auto fumes—are local in origin and can be solved or reduced locally. For years the city has been concerned about restoring its riverfront houses. But new paint and flowers in the squares are not enough to restore Savannah. The editors and reporters of the *News-Press* have recently shown true leadership in keeping the environmental issue before the citizens of Savannah, and they should be urged to keep it up. Meanwhile city and county officials should appoint an environmental watchdog—with enough national stature to make his bark heard, and enough local law to make his bite felt—to supervise both the parks and restoration programs and an all-out attack on pollution. So far the pollutors have acted with remarkable ingenuity in delaying the sewer system, in twisting the city's history, in hiding the facts about their pollution, in manipulating the tax structure. If the people of Savannah show anything resembling this ingenuity, they can turn the city around.

If it costs more, so be it. Forty billion paper bags are produced in the United States annually, two hundred for each American citizen. If the price of these bags were increased by just one cent, the $400 million generated annually (only $2 per person per year) would pay for pollution controls for the entire U. S. paper industry in one to three years—two to six dollars per person to eliminate one-fifth of the BOD thrown into all our lakes and rivers by all our industries and people (Table 2-3). And if Union Camp, which produces one-fifth of those paper bags, were to increase its prices by only one-tenth of a cent per bag, two years' sales would more than pay for a complete pollution control system for its Savannah plant. Moreover, slight as these costs are, only a fraction of them need be passed on to the consumer; most industries can well afford to pay for pollution control out of their own pockets.

And should. For years the citizens of Savannah have paid many of the costs of Union Camp's doing business. They have paid by permitting the mill to pour its filth in their river; by letting Union Camp get away with a minuscule rent and tax bill while private citizens' taxes soared; by prostituting their civic pride to a belief that Union Camp saved the town from ruin. It is time the company, which has taken so much from Savannah, paid its own way, just as it is time U. S. Steel paid its way in Gary and Consolidated Edison in New York. In some cases and to some degree the costs of cleaning up the environment will be passed on to the consumer in the form of higher prices, but this should not deter citizens from pressing for immediate pollution control. The present system, whereby industry skims a farthing off its prices by not cleaning up its waste, is a perverse and false capitalism. We pay now for pollution, each time we pay our taxes; and if industry does not assume the costs of pollution controls, we will pay still more in taxes, because government will have to pay to get the job done. When children are young, their mothers work to bathe them and clean up after them; as they grow up they are forced to clean up after themselves. If industries behave childishly, the government must handle the clean-up; it is time for industry to grow up.

Like growing children, industry will accept adult responsibilities only when this will yield profits—or when compelled to do so by the government. Some laws are already on the books to fight against pollution, the technology to stop it is there, but because corporations are not willing (except occasionally) to spend the money, and governments are not willing (except occasionally) to enforce the law, and because the people are not organized (except occasionally) to press for enforcement, nothing is being done—except occasionally.

The citizens of Savannah are at least somewhat fortunate. In Rock Howard they have a spokesman and defender for their rights to clean water. But what if, in future years, Howard is cashiered by a governor dependent on the favors of industry? And what of the air pollution in Georgia, whose opponents are shackled by the law? And what of the rest of us—citizens, perhaps, of states with no strong environmental protector, dependent on the scandalously weak federal efforts to clean up the environment? This report was not written by a team from "Mission Impossible." What we have done can and should be done by citizens elsewhere; what Savannah can and should do can and should be done by cities elsewhere. In Savannah and beyond Savannah, the evils are no longer sufferable; it is our right and duty to provide new guards for our future security.

Appendix 1

The Other Side: John E. Ray III's Speech to the Savannah Rotary Club, October 19, 1970

First of all, I would like to thank you for your courtesy in inviting me here today, and for giving me this opportunity to speak with you. What I will have to say will not take more than 20 minutes. Afterwards, I will, to the best of my ability, try to answer questions you may have.

I am here in two roles. One as a representative of Union Camp. The other, to speak for myself as a private, concerned American citizen.

In recent months, Union Camp has been the target of inflammatory charges relating to the deterioration of the Savannah River. Moreover, my company has been placed in the role of arch polluter and despoiler of the natural resources of the Savannah community.

However well-intentioned, certain charges made against us are wrong in fact and in substance. Some have been stated out of context. And others are scientifically meaningless. Nonetheless, the ensuing publicity and notoriety are unjustly damaging, not only to Union Camp, but to the Savannah community as well.

In fairness to Union Camp, its employees, and the citizens of Savannah, I welcome this opportunity to visit with you today to try to put the pollution dilemma into some rational perspective.

Before we examine some of the specific charges, it might be useful to agree on terminology as it relates to the whole area of pollution.

If by pollution we mean using nature's bounty and leaving it less pure than we found it, then yes, we have been polluters.

But then so is the housewife who does her weekly wash, or even her dishes for that matter. And her husband who commutes to work and back each day by car. And also town councils which are still trying to decide whether to propose a bond issue for a new sewage treatment plant. And the tens of thousands of picnickers and campers in search of unspoiled beauty, who leave souvenirs of their visit.

I don't mean to insult your intelligence by comparing the effects of one lady's laundry, or one man's car exhaust to those of the largest paper mill in the world. Individually, one polluter doesn't matter a bit. Collectively, many do. The exhaust from one car may seem insignificant, but all motor vehicles put together—and this is according to the U. S. Public Health Service—all motor vehicles account for 60 per cent of air pollution in the United States. By contrast, *all* paper mills, all chemical plants, and all refineries and steel furnaces, all factories big and small—altogether account for only 17 per cent of *air pollution*. Less than a third as much as transportation.

But all this is not to evade the central issue—the making of pulp and paper entails "pollution" too—and in this respect, Union Camp contributes more, but only by virtue of its size since our Savannah plant is the largest paper mill in the world. Nevertheless, things are not as bad as they have been painted.

For example, it has been charged that: *Union Camp is threatening the water resources of Georgia.*

But what are the facts in the matter? Let's refer to an authority on the subject, the United States Geological Survey. For many years they have been monitoring the Ocala Aquifer—the source of our ground water. Based on data collected by them, there has been very little change during the last ten years in its water level or chloride content.

This indicates that the capacity of the aquifier, which holds and replenishes Georgia's water resources has not been exceeded. Indeed, the scientific evidence is that it has not even been strained.

The aquifer is not an underground lake. It is in fact a slow-flowing river. Its size is immense—being 300 to 400 miles wide, 50 to 250 feet deep and having a current flow estimated at one mile in 50 to 100 years. Water not used eventually flows into the ocean at the Continental Shelf and is lost to man's use.

For the record there are two pertinent facts that I should bring to your attention:

> Among the users of the aquifer in Georgia, Union Camp ranks third in volume. Believe it or not, there are others drawing substantially more water than we.
>
> It takes a lot of water to make paper. However, we are constantly striving to be more frugal in its use. For instance, we now re-use each gallon of process water an average of 12 times.

Now let's take a moment to examine another sweeping charge: the one that implies that *Union Camp has polluted the Savannah River beyond redemption.*

Well ladies and gentlemen, even if we didn't believe anything to be beyond redemption on religious grounds, science would come to our rescue. The Savannah River happens to be one of the great river systems in America. Its average *daily* flow for a 20-year period was 7 billion, 330 million gallons.

On the other hand, Union Camp discharges less than 40 million gallons a day, of process water. After discarding a lot of zeros—I think this is *five-tenth of one per cent* of the average flow of the river. It seems to us that the dynamic flow and diluting effect of the Savannah River itself, is the best safeguard against putting it beyond redemption.

However, as you will see later, we are not putting the whole burden of redemption on the river itself.

But first may I ask you to back up a moment to take up specific elements of pollution.

Among the things considered to be major river pollutants are:

Mercury
Oil
Sanitary sewage
Settleable solids and
Organic matter.

Let's consider these one by one.

We do not use mercury in *our* manufacturing process and hence it is not an element of our effluent. As a matter of fact, on the basis of a preliminary report released by the Georgia Water Quality Control Board the mercury level in the sea life of the Savannah Estuary has been declared safe.

As to oil, we had an accidental spill of fuel oil in June of 1969. This incident has been disposed of to the court's satisfaction in April of 1970. We can't guarantee that accidents won't ever happen again, but I can assure you that extensive additional safeguards have been established to prevent them.

Our proportion of sanitary sewage is now minimal. We are preparing to eliminate even that by separately collecting all such wastes for treatment at the new municipal treating plant scheduled for completion in 1972. And, of course, we will pay for the cost of treatment.

As to solids, our new clarification system installed in 1968 already removes 90 per cent of all settleable solids and floating materials. And we are working to improve that ratio.

It seems that *our cardinal sin is the discharge of organic matter,* which is a by-product of cooking pulpwood. This is broken down by naturally-occurring organisms in the river.

In the process they use up dissolved oxygen which exists in the water. *And it is this depletion of oxygen that is harmful to fish. It does no harm to man.*

I'm not saying it's good to impair the natural habitat of marine life. But, as far as we know, we have not been responsible for any fish kill in the Savannah River. Nonetheless, and what is certainly more important to you, we are in the process of developing supplementary treatment facilities, which by late 1972, should remove 85 per cent of the oxygen demand in our effluent.

I might say that these things are being done under the direction and guidance of R. S. Howard, Executive Secretary of the State Water Quality Control Board. The Board set new standards of compliance for us and our neighbors using the Savannah River.

Still another charge directed our way implies that: *it is a myth to say that the smell of pollution is the smell of progress.*

Maybe that one is directed to all Southern kraft pulp and paper mills because the kraft process consists of cooking wood chips—and that's where the odor comes from. And we all use essentially the same type of wood and similar cooking processes.

So cooking odors relate to what is being cooked—be it a garlic sauce, onion soup, cabbage, pecan-pie or what have you. Some are pleasant—some are not. Kraft mill odors are not harmful. They are esthetically offensive, especially to people not accustomed to them.

And we haven't taken that for granted either. Even though our Savannah plant has increased its output from the original 75 thousand tons, to nearly 1 million tons annually, our odor concentration has been substantially reduced over the years.

The Savannah mill was one of the first in the East to install a black liquor oxidation system which treats and substantially reduces odor-causing compounds. We are also evaluating a technique which involves the collection and burning of vent gases.

The difficult aspect of the odor problem is that the human nose is extremely sensitive to even minute, infinitesimal amounts of it. So unless they are eliminated completely, they will always be more or less noticeable, depending on the degree of individual sensitivity.

The ultimate solution, especially for mills built many years ago, will require new technology and significant investments. Uniform standards of air quality have not yet been promulgated. Nonetheless, we recognize the problem and are pursuing it aggressively through resources within and outside our company.

Meanwhile, we think it not a myth that a tolerable level of odor with prosperity, is a more desirable alternative than an idle plant. And we hope you do too!

Before I leave the question of our air emissions, just a word about particulates—the fancy word for dust, particles and soot.

Here in Savannah, our chemical recovery boilers have been equipped with electrostatic precipitators some of which can attract up to 95 per cent of the particles from the recovery process. Our solid fuel burning boilers and lime kilns use cyclone and wet scrubbers. Currently they pick up about 90 per cent of the particles in the exhaust gases which they treat. This was the most feasible equipment available to us when we installed it. We're working to improve it. Actually we're aiming to remove substantially more materials in these gases—and make a very significant improvement over our already effective treatment.

The charges against us and any variations of them yet to follow are a challenge to Union Camp. I might add that you have been challenged too! The charge against you is that you have sold your birthright for a payroll; that you have permitted and abetted insidious, pervasive influences to infect your local, county and state governments.

I won't presume to answer these charges on your behalf. Union Camp has been a citizen of your community for 35 years. We were small when we started, but together we have grown. Today, we are the largest industrial employer in Savannah, and the fourth largest in Georgia.

To some people, this fact may have sinister connotations. To us, it simply means that 5,000 people from this community work for us directly, and at least half as many again, indirectly, in the forest. We are proud and delighted to have every one of them. They are fine, productive, hard-working men and women, and I do not believe that *they* feel they are accomplices in betraying your birthright by working for us.

It is easy to make charges and call people names, and it usually succeeds in attracting attention. What it does *not* do is solve problems.

The fact is that we do have problems. And by "we" I don't just mean Union Camp and the city of Savannah. I mean all of us in this country—in industry, in communities, as private citizens, even as campers looking for a peaceful corner.

The problem is that, to some extent, we are all polluters. By our very existence, by the requirements we place on our environment, we all draw against nature's balance. And we're discovering that this balance is not inexhaustible.

The fact—that we are all polluters—does not excuse any of us, individually or collectively. Nor does it mean that we should abolish the twentieth century and try to restore the wilderness.

No! I think that armed with the awareness of what we are doing, and aware too of what we want out of our lives, we must assess our individual actions and take full responsibility for them.

This is the American credo. We want not only a good life, but a continually better life. We want cars and boats and houses. We want comfort, convenience, security, a better education and the chance and the means to enjoy our leisure. These, too, are elements essential to a quality of life. And to attain them, we have made a national commitment to growth. If you call growth by its other name, progress—it is progress which has contributed to our problem.

It has become apparent that the same environment which effortlessly accomodated 150 million people 20 years ago, and 179 million people ten years ago, is having trouble accomodating 205 million people today.

This is the core of the problem. And it isn't just that there are more of us, but that we have more, we do more, we want more. And compounding the problem is that by choice we tend to crowd together more. Seventy per cent of our population lives and works on less than 12 per cent of our land. This creates a patchwork of interlocking cities and industrial complexes, which on the East Coast is already straining our resources from Miami to Portland, Maine.

No two plants are alike, not even two paper mills, *and not even two paper mills in the same company*. The technological problems we are struggling with here in Savannah are not the same as those that faced us in Franklin, Virginia, or in Montgomery, Alabama. So even if the money were available, I don't think we would be able to purify our waters overnight.

For air pollution even a guesstimate is hazardous because it assumes that the technology is available to do the job. The fact is, to the best of our knowledge, much of the technology does *not* exist.

We tend to talk and think about pollution in national terms, but there is a whole lot of difference between what the word means to the people of Aspen, Colorado, and to those in Gary, Indiana.

And for that matter to those in Savannah, Georgia.

This is your community, and we are one of its citizens. You make the rules and we live by them. That is the way it has been in the past, and that is the way it should remain in the future.

We have been working with the appropriate responsible people on the local and state levels. They know—and we know—that words like pollution are relative. I do not believe, for instance, that with the best intentions in the world, and with the full cooperation of every industry and community in this area, we will ever succeed in making the lower Savannah River into one of the great fly-casting streams of North America.

They know—and we know—that it costs a massive amount of money to do a massive cleaning job. And wherever it's done, there is only one place the money can come from. It may be funneled through public authorities, or corporations, or government bodies. In the final analysis it comes from you and me. Where else?

I said at the start that I was here in two roles. I've spoken for my company. Now I'd like to add a few last words as just a plain, private citizen.

As Jimmy Lientz said in his introduction, I was born and brought up in Franklin, Virginia. In 1938, we started to produce pulp and paper there, and in the years since our mill has grown eightfold. I have many close relatives who still live in Franklin. A number of them are in their seventies and eighties and quote "pollution" unquote or not, most of them are still active, hale and hearty. As for myself, my job required me to move to New York City eight years ago, and even the most positive thinking of local boosters have very little cheerful to say about New York City's environment.

The point is, I know what pollution is. It happens I also enjoy boating and fishing, and the pleasure of getting outdoors and lunging at a golf ball. I want to keep on enjoying these things, and I want my children and grandchildren to be able to enjoy them too.

I know that if industry—or any user of air and water—is permitted to abuse its access to these resources, they can be ruined for all of us.

I also know that if unrealistic demands are imposed on industry—or any user of our common air and water—if a punitive rather than a productive climate is created; if anger replaces reason, and if irresponsible statements are allowed to linger unchallenged; then maybe we'll all be in trouble. The whole question of "Should we grow at this rate or at that rate" would become academic.

And I say this as Jack Ray, the citizen, not as executive vice president of anything.

I mentioned that making paper isn't glamorous. It isn't. Yet one of the surest measures of a country's economic development and well-being is the amount of paper it consumes a year. In the United States, that amount is 576 pounds per person. In the Soviet Union, it is 57 pounds. In India just a little under four pounds.

So as we evaluate the alternatives available to us, I think we must carefully think of what the consequences would be if we chose, as a solution, to make less paper, or fewer automobiles, or plastics, or fertilizer, or what you will.

We, as a company do many things here in Georgia. Among them we grow trees and make paper. Now, trees are a natural resource, too, and a renewable one—like air and water.

We use a lot of trees in Savannah—15 million a year and the equivalent of another five million by using waste from lumber operations. But for more than 15 years we have been regenerating our forests at the rate of eight trees for every one we've cut down. We now raise 400 to 500 trees per acre on land that once supported only 60 to 100.

We've developed techniques that make the land—which is really the base of our ecology—increasingly productive. We've transformed barren fields into healthy forests, and we are now growing many more trees than we started with, despite the fact that our consumption of trees has multiplied during the years.

We have been commended for these efforts and for some of our approaches to pollution abatement. What we have done with one renewable resource, we believe we can do with others. You have our pledge that we shall not relax in our determination to attain this goal.

With your support and cooperation, I'm sure we will succeed.

Thank you.

Appendix 2

What to Look for in Your Environmental Quality Control Law

An ideal statute for environmental quality control cannot be conceived in an academic vacuum, dictated to all 50 states, and be expected to work. Each state has different requirements because of the magnitude and quality of the problem, the degree of popular support for reform, the existing structure of government, and its financial resources. Each state therefore requires modifications in the "ideal" law to suit local conditions. Although the following provisions are offered only as guidelines, if a particular clause is missing, the concerned citizen should ask his legislators why, and demand specific answers.

Policy: Every piece of legislation begins with a declaration of policy. It should be the law's policy to maintain and *restore* the quality of the subject of the legislation, whether air, water, or the whole environment.

Enforcement: The agency's legislation always has an enforcement provision that begins: "It shall be unlawful to . . ."; there is also a clause empowering the agency to prosecute violators. For example: the Georgia Water Quality Control Act says that it shall be unlawful to pollute "except in such a manner as to conform to and comply with all rules, regulations, orders, and permits" issued by the Board. Effective legislation should have a more direct statement of enforcement power—for example, that it shall be unlawful to degrade the waters of the state. Otherwise, penalties and court suits rest entirely on interpretations of the regulations. A positive policy statement in the enforcement clause would also ease the burden of proof on plaintiffs in private suits.

Private suits: The relation between a state's legislative scheme and private citizen action may determine the ultimate effectiveness of environmental legislation, especially in states where there is possible industrial influence over the pollution control agencies. A legislative scheme that aids private actions has great potential benefits. As private actions become more feasible, they should become more common and so ease the pollution control agency's burden of dealing with recalcitrant polluters, thus allowing the agency to devote itself to more appropriate jobs of planning, extending research, and setting standards.

In Georgia, both the air and water laws forbid the use of agency information in private suits, although Howard will ask the legislature in 1971 to delete this clause from the Act. Even if the records were admissible, rules of evidence usually demand personal testimony to support the validity of the evidence. In a water pollution suit, for example, a Water Board engineer would probably have to testify in court about how the information was gathered. This kind of duty could be a serious drain on manpower and time; with adequate staffing, it could be understood as one of the staff's proper functions. There is also the problem of potential abuse of agency records. It is conceivable that agencies would collect information for the specific purpose of giving it to private litigants preparing suits to collect money damages, to improve property values, or out of pure malice.

The most common defense of making the records inadmissible in court is that their use would impair cooperation between the agency and the industries it regulates. Howard, who would like to see his records used in private actions, answers this argument by saying that getting candid information is already so much like pulling teeth that making it admissible would not really change the situation. The industries already following antipollution legislation would have little to fear from private suits. Even if the threat of private litigation were to cause temporary interruption in the flow of information from company to agency, the potential power and benefits of an alliance between private citizens and the state agency should thoroughly justify the inconvenience.

The legal obstacles to making state records available to private litigants are not necessarily insurmountable; at least one Georgia agency, the Department of Public Health, already lets its records be used in private suits.*

There is a final reason for allowing citizens to use state records. Too often regulatory agencies act to cushion industrial polluters from any serious public action or scrutiny. If any agency knew that its files would be open to the public, and that citizen groups might take up cases the agency had been too timid to prosecute, it would be much less likely to become an industrial lap dog.

Precise provisions of a public access clause could take several forms, ranging from allowing the public to use

* 88 Georgia Code Ann. Sec. 303.

agency records in court to giving citizens legal standing to file a *qui tam* suit and collect a reasonable portion of any fines imposed. By providing citizens with legal standing in cases against large polluters, an environmental act could greatly encourage individual action.

Investigatory power: Before they can make rulings, regulatory agencies need information, for which they are often totally dependent on the industries they are supposed to regulate. For example, the Georgia Water Board has no subpoena power to force information from recalcitrant companies. The Georgia Air Board is further hindered because a public hearing is required before it can even find out what a company makes. Any effective law would give the agency the right to inspect the polluter's factory and premises, and the power to subpoena information about discharges into the air and water.

Judicial review: Under many environmental laws—including the present Federal water law and the Georgia air and water laws—any attempt to get the court to enforce an agency order requires a *de novo* hearing. This process, which amounts to a complete rehearing of all the facts and issues of the case, bogs down and complicates the legal proceedings; it often makes the agencies unwilling to even try to prosecute. Under a strong environmental protection law, the courts would be instructed to accept the agency's determination of fact—for example, how many pounds of pollutant a mill is discharging. Judicial review would then be limited to weighing points of law.

Standards: Although the distinction is not well publicized, there are two different systems for setting pollution standards; the choice of the system is one of the most important steps in guaranteeing a useful law. The first, most common system is standards based on the general quality of the air or water. Such a standard might say, for example, that the dissolved oxygen of a river should never be less than four parts per million, or that the particulate pollutants in the air should never be more than 80 micrograms per cubic meter. The second system is more effective, for it sets specific limits for the amount of pollutant that a pipe or smokestack may discharge. The general pollution levels often depend on factors beyond any industry's control; the dissolved oxygen of the water, for example, inevitably drops when the water temperature goes up, and the level of air pollution usually depends on the wind. These factors not only complicate the problem of trying to identify sources of pollution but also pose the serious danger of short-term emergencies. Companies may release large amounts of pollution when a strong wind is blowing or when a rainfall will dilute their liquid wastes; when the situation is reversed, the industries may argue that there is nothing they can do about controlling nature. In this way the amount of pollution that might be tolerable in normal situations can quickly reach lethal levels, as the East Coast learned the hard way during a protracted thermal inversion in the summer of 1969. Even if the long-term average level of pollution is within safe limits, brief incidents can be enough to purge all life from a river or do irreparable harm to the health of a human community. The only effective way to control the general pollution level is to regulate the pollutants as they leave their source.

Economic qualifications: The Georgia Air Law, inspired by Union Camp's Glenn Kimble, states that Georgia's policy is to "preserve, protect, and improve air quality . . . consistent with providing for maximum employment and the full industrial development of the state." Statements about "maximum employment" and "full industrial development" are too vague and ambiguous to offer any real guidance to courts and administrators; their net effect is to confuse and debilitate the law. The old ideas of "maximum employment" ignore current theories of economics, which stress the responsibility of industries to absorb the environmental cost of their production. With an "economic feasibility" clause like that in the Georgia Air Law, few judges would be moved to saddle a company with a $10-million pollution treatment plant. In light of other economic and ecological theories, the cost would seem not only reasonable but also necessary.

Penalties: No law can hope to meet the complex threats to the environment unless it can be enforced with a flexible range of penalties. Each law should give regulatory agencies the full arsenal of penalties—criminal sanctions, injunctive relief, and civil penalties (fines and damages). In many cases, criminal proceedings are necessary to reflect the importance of the offense. Purely criminal provisions sometimes have drawbacks; judges, juries, and agency officials are usually reluctant to apply criminal penalties to a respected corporate officer. That is why both injunctive power to make a polluter stop or reduce his polluting and civil sanctions are valuable complements to criminal enforcement. The fines that a polluter pays in a civil settlement can serve several purposes; they make environmental destruction costly to the polluter, they can help finance future environmental protection efforts; and they can partially repay some of the damage done by the pollution.

Administrative discretion: If all environmental agencies were sincere, dedicated to the public interest, and honest, there would be no danger in giving agency officials complete discretion in how and why they should enforce the law. The only long-term solution to the problem of biased agencies requires a new breed of civil protectors, or a public interest lobby as potent as the industrial lobbies. The best immediate defense may be simply to limit the agency's amount of discretion. Certain important functions, like issuing abatement orders when all other steps in the enforcement process are finished, should be mandatory duties, not potential powers. There is often a large gap between the powers allowed by law and the powers the agency actually uses. Citizens interested in closing the gap should first examine the language of their state's environmental law. The important semantic difference between the powers that the agency "shall" use and those it "may" use is the difference between having no discretion and being able to find loopholes for compromise or retreat.

Enforcement responsibilities: Any environmental agency should have its own legal staff and the power of legal enforcement. When the agency must rely upon other parts of the state's political machinery—usually through the attorney general's office—enforcement may become so cumbersome or so mired in politics that the agency learns to avoid it.

This brief check list does not pretend to be a complete discussion of the provisions necessary for good environmental control laws. It says nothing about many topics which are just as important as those mentioned—the benefits of regional planning groups; the mechanisms by which a state can select, buy, and protect a natural area; the need for unifying functions now split among many agencies; and the eventual necessity of giving environmental protection agencies sweeping powers to plan and regulate the use of natural resources.

These areas and many others will open up after citizens make sure that the more rudimentary provisions are written into their environmental protection laws. In many state legislatures and regulatory agencies, there are men eager to pass and enforce good laws; for years they have faced pressure from only one interest group, the industries who face regulation. The only way to correct the balance is for citizens to start pushing too. As the group which bears the burden of pollution, citizens have a literally vital interest in the way laws are written and enforced; so far, their welfare has only rarely been protected by law. Companies learned long ago to protect their interests at every step; they shepherd bills through the legislature and make their influence felt on the regulators. The general public has been slower to catch on, but now political sophistication is growing, as one would expect any skill to improve as it becomes a necessity for survival.

Appendix 3

The Second Oil Spill

Under the authority of Title 33, United States Code, Section 411, we, James M. Fallows of Redlands, California, Neil G. McBride of Atlanta, Georgia, and Terence J. Seyden of Savannah Beach, Georgia, wish to inform you of what we believe to be a violation of Title 33, United States Code, Section 407 (The Refuse Act of 1899).

It is our belief that on May 8, 1970, at approximately 1630, the Union Camp Corporation of Savannah, Ga., discharged a quantity of oil into the Savannah River, a navigable river. In support of our belief we offer the following information:

1. A United States Coast Guard report, dated May 13, 1970, states that on May 8, 1970, at 1630, oil was found to be discharging from a ditch near the American Oil Company and the Union Camp Corporation. The inspecting officer is listed as ENS. Denny M. Dobbs.

The report states that samples of the oil were taken by SN Johns, and that sampling was witnessed by ENS. Dobbs. The report is signed by R. S. Cutler, LCDR, USCG, COTP. A statement attached to the report, signed by Jimmy R. Johns, says of the oil spill:

> We tracked it back to their (Union Camp) factory and lost it under the buildings. The Union Camp officials said they would find the source as soon as possible and stop it.

The report suggests that the spill took place over a period of hours. A statement by the investigating officer says, "The oil would almost disappear, and then come out in larger patches almost following a cycle type pattern." The report also suggests that the Union Camp Corporation failed to mitigate damages after the discharge began. The investigating officer's statement concludes:

> When I first talked with the yard and woodyard foreman I suggested that they put straw or grass or something into the ditch to trap the oil. I made this suggestion several times but to my knowledge nothing was ever done.

According to the statement of Randall B. Guidry, also attached to the Coast Guard report, "The spill stretched from American Oil Co. to Savannah Machine and Foundry." The distance he describes covers about a mile of the river.

A copy of the Coast Guard report is attached to our statement.

The files from which this report was copied are public information under the provisions of Title 5, United States Code, Section 552. We are currently engaged in a study of pollution in the Savannah River. The discovery of this report was the result of a routine examination of the Coast Guard files.

2. Upon learning of the report of the violation, we questioned ENS. Dobbs about the incident. During an interview on August 11, 1970, ENS. Dobbs confirmed that he had seen an oil spill originating at the Union Camp plant site on May 8, 1970.

3. During an interview with James Fallows and Terence Seyden on August 12, 1970, James Lientz, vice-president of the Union Camp Corporation and resident manager of the plant at Savannah, stated that the plant did discharge oil into the river on May 8, 1970. Mr. Lientz said that the oil involved was "tall oil" from the plant's chemical by-products division, and that the discharge into the river came from oil deposited on the sides of an old drainage ditch. He said that he was "fully aware" of the incident.

Also present at that interview were Miss Susan Fallows of Redlands, California, Dr. Richard Miksad of Yonkers, New York, and Miss Deborah Zerad of Cincinnati, Ohio, as well as plant officials William Binns, public relations director, and Harry Harriman, technical director.

4. The current Coast Guard regulations treat any discharge of more than one quart of oil as a possible violation of the Refuse Act. Since this spill is said to encompass at least a mile of the river, we allege that the Union Camp Corporation discharged an undetermined but large amount of oil into the river, calculable by any judgment to be greater than one quart.

5. The discharge of which we are informing your office was witnessed, we believe, by the following persons:

ENS, Denny M. Dobbs, USCG
17 Hampstead Avenue
Savannah, Ga.

Jimmy R. Johns, USCG
Chatham City Apartments
Savannah, Ga.

BMC Billy R. Russel
Savannah, Ga.

Randall B. Guidry
Savannah, Ga.

The following persons have knowledge of the discharge:

James Lientz
1410 Bacon Park Drive
Savannah, Ga.

Richard R. Chase
402 East 46th Street
Savannah, Ga.

James M. Fallows
137 Whittaker Street
Savannah, Ga.

Neil G. McBride
137 Whittaker Street
Savannah, Ga.

Terence J. Seyden
137 Whittaker Street
Savannah, Ga.

The Coast Guard report and conversations with the plant manager suggest that the discharge was witnessed by a number of yet-unidentified plant employees.

6. The Union Camp Corporation does not have a permit issued by the Corps of Engineers to discharge oil into the Savannah River. On April 27, 1970, the Union Camp Corporation pled *nolo contendere* to another violation of the Refuse Act and was placed on one year's probation because of its oil discharge. *United States v. Union Camp Corporation* (S.D. Ga. #18044, April 27, 1970).

That oil spill is recorded in Coast Guard files in a report dated August 13, 1969. The violation occurred on June 30, 1969, on the Savannah River "at Union Camp dock." The pollution was reported by BM3 H. G. Rost, and the investigating officer was R. S. Cutler. A copy of that report was obtained from the United States Coast Guard District Headquarters, Miami, Florida.

In view of the potential recurrence of this type of offense, we request that you immediately seek an injunction against the Union Camp Corporation to cease their violation of the Refuse Act, in addition to monetary penalties for this and future violations of the Act.

We understand that the Federal Water Quality Administration, pursuant to the Water Pollution Control Act and the Water Quality Improvement Act of 1970 (public Law 91-224, April 3, 1970), has concurrent jurisdiction with the Justice Department, under the authority of the Refuse Act, to regulate discharges such as the one we are reporting. We are confident, however, that this violation is of the kind uniquely suited for remedy under the provisions of the Refuse Act. The United States Department of Justice, in a memorandum entitled "Guidelines for Litigation Under the Refuse Act (33 U.S.C. 407)" states as its policy that the Refuse Act be used not in competition with the Federal Water Pollution Control Act but rather to "supplement that Act by bringing appropriate actions either to punish the occasional or recalcitrant polluter, or to abate continuing sources of pollution which for some reason or other have not been subjected to a proceeding conducted by the Federal Water Quality Administration or by a state." We contend that both conditions exist: the discharge is occasional and the offender is recalcitrant. Though the Union Camp Corporation is subject to a proceeding conducted by both the State and the Federal Water Quality Control Agencies, those proceedings have dealt exclusively with the continuing waste from the plant's production processes, not its occasional discharges of oil or other waste material. Our reading of the Federal proceedings conference, October 29, 1969, and of the State Water Quality Control Board files in the matter of the Union Camp Corporation, confirm this definition of the State and Federal areas of concern. The April 27, 1970, judgment, of course, further suggests that this violation is the rightful concern of the Justice Department. The Justice Department memorandum gives United States Attorneys specific power, without authorization, to initiate actions to enjoin the discharge of oil, even where the violation is reported by private citizens.

In requesting that you take this action against the Union Camp Corporation, we do not intend to imply that the formal governmental agencies which deal with these problems from day to day are not adequately protecting the interests of the river and of the people of Savannah. To the contrary, the Coast Guard has constantly demonstrated keen interest in safeguarding the navigable waters of their area of concern.

The Act's judicial mandate is that its reading be "charitable in light of the purpose to be served" and that this purpose "forbids a narrow, cramped reading. . . ." (*United States v. Republic Steel Corp.* 362 U.S. 491 (1960)). Given this reading, and the statutory mandate that the Attorney General "prosecute vigorously" violations reported to him (33 U.S.C. 413), a citizen complaint should be entertained to prevent further delay in the prosecution of this complaint. Several months may be an acceptable lapse of time for a governmental agency to report its findings of the usual violation, but here, where the discharge followed by a mere two weeks a conviction for an earlier violation, a local resident should be allowed to pursue his statutory right to discourage future violations of Federal law. We also believe that the law, in allowing the reporting citizen to retain half of any fines the court may impose, meant to encourage the participation of private citizens; this participation should not be discouraged merely because there exists a governmental branch with jurisdiction over the same problem. Private participation need not be seen as in competition with a governmental agency. It is rather an effective aid and complement to existing governmental efforts.

We are requesting, therefore, that should any of the information we have forwarded to you be used as the basis for a criminal complaint or in the trial of this case, and results in a conviction and the levying of a fine, that we be allowed half of the fine collected, pursuant to Title 33, United States Code, Section 411. If such a fine is imposed, we request that our share be placed in trust for the people of Savannah, to be used for the purpose of conserving their natural environment, and that we, James Fallows, Neil McBride and Terence Seyden, be named as trustees for the fund.

Please inform us as soon as possible as to whether you intend to prosecute the Union Camp Corporation for this violation. If you do not decide to prosecute this violation, we would like to know, so that we may begin the consideration of a *qui tam* suit to try to prevent the recurrence of this kind of discharge in the future.

We swear that the foregoing statement, to the best of our information and belief, is true.

(signed)
James M. Fallows
137 Whittaker St.
Savannah, Ga.

Neil G. McBride
137 Whittaker St.
Savannah, Ga.

Terence J. Seyden
137 Whittaker St.
Savannah, Ga.

Sworn to and subscribed before me on this 13th day of August, 1970. (Signed) *Betty A. Pizinski,* Notary Public, Chatham County, Georgia. My Commission expires Nov. 24, 1973.

Notes

Chapter 1—The River

1. "Plan for Development of the Land and Water Resources of the Southeast River Basins," Appendix 1, Savannah River Basin, U.S. Study Commission, 1963, pp. 1–7.
2. Report of the Flood Control Subcommittee of the House of Representatives, "Savannah River Basin Inspection," 1969, Greenwood, South Carolina, p. 9.
3. *Savannah News-Press,* May 10, 1892.
4. *Savannah News-Press,* September 11, 1879.
5. Anna Hunter, *The Eyes of Savannah*
6. *1937 Report of the East Georgia Planning Council,* "Commercial Fisheries of Georgia."

Chapter 2—The Last Resource

1. U.S. World Almanac, 1970.
2. "Estimated Use of Water in the United States, 1960," Geological Survey Circular 456, United States Geological Survey.
3. Leroy E. Burney, M.D., "Clean Water," proceedings of the National Conference on Water Pollution (PNCWP), 1960, United States Department of Health, Education and Welfare, p. 6.
4. *Handbook of Applied Hydrology,* Van Te Chow, editor, McGraw-Hill Book Company, pp. 1–3.
5. *Ibid.*
6. Clarence W. Klassen, "Water Quality Management—A National Necessity," PNCWP, 1960, p. 139.
7. Quoted by Leonard E. Posek, "The Needs and Obligations of Industry," PNCWP, 1960, p. 310.
8. Geological Survey Circular 456, p. 10.
9. *Ibid.,* p. 2.
10. Albert E. Forester, "A Matter of Survival," PNCWP, 1960, p. 15.
11. Klassen, *op. cit.,* p. 140.
12. "Water Use in the United States, 1900–1980," United States Department of Commerce, Business and Defense Services Administration.
13. Klassen, *op. cit.,* p. 140.

Chapter 3—The Floating Crap Game

1. *Savannah News-Press,* August 2, 1970.
2. *Ibid.,* July 18, 1970.

3. Interview with Malcolm MacLean, former mayor of Savannah, summer 1970.
4. Memoranda from city manager Picot Floyd to Savannah city council, February and June 1968.
5. Letter from R. S. "Rock" Howard, Georgia Water Quality Control Board, to Savannah mayor J. Curtis Lewis, April 30, 1968.
6. *Ibid.*, May 27, 1968.
7. Letter from J. Curtis Lewis to Rock Howard, June 4, 1968.
8. Telegram from Rock Howard to J. Curtis Lewis, August 5, 1968.
9. Letter from J. Curtis Lewis to Rock Howard, August 22, 1968.
10. Rock Howard, at the Conference in the Matter of Pollution of the Lower Savannah and its Tributaries, October 1969, p. 186. Conference sponsored by the United States Department of Health, Education and Welfare, proceedings.
11. Benjamin Garfunkel, member of the Savannah city council, at the Conference in the Matter of Pollution, October 1969, p. 47.
12. Interview with Arthur Gilreath, mayor of Thunderbolt, July 30, 1970.
13. Interview with Savannah Beach councilman, summer 1970.

Chapter 4—The Lesser Evil: American Cyanamid

1. Georgia Water Quality Control Board Study, "Water Quality Investigation: American Cyanamid Company and the Savannah River," May 19–20, 1969.
2. *Ibid.*
3. California Water Criteria Book, Sacramento, 1970, p. 236.
4. GWQCB, *op. cit.*
5. Interview with American Cyanamid plant manager C. W. Sieber, June 22, 1970.
6. GWQCB, *op. cit.*
   Conference in the Matter of Pollution of the Lower Savannah and its Tributaries, October 1969, p. 91. Conference sponsored by the United States Department of Health, Education and Welfare.
7. *Ibid.*
8. Chatham County Health Department Report, June 17, 1968.
9. *Savannah News-Press,* June 12, 1968.
10. *Ibid.*
11. Charles Lindsey, Senior Sanitarian of the Chatham County Health Department, quoted in the *Savannah News-Press,* June 17, 1968.
12. Interviews with Sieber, June 22 and July 13, 1970.
13. *Ibid.*, June 22, 1970.
14. Letter from R. S. "Rock" Howard, Georgia Water Quality Control Board, to Sieber, September 8, 1969.
15. GWQCB, *op. cit.*
16. *Ibid.*

Chapter 5—Papering the Earth

1. *Pulp and Paper,* January 1970.
2. *Cleaning Our Environment: The Chemical Basis for Action,* American Chemical Society, Washington, D.C., 1970.
3. *Paper Trade Journal,* December 1, 1969.
4. *Ibid.,* November 3, 1969.
5. *Southern Pulp and Paper Manufacturer,* November 10, 1968.
6. John Kenneth Galbraith, *The Affluent Society,* p. 14.
7. Union Camp annual report, 1965.
8. *Ibid.*
9. *Ibid.,* 1967.
10. *Paper Trade Journal,* June 23, 1969.
11. *Ibid.*
12. *Ibid.*
13. *Ibid.,* February 2, 1970.
14. "About Our Savannah Plant," Union Camp pamphlet, p. 25.
15. *Contact,* Union Camp quarterly magazine, Autumn 1967.
16. *Ibid.*
17. *Pulp and Paper,* May 1970.
18. John E. Ray III, executive vice president of Union Camp, at a January 1970 address to Virginia Forests, Inc.
19. Union Camp annual report, 1969.
20. "About Our Savannah Plant."
21. *Pulp and Paper,* December 1969.
22. *Pulp and Paper,* December 1969.
23. *Ibid.,* July 1970.
24. *Ibid.,* January 1970; also cited in *Paper Trade Journal,* February 24, 1969.
25. *Paper Trade,* June 16, 1969.

Chapter 6—Polluting the Earth

1. "Water . . . How Southern Pulp and Paper Mills Manage This Natural Resource," Southern Pulpwood Conservation Association pamphlet, Atlanta, Georgia, pp. 4–5.
2. "Water Requirements of the Pulp and Paper Industry," USGS Water Supply Paper 1330-A, 1961, pp. 31–33.
3. *Southern Pulp and Paper Manufacturer,* September 1968.
4. *The Cost of Clean Water,* Vol. I, FWPCA, 1968, p. 17.
5. Southern Pulpwood Conservation Association, *op. cit.,* p. 1.
6. Michael Waldichuk, "Some Water Pollution Problems Connected with the Disposal of Pulp Mill Wastes," *Canadian Fish Culturist,* October 1962, p. 7.
7. *Cleaning Our Environment: The Chemical Basis for Action,* American Chemical Society, Washington, D.C., 1970, p. 141.
8. A. E. Werner, "Sulphur Compounds in Kraft Pulp Mill Effluents," Fisheries Research Board of Canada, Bulletin #796.
9. *Southern Pulp and Paper,* September 1968.
10. *Ibid.,* January 1970, p. 97.
11. *Cost of Clean Water,* p. 17.

12. *Southern Pulp and Paper,* February 1970, p. 120.
13. *Ibid.,* September 1969.
14. *Cleaning Our Environment,* p. 139.
15. *Southern Pulp and Paper,* April 1970.
16. *TAPPI,* magazine of the Technical Association of the Pulp and Paper Industry, June 1965, p. 43.
17. Testimony presented by the National Association of Manufacturers before the Subcommittee on Air and Water Pollution, United States Senate Committee on Public Works, May 27, 1970.
18. *Southern Pulp and Paper,* July 1969.
19. "Georgia-Pacific and the Environment," Georgia-Pacific pamphlet, 1970, p. 10.
20. *Southern Pulp and Paper,* December 1969.
21. *Ibid.*
22. *Cooperation,* Kimberly-Clark publication, Spring 1970.
23. *Paper Trade Journal,* January 27, 1969.
24. *Wall Street Journal,* Vol. CLXXV, No. 124, p. 1.
25. *Paper Trade,* April 13, 1970.

Chapter 7—Three Pulp Mill Towns

1. Most of the information on Interstate gathered during author's visit there, summer 1970, and confirmed in talks with GWQCB later in summer.
2. Union Camp manager James Lientz at 1965 Federal water pollution conference, *op. cit.,* p. 131.
3. 1965 conference, p. 27 d.
4. *Ibid.,* p. 129.
5. *Ibid.,* p. 134.
6. *Ibid.,* p. 131.
7. *Ibid.,* pp. 137–138.
8. Letter from Lientz to R. S. Howard of the Georgia Water Quality Control Board, January 7, 1969.
9. Letter from Howard to Lientz, January 8, 1969.
10. Union Camp, 1969 annual report, p. 7.
11. *Savannah News-Press,* July 1970.
12. Georgia Water Quality Control Board hearings, January 17, 1967, p. 2.
13. *Ibid.,* pp. 2–3.
14. Interview with Lientz, August 12, 1970.
15. Report filed May 27, 1955, by Frank T. Knapp, Chief, Research Unit, Georgia Department of Public Health.
16. Sirrine Engineering Report, filed with the Georgia Water Quality Control Board, May 14, 1970.
17. Letter from Howard to Gilman manager George W. Brumley, April 17, 1970.
18. Testimony of Brumley before Georgia Water Quality Control Board panel, January 29, 1967.
19. *Ibid.*
20. *Ibid.*
21. Jacksonville, Florida *Times-Union,* June 26, 1970.

22. *Savannah News-Press,* December 10, 1969, p. 2.
23. *Camden County Tribune,* June 25, 1970, p. 1.
24. *Savannah News-Press,* February 7, 1971. Other information on the rape charge comes from the Georgia press and from informants in St. Mary's who have asked us to preserve their anonymity.

Chapter 8—Union Camp's Divining Rod

1. C. L. McGuinness, *The Role of Ground Water in the National Water Situation,* United States Geological Survey Water Supply Paper 1800, Washington, 1963, pp. 21, 23.
2. K. A. Mackichan and J. C. Kammerer, *Estimated Use of Water in the U. S., 1960,* USGS Circular 456, Washington, 1961, p. 16.
3. *Op. cit.,* McGuinness, p. 85.
4. George Whitlatch, *Summary of the Industrial Water Resource of Georgia,* Industrial Development Division, Georgia Institute of Technology, Atlanta, June 1964, pp. 1, 41.
5. Ven Te Chow, *Handbook of Applied Hydrology,* New York, 1964, pp. 13–14.
6. Chatham County Ordinance, July 30, 1943.
7. Harland B. Counts and M. J. McCollum, *Relation of Salt-Water Encroachment to the Major Aquifer Zones Savannah Area, Georgia and South Carolina,* USGS Water Supply Paper 1613-D, Washington, 1964, p. D16.
8. Bill Carpenter, "Going Down," *Savannah News-Press,* July 13, 1970.
9. Interview with Ed Morgan, Chairman of Savannah's Industrial and Domestic Water Supply Commission, July 1970.
10. Compiled from information on pumping in principal artesian aquifer received from Dean Gregg, USGS, Brunswick; City of Savannah; Union Camp Corporation; American Cyanamid; "Some Top Water-Use Limit," *Savannah News-Press,* July 14, 1970.
11. Whitlatch, pp. 99–100.
12. Interview with Dean Gregg, July 20, 1970.
13. Computed from total pumping rates in Savannah supplied by Harland B. Counts, Georgia Ground Water Director, in interview, July 1970; information on city and industrial rates supplied by the City of Savannah, Savannah Beach, and Port Wenworth.
14. Union Camp Corporation and City of Savannah Water Department.
15. Letter from Union Camp Corporation to Chatham County Commissioners, 1953.
16. Union Camp yearly pumping information from 1936–69 from William Benz, Union Camp Public Relations Director, August 1970.
17. *Savannah News-Press,* November 1, 1970, p. B1.
18. Interview with Jack Carlson, Layne-Atlantic Company, Savannah, July 1970.

19. Conversation between Albert N. Cameron, Special Assistant to the National Director of the USGS, and Bill Carpenter, reporter for the *Savannah News-Press,* July 1970.
20. Letter from American Cyanamid to Georgia Water Quality Control Board, October 16, 1969.
21. Interview with Dean Gregg, July 20, 1970.
22. *Ibid.*
23. Interview with Everett Zimmerman, USGS, Brunswick, July 20, 1970.
24. Interview with Robert E. Carver, Department of Geology, University of Georgia, and Don Duncan, geologist, South Carolina Water Resources Commission.
25. Interview with O. B. Odum, USGS, Savannah, July 27, 1970.
26. Letters from the City of Savannah to private well owners within city limits, July 13, 1970.
27. Interview with Richard R. Chase, Union Camp Division Technical Director for Unbleached Products, August 1970.
28. Interview with Harland Counts, July 1970.
29. *Ibid.*
30. Letters from O. B. Odum to Earl Robbins, Savannah City Manager.
31. J. T. Callahan, L. E. Newcomb, and J. W. Geurin, *Water of Georgia,* USGS Water Supply Paper 1762, Washington, 1965, p. 56.

Chapter 9—The Smell of Money

1. *Atmospheric Emissions from Sulfate Pulping,* proceedings of conference sponsored by the Public Health Service, National Council for Air/Stream Improvement, held at the University of Florida, April 28, 1966, pp. 74–75.
2. *Ibid.*
3. *Ibid.,* pp. 76–77.
4. *Ibid.,* p. 76.
5. John Esposito, *Vanishing Air: Ralph Nader's Study Group Report on Air Pollution,* Grossman Publishers, New York, 1970, p. 131.
6. *Ibid.,* p. 130.
7. "Air Pollution Aspects of Hydrogen Sulfide," report prepared by Litton Industries for the National Air Pollution Control Administration (NAPCA), Contract PH-22-68025, September 1969, p. 66.
8. Berton Roueche, "A Woman with a Headache," *The New Yorker,* January 31, 1970, p. 66.
9. "Air Quality Criteria for Particulate Matter, NAPCA publication AP-49, United States Department of Health, Education and Welfare, Public Health Service, January 1969, p. 12–20.
10. *Ibid.,* pp. 12–18, 12–19.
11. Warren Winklestein, Jr., "The Relationship of Air Pollution and Economic Status to Total Mortality and Selected Respiratory System Mortality in Man," *Archives of Environment,* 14: 162–169, 1967.

12. "Air Quality Criteria for Sulfur Oxides," NAPCA publication AP-50, U.S. Department of HEW, Public Health Service, January 1969, pp. 161–62.
13. Registration forms sent to Georgia Department of Health, Air Quality Control Branch by American Cyanamid and Continental Can.
14. Telephone interview with American Cyanamid plant manager C. W. Sieber, summer 1970.
15. Interview with American Cyanamid Pigments Division Manager J. Ludden, summer 1970.
16. Registration form sent to Georgia Department of Health, Air Quality Control Branch by American Cyanamid.
17. *Ibid.*
18. "Carbon Monoxide on the Highway," *Scientific American,* 212: 52–57, May 1965; L. Friberg and R. Rylander, "Scientific Basis for Some Medical Air Quality Guides," *Journal of the Air Pollution Control Administration,* 15: 531, November 1965.
19. *Pulp and Paper,* April 1969.
20. Union Camp Technical Director Glenn Kimble, testimony before Air Pollution Study Committee proceedings, December 9, 1966.
21. Interview with Union Camp plant manager James Lientz, July 16, 1970.
22. Georgia code 88-901.
23. Georgia code 88-910 (3).
24. Georgia code 88-906.
25. *Ibid.*
26. *Ibid.*
27. Georgia code 88-912.
28. Esposito, pp. 198–199.
29. "Air Quality Criteria for Particulate Matter," NAPCA Publication AP-49, January 1969.
30. Interview with Chatham County Health Department Engineer Mark Harbison, summer 1970.

Chapter 10—The Making of a Company Town I: A Present for Mr. Calder

1. Savannah mayor Lee Mingledorff, in "Georgia's Ocean Gateway," Manufacturers Record Area Survey, May 1958.
2. *Savannah News-Press,* April 29, 1956.
3. *Ibid.,* December 23, 1947.
4. Interview with Tom Johnson, senior partner of the Johnson, Lane, Space and Co. investment firm, 1970.
5. *Op. cit., News-Press,* December 23, 1947.
6. Thomas Reed, "Financial Survey of the City," National Municipal League, New York, 1937.
7. Agreement between the City of Savannah and Union Bag and Paper Corporation, signed March 11, 1935, amended March 11 and 15, 1935.
8. *Op. cit., News-Press,* July 6, 1951.

9. *Journal of Commerce,* 1955.
10. Union Bag Report to Stockholders, 1937.
11. *Investor's Reader.*
12. Speech by Congressman Paul D. McCloskey, Jr. to the Conference on Law and Environment sponsored by the Conservation Foundation, Warrenton, Virginia, September 11, 1969; printed in the Conservation Foundation *Letter,* September 30, 1969.
13. Union Camp vice president and Savannah plant manager James R. Lientz, from proceedings of the 1965 Federal conference, pp. 129–130.
14. Water . . . how Southern pulp and paper mills manage this natural resource, p. 3.
15. *Post's 1970 Pulp and Paper Directory,* Miller Freeman Publications, San Francisco, 1969.
16. Georgia Institute of Technology Report, Engineering Experiment Station, Project A-787, 1967.
17. H. F. Griffies, "A Tourist Development and Promotion Program for the City of Savannah," Georgia Institute of Technology, Industrial Development Division, Project A-834.
18. "Immediate Water Pollution Control Needs—Savannah River Basin, Georgia-South Carolina," United States Department of the Interior, Federal Water Pollution Control Administration, Atlanta, February 8, 1968.

Chapter 11—The Making of a Company Town II: Representation Without Taxation

1. Interview with Union Camp plant manager James R. Lientz, July 16, 1970.
2. Interview with Union Camp executive vice president, John E. Ray III, July 16, 1970.
3. Interview with former Savannah Finance Director Herb O'Keefe, July 24, 1970.
4. Letter from financial consultant and Maryland tax expert, Alex K. Hancock, to then chairman of the Savannah-Chatham Joint Tax Board, Richard Heard, October 3, 1967.
5. Letter from Assistant Attorney General of Georgia William L. Harper to Richard Heard, June 18, 1970.
6. *Savannah News-Press,* June 23, 1970.
7. *Atlantic Constitution,* March 13, 1969.
8. Interview with County Administrator Joseph Lambright, June 29, 1970.
9. Union Camp Annual Report for 1969, p. 23.
10. *News-Press,* August 12, 1970.
11. *Ibid.,* August 26, 1970.
12. *Ibid.,* May 2, 1969.
13. *Ibid.,* July 16, 1965.
14. Interview with James Lientz, July 16, 1970.
15. Interviews on June 29, 1970, and July 21, 1970.
16. *News-Press,* August 1, 1970.

17. *Ibid.*, August 12, 1970.
18. *Ibid.*, August 22, 1970.

Chapter 12—Bringing Down the Law

1. *Pennsylvania Coal Co. v. Sanderson,* 113 Pa. St. 126, 6A 453 (1886).
2. *Ibid.*
3. *Whalen v. Union Bag and Paper Co.,* 208 NY 1, 101 N.E. 805 (1913).
4. See "Toward a Constitutionally Protected Environment," *Virginia Law Review,* Vol. 56, No. 3, April 1970. (Articles on constitutional theories are not cited as definitive critiques but rather as starting points from which the lay reader may become more familiar with the legal issues involved.)
5. See E. Roberts, "The Right to a Decent Environment: Progress Along a Constitutional Avenue," paper presented at the Conference on Law and the Environment, Warrenton, Virginia, September 11–12, 1969, to be published in *Law and the Environment,* M. Baldwin, editor. (*Law and the Environment* will include articles of interest to both the lay reader and the practicing attorney.)
6. *Boomer v. Atlantic Cement Co.,* Cir. No. 242. (For a discussion of this problem and a general examination of private action against polluters, see "Private Remedies for Water Pollution," *Columbia Law Review,* Vol. 70, No. 4, April 1970.
7. For a concise discussion of the possible relationships between common and legislative law, see "Water Quality Standards in Private Nuisance Actions," *Yale Law Journal,* LXXIX, 1969, p. 102.
8. Proceedings of the Federal Water Pollution Control Administration Conference, Savannah, October 1969, pp. 161–162.
9. Testimony of David Zwick before the Senate Subcommittee on Air and Water Pollution of the Committee on Public Works, June 10, 1970.
10. Hearings on S.649 before the Senate Subcommittee on Air and Water Pollution of the Committee on Public Works, 88th Congress, 1st session, 1963, pp. 199–122.
11. *Savannah News-Press,* January 18, 1970.
12. See *Adams, qui tam v. Woods,* 6 US (2 Cranch) 336 (1805); *Marvin v. Trout,* 199 US 212 (1905).

    The Conservation Foundation *News Letter* of August 1970 reported a curious story. An oil company employee in Maine accidentally left the valve open on an oil storage tank; when he discovered the resulting oil spill, he reported it to the U.S. Attorney's office. His company pleaded guilty and was fined the maximum of $2,500. The employee was then given half the fine for reporting the spill.

    For a complete discussion of citizen use of the Refuse Act, including references to *qui tam* actions, write Congressman Henry Reuss of Wisconsin and ask for his kit describing the Act and its possible applications. An important feature of

the Act, as Congressman Reuss' discussion points out, is that citizens do not need formal legal advice in order to make complaints.
13. *US v. Republic Steel Corp. et al.*, 362 US 482 (1960).
14. Department of Justice memo to all U.S. Attorneys, June 15, 1970.
15. *Ibid.*
16. For a scholarly analysis of the legislative history of the Refuse Act, see Mr. Justice Harlan's dissent in *United States v. Republic Steel,* 362 US 911 (1960).
17. See *United States v. Florida Power and Light Co.*, USDC, SD, Florida, March 13, 1970.
18. *Zabel v. Tabb,* No. 27555, 5th Circuit, July 16, 1970.
19. Conservation Foundation *News Letter,* August 1970.
20. *United States v. Standard Oil Company,* 384 US 244 (1966).

Chapter 13—Bringing Back the Water

1. Claire Schelske and Eugene Odum, "Mechanisms Maintaining High Productivity in Georgia Estuaries," Gulf and Caribbean Fisheries Institute, 14th Annual Session, November 1961.
2. Eugene Odum, quoted in *The Frail Ocean* by Wesley Marx, Sierra Club-Ballentine Books, 1967.
3. Eugene Odum, "The Role of the Tidal Marshes in Estuarine Production," New York State Conservation Department Information Leaflet.
4. Eugene Odum, "Natural Production in Estuaries, a Source of Food for Oysters," Institute of Ecology, University of Georgia, Oyster Culture Workshop, Sapelo Island, Georgia, July 11, 1967.
5. Experiments by Dr. Robert Lunz at Bears Bluff Laboratories, South Carolina, recorded in *Life and Death of the Salt Marsh,* by John and Mildred Teal, Boston, 1969.
6. Dave Gould, Atlantic States Fisheries Commission, *Clean Water for the Nation's Estuaries,* Jekyll Island, Georgia, February 29, 1968 Conference proceedings.
7. Proceeding of the Conference on Pollution of the Interstate Waters of the Lower Savannah River and its Tributaries; South Carolina-Georgia, February 2, 1965.
8. Interview with Sieber, June 22, 1970.
9. Georgia Water Quality Control Board Survey, May 20, 1969.
10. McKee and Wolf, *Water Quality Criteria,* second edition, California State Water Quality Board, Sacramento.
11. Report of the Committee on Water Quality Criteria, Federal Water Pollution Control Agency, April 1, 1968.
12. Kenneth Mackenthun, The Practice of Water Pollution Biology, Federal Water Pollution Control Agency, Washington, 1969.
13. Eugene Odum, "The theory of the estuarine ecosystem in relation to use, management, and pollution," *Clean Water for the Nation's Estuaries.*

14. "Environmental Requirements of Fish and Wildlife," *Biological Problems in Water Pollution,* Third Seminar, United States Department of Health, Education and Welfare, 1962.
15. *The American Oyster,* Fishery Bulletin, Volume 64, United States Department of the Interior, Fish and Wildlife Service, Bureau of Commercial Fisheries, p. 213.
16. McKee and Wolf, *op. cit.*
17. Report of the Committee on Water Quality Criteria, *op. cit.*
18. "The Effects of Waste Disposal in the New York Bight," Interim Report for January 1, 1970. Report to the Coastal Engineering Research Center, Army Corps of Engineers, Washington; prepared by the Sandy Hook Marine Laboratory, United States Bureau of Sports Fisheries and Wildlife.
19. Michael Waldichuk, "Some Water Pollution Problems Associated with the Disposal of Pulp Mill Wastes," Fisheries Research Board of Canada, Nanaimo, British Columbia.
20. McKee and Wolf, *op. cit.*
21. Speech given by Union Camp executive vice president John E. Ray III to the Savannah Rotary Club, October 19, 1970.
22. McKee and Wolf, *op. cit.*
23. Waldichuk, *op. cit.*
24. South Atlantic Fisheries, Historical Catch Statistics.
25. Report from Bears Bluff Laboratory, South Carolina, in *Fish and Man, Conflict in the Atlantic Estuaries,* American Fisheries Society, Special Publication No. 5.
26. *Ibid.*
27. J. L. McHugh, "Management of Estuarine Fisheries," in *A Symposium of Estuarine Fisheries,* American Fisheries Society, Special Publication No. 3, 1966.
28. Paper presented by Charles M. Frisbee, Marine Fisheries Supervisor, Georgia Game and Fish Commission, at the *Marshlands—Not Wastelands* Symposium, Brunswick Junior College, May 8, 1969.
29. *Symposium of Estuarine Fisheries,* Joseph Kutkuhn, "The Role of the Estuaries in the Development and Perpetuation of Commercial Shrimp Resources."
30. Wally Hitchcock, *The Atlanta Constitution,* September 8, 1970.

Index

acid, 10, 40, 42–44, 102–103, 123, 222, 224, 230, 232–233, 240–241
acid-alkaline balance, 41
Activated Sludge system, 69, 145
Adams, Mary, xxi
aerators, 69, 80
aerosols, 134
Affluent Society, The, 64
Air Pollution Emissions Inventory, 132, 151
Air Pollution Study Committee, 146
Air Quality Criteria for Particulate Matter, 149
Allied Container Corporation, 162
American Can Company, 72
American Cyanamid, x, xx–xxi, 8–10, 40–45, 55, 122–123, 128, 133, 138, 141, 144–145, 173–174, 197, 224, 228, 231, 233, 248, 251
American Motors Corporation, 51
American Oil Company, 97
American Paper Institute, 52, 73
Anderson, Donald, 130
Appalachia, 167
artesian aquifer, 116–126, 248–249; wells, 113, 115, 126
Associated Industries of Georgia (Air and Water Resources Council), 146
Atomic Energy Commission, 236

Baby-Scott, 55–56, 58
Barker, Dr., 111
BASF, 108, 123
Battle, Joe, 186
Bayh, Birch, 209
Bears Bluff Laboratory, 240
Beaufort, 117, 123
Bloodworth, Dr., 111
BOD (Biological Oxygen Demand), 9–10, 23, 41, 68–69, 72, 76, 78, 80–81, 83–86, 88–91, 100, 102, 105, 225, 228, 230–232, 251–253
Boise Cascade, 51
Bouhan, John, 184
Bouhan, Lawrence, Williams, and Levy, 147
Brumley, George W., 102–103, 105–107, 109
Brunswick, 120, 123–124, 168
Brown, Victor, 62–63
Burke, Edmund, 244
Business Week, 53
Butler, Nancy, 221

Cabbage Island, 183, 218
Calder, Alexander, 156–157, 160–163, 184
Calder, Alexander, Jr., 52, 92, 95
Camden County, 106–107; Commission, 122; Recreation Authority, 108–109
Camden County Tribune, 110
Cameron, Albert N., 123
Camp, Hugh D., 92, 95
Camp Manufacturing Company, 162

carbon monoxide, 133, 138, 145
Carnegie, Thomas Morrison, 104
Chamber of Commerce, 76, 173
Chase Manhattan Bank, 52
Chase, Richard, 95, 125
Chatham County, 36–37, 116, 139, 155, 172–174, 176–177, 180, 183–184, 188, 249–251; Commission, 29, 115, 175, 179, 184, 186; Grand Jury, 196; Health Department, 27, 38, 45, 137, 141, 148–152
Chatham-Savannah Board of Tax Assessors, 179
chloride, 72, 141
chlorination, 38
chlorine gas, xxi, 45, 133, 138, 141, 144–145
Chrysler Corporation, 51
Citizens and Southern Bank (C&S), 29, 157, 184
clarifier, 68–70, 77, 84–85, 88, 90–91, 93, 199, 203, 226
Clark, Judge, 189
Clayton Anti-Trust Act, 162
clear-cutting, 59
Clearwater River, 73
Clifton, Pete, 185
COD (Chemical Oxygen Demand), 9–10, 41, 228
Color Removal Tank, 77, 79
Colorado River, 199
Condemned Oyster map, 221–222
cone of depression, 116–117, 121, 126
connate water, 117, 120
Conservation Foundation *News Letter,* 211
Consolidated Edison, 254
Container Corporation of America, 62
Continental Can Corporation, xx, 9, 38, 40, 51, 65, 131, 138–139, 145, 174, 186, 197, 250
Counts, Harland, 125
Cretacia, 166–167
Cumberland Island, 104–105, 107–109
Cumberland Sound, 102, 105

DDT, xiii, 134, 220, 234
diffusion header, 43–44
disposables, 54–56, 61
dimethyl sulfoxide (DMSO), 71
dissolved oxygen (DO), 9, 41, 68, 78, 82, 102, 224–226, 229–230, 233
Dobbs, Denny, 97
Doremus, Ogden, xxi, 187
Douglas, Justice William O., 206–207, 216
Drury, Carl, 109–111

Eastern Box Company, 162
Eagleton, Thomas, 209
electrostatic precipitators, 145
Elks Club, 29
Engineering Science, 32–33
Environmental Protection Agency, 248
escherichia coli, 221–222
Essays in Taxation, 171

Factor's Walk, 3, 169
fecal coliform, 27, 221–222, 241
Federal Aviation Administration, 109, 129
Federal Communication Commission, 30
Federal Trade Commission, 162
Federal Water Pollution Control Act, 197, 208

Federal Water Pollution Control Administration, 10, 33, 197, 235
Federal Water Quality Control Administration (FWQA), 79, 195, 197, 199–200, 208, 210, 252
Fields Cut, 229
Fletcher v. Rylands, 189
Floyd, Picot, xxi, 32, 34
Folkston, 107
Ford Motor Company, 51
Fortune, 53
4-H Clubs, 59
Frady, Marshall, 128
Franjo, Incorporated, 183
Fraser, Charles, 108–109
Funk, Arthur, 175

Galbraith, John Kenneth, 53, 64
Gamble, Mayor, 160
Garden City, 37
Garfunkel, Benjamin, 35, 175
General Motors Corporation, 51
Georgia Air Board, 247
Georgia Air Quality Control Act, 139, 147
Georgia Air Quality Control Branch, 45, 139, 141, 144, 146–148
Georgia Board of Registration for Professional Engineers and Land Surveyors, 32
Georgia Code, 176, 179
Georgia Institute of Technology, 166, 169
Georgia-Pacific, 51, 71–72
Georgia Marine Institute, 113
Georgia Mines, Mining, and Geology Department, 123, 196
Georgia Parks Department, 182
Georgia Public Health Department, 102
Georgia State Game and Fish Commission, 204
Georgia State Mineral Leasing Commission, 204
Georgia Water Quality Control Act, 38, 202, 246
Georgia Water Quality Control Board (Water Board), xxi, 8, 10–11, 28, 31, 33, 36, 40–45, 76–77, 79, 81, 85, 89, 93, 101, 105, 107, 196, 198, 200–203, 225–226, 228, 246–247, 252
Georgia Resolution #688, 108
Gilman, Charles, 101
Gilman, Charles, Jr., 101, 110
Gilman, Howard, 101
Gilman Paper Company, 75, 100–108, 110–112
Gilreath, Arthur, 37
Glatfelter Company, 72
Gowen, Charles, 204
Gregg, Dean, 124
Groves, Robert, 160
ground water, 17, 113–116, 120–128, 248–249
Grumman Aircraft, 175
Guidelines for Litigation Under the Refuse Act (33 USC 407), 207
Guidry, Randall B., 97

Habersham Woods, 30
Hammermill Paper, 54
Hancock, Alex K., 177
Harper's, 128
Harriman, Everett, 98
Harrison, Robert, 107–111
Hart, E. L., 79
Harvard Crimson, 71
Hayner's Creek, 27–28
Hays, Wayne, 61

Heard, Richard, xxi, 179, 186
Hendrickson, Dr. E. R., 147
Hercules Powder Company, 147
Hickel, Walter, 200
Highland Container Corporation, 162
high-volume sampler, 149
Hilton's Head Island, 108
Hohenstein, Louis, 176
Holmes, Justice Oliver W., 206
holding pond (aeration pond), 41, 69, 72, 77–80, 90, 100, 105, 145, 226
Howard, R. S. "Rock," xxi, 24, 31–32, 34–35, 38, 42, 76–77, 81, 83–84, 105, 122, 196, 201–204, 246, 248, 255
Hudson River, 199
Hunnicutt (tax appraisers), 176
Hussey and Gay, 29
Hutchinson Island, 173
Hutton, Joseph, 33
hydrocarbons, 133, 138
hydrochloric acid, 138
hydrogen sulfide, 8, 67, 129, 131, 138

Ideation Group, 53
Industrial and Domestic Water Supply Commission, 120
Industrial Committee of Savannah, 155, 159–160
industrial zones, 173–176, 179, 226, 251
Institute of Oceanography, 235
Internal Revenue Service, 176
International Paper, 51, 71
International Telephone & Telegraph, 51, 71, 131
Interstate Paper Company, 61, 68, 75–80, 89–90, 93, 113, 117, 165–166, 202–204
Investor's Reader, 160
ion exchangers, 69, 72
iron, 10, 41, 228, 233
The Islander, 221
Isundiga, 3
ITT Rayonier, 73–74

Johns, Jimmy, 97
Johnson, Tom, 157
Johnson, Lane, Space, and Co., 157
Journal of Commerce, 161

Kaiser Chemicals, 151
Kelly, Tex, 185
Kendall Company, 55
Kennedy, John G., 173
kerosene, 102–103
Kerr, Robert, 13
Kerr-McGee Company, 183, 204
Kimberly-Clark, 72–73
Kimble, Glenn, 92, 139, 141, 146–147
K-Mart, 175
Knapp, Frank T., 102
kraft mill, 66–67, 76, 130–131, 137, 221, 224, 231–233, 241
Kravitch, Aaron, 187

Lake Erie, 199
Lambright, Joseph, 182, 186
Land, Wood, and Water, 13
Lane, Mills B., 157
Lane, Remer Y., 185
Lawrence, Alexander A., 97
lead peroxide candle, 137, 149–150
Letters From The Earth, 46
Lewis, J. C., 1, 29–36, 175, 187
Liberty County, 76

Lientz, James, 82–85, 93–95, 98–99, 105, 147, 163, 176, 185, 214–216
lignins, 9, 67, 70–71, 232
lime, 77, 106, 190
limestone, 116, 123
Little, Arthur D., 55
Little Tybee Island, 183
Litton Industries, 131
Locke, Edwin A., 73
Louisiana Brimstone, 128–129
Lovett, Robert F., 179, 184–185
Ludden, J., 144

M & M's, 40, 145
MacLean, Malcolm, 29
Maddox, Lester, 204
Manufacturing Chemists Association, 147
Martin, Benjamin, 111
Masonite Corporation, 72
McBay, Glen, 42
McCloskey, Paul D., Jr., 163
McCorkle, Robert, 185
McNeal, William, 185–186, 188
McWhorter, Edwin, 187
Mead Paper Corporation, 147
mercury, 8–9, 209–210, 234–235
Mendonsa, Arthur, 28–29
methane gas, 8
methyl mercaptans, 67, 129, 138
Metropolitan Planning Commission, 37
Mingledorff, Lee, 29, 155
Mirex, 234
Mitchell, John N., 209–210
Murphy, William, 160
Muskie, Edmund, 200, 209

Nader, Ralph, xx, 201, 244–245, 253
National Air Pollution Control Administration, 131
National Environment Policy Act of 1970, 197
National Industrial Pollution Control Council, 144
National Park Service, 108–109
New River, 224
New York Court of Appeals, 194
Ninth Amendment (U.S. Constitution), 193
Nixon, Richard M., xix, 144, 212
North Channel, 43–44, 222
North River, 102, 105–106

Odum, Eugene, 113, 225
Oglethorpe, James, 2–3, 154, 236
Ohio River, 21
Oil Pollution Act (33 US 1001), 96
oil spill, 96–99, 206, 211–212, 216
O'Keefe, Herb, 177
Olin Corporation, 8, 235, 242
Ossabaw Island, 218
Owens-Illinois, 72

Parris Island, 117
Parsons School of Design, 53
particulates, 133, 135, 137–139, 149
Peagler, G. Miner, 178, 180, 182–188
Pennsylvania Coal Company, 189
Petroleum Council, 147
pH, 41, 43, 224, 231–233, 235
Pillsbury Space Food Stick, 47

pollution abatement
surcharge, 36
Pooler, 37, 115
Population Equivalents
(PE), 9–10, 228
Populists, xiii–xiv
Port Wentworth, 37–38, 250
Potlatch Forest Mills, 73,
131
Potomac River, 199, 201
primary system, 70, 105
Pulp and Paper, 62
Pulp and Sulfite Workers
Union, 111
Public Law 660, 35
Purvis, Devant, 74

Randolph, Jennings, 209
Ray, John E., III, 46, 60, 95,
99, 113, 122, 176, 232,
248
recovery boiler, 106–107,
111
Refuse Act of 1899, 96–97,
99, 197, 205–215
reverse osmosis membranes,
69
Reuss, Henry, 206, 214
Reynolds, R. J., 113
Riceboro, 68, 75–76, 78, 93,
113, 165, 202
Riceboro Creek, 78
Ringleman Scale, 149
Rivers and Harbors Act of
1899, 210
Roach, Quinnie, 37
Rogers, Herbert, 83
Rousakis, John, 36, 175,
185, 252
Ruckelshaus, William,
248
Ruffin, Arthur, 242

St. Joseph (Mo.), 198–199
St. Mary's, 100–103, 105–
110, 112, 200
St. Mary's Kraft
Corporation, 103
St. Mary's River, 102–103,
105
St. Regis Paper, 62
salt water, 115, 117, 120–
122, 124, 126, 222
Sanders, Carl, 196
Sanderson, (J. Gardner and
Eliza), 189–190, 193
*Pennsylvania Coal vs.
Sanderson,* 190–192
Sapelo Island, 113
The Savannah, 1
Savannah, Ga., ix–xi, xv,
xix–xxi, 1–11, 13, 23–25,
27–29, 31–36, 38, 40, 45,
56–58, 81–82, 93, 95,
114–122, 124–125, 128–
130, 133, 135, 138, 141,
146, 153–165, 168–169,
172–176, 182–183, 187,
196–203, 212, 217–218,
225, 230–231, 235–236,
244–246, 248, 250–255
Savannah Beach, Ga., 28,
37–39
Savannah Board of Tax
Assessors, 179
Savannah-Chatham Joint
Tax Board, 177
Savannah Machine and
Foundry, 97
Savannah News-Press, 160,
175, 248, 252–253
Savannah Port Authority,
154–155, 158, 175
Savannah River, x, 4–9, 12,
25, 27–28, 40–44, 56–57,
61, 68, 81, 90, 93–94, 96,
98, 100, 105, 117, 121,
128, 169, 174, 218–219,
221–222, 224, 226, 230,
232–237, 244–245, 249,
252
Savannah Rotary Club, 122,
232
Savannah Sugar Refinery, 6,
29, 38, 40, 174–175, 178,
250

Scenic Hudson Preservation Conference v. Federal Power Commission, 195
Schoenhofen, Leo, 62
Scott Paper Company, 55, 71
secondary fiber repulping, 61–63
secondary treatment (biological stabilization), 69–70, 83–84, 100, 105
Secretary of the Interior, 198, 200
Seligman, Edward, 171
Senate Select Committee on National Water Resources, 19
septic tanks, 28, 37–38
settleable solids, 66, 86, 88–91, 102
Sewell, Dan, 30–31
Sewell-Wiedeman feud, 30
Sieber, C. W., 43–45, 141
Siverd, C. D., 55, 144
Skidaway Island, 34, 182–184, 188, 235
Skaghall Mill, 73
Smith, R. Jackson B., Jr., 212
Sognier, John, 176
South Carolina Water Resources Commission, 124
South Channel, 43–45, 222, 224
Southern Nitrogen, 174
Southern Pulpwood Conservation Association, 65
Southern States Phosphate and Fertilizer, 151
Spong, William, Jr., 209
Starling, Charles, 10, 85
Stell, Rev. Scott, 185
Stein, Murray, 83–84, 197, 200
Stockman, R. L., 130
Storm King Mountain, 195
Stokes, Thomas, 1
sulfate process, 232
sulfite mills, 66, 68, 70–71, 74
sulfuric acid (H_2SO_4), x, 8–9, 40–43, 123, 137, 190
sulfur compounds, 67, 138, 232
sulfur dioxide (SO_2), 137–138, 193
sulfur oxides, 134, 137, 150, 152
sulfur trioxide (SO_3), 137–138
Supreme Court, 191, 205–206

Technical Association of the Pulp and Paper Industry (TAPPI), 61
tertiary treatment, 69
thermal pollution, 79, 210
Thomans, Huguenin, 173
Thorold Paper Company, 71
Thunderbolt, 37–38
Time, 53, 73
titanium dioxide, 40, 45, 138, 141, 145
Travis Field, 129
treatment plants, 11, 25, 28, 30–31, 34–38, 45, 71–72, 76–77, 84, 121, 172, 250, 252
Twain, Mark, 46

Union Bag and Paper Company, 6–7, 57–58, 154–163, 168, 184, 190–191
Union Bag-Camp Paper Corporation, 162, 164
Union Camp Corporation, x, xv, xx, 6–7, 9–11, 28–29, 40, 46, 49, 51–54, 56–58, 60–61, 65–68, 70–72, 75–77, 79–86, 88–98, 100–102, 105, 113, 116–117, 121–123, 125, 128–

129, 131, 136–139, 141, 145–147, 152–155, 158, 162–166, 168, 172–175, 178, 180, 182–186, 188, 190, 193, 197, 199, 202–203, 208, 211–214, 228, 230, 232–233, 245, 248, 251–252, 254
Union Paper Bag Machine Company, 57, 156
U.S. Army, 207
U.S. Army Corps of Engineers, 4–5, 7, 96, 98, 196, 207, 210–213, 222, 224, 226
U.S. Attorney General, 198, 212
U.S. Coast Guard, 96–99, 196, 206, 212–215
U.S. Geological Survey (USGS), 18, 123–126, 248
U.S. Department of Health, Education and Welfare, 83, 149–150
U.S. Department of Interior, 207
U.S. Department of Justice, 207–210, 214
U.S. Public Health Service, 19, 28, 134–136, 138
U.S. Plywood-Champion, 51
U.S. Steel Corporation, 254
United States v. Standard Oil Company, 216
Universal Paper Bag Company, 162
University of British Columbia, 130
University of Georgia, 113, 124, 184

Vernonburg, 27–28, 36–38
Vernon River, 27
Veross, William, 78–79
Vicksburg, 222

Wall Street Journal, 71, 73
Washington State Department of Health, 130
West-Gaeke system, 150
wet scrubbers, 76, 145
Weyerhaueser, 54
Whalen vs. Union Bag and Paper Company, 190–193
Wiedeman and Singleton, 29, 31
Wiedeman, Theodore, 31–32
Williams, George, 147
Wilmington River, 42–44, 222, 229, 231
Windom, Dr. Herbert, 235
WJCL, 30
WJXT, 74
Wolle, Francis, 57
Wright River, 224

Xylose, 70

YMCA, 30

Zwick, David, 199